WHAT ABOUT AFTER

Quinn Coleman

Copyright © 2023 by Quinn Coleman

This is a work of fiction. Names, characters, places and incidents either are the product of the author's imagination or are used fictitiously. Any resemblance to actual persons, living or dead, events, or locales is entirely coincidental.

All rights reserved. This book or any portion thereof may not be reproduced or used in any manner whatsoever without the express written permission of the publisher except for the use of brief quotations in a book review.

Printed in the United States of America

First Printing, 2023

Cover by Quinn Coleman

ISBN (paperback) 9798-3704-5130-0

To all those who have only ever felt like the sidekick.

You're the hero in your story.

You're worth the happy ending.

I pinky promise.

Chapter 1

He's been all over my phone since last night. I shouldn't be surprised; he's got a new movie releasing later this summer, and he recently finished a season finale playing TV's biggest heartthrob. (No, I've never watched a single episode of the show and yes that is an intentional choice.) Just call me Scott Everett Boscoe, leader in the group of 'if the mistake isn't in front of me rearing its ugly-yet-sexy face, I can pretend it doesn't exist'.

Instagram? Boom, reposted by three different people, including my friend Charlotte. Explore page, there again, in gif format to boot. Twitter—*abhor* Twitter, but I thought I could escape his endless fame by stalking Silversmith Publishing House, the organization I've been waiting to hear back from for the last week.

Honestly, I was checking to see if the job I applied and interviewed for was still up; if it was gone, then they found someone else. (And I could then safely go full Brontë and lock myself in the attic of my grandpa Mitch's absurd Californian mansion, Mr. Rochester style. I suppose the extra levels then would have their perks.)

No post on the job. Posts about him though? Thirteen. By five different magazines.

Don't get me started on Spotify. I went to load up my playlist as I got ready this morning and in seconds, Fleetwood Mac was interrupted by an ad for a podcast he'd be joining, talking about Top Ten Craziest Movie Stunts in the last year with Buzzfeed journalists.

He's done five out of the ten I'm fairly sure. (In movies I've *also* refused to watch.)

Attempted to avoid him by talking to my younger sister Bevett for a few minutes this morning; I went into town this weekend only for our grandpa's seventieth birthday. Staying an extra day was torture enough, but it's what I get for having Fridays and Mondays off my senior year.

We still had streamers up from Grandpa Mitch's party on Friday, but it looked like someone had already started to decorate for Valentine's Day today. The staff member who bought those frilly hearts and cupids and put them up deserves a high five for unintentionally irritating Mitch with an overload of reds and fuchsias.

Bevett and I had a *super* mentally healthy chat. She's been accepted into the National Junior Honor Society at her middle school, and she's stressing already.

I can't blame her, it's a family trait we share; she's our dad's kid from his second marriage after my mom died years ago. Although her skin is a few shades darker than mine, like her mom Cassidy, and she didn't get the 'shoot straight up like a beanpole at eleven' gene, we did both inherit Dad's brown eyes, anxiety, and his lack of boundaries when it comes to school and work.

But then, who popped up the moment she unlocked her phone when she decided she was done panicking about NJHS? (And making *me* panic about *my* school cause we suffer in solidarity here.)

Him. And that handsome, hollow movie star smile along with some trashy, bubblegum pop article title.

"Valentine's Day Drama—David Después has done it again, leaving behind another broken heart! So much for being the 'cherub of Hollywood'—Hershey's kiss? More like a rotten candy apple!"

Magically, I escaped with my backpack without reading the article over Bevvy's shoulder, and without answering her question on if I'd be back for her birthday in a couple of weeks.

Oh, and without acknowledging her when she screamed, "Oh shoot, guess who broke up with his girlfriend! *Again!*"

You'd think seeing your ex best friend from high school all famous and flashy on the Internet would be a cool thing.

Like, "Wow, I knew that guy when he'd pretend to stay up late to watch Gargoyles, when really I know he just liked watching Sailor Moon on the other channel." Or even, "Golly, the dude sure got hot when he stopped wearing jeans two sizes too big and decided hunching his shoulders was actually super bad for his back and self-confidence."

I've ended up on Paramount Street, waiting for Charlotte to text me to let me know her and her fiancée Mei are ready to go back to the school we attend and Mei works at. Mei is TA for three different classes in the art department at Jethro University—my soon to be alma mater—and some of those classes require weekend work. (Apparently, the basket weaving course takes up most of her time. Who'd have thought?)

Paramount is a good street to bumble around on, though. It's busy, but not shoulder to shoulder bustling like Main or John Heavens Drive that runs under the highway. There are some homeless people, the occasional hot dog stand and street artist or musician, and it always somehow smells like churros.

Bad thing about Paramount Street? Magazine peddlers. By the dozens. And they're worse than the social media apps I have an unhealthy relationship with. Don't normally notice the carts, or care about whatever they're selling. But since I've applied to a publishing house and I'm waiting to hear back from them with my hand literally wrapped around my phone in my pocket, everything literature, even tabloids, has me reading more.

I stop at one that doesn't have a flock of Californians around it, nod to the seller chick who looks bored and hungover, and I squint at the glossy covers. *Good Living* is all about how to make your Christmas trees last year 'round, including decorating your ferns for the Fourth. *Nat Geo* is talking about penguins, again.

Because I've given up avoiding him (bullshit, everything I've said until now has been a lie—I listened to that Spotify advert all the way through) I pick up the new edition of *People* and stare at the yellow words that take up half the front:

"**David Después and Sasha Newman—over already? Fans shocked after Just Biding Time co-stars' messy argument outside Starbucks. What—or who—will David do next?**"

Photo's a little blurry, probably taken through a bush, seeing how distorted it is. Sasha's back is to the lurking paparazzi, and her finger is pointing at something off camera.

It's clearly meant to be a dramatic shot; they're both dressed in fine, going out clothes, her blonde hair all done up super snazzy just for her caramel latte.

But I can't stop staring at his face. Thick brow heavy over his eyes, cheeks covered in more freckles. His skin is bronzer now—I think his Twitter showed he'd just finished filming something in New Mexico. One hand up in his short, light brown hair, the other resting on his hip. He doesn't even look like he's trying to win whatever argument they were having.

Grainy quality or not, he looks miserable. He's looked pathetic in every photo I've seen of him for the last year, but in this one, he just seems hurting and sick.

Thank goodness we stopped talking before I ever saw him look so disappointed in person.

Can't tell Bevett he's the real reason I'm so anxious.

I told her it was because I was worried about the background check and piss test I was forced to take after interview two. Even if I haven't shot up in years, handing over that little cup for judgement still had my heart in my throat.

I don't just want the job at Silversmith. I *need* it.

It's nothing fancy; part-time assistant work to the editorial manager Mona Vermont. When I talked to her last, she said more or less my job would center around helping her out with deadlines, running errands, filling her coffee cup; said I could flex when I came into the office if I needed to, until I lived closer.

Eventually I'd graduate, get a second job, maybe a third. Rent a studio outside the city. Live lean as hell, cut down on how much I use public transport or Ubers and just bike until my knees break. Could totally do that.

What I'm terrified about is…I shouldn't be here in the first place. Not in California, not nearly graduating from Jethro, not potentially getting a nice job right out of college that could be my first, professional step in the right direction with my writing.

Let me explain. I went through the door on my own.

Took the first solo step over the threshold and each step after that nearly sent me on a bender of Ben and Jerry's Cookie Core and cream soda. (Only the classiest of vices for Scott Everett.)

When I fell, I picked myself up, dusted myself off, and kept going. And I'm gonna keep going until I reach the end, then I'm gonna get $100 from Charlotte cause she dared me on the first day of freshman year that I'm too chicken to do a dab on the graduation stage. Just watch me, I'll do anything for a crispy hundo.

Yeah, even with supportive friends and Bevett cheering me on, I've done it all on my own.

However. *Teeny* detail…

The key that unlocked said door, the way I got into Jethro in the first place?

I stole it. From none other than my childhood best friend turned world-wide famous celebrity, David Después.

Also known as After by his best friend Charlotte and former BFF me. (His last name, Después, means 'after' in Spanish. Obviously, seven-year-olds are *incredibly* clever.) Everyone else called him Afterthought, cause they were all unfunny, uncreative assholes who loved to pick him last for everything.

I mean, clearly, *I'm* the perfect picture of non-asshole.

Only plagiarized an essay After worked his ass off to write, then used it to get into a spectacular college before he could submit it himself, breaking After's heart and destroying eleven years of trust and friendship in the blink of an eye.

Otherwise…I mean I'm overall an okay dude. Haven't killed anyone. Got that going for me.

Two times I applied for Jethro with my own writing. Two times I got rejected and received the cold shoulder and threat of homelessness from Grandpa Mitch.

At the time, I did the only thing that would get me accepted, even if I didn't care about anyone but my own damn self when I did it. Only regretted it the moment I got in, but I guess not enough to decline the acceptance letter.

It's more complicated than that. It's a *lot* more complicated, but anything I've got to say around it just sounds like an excuse.

My phone goes off. I try to pull it from my pocket and end up fumbling with the magazine, accidentally ripping a page. I flinch at the sound and hope the seller in the booth didn't hear it. "That's $4," she says. I glare at her and she glares right back, fiddling with her nose ring.

Answering my phone, I press it between my ear and shoulder and pull out my wallet. "This is Scott Everett."

"Hi Scott, this is Mona—" I nearly drop everything in my hands at once.

"Hi—hello, Ms. Vermont, hi—" The clerk laughs at me, and I shove four bucks at her and rush off with my unwanted magazine rolled in one hand.

Mona chuckles over the phone. "Did I call at a bad time?"

"No, not at all, how can I help you?" I sound like a cardboard cutout. I clear my throat and prepare something a little more chill for whatever she says next, even if it's, 'Hey, no snazzy savior job for you, ya big gnarly-lookin' fraud'.

"I'm calling to let you know that, uh—well, you got the job! Sort of?" I was ecstatic for 0.4 seconds, then I frown and mouth 'sort of'? "But. We'd like you to come in today, if you've got time?"

"Wha—um…" I look fast at my clothes. Khakis, but they're so old they're faded at the knees, holes in the pocket from the corner of my phone and keys. Dad's old bomber jacket, grungy boots. There's a spaghetti sauce stain on my t-shirt and not even God knows how old it is.

Silversmith is a ten-minute walk down Paramount, then east on Settler's Road. Jethro and a chance to change into nicer clothes are a half hour taxi ride in the other direction. I've already been too in-my-own-head today, and if I wait another minute longer, I'm liable to think myself out of this job I apparently already have. How impatient am I?

"I...I mean I can come in right *now*, but...I'm not really dressed—"

"You don't need to be in dress casual or anything. I mean, ever, truly, that's not the vibe of Silversmith. Anyway, Jackie's here now, wanting to meet with you..."

I don't hear shit after that. Jackie Silversmith? *Director* of Silversmith? Wants to meet…

Oh shit, here comes Pop-Tart from breakfast up my throat for round two. "I—I—yep, okay, yep, can, can do, I'll be there ASAP." I went from cardboard to *wet* cardboard all icky and squashed to the concrete. I have no in-between chill.

"Great! We'll see you soon, Scott."

After she hangs up, I stand there for a solid minute before my brain slams my body forward down the street, forcing my legs to reach new loping speed.

Pulling the straps of my backpack tight, ascending to ultimate nerd-in-a-rush levels, I look at the magazine still in my hand.

Every trashcan I pass, I think about tossing it. It ends up unceremoniously shoved into my back pocket, and I yank my shirt and jacket down over it.

Kind of a funny thought. More sick than funny, maybe. David Después, After, still in my back pocket, helping me along with just one thing he gave me unwillingly years ago. Got the job, cause I got the degree, cause I got into the school, cause I stole his essay.

And, cause I'm fucked up, I'll ride the lie along until I die. Or until I get caught.

Chapter 2

This *has* to be a new record for karma.

Fifteen minutes and thirty-three seconds ago, when I rode the elevator up, after power walking to get to Silversmith, parting crowds with my glare alone cause ain't nobody was getting out of my 5'10" way fast enough, I didn't care.

Forty minutes before, when I left the house, I didn't care.

Three hours ago, when I was lying awake too early, too stressed out over this job, I wasn't even *thinking* about the old mistakes that got me into a school I won't be attending in a few short months.

I mean, I'm inches from my degree and I've been dumping money at the establishment by the buckets for years.

If they get their pound of flesh, they won't care about any scheming I did to get into the school in the first place. Right?

I mean, theoretically, *they* wouldn't.

But Silversmith would. They'd care a shit ton.

Primarily the founder herself, Jackie Silversmith, who's currently sitting at her desk across from me with linked fingers and a pearly smile I suddenly don't think I deserve.

Can I just go back a few minutes, to the part where I was drooling over the kitchen right down the hall from Mona Vermont's office? Seriously, the kitchen, the break room, the vending machines. There's a *Nespresso* for God's sake, a water cooler. I was already excited about the idea of water cooler gossip. So much better than my time spent at Chili's.

Break room shenanigans and coffee dreams shattered the moment I walked in and sat down and heard the real reason Jackie wanted to meet me today. If a trap door opened below me and a guillotine flew out from the side of the wall, I would not even blink.

"So, you think you're up for it?" Jackie asks.

I start to open my mouth to squeak or cry or do something else super demeaning, but she raises a bejeweled hand and shakes thick orange curls from her eyes. I've never seen someone with such disarmingly gigantic green eyes. She *peers* with them. It's worse than a guillotine, I think.

"No rush on the first article. I know you gotta dust off some cobwebs. To be blunt, the blurbs you wrote aren't the reason I'm wanting to push you up." Are *blurbs* two thousand words long? When did *that* change? "The samples you sent in were uh…well, they were nice, Scott."

Nice? Nice! Eeeh, y'know what's *nice*? Macaroni art your toddler botches together. Not writing samples I fought to perfect for weeks before sending them in. (I even hid away enough of my ego and fear and asked Grandpa to proofread them, and his secretary, and *her* secretary.)

Nice. Put that in my obituary. RIP Scott Everett Boscoe: He was a'ight at, like, everything.

"But your credentials were all there, and I just knew, I *knew* you had to be hiding some creative genius up your sleeve, and lo and behold! I just had to dig a little back!" Dig me deeper into the grave is more like it.

"That essay you used when you applied for your university—I know it's old, sure, a little stale after four years, but that style, that voice of yours…"

Jackie puffs air through her cheeks and her curls do another dance. "Gracious, Scott, I think you'd soar on the publicity team. You'd be in charge of writing about the books, summaries—I love authors, truly I do, but they can be clueless when it comes to summing up their own stories in four paragraphs.

"You spit-shine up that old style of yours and I can just see the books flying off the shelves. A lot of times, a novel could be spectacular but the publicity it gets is just junk, and no one even cracks the spine open, so the author can't get a damn upswing. They just need someone amazing on their side to represent them. You're gonna be the one to get people to pick the books up, Scott, I can *see* it."

Alright, listen. I know my writing isn't good enough for JU. Hard truth accepted.

But when Jackie opened the door to her office, shook my hand, and said, "Let's talk about your writing!" I thought maybe it could be good enough for Silversmith, and I floated to the ceiling.

There was one little blip where I truly believed she was going to say they wanted me on the publicity team because of my writing. *Mine*. My style, my short and clipped voice that hits the gut with every punctuation.

Mom said she loved it even when I *was* just writing stories to go along with my macaroni art. She'd hang my nonsense on the fridge until the magnets wore out.

Cassidy cried when I first gave her a poem about the color of her eyes. Dad said I could really do something with my voice, if I ever wanted to. And Bevett likes it, too, but she signed a contract that explains if she ever says otherwise, she'll be turned into a mushroom.

Dashed, I tell you. All of it. On the rocks, bloody and broken. Leave me to the side to be pulled out to the sea in pieces.

Jackie's probably taking my lingering silence as something more innocent than guilt. Like excitement, shock.

How many newbies ever get to meet with the lady in charge of the publishing house to be given a spectacular job like this in person? How many have been awarded an opportunity as incredible as this right out of the gate—or before they've even *left* the gate?

She grins and crosses her arms on the desk. "I know you've still got a semester left at school, so I'm not expecting you to get started until maybe spring break—that's in March, right?" She accepts my croak as a 'yes'.

"Right, excellent. So you'll be starting as PT assistant to Mona in editing—you said you don't have a place in LA yet, no problem, we can send you some work to do remotely at your dorm so you're not having to commute so much, come into the office when you can. And I'm thinking we can scoot you up bit by bit over the next couple projects. By the time you've graduated, you'll be working on the pub team! Whadya say? I'll write up a formal offer of course, just like I did for the other position. Please make me one very happy woman and say yes?"

Lordy, that was a lot, Jackie. I stopped listening after her mentioning me finding a place to live at in LA.

The magazine with After's face printed all over it digs into my back under my shirt and jacket.

"Well, um." Apparently I've been transported back to thirteen. I clear my throat. "Yeah, I can do that." Better, at least I don't sound like I've hit second puberty.

Jackie gives a loud laugh and juts her hand in my direction. I wipe my palm on my knee and shake it, counting the seconds until I can leave and go find a potted plant to vomit in since her corner office was six miles from the nearest bathroom.

I'm in the hall, walking past that glistening break room and Mona, who waves an encouraging hand and shouts out her excitement at seeing me soon.

My phone lights up with a text from Charlotte. She lets me know she's done with her nail appointment and can meet me in thirty at Honeydew's while we wait for Mei to finish up at her mom's.

I'm outside, shivering in my layers, staring at the rush of traffic. My right leg desperately wants to move me forward, straight into the lanes. I direct it to take me down the street instead.

I'm crying. Hadn't noticed that with all the shaking. At least I can blame my pink nose and cheeks on the cold.

I'm dead. I'm caught, and I'm so, *so* dead.

Chapter 3

I'm halfway through a slice of cake at Honeydew's and it's not helping. My foot's tapping so fast, it keeps thumping the underside of the table, disrupting my elbows, and therefore shaking my head around as it rests in my hands. I'm a jittery, cake-filled mess, and I just keep glaring at the magazine opened on the table.

After's moved up in the ranks. According to this morning's edition of *People* that I can't *believe* I'm *actually* reading, he's now number four in their 'Top Ten Bad Boys'. Six months ago he was maybe eight. Not that I'm keeping up with any of that. But bad boys? *Seriously?*

Literally a year ago he was leading the pack in the poll of 'who'd you bring home to introduce to Momma'. Dude gets a tattoo sleeve and suddenly he's a 'your daughter calls me daddy, too' kinda guy. Unbelievable.

I blame the haircut he picked last summer; finally got rid of the wisps that hung around his ears, donning a fade and shorter bangs. Then every teeny-bop article went on and on for months over a leak of shirtless pics taken of him at his dad's house in Spain.

All that lead to him getting an upgrade in publicity, and he went from gracing the cover of *Glitter*, to smeared all over *Us Weekly* in skimpy swim trunks. I don't see what all the fuss is about. Really. He's tall, but not taller than Chris Evans, jacked but not like Tom Hardy. Ears still take up half his dorky-ass head—looks like a two-handled tea pot with lashes.

Most ridiculous is the constant description of hazel eyes. His eyes are boring and brown like mine. Hazel eyes are a scam made up by Kelly Clarkson, I swear.

"**David can be adorable *and* sexy**," said some flippant article both Bevett and Charlotte showed me at Christmas. (He was wearing the most hideous holiday sweater I've ever seen. And not even 'ugly Christmas sweater' ugly. That thing was *horrid*.) Teen Vogue once had pages with absurdities like, "**How to get Thick Brows Like David Después**," and, "**Want a Cool Brow Cut like DD? Here's How!**"

I was shocked (I wasn't) when the first paragraph didn't read:

Step 1.) Get in face/forehead collision with fellow seven-year-old.

Step 2.) Get sent to the nurse's office, then the ER.

Step 3.) Leave hospital with six stitches each and a new best friend.

Step 4.) Ruin friendship eleven years later.

No one ever wrote anything like, 'Looking to Get a Neat-o Jaw Scar Like Scotty? Look No Further!'

I roll my eyes, take another bite of cake, and flip to the page about him and Sasha's argument. *Why* do I flip the page? Waste of my time, straight up. But Charlotte's not here yet, so...

According to this super reliable source, After and Sasha were fighting over where their relationship was gonna go. She wanted to take it further, says she was even—gasp—looking at wedding dresses. They've included a shot of her from the big bridal breakup scene in Just Biding Time, arguing with on-screen boyfriend Giddings who's played by, you guessed it, After. Oh, the irony.

"**He's always so secretive!**" whines—excuse me, cries—Sasha Newman. When the hell did she even give someone her statement? Probably had it prepared, tucked away in her fancy dress pocket right outside Starbucks."**I don't get it. I thought we were really getting somewhere. Three months of dating is a lifetime in Hollywood! He's a commitment-phobe!**"

Maybe, just maybe, if I stare at her little heart-shaped face in that wedding dress shot, mascara running down her cheeks in perfect movie-makeup streaks, I can set the magazine on fire.

There's a vibration under my elbows, and I admit my eyes widen cause I legit think the table might explode from my newfound superpowers. But it's just my phone, lighting up with a text from Charlotte.

[Cat-cat] 12:22: Where you at, stud muffin?

Before I text back, I look up and around, and I spot her walking my way down Settler's Road. I smirk at her wiggling her shoulders along to whatever she's listening to, headphones clunky on her head with cat ears on the band.

[Me] 12:22: I like your cute plaid pants.

She stops, tilts her head, then turns in a circle as she takes off her headphones, looping them around her neck. I laugh and stand, and she whips back to grin at me.

"Hi!" she screams, even though there's still four restaurants between us, and dozens of people sitting outside under awnings eating lunch. Three of them look up, one even starts to get out of his seat. "Not you, return to your salads, plebeians," she says, waving a hand at them as she rushes for me.

I'm hardly stepping away from the table when she crashes into my arms, looping hers around my neck as I bring her to her toes.

"Well, howdy," I chuckle, dropping her to her boot heels. She acts like I haven't seen her in a thousand years; she just dropped me off at Mitch's on Friday. "How was your weekend?"

"Excellent! Lots of food, lovely sex, slept in until three yesterday."

"Naturally."

"How was *your* weekend, shnookums? You said you had an emergency—" She glances once at the cake, twice at the magazine, and smirks back at me as my face starts to tingle. "Sure as shit looks like it. Can I have bitesies?"

"Of course," I reply, sitting back down as she plops into the seat across from me. Charlotte Montague is like, if you took a cherub with a lingering Texan accent, gave it a slightly uneven shoulder length haircut, and taught it how to kickbox and break your legs. And if it had an obsession with manicure art.

"I like what you got done today," I tell her, taking one of her petite hands and inspecting the long, purple nails adorned with jewels. There's a moon charm hanging from one by some mystery magic.

"Thank you, but no distracting from the emergency. What's got you reading a magazine and eating cake like a broken-hearted tween? Is this your second slice? Be honest."

"No, but if you took five minutes longer, I would've gotten another."

"Oh, Lord, what happened? Is it Silversmith?"

I grimace and she groans for me. "No, not like that. I mean. I got a job."

"You what!"

"But it's for publicity."

"You what?"

"To write articles and summaries for books."

"You...you what?"

I nod and she mulls my words over as she eats a slow bite of cake. "I'm...confused. Why aren't we celebrating? That sounds spectacular and way better than you were expecting."

"It. *Is*. But..." I chew the dickens out of my lower lip until she reaches and pokes under my nose with a pointy nail. "Sorry, thanks. Um. So Jackie Silversmith, I met with her—head honcho of the house—she wants me to write all sorts of stuff. But she didn't like the voice of the...*blurbs* I sent in. She wants the voice of my entrance essay to Jethro, which is not in. *My* style."

"She doesn't want your style. Then how else are you supposed to...write..." I stare at the table as her sentence falters, drawing circles with the moisture pooling around my iced tea. "Oh, massive, flying dicks."

"I can't honestly tell if you meant to say ducks, and I'm going to look up and see a flock overhead. Or if that's you freaking out as you come to the same realization of how absolutely shitty this situation is."

I peek back at her and her bugging, glittery blue eyes letting in all the light around us. "Bro, you're fucked."

"With a prize-winning cucumber at the county fair."

"Vivid. What're you gonna do?"

"Move to Morocco, obviously."

"You'd roast alive, you pathetic little vanilla boy."

"I'm well aware."

"So, let me get this straight, in case I'm misreading literally everything," she says, eating more cake.

She squints as she chews, point of her moony little nail tapping at her chin. "Big boy publishing house wants you off the bench to write for them."

"Check."

"However, it's not in a style that's yours."

"You got it."

"It's in the style you plagiarized from After when he was planning on applying to Jethro back in high school."

"Ding, ding," I say with sad jazz hands. Should've ordered another slice of cake. "She emailed me the offer letter a few minutes ago, told me to take my time to think about it—though she was over the moon when I accepted the verbal offer. So I highly doubt she really wants me to take my time."

I'm nauseous when I admit the number out loud. "Cat, they're offering me $60,000 annually if I take this position." Charlotte's eyes round even more, and her mouth does a little 'o'. "The part time gig for Mona? Was $23 grand a year."

My face lands in my hands. "I can't—I *can't* lie about the writing all over again. But I can't take that small amount if sixty k is right there on a platter. Grandpa Mitch would never forgive me."

"Fuck your grandpa."

"Please don't."

"No, I'm serious—geez, Scotty, I've hated that man ever since the hell he put you through after El Paso."

I'm shaking my head with a weak argument building, and she reaches and runs her fingers through my hair, making my bangs sit straight up like a cockatoo. "C'mon, bubba, chin up! If he kicks you out, you can live with me."

"In your two hundred square foot flat with you and your fiancée and three cats and strict as hell landlord?" I wince and she makes a face of defeat and agreement. "Face it, Charlotte. There's no 'if', not after last time."

She can't argue with that cause she knows it's the truth. I had one path my last year of high school: get into JU, mega esteemed school that not only gets funds from high and mighty Judge Mitch Norman annually, but is also his alma mater. I was to make him proud and correct my laundry list of mistakes I made in El Paso by any means. Or I'd be sent packing back to Texas to an uh…he called it a *reformation* school. California might have laws against those kinds of things, but the good ol' Lonestar state still doesn't. It was one school or the other, and that was that.

Charlotte's quiet for a heavy ten seconds. "What about after?"

"After what?" I mumble, wiping at my face so hard it stings.

"No—After. David Después. Why don't you talk to him, get him to help you learn to write like he wrote?" I gawk at her, and she reaches and taps my mouth closed. "I'm just saying. If he can mentor you to write like they want, then you can change your style enough that they don't even notice a ripple. Everything here on, well, after *After*, it's just your own voice."

I find said voice with a coughing choke. "No ma'am—I'm not reaching out to him, are you *joking*?"

She pouts with cheeks full of cake. "Why not?"

"Cause he's who I plagiarized in the first place! Why would I return to the scene of the crime and ask him to help me do it all over again?"

"Don't y'all have your weird little favor thingy?" I mutter 'favor thingy' with a scowl and she rolls her eyes. "You said it was like uh…like a hand-slash-pinky shake? Told me about it orientation week years ago."

"Oh." I blink down at my hands on top of the magazine, and I move my fingers aside to look at After's face.

Twelve years old, busted up after fighting some bigger jerks off, we stood barefoot in the grass in my front yard. With no fingers, no toes crossed, After and I made a deal with a handshake and a pinky-swear over it.

No matter how old we got, wherever we were in life, we'd have one opportunity to ask the other person for a giant, life-changing favor. From being, like, godfather of each other's kids, to escaping the country with a backpack of cash, we promised to go through with it. Cause it's what best friends did. Be there for each other. Was what we used to do.

My ears heat up and I chew on my lip, remembering to stop before I get a fingernail poked at my face again.

"I doubt he'd take that seriously after everything that happened," I mumble to my lap.

Charlotte hums, and a piece of cake appears on a fork in front of my nose. I smile and accept her feeding me the bite. "Worth a shot. What's the worst he could say? 'Bye loser, never talk to me again'?"

"Throw in about a dozen more expletives and a restraining order from his three thousand agents. How would I even get in touch with him? He's world famous, I doubt he'd take my call."

She shrugs and prepares another bite of cake. "He takes mine. We FaceTime." Charlotte does a doubletake to my look of shock, and she snorts. "What? He likes me. Unlike others at this two-seater table, I didn't betray his trust and break his heart."

"Touché," I grumble, taking the fork to feed myself.

"Dems da facts, sugarboo." Her phone vibrates against at least ten different bottles of nail polish in her purse, and she extends her arm under the table for it. She reads the text with a tiny, blushing smile. "Mei says she got out of her mom's luncheon early. You ready to go back to JU?"

Ready as I'll ever be until I decide what mistake I wanna make next.

Chapter 4

Add this to Scott Everett's stupidest decisions made in his lifetime.

Not just meeting my ex-best friend after avoiding him since high school. I'm gonna ask him for help. Claim a promise we made forever ago.

I'll be dead the moment he sees me, I guarantee it. Plaster *that* on *Us Weekly*: "David Después—bangin' hot, even when he's choking out the dumbass who destroyed his chance at going to a prestigious mega university and getting a degree in English Lit like he'd talked about for, oh, only half his life! How to kill a man with one hand—tips and tricks on page 14."

Maybe I should text Bevett. Don't believe what the news tells you, pooch, I did *not* piss myself the second I died.

I keep rattling one thing around in my head.

Is he gonna ask me why I stole his paper?

He never did, that spring of senior year. And I didn't call and tell him, I just ignored his flooding texts asking if I was okay the rest of that week. Didn't have to show him what I did anyway—by that Friday, after I applied with his stellar essay, the school page posted quotes from it as an example on how to write something glorious and heartfelt in order to get accepted.

I knew he saw it; he'd been refreshing the page daily just like me, waiting to see if they'd announced those who'd gotten through the late admissions waitlist. One single line from it would've told him it was his paper with my name attached to it.

They used three paragraphs. He stopped checking up on me. And he never asked me why.

That's probably most upsetting, if I'm being honest. The fact that he never even tried to find out broke me. I wanted to scream and cry and hit myself and tell him why.

Maybe if all this goes through and he somehow agrees to help me, I'll tell him what happened and what drove me to leave Texas in the first place.

As it stands, though, I'm currently waiting outside a, no joke, fucking Starbucks, staring off into space, wondering if I'll be able to do an open casket—or if After will destroy my face so much that not even Mom, Cassidy and Dad will recognize me the moment I show up at Heaven's gate, there long enough to wave and say, "What up, fam," right before I drop to hell.

I check my phone again cause it's glued to my palm. Charlotte said this was where to meet him. She texted me last night to let me know that, after four days of struggling to get him when he wasn't busy, she'd successfully talked to him.

Was expecting a month or two to prepare, not a week. Booked it with an Uber to get here on time from campus, and I've been shivering and sulking outside in the cold for an hour. At least I dressed a little nicer today than when I met Jackie.

But it's ten minutes later than the time Charlotte specified, and I've never known After to be late. Could be that it's part of his new 'bad boy' charm or whatever the fuck.

I give up and shove my phone in my pocket and I turn down Edgar Drive, heading to the big house. Bevett doesn't know I'm back in town so soon, maybe she's home from school by now and she'll be up for eating feelings today. We can see if the Five Guys they're building is finally open—

I slam into Burberry, black turtleneck, and something that smells expensive and familiar all at once.

"Oh, shoot, I'm so sorry," After chuckles, taking my arm and trying to politely steer me out of his way. He looks at me once. "Are you alright?"

Knew he'd gotten taller but like—this is—my neck aches, staring straight up at him like an idiot. His chin is perfect height to hit me square in the forehead. "Hi, After."

There's a second of confusion, then flooding recognition when his eyes flicker to the scar on my jaw. Whoop, there it is. "Scott Everett?" After mumbles. He frowns at me with similar shock. Though I'd say his is laced with disgust the longer he's looking at me. "Boscoe?" Those are all three of my names, yes.

"Uh. Yeah, hey. Hi." His hand jolts away from my arm like it's a hot iron, and he squeezes his gloved fingers into a fist, head swiveling around. "Charlotte uh…"

"She—she said to meet her here," he says.

He turns in a circle, and as nice as he's dressed, I'm oddly more focused on his voice; it's deeper in person than I expected. Didn't sound like this over the phone during spring break, a week before I sent in his essay as my own.

Maybe that's because we spent most of the call laughing all squeaky and stupid at three AM, and I was already sunk in a hole I couldn't claw out of yet.

"It's just me, After. I need to talk to you," I reply. I swallow and his eyes dart to my throat, no doubt trying to find the best way to sever my carotid artery. He stands his full height and the shoulders of his tan coat stretch. "I'm sorry. Charlotte's not coming. I needed to meet you, but you wouldn't have talked to me—"

"Damn right I wouldn't."

"Please, dude, I need your help."

After laughs and it's horrid. "Bye, Scott Everett, never talk to me again." He flicks a hand at me and turns to walk down the street. He gets three feet away. Five. Ten. Tears blaze to the fronts of my eyes.

Homeless. Or dead. Third option is leaping off a bridge, but at least I can pray there might be water at the bottom to catch my fall.

"I'm cashing in my favor, After!"

He freezes. His hands flex and splay at his sides. I look for claws to rip out of his gloves. When he turns on me, he turns fast, and he only needs to take two gigantic steps to be standing right against my chest, bumping me backward. I catch my balance and his nostrils flare.

"Say that again."

Nope, I'd rather not.

"I'm…I'm cashing in my favor." Voice crack. *So* dignified. Too little too late I realize that was probably a rhetorical question.

He brings his hand up, inches from my face, curls his fingers into a tight fist. The leather glove he's got on squeaks around his knuckles, and he cocks his head and leans in even closer.

There's a puff of air from his nose; my eyelashes twitch. I can sense people starting to stare, but I'm not about to look away from him.

Another altercation outside Starbucks. They should sell tickets.

After raises a finger and points it *real* close to my eye. His lip curls back. I bet you he got his canines sharpened or something; I don't remember him ever looking so menacing before. Newest trend: get your incisors surgically altered to look like Davy D, perfect for tearing out throats.

Well. See you later, life, it's been fun.

He spits it through clenched teeth and my legs wobble. "Go. Straight. To hell."

In a rush of Dior and fury, he takes off back down the street, flipping his collar up against the cold. And I groan, and sputter, and topple, flailing out a hand to steady myself on a nearby table. Only I horribly misjudge how close I am to it and drop onto a knee, smashing my face into a potted plant in the process.

—

Like an absolute fool, I previously believed staying the night at the big house with Mitch and Bevett was better than trying to get my ass back to school. Of course now, with no way out of the house (that *doesn't* look like I'm leaving for a late-night booty call), I'm trapped until tomorrow. And, no, they haven't finished building the Five Guys. Fuck my life.

Being a Thursday, I don't have classes tomorrow, and I'd be lying if I said I hadn't sort of, kind of, planned to have been in LA a little while longer. What can I say, I was holding out for my hero After to magically be like, y'know what Scotty, I see you, I gotchu bro, I'll help you out and forget about the shit we put one another through that last year we talked.

Dashed. Have I overused that word yet? No, I've decided I haven't. After didn't just dash my little lifeline, he like…ran over it with a monster truck, set it on fire, and shoved it into a garbage chute. I know I have to tell Bevett something, cause she's nosy and knows me and every little nervous tic and twitch of my scraggly body. As excited as she was to see me, she knew something was wrong the moment I showed up to the house.

So after dinner (we ate salads. *Salads.* I just want some goddamn French fries to fuel my feelings but *noooo*) I tell her I emailed Jackie back and accepted the job, simple as that. Don't tell Bevvy which job, seeing as she didn't know there was a second one.

Grandpa Mitch had asked me repeatedly ever since I applied how much I'll be making, and every time I got away with the lie that I don't know, they didn't have a set number on the application (true) and I wasn't given the option of asking for a certain amount. (Not true.)

Sitting in the living room, looking like the Godfather next to a massive, unnecessary fireplace, he asks the book in his lap how much I'll be earning. I pause shoveling more ice cream into my bowl. (Lovely Bevvy took pity on me with the salads.)

I gulp in bravery and turn to face him. "The offer said—" Aaand I fumble it. Started off *so* confident, too. What's a good middle ground that'll keep him off my back? "Offer said—said uh. Forty grand a year." Bevett whistles and elbows me with congrats, but I've got my sights on Grandpa.

He nods once, flips the page of his book, and nods a second time. He's been stressed as hell with court lately, so him not acknowledging me is a good sign this time. I release a shaky breath through my nose and take my sweating bowl of ice cream up to my room, where it promptly ends up on my bedside table, ignored and melting slowly for hours while I write nonsense on my Mac.

There's a new text I see pop up on my laptop first, and I check it there. If I unlock my phone in the mental state I'm currently wallowing in, I know I'll go straight to After's Instagram, a page I've blocked and unblocked a dozen times just to pretend I've got some sort of control over my obsession with my ex-best friend.

[Unknown] 02:28: In-N-Out on Third and Kokellen. Tuesday the 23rd, noon.

Okay. Um. So, either this is After, or it's an ax murderer with a taste in greasy fast food and planning ahead. I text the number to Charlotte, but she doesn't recognize it. Seeing as how I saw my pitiful life flash before my eyes earlier, I'd *really* rather never look at After again. So, honestly, I'm hoping it's an ax murderer.

But I'm shaking my head before I've even replied; Tuesday's not gonna work. (To meet After or get axed.) I've got class—I'm not so desperate as to skip more school than I already have, I refuse, I'm too close to getting this shit storm handled.

Plus, I have no way to get back to town on such short notice without bumming another ride from Charlotte or braving the bus. I'm already spending too much money on Ubers, and it's a thousand-hour bike ride from JU.

[Me] 02:30: Hi. I actually have class on Tuesdays at that time.

[Me] 02:31: I also don't have a ride, just my bike. There's a DQ ten minutes from campus. Would that work? I think there's another one near Henrickson, too. That's close, I can bike there from my house.

[Me] 02:32: I can do Monday, the 22nd. I'm off Fridays and Mondays. But, again, no ride.

[Me] 02:32: Or, today. Later today. Friday the 19th. I'm still in town, haven't gone back to JU yet.

[Me] 02:33: This is Scott Everett, by the way.

[Me] 02:33: Scott Everett Boscoe. Sorry about my weird school schedule. And lack of vehicle.

So, there's overkill…

Then there's overkill, running said kill *back* over, kicking it, potentially pissing on it *and* setting it ablaze, then yeeting it into the void. I did all that and then some. (Hi, Scott Boscoe, king of exaggeration, great to meet you.) I'm irritated at myself, I can't imagine how this person's feeling, whoever it is.

[Unknown] 02:40: Okay. Today, the 19th, noon, DQ off Henrickson and 8th. Work for u?

At least they're a considerate murderer. After or otherwise.

[Me] 02:41: I'll be there.

Chapter 5

I'm early cause I'm freaking out.

I only got a soda, didn't even think about getting food. The last thing I want to do is start choking on a burger while After just sits there with his arms crossed like, 'You brought this on yourself, dipshit'.

As hungry as I am, I've been sitting here with my knee wiggling under the outdoor table, looking around like a fidgety madman. Big open place, next to a water fountain, couple other restaurants. At least there's a few witnesses to my oncoming demise. Get a good picture of me, paps, make my death spectacular.

"Hey." I leap into the table and look up to After. He squints at me, holding a basket of fries in one hand, other hand tucked into his leather jacket pocket.

No fists free to knock me out, but he could still kick my face in with those combat boots he's wearing. He's got on *cargo pants*, there's, like, six dozen pockets on them that could be holding all *sorts* of weapons. "You're early," he adds.

And suddenly feeling underdressed in my jeans, hoodie and sneakers. Why didn't I just wear the nice shirt I had on yesterday? Oh, right, cause I sweated through it and it's still in the laundry hamper at the house. "I uh…yeah," I mumble. He sniffs. "Was— was that your new number you texted me from?"

He sniffs again. Good talk.

"Let's get one thing clear," he says.

He drops his basket of fries to the table, and just the glare he sends me has me keeping my hands tight in my lap, no matter how delicious his food looks. "I am doing you a *massive, goddamn* favor coming here today."

"Right. Yes, yeah, thank you—"

"And I'd rather be literally *anywhere* else, like even on the fucking sun, *burning* alive, than sitting and talking to you," he says next, thumping into the chair across from mine.

He extends his legs out on either sides of my chair, and I keep my feet crossed at the ankle. Immediately, I'm boxed in. "I'm only doing this because I actually have an honor code I keep to. And that's that."

"Right. Yeah," I repeat. After scowls at me, lines in his jaw rocking with calculation. "Thank you."

"Fine. What is this favor you so *desperately* need," he asks, going for a fry.

"Um…okay, um." I sit up straighter and take in a deep breath, and he quirks a brow with mild yet irritated interest.

"I got a job at a publishing house. I start part time soon but I go full time as soon as the semester ends and I graduate."

"Good for you." He's eating those amazing looking fries slow on purpose, I swear. He juts his chin at me. "Go on."

"Yeah and I uh—well. I was just gonna do assistant work. But um. But…" Man, could I have just *one* fry? Like a last measly meal before I get my throat cut open by After and his sharp as a knife glare. He's gonna kill me as soon as I say the rest of this, I know it.

"Jackie, the director of the publishing house, read some of what I wrote through college and it wasn't really her…her flavor. But she liked some of my…earlier work. From when I first got to Jethro."

After pauses with a fry nearly to his mouth. "Specifically what got me *into* Jethro," I add.

I'm expecting rage. I get a wide, pleased with himself grin. "She liked my stuff, didn't she?"

"I...yeah." He beams and I slouch. "She loved it. Like, *oozed* about it. And she wants me to write like that—"

"Oh shit."

"As part of the publicity team. Writing summaries and blurbs for novels."

"Oh. Shit." He throws his head with a sharp, throaty laugh. "Dude! Dude, you are *fucked*!"

"Sideways with a fine-toothed comb."

"Vivid!" He cackles at my expense and wipes a fake tear from under his eye. "Oh my God, you're like that—like that meme!"

My face is on fire and I don't know when I crossed my arms, pouting like a child, but I struggle to uncross them now. I think if I tried to escape with my fractured dignity on my bike, he'd chase after me like a fucking cheetah. "*What* meme?"

He waves his hands about and shrieks at a voice-cracking falsetto, "I lied on my resume!"

"That's not a meme—"

"I haven't *had* any training!"

"Bro—"

"I'm not writing anything else for you to steal, Scotty," he says, continuing to snicker so much his shoulders wiggle. "You're on your own, man."

"No, don't—don't write it *for* me, just teach me how to write like that. Or at least sort of like that. So I can, I don't know, get the hang of it, start to make a voice of my own, and maybe they won't notice the difference—"

"You're not clever enough to have concocted this plan, did Charlotte help you? Did you copy her idea, too?"

I reach for my soda just to have something to do with my shaking hands. "Yeah."

"Incredible." He's still grinning and my neck stings. "I can literally hear—there's a whistle, like a cartoon whistle in my ear right now. It's you, falling to the Earth. Splat, Scotty Everett."

After shakes his head with a sigh, one last chuckle, and goes back to his fries. "Yeah, I'll do it."

Whiplash. "Wait, what?"

"But you gotta do something for me in turn." I frown and he takes in a long breath. "You gotta be my cover."

"Cover for…?"

"To help me escape the tabloids."

"I'm not following."

He rolls his eyes and thumps back in his seat.

"I want to come out publicly. Show myself with a dude and parade around a big, fat, fake romance that will get people off my back, followed by a catastrophic break up. Then, if it goes according to plan, I'll be forgotten for a while. Forever, if I can swing it."

Come out? Romance? The fuck? "But I didn't even…I didn't think you were…y'know." I chew on my lip. He munches a fry and shrugs. There's a lot unsaid in that shrug.

I raise a hand. I let it fall with a bent wrist, and he snorts with a twitchy eye. "You didn't think I was gay? Yes I'm gay, Jesus."

"You're gay Jesus?"

"What—no—" After lowers his head and laughs, with me, not at me this time. Seems like nothing's changed in that split second.

Then he looks up at me without a smile, clears his throat and frowns, and I remember everything's changed all over again.

So he's using 'gay' to describe his sexuality. Good for him, glad he's comfortable with the term. Too bad he didn't figure it out before I was yanked out of Lubbock and thrown to the sharks in El Paso, but I'm not one to point fingers about that, or judge. Thought he might be something other than straight for a long time anyway.

But then he fucked Missy Davis, spring of our junior year, and that's when I started to believe all our 'almost' moments were just…I don't know. Guys being dudes.

Has he kissed a dude before? He never kissed me. Kissed Missy.

Those 'almosts' start piling up in my head, and I scratch my knuckles in my lap, picking at the old scabs on my fingers from the bad habit. "Well. Congrats. Thanks for telling me."

"Yeah, sure. It's why Erica—my agent—why she's been so hellbent on having me seen with girls. She's afraid that me coming out will hurt my chances in upcoming shows and shit. She's been like that ever since I signed with her."

"When *did* you sign with her?" I take a fry, surprised he lets me.

"Nineteen, summer I graduated James Bowie."

God, he was just a baby. He's still just a baby at almost twenty-three. I shouldn't be thinking about baby After, it's just making my heart hurt. "Wow. Why's she afraid of that?"

After swirls a fry around in ketchup before abandoning it, wiping his hands in the air. "Think about it. Every single role I've ever had. Even in the action movies, the scary ones, the comedies—what've they got in common?"

"They've been 'straight to videos'?"

I think that was a hint of a smirk. "*Ha.* No, there's been a goddamn romance shoved in there, right in your face. Like the dead cat buried in Pet Semetary. Just keeps coming back, over and over, with a fresh new babe and sparkling new—but totally *not* new—subplot. So imagine, suddenly *People's* number 2 on the 'hottest twenties' is hella flaming gay. It's also why she hasn't let me do any stage work like I did in high school—loved that shit, but she thinks it'll chalk me up as the stereotypical theater queer. Erica believes once I'm out, I won't get hired for all the regular shit I've been cranking out for the last four years straight. No pun intended."

After sucks in a hard breath and huffs, picking up his fry again. Don't think he took a single gulp of air the whole time he was talking. Fuck, how long as he been dying to get all *that* out there? "So…" I fidget and he glances once at me, "so your agent is nervous that if you come out, you won't get any work?"

"No. She's nervous I won't get the *easy* work. She *hates* a challenge. Loves to roll me out, project after project, dressed in my usual hetero suit, snatchin' up low-hanging fruit. It's a no-brainer for her."

"That's so homophobic."

"Straight up."

"No pun intended."

He taps a fry at me.

"Why don't you fire her?" I ask.

After grimaces and either shrugs or shivers. "Can't. Contract I signed? It's for ten years."

"So…just wait out another—"

"Another six years?" He stares at me like I slapped him. His wide shoulders slump for just a second before they go rigid again. "Man, I can't. I fucking refuse."

The red blooming around his eyes makes my foot tap to the concrete. "I'm um. I'm still not sure how I'm gonna help you, dude, I'm sorry."

After blinks, cracks his neck, and takes another sharp sniff in to recover whatever flash of human I just happened to glimpse. "Like I said, you can be my easy out."

"I don't get it."

"Guess how many times I've reminded Erica that I'm gay?"

"Three?"

"Ten." I scoff and he adds, "This year alone."

"It's *February*."

"Guess how many times she's listened."

"Goose egg." He pops his lips with a nod, and I go back for my drink. "You're like Jim Parsons from Big Bang Theory. Twelve years of Sheldon Cooper and kissing women."

"Right? Y'know Kassandra Clements—the Internet kept calling her and her girlfriend 'gal pals' for months, even with pictures of them making out. Could've been photographed mid-scissoring and the caption would be like, 'best friends help you stretch out after yoga!'"

I choke on my soda. "Good grief—"

"Yeah, so you get my frustration."

"I *still* don't see how I'm an easy out. I'm not that flexible for scissoring."

That looked like a smirk, for sure. "Hilarious, Scotty. You're photogenic in a super boring, white boy from Pinterest way."

"Thank you?"

"You're good-looking enough to get their attention, then dull enough to be forgotten about. It'll work cause I know you. You're just for show, I don't even have to *like* you."

"Um...thank you...?"

"Yeah, so here's my idea," he says, "I thought this up yesterday after you appeared out of the blue like a rock in my shoe I thought I got rid of years ago."

Fair, but ow.

With a flourishing adjustment of his sleeves by his elbows, he holds his hands out at me like 'picture this'.

I only get the lower half of his sleeve tattoo on his left forearm, but it's some sort of flowers and wings, and it goes all the way to his fingers.

"I get seen with you repeatedly, like five times total maybe, doing couple shit, holding hands, whatever. It gets all over Tumblr, all the way to Buzzfeed, that David Después is a rainbow totin', dick lovin' gay boy."

"Alright...and what about after? We just go on to fake get engaged and have fake babies and buy a fake house, until we fake die at each other's bed sides?"

"I'd fake die first so I can haunt you," After laughs. As much as I was kind of hoping for a little smile in my direction from my ex-best friend, I suddenly miss the scowling. "No, after all that, my agent, and therefore every person who's obsessed with my love life for whatever fucking reason, will leave me alone and stop forcing me to try and hook up with my lady co-stars. Then, we have a big blown out break up, and tada, no one ever wants to date me again."

That's the stupidest thing I've ever heard. "You're an idiot," I blurt.

After pouts, returning to his fries with a scoff. "I worked on it all night."

"Is this like…like that trope?"

"You did *not* just use trope in an *actual*, real-life conversation."

"Y'know the uh—the one…" I cringe at my own words, and he darts a look at me from under his brow. I use air quotes like that'll help. "Like…*fake dating*? I said fake engagement and you didn't blink."

After snorts and points an aggressive fry at me. "That's because you're *not* my date. You're my cover. Really, I'm using a page from Erica's 'rebound book'. It took about five outings with Sasha to get the press off my back about Greta, and about five or six what-have-yous with Greta to get them to leave me alone about Jolene. And those were just the last couple years. I'm the T Swift of the gay world; can't keep a woman—cause, surprise, I don't like them."

"So, what, I'm your 'turn the printer off and on again' to get you another fresh-ish start?"

"Bingo."

"But if you come out as gay and Erica's right and you don't get any more work for a while, or ever, what're you going to do?"

After sits up, closes his eyes, and leans his head back with a hard sigh. "Breathe."

Oh. Well, *that's* depressing. Dramatic motherfucker.

"Sounds like you're getting more out of this deal than me," I squint. He looks back at me longer. Okay, fine, his eyes *are* hazel.

I barrel on and lose steam in my argument at the same time. "I mean—well, you get your nice publicity, and I get dragged alongside you, thrown into the spotlight even more than I already am with a judge for a grandfather." I don't mention all I've done to stay *out* of the spotlight. Not looking forward to jumping in ass first.

Kicking his leg up over his knee, he links his fingers behind his head. "Either you're in the spotlight for standing next to *me*, or you get the spotlight for being the plagiarizing, dickhead grandson of a judge who, may I add, is already struggling to keep in the publics' good graces after his most recent case had innocent people going to jail."

He says it so solid and flat that I sink an inch in my seat and suck on a tooth, looking back to the fountain. Guess he pays attention to the news more than I hoped he did.

"I mean…I don't think my shit would destroy his cred *that* much." Big ugly, desperate lie.

After hums an 'mmmmhm', and I squint back at him as he pretends to open his palms like a book.

"Sure, let's just open up next Saturday's first page of *Us Weekly*—oh look, there's you and good ol' Grandpa Mitch! What's that say there…" he squints and mimes putting on readers, "'Judge Mitch Norman—Man of Change or Chicanery? Only grandson has been outed as having lied his way into esteemed university, a college backed by non-other than the big cheat himself. Jail for Judge Norman? Or is having a disgrace of a grandchild enough of a punishment?'"

He clicks his tongue, closes his fake book, and sits back in his seat, and I manage to close my dropped jaw just to huff out, "Wow."

Someone catches his eye behind my head, and he directs a glowing smile to them, tossing up a peace sign.

Still in shock from a slap I totally deserved, I frown and turn. There's a couple giggling girls with their phones out. They see me scowling and dart away, chattering over their pictures together. "Well…how'd *that* feel?" I ask, looking back to After. He makes a face like he doesn't know what I'm talking about, and I try not to roll my eyes. "Getting all that repressed anger out after four years."

"Ah, nah, nah, Scotty," he smirks, arching his scarred brow. I don't want that smirk anymore; it can fuck off. "Getting my repressed anger out would've been curb stomping you the day you ruined our friendship. I'm all hunky dory now."

Can't believe those words came from the same guy that used to sob watching Land Before Time.

I eye the large boot crossed over his knee, tapping up in the air along to music crackling over the outdoor speakers. "Sure...so. You're saying if I *don't* help you, you'll out the plagiarism?"

After cranes his neck back and actually looks hurt. "Dude. No. You fucked up, but I'm not gonna ruin your life like that. Believe it or not, but I forgave you years ago. Holding onto that shit was gonna destroy me."

Believe it or not? Definitely not. Nice that he's moved past it, but I can't seem to break off the ball and chain of guilt I've been lugging around all this time. The fountain is suddenly much more interesting than this life-changing conversation.

"Though—I mean, I know you. You won't be able to hold onto this much longer before you implode and take half the block down with you. You don't keep secrets well, you never have."

Don't have anything to say to that. It's his turn to fidget now. He clears his throat, and I force myself to meet his eye. "So. We got a deal or not? This is my big promise to you, fulfilled. You'll never in your life be able to ask for another one."

"This is me fulfilling *my* big promise to you, too—"

"Nope, sure ain't."

"What?" I glare and cross my arms, self-pity thrown aside as I grapple for the defensive. "Like all fuck hell it is!"

"That makes no sense."

"Makes *perfect* sense—I'm doing you a favor with this cover up shit—"

"You're asking *me* for a favor with *your* writing," he corrects, jabbing a finger at me. "I'm merely adding flavor to it. Flavor to the favor. I like that."

"You can't change the rules." I sound like I'm twelve.

He nods in fake thought and taps at his chin. "In that case...I wonder if you can get a job at Chili's again. Maybe Wendy's would take you after you get out of prison—"

"Fine." I'm about to raise my hand from under the table when his eyes dart over my head again. I'm expecting more ogling girls, but he's not smiling like last time.

There's a sound like fluttering bug wings right in my ear, and I start to turn, when he moves his foot off his knee and kicks me in the shin. Not out of anger, more like a tap to get my attention.

Maybe. Might've been out of anger, who knows. "Camera shutter. We're gathering a crowd. C'mon." He gets up and goes to reach for my arm, when his hand draws back, and he angles his chin down the street. "Park nearby, more secluded."

Chapter 6

He's snaky and sneaky and I struggle to keep up with him, rolling my bike along and fighting to ignore the amount of rubberneckers that watch us as we nearly gallop through the streets.

I'm almost to the point of telling him to just run like I know he wants to and I'll follow on my bike, when we end up at a soccer field. Not too many people out, mid-afternoon on a Friday; most kids are back in schools, people ending lunch breaks. Just the occasional lady out jogging, dads pushing strollers. Lot less eyes on us than at DQ.

"Before I sign my soul away for public humiliation," I begin, setting my bike against a tree, watching an older woman power walk with a schnauzer at her side, "what're the five things you want to do together?"

"Murder."

"All five of them?"

"Yep, got a list."

"I've got shovels."

He chuckles and puts his hands on his hips, staring out at a couple of toddlers tripping over a soccer ball while their parents chat on a park bench. "But uh. Nah, I've got some ideas."

"Let's hear it. If…if I can ask that," I add and rub at my neck under my hoodie. He glances at me, looks between my eyes, before his own drop to the ground.

In this quiet moment, my brain reminds me I still haven't apologized for what I did. I take in a breath, but he talks over me. "Let me ask first, cause this is your favor: when do you need to have the first piece sent to your boss? How much time do we have to work on your writing?"

"Jackie's given me until March, spring break, to get the first article written. Said she understood that I needed to—" I wiggle a hand in the air— "dust off some cobwebs."

"Kind of fitting for this, too," he replies, wiggling his hand between us like I did.

"True."

"How often have you been writing? Like, have you been keeping up with it?"

I nod and kick my heel to the grass. "Yeah. Off and on, best as I can. When she first said she read some of my work that I'd done in college, I just…" My hoodie's too warm. I shiver anyway. First sign of anxiety building up, know that by now. "I felt hopeful that, for once, my own stuff was enough; that what I had to offer was good enough to give me a chance."

I dart a look at his face and that furrowed, scarred brow. "Anyway, not until March, so I guess we can work around your schedule. Didn't you just finish filming something? What's your downtime like?"

After's still frowning, but he rolls his shoulders back with a hum. "Let's see uh…well, Erica's trying to run me ragged, but this whole dumb shit with Sasha's given me a couple weeks to chill. Her agent was demanding that I clear up my schedule so I could spend time with her. Ended with me having to cancel a bunch of things. Now that we're over, I've still got those weekends open."

"Okay, so weekends. I've got my dorm on campus."

He nods. "Cool. What's your roommate like?"

I scratch at my arm. "No roommate."

"How's *that* possible?"

"Grandpa Mitch. Didn't want temptation."

"Not sure what *that* means," he mumbles. And it's gonna stay that way.

I hop us back on track, or at least, away from anything related to me. "So you've got weekends. Are you free the first Friday of March?"

"The fifth? Should be, or Saturday. We can start with one of those, I'll let you know."

"Okay, good plan. Now what about *your* side of things?"

After starts to pace, tapping a rhythm on his chin. "I think small things would be a post or two on Instagram, maybe Twitter. You got a Twitter?"

Unfortunately, cause I can't help myself. "I tweet, yes."

"Sweet. On top of those things, Mom's got a fundraiser March 20th. Was one of the events Sasha wanted me to not go to."

"Why was that?"

After stops pacing to dig a boot toe into the grass. "No idea. But it was a deal breaker. I mean that and the—" he grins and flips a wrist at me, and I roll my eyes— "so you can go with me to that."

"You think your mom will be fooled by us?"

"I mean she *knows* I'm gay. She's more supportive than Erica, but she doesn't…" He takes a step to start walking again, then pauses, rocking back on his heels.

After scratches furiously at the fade in his haircut on his neck. "Mom doesn't really fight for me. I mean, I signed the contract as a legal adult. I get that. Would just be nice to have someone standing up on my side."

I take a breath to say something like, that's rough buddy, but he keeps talking, and I don't want to interrupt. Seeing After with slumped shoulders as he shares his personal thoughts is as rare as— shit, I don't know. Seeing a jackalope.

"I don't *think* she's homophobic, at least to me, but she's never forgiven Dad for breaking up their marriage and going off with a man. Y'know what I mean?"

Don't know if that's rhetorical or not, so I just shrug and nod. "Yeah like—like how he asked for the divorce out of the blue—married a dude two months after the official split. She's always been...weird. About *him*. Being gay. Sometimes she's weird about *me* being gay, like. Like, look, but don't touch the boys, y'know? I dunno. Maybe she *is* homophobic. I don't fucking know..."

His eyes flash to mine, and he sniffs and picks up his pacing. Always with the sniffing. I think homeboy's either got some serious allergies, or someone once said it made him look macho. I bet it was this Erica person. "Mom knows you from Lubbock, that's what matters. She knows we were super close and will probably say, 'Oh, goodie, you ended up with a sweet southern boy from your hometown, and not a California crack addict,' or whatever."

Just an ex-Texan crack addict, but that's semantics. "Cause those are your only two options."

"Obviously. So fundraiser, then I think if people see you coming and going from my house after staying the night, they'll really lose their shit. You can meet Chicken."

"You have a chicken?"

"Chicken is my dog."

I make an 'are you kidding me' face, and he smirks. "I was drunk, he answered to it, it stuck. Moving on. There's a black-tie event in early April for the movie I finished filming last year, big viewing party thing."

"I don't own black tie—I mean, I own a *black tie*—"

"It's cool. Yvonne, she's a fashion designer friend, she can make you something snazzy. She's been working on mine for over a month. No doubt she'll have a blast designing something for you, too." I turn in a slow circle and watch him as he moves and nods to his own ideas. He really *did* think all this out.

"Alright, so far I'm just pasty arm candy, there's a sleepover and a chicken. What's next?" He sends me another real deal After smile. Every time he does, it's like those smiles are getting more and more genuine, and I'm getting more and more relaxed back into this friendship. That's super unsafe.

"I've got another buddy, Nicholas Starr, he's a director. Him and his brother Harry are filming a TV show in Tennessee; they've asked me to guest star in an episode. So I gotta go do that for a few days in late April. You said you're off Fridays and Mondays?"

"Yep, you got it. Tennessee, nice, never been there."

"I know, I thought you might like that one; you used to talk about visiting Dollywood one day."

My ears tickle and I scratch at one. "I uh—yeah, I did."

"Lastly, I'm celebrating my birthday with Dad."

"Cool."

"In Spain."

Oh. International. I go through six faces, and he smiles at them all. "Um. Spain." He nods. "In…in May." He nods twice.

"You look like I've lost you," he says, putting his hands on his hips again and swaying side to side.

"No, no, still here just. Shocked."

"Spain shocked you, but not fake boyfriends?"

"So we *are* fake dating!"

He squints at my celebratory finger jab in the air. "Yes, fine. We fly out early May 21st and we'll be there until the 25th. You'll be graduated by then I think?"

I shake my head. "A'ight, at least you'll be done with your finals?" I nod my head and he mirrors me. "Sweet. So we can celebrate both my birthday and your upcoming graduation that weekend."

"I don't wanna steal your birthday celebration, that's fucked up."

It's like around him, 'steal' is a four-letter word. He didn't seem to notice the way I cringed when I said it. "What do you think, Scotty, sound doable? We can work on your writing on the weekends, or during the week around other stupid shit I've gotta handle that's Sasha-cleanup crew related."

"Y'all dated for three months and you have to do that much housekeeping?"

"You should've seen the mess after me and Jolene broke up. Dated for ten months. Even did the dirty with her a few times to get her off my back, cause she started suspecting I *was* gay, or incompetent. Erica's idea. 'What's a few little pokes to keep the press away,' she said, 'let the brat go on and on about what a stallion you are'…" After sends the trees a lip-curling glare. "Can't do another year with her, man. Not one.…"

I blurt it out cause I'm a total jerk. "How'd you manage to have sex so much if you're gay?"

He looks at me for a long moment, gives a solemn nod. "So…that's a good question," he says softly. "First you…"

He raises his hands. Points one finger and starts to move it to the hole he's made with his other hand. I smack at his arm, and he swats me back. "How the hell did you think I had sex?"

Oh, sir, I most *definitely* know how *you* have sex.

"I just meant that must've been upsetting. I don't know how you got through it so many times."

"I got very, very drunk," he deadpans.

I shift my weight and rub at my arm under my hoodie. Could apologize out of empathy, pity, shame, dealer's choice. I choose to change the subject. "Sooo…okay, cool—well. I'm game for mission 'break After out of the closet'. Thanks for explaining your plan."

"Sure." After crouches and starts unlacing his boots, and I stare at him for a moment before I remember it's part of the promise: no toes crossed. I pull my sneakers off one at a time with my toes on my heels, and I yank off my socks, losing balance on my second foot.

He stands half an inch shorter without the boots, and I smile at his toes curling into the cold grass, feet half-hidden under the cuffs of his cargo pants.

"Alright," he huffs, wiggling out his shoulders. "Let's do this."

"Ready?" I ask myself more than him.

He nods. "Ready."

I feel the need to adjust my stance, spreading my legs an inch more and bending at the knees like I'm about to go Super Saiyan. I start to think he might make fun of me for it, but After does the same thing. I send my right hand out, cross my left hand over it with my pinky raised.

He smiles for some reason and shakes my right hand with his. Inches from hooking his pinky around mine, he pauses.

"What? Suddenly deciding you don't want me to sully your limelight?" I ask.

After's smile fades. His eye twitches from my face to our hands. What I think he's thinking is: this is it. I doubt he'll ever have any reason to come ask me for *his* big favor, not with how different we are, how successful he is. This is a weird happenstance for me; I never thought I'd be trying to claim the promise after we stopped talking years ago.

Once he helps me smooth things through with this new job and with my writing, and once his five stupid things are done, then. *We're* done. For good.

What he says though is totally unexpected. "I'm just thinking you're gonna wanna get a spray tan. Any pictures of me next to you are gonna get all blown out; you're the palest Californian here. It's embarrassing."

"Oh, fuck off," I snap, snagging his pinky as he grins.

Chapter 7

Willa and Veronica are on their way over for Bevett's fifteenth today. We've got fluffy boas at the ready, glitter cannons around here somewhere, and someone's dropping off a cake any minute now. It's the third one I ordered. Bevett tried to tell me we only needed one, but I just had to briefly mention the chaos of her thirteenth, when her and her besties devoured an entire sheet cake between them before we'd even opened presents; she agreed a third was most likely necessary if we are to have leftovers this time.

Everything's set up and ready to become a teenage disaster, and yet I can't find the birthday girl herself.

I check her usual hiding spaces (a music room on the third floor, a window bench she's re-purposed as a teeny reading nook, and a cabinet under the stairs leading to the second floor) but I'm coming up empty. Scratching at my nose, I send her a text.

[Me] 12:22: Where you at, booboo?

No reply, but I swear I heard the tinkling *dingaling* of her phone going off somewhere nearby. I send another.

[Me] 12:24: marco...

There's a muffled, "Polo," to my left, and I smile and shake my head, going for the closet to my side.

Bevett likes to hide, like me. But unlike me, she sometimes does it in obvious places, where she knows she'll be found sooner or later; as much as she shuts down on occasion, bottling up things that upset her, she doesn't explode like Dad or me.

She simmers, opens the cork of the bottle slow with just a question or two to coax what's wrong out of her. Bevett likes to be helped, she just doesn't like to ask for that help.

I rap my knuckles on the door in a 'shave-and-a-hair-cut'. When I get a 'two-bits' knock back, I open the door. She's perched on the ground between a vacuum and a wardrobe box of Mitch's winter coats. Clearly she attempted to braid her coily, dark brown curls, but most of the shorter strands have freed themselves, giving her a perfect Ms. Frizzle look.

"Hiya, Bevvy." The hall light coming in behind me accentuates the shadows under her eyes. Pretty sure she went to bed last night before me, too.

"Hi," she mutters, thumb tapping around at her phone. I don't have to see the screen to know she's poking at nonsense just to not look at me.

"You got the birthday blues?" I ask. She hums and clicks her phone closed. "Anything I can do?"

Looking at the vacuum, she trails her nail down the kinked hose on the side. "No. Not really. I just need to get through it."

"But not alone, you know that."

"I know," she smiles, leaning her head to the wall. Her lip shakes and she forces her smile wider. As soon as I sit and kick my feet out with my arms open, she's crawling into my lap, letting me hoist her knees over my leg. She puts her temple on my collarbone and I kiss her hair, rocking her with my cheek to her head.

"What set it off this time? Another year without them? Or not the friends you want to be seeing today?"

"Bit of both. I said a prayer to Dad, Momma and Georgie this morning. There was a big fat monarch on my window and I told myself it was them. I know that's silly, but I remember you once said those were Georgie's favorite."

"You're right; my mom used to grow milkweeds just for the butterflies. And it's not silly. Y'know when it rains, and there's that nice smell afterward? I think it's all three of them, saying hello."

Bevett's quiet. "That's so nice, grump," she whispers.

"What else did you do today?" I ask, tucking a loose curl behind her ear.

"I facetimed Mill earlier. Hattie was busy; it's dinner time in El Paso. But she sent me a long text this morning about how much she misses me. I only knew them a few months for fifth grade and…I know I'm young, I'm sure I'll make more friends. Eventually."

She squishes tighter to me, fingers pulling at my sweatshirt collar. "But we've been here for four years and—and I haven't met *anyone* with as nice a laugh as Mill. Or with soft hands like Hattie—she taught me how to do a French-tip manicure on my own. Showed me over Zoom."

"I know, pooch," I nod. She sniffles and I wipe under her nose with my sleeve cuff. "Why don't we um," I hope I don't regret this, "why don't we try to visit them after I graduate? Go to El Paso in the summer."

Her head shoots up so fast she nearly clocks me in the jaw. "You'd go back to El Paso for me?"

"You know I'd sell my soul for you, Bevett." Her eyes water, and I tap at her lashes with my thumb.

"Would Grandpa even let us go back there?"

"Wouldn't hurt to ask, would it? And just because you only knew them for a little bit doesn't mean they won't stay lifelong friends. You can know someone for a day and know you're meant to be there for each other forever. Or for years. And you drift apart."

Bevett's brow wrinkles and she hums, circling her arms around my waist. "But not you and David. Y'all worked it out, you said you're talking again after all this time."

"Sort of. Yeah."

"I don't know if I told you, maybe I did. But I'm so glad y'all are friends again. I really missed him. I love him. He's family."

I nod and bury my face in her curls, glaring off at the box of Grandpa's coats. "Right. Family."

"Let me think about El Paso. I'm not sure I…I mean. I *want* to see my friends, but. If Aunt Devon and Kendra found out we'd be in town." Her inhale shakes us both. "I don't ever want to see them again. Does that make me bad—"

"No, never. Never. I don't either, Bevvy. Doesn't make us bad. I'm only sorry I let it go on for so long. And that I didn't tell you what was happening until it was too late."

Bevett leans away from me, so far that she pulls out of my arms. She puts her hands on my shoulders, and in a flash, she's twenty-two, and I'm fifteen. "Don't. Don't apologize anymore for El Paso." She squeezes my cheeks in her warm hands until I nod, and she smiles. "I'm still sad."

"It's okay if you are."

"Tell me about fifteen years ago."

I laugh and take her wrists and make her smack herself in the head with her own hands. "Again? You just love hearing about yourself."

"Who doesn't? Do it, please? I like hearing about them, too—it puts them here with us."

"In here?" I smirk, squinting up and around the small closet. "Jesus, it'd be cramped with all of us in here."

"We could snuggle," she chuckles. "Puppy pile. Like what Momma used to ask for, when she'd come home from work and would kick off her heels."

"Alright, assume the position, bub." She jerks backward, sits against the box of coats, and brings her knees to her chest, eyes sharp on me. "February 27th, 2006. 'Twas a dark and stormy night—"

"Was not!" she laughs.

"Am I telling your birth story or are you? Girl, you weren't there yet!"

"I'm gonna be! Early and with flair."

"With a ton of screaming, that's for sure—"

"Skip to when you nearly dropped me—"

"I did *not* nearly drop you!"

"Dad said you freaked out cause I was all icky."

"Rumor has it, I continue to freak out around you to this day, cause you're *still* all icky—" She slaps me in the arm, and I go for her big ears, making her shriek. It turns into a screaming tickle fight that ends with me alligator rolling away from her, out of the closet and into the hallway, as she goes for my belt loops in an attempt to give me a wedgie.

—

I keep a close eye on Bevett until her friends show up. Willa parades in with fifteen hot pink and lime green balloons. In her delightful, on occasion unintelligible, Michigan accent, she announces that she's here for the best birthday girl ever, and plants a big kiss on Bevett's cheek that has her stuttering and giggling.

And when Veronica comes in and presents Bevett with a handmaid knit hat, complete with two fluffy pompoms that take up most of the top, I know I have nothing to worry about. Especially once Bevett meets my eye as the girls go straight for cake number one, and whispers she thinks she might be wrong about not having super close friends like she thought.

The three cakes were a bad idea. We blow through the first one before the pizza arrives. While we wait for homemade tortilla chips to cook, we play a game of hide and seek that ends up lasting two hours, cause Willa can't listen to directions and the little weirdo hides outside.

Then it's time for cake number two, which includes dance party and dress up. Veronica insists she just has to wear the yellow boa because it matches her braces and her hijab, and I mean who could argue with that logic?

Willa's grumpy until I reveal a rainbow one, then her squeal echoes through the house. Bevett takes five for herself, leaving me with the lime green boa because it 'matches my eyes', claims Willa. Yes, of course, how silly of me.

As soon as they discover I'm moderately decent at the piano, I become the source of entertainment. Veronica begs me to play

Miley Cyrus, and Willa demands Megan Thee Stallion. (On the piano? Also you're fourteen, what the fuck?)

But it's Bevett's idea to start off with something easier. Like American Pie by Don McLean. I think I would've preferred Ms. Stallion.

That was my thinking anyway. Except on the third run around of the chorus, in his distant first floor office, we hear Grandpa singing along. I find my rhythm after that.

By cake three, Mitch finishes work and makes an appearance, accepting a neon blue boa from Bevett. I'm concerned he might be on edge (his most recent case has gone on for longer than he said he'd liked) and last year, he didn't come out of his office at all except to sing her Happy Birthday.

This time, he actually smiles next to her and the girls as I take a photo, and he says I can post it on Instagram if I want to. Though, those aren't his exact words.

"Yes, you may share that with your 'grammers' if you choose. Hashtag—" straight up says 'hashtag' in the middle of his sentence along with air quotes, I shit you not— "'Fun family times'." Bevett has to hide in the pantry so he can't hear her squeaking laughter.

Cake three, though a mistake at the time, is my savior, because it knocks all three of them the fuck out as soon as one AM rolls around. I get a notification on my phone from Instagram, and I check it as I clean up after the tyrants.

Willa posted a video of me singing and playing piano for the girls while they danced earlier; hadn't even noticed her filming. I sound like a cat stuck in a thunderstorm. Lovely. And there's no way for me to take it down.

Okay hold up, let me get this out real quick and I swear I won't mention it again—no, really, I promise. I *hate* social media. I have maybe eighty Instagram followers on a good day. I post snippets of my writing, things that inspire me, miscellaneous selfies with me and Charlotte or me and Bevett. It's not my first account, either; I had to delete the one I made in Junior High.

Couldn't tell you what was on it, but I do know it had a lot more smiles and happy memories. And probably a lot more After.

All that had to go when I left El Paso and moved in with Mitch. Along with my old Twitter and Tumblr. (Made up of Chris Pine and Lord of the Rings smut. No, not mixed together, and no, I will not explain myself.) Truth be told, I wasn't too broken up about those.

I only got to keep my SIM card, number and all my data, cause it had old voicemails and texts from Dad and Cassidy, and Mitch took pity on me since I had nothing left of Mom. But he wiped me of everything else though, down to LinkedIn. Like I was hooking up with people and getting dope using flippin' *LinkedIn*.

Exiting out of the video before it starts to torture me all over again on repeat, I post a couple different shots in a carousel, including the one with Mitch. I start it with Bevett, Willa and Veronica, all wearing their boas. And there's me, grinning in my own green boa, planted near the bottom, holding the phone cause my arms are built in selfie-sticks.

"**Happy fifteenth, pooch!**" I caption it with no hashtags or filters. What would I even hashtag it? 'Family fun times' like Mitch said? Maybe I'm always doing it wrong and that's why I have next to no one following me. I don't know.

After likes it less than a minute later. He went through and randomly spam-liked a dozen of my old posts the moment he followed me yesterday, too. I smirk and close my phone.

Gathering a dozen popcorn bowls and eating the remaining M&M's that had fallen to the bottoms, my phone goes off in my pocket in quick succession, vibrating non-stop like. Well. Like a vibrator, straight up. My notifications say I just gathered ten followers since I posted that photo five minutes ago.

I frown and open the app, munching on candy. Then choking on candy.

After took my photo and shared it to his story, adding at the bottom, "**Only the best birthday ever for goose**." He's only ever called her that nickname, for whatever reason. Not even Dad or her mom used it, or me.

Another thing from him pops up on my newsfeed: he filmed a reaction video to the one Willa made. He's grinning and dancing around in his gigantic kitchen, wearing sweats and a loose tank top that shows off his collarbone and a shit ton of man cleavage.

First thing I notice is he's still got on the necklace his dad sent him for his sixteenth birthday; a leather choker with a black pearl. That makes me smile, cause I still have the bracelet Pedro gave me, too.

Then I notice a bottle in his hand as he jams along to the music. Likes are flying in, people wanting to know what he's drinking, how's his night. He takes a sip from the bottle before singing out the lyrics, and I get an uncomfortable tightness in my chest when I see it's just soda.

He's tagged Willa cause it's her post, Bevett, and me and—look, six more people just followed me, commenting on *my* post now. My now hundred followers on Instagram turns to a hundred and forty-three—forty-seven—sixty-five—

Then suddenly Twitter's sending me a notification.

@DavidDespués has started following you.

And Twitter *explodes*.

I pull up my texts and shoot a fast message to the last number After talked to me from.

[Me] 01:31: Is this all you do now? Swarm my social medias and send your Double D girls after me? My twitter follower count just went up to three hundred. It was seventy-two ten minutes ago.

[NEW-After] 01:33: Ur singing hasn't improved much. Not even Soundhound could help me figure out wtf u were screeching.

[NEW-After] 01:33: Also, Double D girls? OMFG please tell me that's what they really call themselves.

[Me] 01:34: I highly doubt your fans are that clever, if they're obsessing over someone like you.

[NEW-After] 01:35: I'm a proud member of the himbo society. I am both too stupid and too hot to care what u think.

I hate that I laugh at that. He doesn't get to make me laugh. I know *I'm* the one that fucked up, but I haven't forgiven myself yet, and I'll continue to be angry and bitter about it. And that includes not finding the person who I hurt so badly funny. I refuse.

[NEW-After] 01:37: Enjoy fandom while it lasts. The moment we breakup, ull be nothing but a fart in the wind.

[Me] 01:37: is this a stagnant wind? A gust? A hurricane? Depending on the wind, a fart lodged in said breeze could be lethal, blown about all over town, impacting thousands. No one is safe.

[NEW-After] 01:38: Sweet Jesus I just snorted soda up my nose

[Me] 01:38: you just snorted coke? Goodness, After, that's how it starts, y'know...

[NEW-After] 01:39: STOP

See, *I* get to be funny. Cause I'm trying to make my mistakes right. Me being silly and over the top is expected as I strive to get back in his good graces. And I get to make fun of cocaine abuse because, hello, Scott Everett, recovered addict.

I think that's how it works. Should probably not make any more snorting jokes in case he takes one of them literally and asks too many questions. Not that After will ask me any questions. Not that I want him to. Oh look, I'm at eight hundred Instagram followers.

Chapter 8

Sometimes when I visit for longer than a couple days, we hook my bike up to one of the chauffeurs my grandpa has on demand. I don't mind those rides; depending on the person, it can be a chatty thirty minutes to Jethro, a pleasant off and on conversation with some music playing, or a hilarious mix of dialects that end in both of us laughing and nodding because we're not sure what the other person is saying.

In fact, the person who picked me up from school back in December spoke strictly Swedish, though she knew—and got very excited about—Billie Eilish, so we bonded over Bad Guy and listened to it on repeat the whole way.

I'd take any one of those over the grueling silence hanging in Grandpa's Cadillac right now.

Being Monday, first of the month, I'm just a drop off, like Bevett was this morning; as soon as he takes care of me, he's off to the office for the day. Now that I'm without my chatty shield, it's just me, him, and his knuckles gripping the steering wheel like he's about to rip it off and hit me over the head with it, Mad Max style.

"So. New job. Forty thousand a year," he says after fifteen minutes have passed with me counting the Chino's threading on my knee.

"Yes, sir," I reply, chancing a glance at him. He hums. Hidden in his trim gray beard making him look like musketeer meets poet meets pirate lord, I can see him chewing his lower lip, just like I do, like my birth mom did.

Still feels like a stretch that we're related at all. He has blue eyes like she had, lighter hair—though his turned silver about two decades ago—and that's where the similarities end. My mom Georgiana died from cervical cancer when I was nearly seven, and I heard from a random man named Mitch a year later, claiming to have been her father and therefore, my grandfather.

I guess Mitch and Mom had a falling out when she married Dad, and he was waiting for time to pass to 'heal all wounds' or 'hide all secrets'. Who knows. Sent me a card or two as I grew up, but that was it. The moment Bevett was born, even without any blood ties to her, he started visiting nonstop, flying all the way from Cali to see her.

And Dad allowed it, encouraged it. Whatever happened between Grandpa Mitch and Mom, I doubt she ever really told him, otherwise Dad wouldn't have let the man back into his house in Lubbock.

Loved Mom with all my heart, even if I blacked out a lot of those last months with her, when she was just a sick corpse I visited in the hospital, a frail echo of her old self with my sharp-slanted nose and long fingers. But I remember, in her prime, she blasted Joan Jett, made the best chicken parmesan and spaghetti, and always wore mix-matched socks.

Loved Dad and Cassidy, too, even if I think Dad moved on too fast; mourning Mom for less than a year, then claiming he met his true soulmate in Cassidy. They had Bevett before they were even married.

Love them all. But I hate that I've always felt like an afterimage of an old love story that's long been buried. Even more so now that it's just me and Bevett.

"When's your first day?" asks Mitch, pulling me unwillingly back into conversation.

"March 29th, right after spring break is over."

"That's only a few weeks away. You must be very excited," he says next.

I nod and trace a circle on my knee with my finger. "I am. It'll be nice to get some experience in before I've graduated."

"Excellent," he nods. "Well done, Scotty." My heart slams out and crashes through the windshield, and I have to tighten my mouth into a line to keep from grinning too wide.

"Thanks, Grandpa." My voice shakes. "Thank you."

"I'm only a little confused," he says, turning us off one highway and onto the other.

"About what?"

"Well…$40,000 is quite a lot. For part-time work."

I watch him from my peripheral as he slows along with traffic. He takes one hand off the wheel and taps it on his leg before running his thumb over the pressed seam at his knee. His suit jacket swings to a pause behind his head like a giant black bat, or like death coming to knock me off the flyover, for thinking I could lie to him about *money* of all things.

"It's um. Well, I actually met with Jackie Silversmith."

He looks shocked at this and checks my face, before accelerating and getting us moving again. "The director?"

"Yes, sir. She's asked me to do some writing on the side. So. I'm getting paid for that as well…"

"You didn't mention that."

"It wasn't totally solidified until recently. Was an add on." How can I make this fluffier for him so he won't look into it too much? "In a way, I'm doing them a favor. That's what Jackie said."

He gives me one of his rare chuckles, rumbling and deep, something I've been gifted on Christmas mornings or when I've killed myself to get straight A's. "A favor for the director of a publishing house. Well damn, Scott. Who'd have thought?"

He could stop there, easily. Not another word needed, doesn't have to elaborate, cause I know exactly what he's talking about. But Grandpa Mitch can't hear my inner dialogue, begging him to shut the fuck up before he makes my day so much worse. (If he could hear *any* of the chaos happening in my head, I'd have been punted out of his champagne Cadillac by now.)

"After everything that happened in El Paso, you've come so far. I admit, the cocaine, the drinking—I really didn't see you succeeding in the long run, let alone staying alive to get to your twenties. Don't get me wrong, I understand Cassidy and Tyler's deaths were hard on you and, well, I'll take some responsibility here."

My hand was creeping along to unlock the car door, ready to fling myself into oncoming traffic, but I frown and look back at him. "Responsibility for what?"

He sighs and takes us onto the frontage road. Only one last turn until the long street to Jethro. It's never felt like such a hopeless trek before in all the years I've made this drive.

"For the people you were living with, where I left you after the funeral. I…appreciate. What my daughter Devon did for you, her and her. Her *roommate* Kendra. But the way they ran their household. Lying to me about it, making you lie to me as well. I should have picked you and Bevett up the moment we said goodbye to Cassidy and Tyler, taken you both home to California. Not let you whore your way through your fall semester as a senior with that 'depressive episode', setting such an ugly example for your younger sister in the process."

Oh, *wow*. Well.

I started shivering as soon as 'roommate' was snarled, instead of acknowledging that his last living daughter is a lesbian in a committed, long-term relationship.

But…to call me mourning my parents a *depressive* episode. To say what happened in El Paso was me being a…it's like he forgot every single other nightmare I told him about during those wicked fall months that tore me apart.

Now I'm shuddering so hard, I'm having to clench my jaw to keep my teeth from chattering. He pats my knee and I coil my muscles tight so I don't snap apart.

"I'm glad you've gotten this far, that's all Scott, and that you've changed up some of your lifestyle. I suppose there's that whole 'it's not a choice' thing, and I'm not disagreeing with that."

Aren't you?— "But you've cleaned up your act, and I'm proud of you. I'd have hated the alternative if you hadn't. Jethro is a good place for you, and I believe you'll do great things at Silversmith."

For every compliment, there's a punch in my gut.

Proud you're not shooting up and snorting coke and drinking and fucking yourself into a stupor from October to December. Like you did months after your parents, the last adults who might've believed in your potential, were in a horrible car accident three days after you turned eighteen that spring.

Glad you're embracing your sexuality enough that I can check off the box that says, 'look, I'm progressive, I've got an LGBT grandchild and a biracial grandchild'—but it's a good thing you're not *actually* living out that lifestyle. Like After said: look, but don't touch.

Super pleased you ended up in the school I pushed you to the limit to get into. Would've hated if you hadn't. Cause then I would have had to send you to conversion therapy, like I may or may not have tried to do to my youngest daughter, Devon. Will neither confirm nor deny.

Y'know, I bet he had. That would explain why he had such an insane, decade lasting argument with my mom. Attempting to force one of his daughters into a reformation 'school'. Maybe that clears up why Devon's the way she is, too. Not that I'm making excuses for her.

Wonder what Mom would have to say, if she knew he'd been threatening her kid with the same torture. I know Devon and Kendra had a lot to say about it, but there wasn't much they could do when Mitch showed up on their doorstep, claiming with a court order that he'd be taking little Bevett with him, and I could either come along, or I'd never see her again.

I was her blood, sure, and eighteen; old enough to care for her. But he was the one with a steady job, steady home, and steady mental health. What choice did I have back then?

Got a choice right now, as I stand on the curb, watching Grandpa's car go back down the drive toward the highway.

Could walk into the street and hope one of the college kids texting and driving hits me. With a tense smile on my face for anyone I pass, I turn and walk toward the dorms.

Chapter 9

Wonder what it must be like, to be a college student with a roommate. Maybe more irritating, sleep broken up by someone tripping into bed at three in the morning after a night of partying. Maybe more frustrating, when we'd disagree over whose turn it was to take the laundry to the laundromat on the opposite side of Fredericks Hall.

Maybe more wonderful than ever, laughing with a new friend to the point of tears with Charlotte and Mei staying over with us well into the night, drinking cream sodas and playing never-have-I-ever like little kids.

Wouldn't know.

Orientation week, freshman year, I never met anyone that shared room 65G with me. A day went by, first classes. Four days. Two weeks.

I talked to the staff member in charge of my dorm hall, asked if there'd been a mistake. She checked her paperwork three times and said no mistake, no roommate, no buddy ever. Then I reached out to Grandpa, since he'd helped me fill out the papers months prior, in case it had been a slip up on our end.

His voice was gruff and short over the phone when I called him that day. "I made arrangements. You won't be getting a roommate," he'd said. There was a *click-click-click* of an irritated pen over the line when I asked why, and he cleared his throat. "Keep you in check this way. No temptations."

I asked why again, what did I do wrong. I'll never forget the way he growled at me, how the line crackled and I held my phone away from my ear like he might fly through it and attack me.

"Jesus, Scott, the *last* thing you'll be bringing back into my goddamn house over winter break is a fucking STD. No drinking, no sex, no roommate that could potentially *foul you up* like that man did in El Paso. You won't sully Bevett anymore than you already have!" Then he hung up on me. And I cried through my last three classes of the day and never asked again.

Was one of the times I nearly called After. I stared at his face in my phone, a filtered selfie that gave him puppy ears and a rosy nose and extra freckles.

Last message received: March 23rd, 2017. "**Hey, are you still there? Did you fall asleep on me again?**" Never replied.

Now I'm in my empty dorm room, and it's three PM on Friday after a full week of school. Classes are fine, if not dull at this point; I took all the ones that would kick me in the teeth already. In fact, I could've graduated *last* semester. Grandpa Mitch doesn't know that.

And he'll never know the reasons I didn't were because I refuse to A) face the world just yet, and B) have to live under his roof again. Because, to my surprise and somewhat horror, he's already offered repeatedly for me to stay in his home, rent free, while I work at Silversmith after graduation.

Like absolute hell.

But it's either that or try to find a place of my own with what little money I have from Mom, Cassidy, and Dad's wills. Might have to pay a few extra grand to JU cause I'm turning into a career student, but as long as I keep doing well enough to get financial aid, it's a price I'm willing to fork over for now. Better than finding a flat in LA like Jackie suggested. It's inevitable that I'll have to move, but I'm holding on to the free-ish rent while I can.

I'm finishing up a homework assignment for my art history class when my phone thrums next to my elbow. Without looking at the ID, I hit accept. "This is Scott."

"Hey, it's me."

Me who? I frown and glance at my phone. After's young, filtered face and name pop up on my screen. He's calling me from his *old* number? He's calling me at all?

"Oh—hi, hey." I kick my feet off the desk and stand from my swivel chair. "Hey—"

"We had an appointment. Thing."

We didn't, but I'm not about to say that. "Right, yeah—"

"I don't know where you are."

"Well, where are *you*?" I ask, checking out my first floor window to the green lawn, full of students playing frisbee and sitting in the sun.

"I'm standing by the campus entrance. There's a fountain, steps up to…looks like Jones Hall?"

"Okay, yeah, you're close, I'll be there in a minute," I reply, shoving my feet into the sneakers by my desk.

"Please hurry." I start to laugh, but his voice lowers. "People are um…staring."

"Got it, on my way." I hang up without another word and grab my keys, pulling on a dark purple Jethro hoodie as I run to the doors of Fredericks Hall. Unlocking my bike from the rack, I zip through campus, standing off the seat and dodging pedestrians.

I see him before he sees me. He's got his left hand in his pocket, and he keeps adjusting the bill of his ball cap over his eyes.

Can hide his tattoo and that scar on his brow, but something about him just exudes 'popular', and sure enough, people are slowing down and watching him curiously. "Hey, dude," I call out, lifting a leg off my bike. After turns as I jog to a stop and nod to him. "Sorry, guess I didn't tell you where my dorm actually is."

"It's okay. It occurred to me I didn't tell you when I'd be by, either."

"You don't need to; you can show up whenever." I mean, he *can't*, I have boundaries. Sort of. Those were always murky when it came to him. "We're this way."

"This is a nice school," he says as we walk. "Bigger than I thought it would be."

"Yeah. Right…" Too many students are stopping and gawking at him now. I grab a fistful of his jean jacket sleeve and drag him toward a brick pillar. "Trade coats with me."

"What, why?"

"You're dressed like a celebrity, whether you meant to or not. Plus, we've got a ways to go before the dorms, and I don't want you mobbed."

"You got here in five minutes."

"I'm on a bike. Can *you* run as fast as a bicycle?" Probably. After frowns but agrees, shrugging off his jean jacket.

I get a good look at his tattoo as I take off my hoodie. Thorny vines and leaves twine around his middle and ring fingers. They trail up his hand to his wrist, where black chevron arrows point down to his knuckles. Further up are yellow and red flowers that circle a hyper realistic swan. It's being choked by coiling thorns, graceful head bent. Above it sits a broken golden crown, a little faded in his tan skin.

He catches me staring at his arm, and I pull on his jean jacket as he slips into my hoodie. It literally takes until that moment for me to realize there's spaghetti sauce on the white JU on the front, too.

The sleeves of his are too long on me, but I roll them up rather stylishly if I say so myself, and as soon as he's brought the dark purple hood up over his hat, he looks a lot more like a student.

"What do you think?" he asks, putting his hands in the pocket.

"Slouch." He slouches. "Better. More like a defeated senior, less like someone who exercises regularly." After smirks and follows along with me, and ten minutes later, walk undisturbed through campus, I'm unlocking my dorm room.

"Alright. Please don't laugh at the sheer um…let's just call it Scotty Blah of my room," I mutter, swinging the door open and going in first.

In my haste to get him, I hadn't tidied up my desk, and the opposite bunk where I fold my laundry still has clumps of clothes on it. "I use the left side of the room for schoolwork. Right side, the other desk, it's for my writing," I explain, waving a hand at each direction. There's silence behind me, and I turn and look at him still in the doorway, hat turned backward now. "What?"

"Well, it's…"

"Messy? Disastrous? Unintentionally minimalist?"

"Lonely," he mumbles. I look back to my room and stare straight out the window. We planned to bunk together somewhere, someday. A flat in England, a little shed in Iceland, a brownstone in Brooklyn, who knows. Share clothes, share snacks, share heartbreak and arguments and secrets.

"It's home," is all I can think to say.

He knows that's a lie as much as I do. But he doesn't push it, and he goes and sits on the writing side of my room. After taps a key on my Mac, and it glows back at him. He doesn't ask as he types in a passcode, and I both hate and love that he knew instantly what it would be.

"You need to change your passwords," he says, reading my mind and bouncing the mouse around on the desktop until he finds what he's looking for, opening a blank document.

"My passwords are perfectly ironclad," I refute, sitting in the second swivel chair and rolling up to his side.

He sends me a raised brow and smirks as I kick my sneakers off under the desk. "PeanutButterBoi43 is most certainly *not* ironclad. And, may I add, you've had it since you were ten and used it on Neopets."

"True on all accounts. What're you doing?" I ask, putting my elbows on the desk.

"I thought we'd try a little assignment."

"Oh, goodie, cause I don't get enough of those."

"Don't you? Well then this won't be a problem," he says with a smile. I don't like how close we are, feels too friendly. I wheel away a few inches, but he grabs the armrest of my chair and pulls me back, planting me in front of my laptop.

"I'm gonna give you a prompt, *you're* gonna write it, then *I'm* gonna write it. This'll be a good starting point, I think; a way for us to compare styles and how we handle talking about things. I dunno. I'm making this up as I go."

"Fair enough." I'm still hyper aware of his hand on my armrest by my elbow. He seems to notice it when I do, and he pulls back.

"Prompt: what would you say to someone who's big on dreaming?"

"That is a *huge* prompt—"

"Two hundred words, you can do a little more or a little less. But write like um…like if someone wanted to try something new, something never done by anyone before. What would you say to them?"

I scowl at him, and he swirls left and right in the swivel chair. "Take your time. Mind if I lay down?"

"Go for it," I reply, nodding to the spare bunk. He goes for mine. I mean, he would, the other one is covered in laundry.

Before I can remind him, he takes off his sneakers and leaves them on the floor, and I glare at the empty Word Doc, crack my knuckles, and start to write. Who's big on dreaming? What do you say to someone who wants to reach for the stars?

Chapter 10

I admit it probably took me too long to write just two hundred words. But everything I started felt fake and forced; I've read and reread After's essay so many times that it's gotten lodged in my brain, influencing little things I've written every now and again, and altering some of my papers at Jethro.

Trying to dig out my own style was near impossible. I want to say that it's a good thing; that we already write so similar, so we won't have much work to do. But it's just as much a farce as anything else at this point.

Think I finally got it, though. I sit back and kick my legs out under the desk, and I glance over at After.

He's asleep, it seems. I'm tempted to chuck a rolled-up pair of socks at him. "Hey, dude—"

He jolts and sits up on an arm, rubbing his eyes. "What, Bo, what's wrong? You okay?"

I stutter. Been awhile since I've heard that nickname. "I'm…yeah, I'm good. Finished the writing thing," I reply.

After sighs away whatever sleep was clinging to him, and he squints with a nod. "Right. Yeah, right, okay."

"You can keep sleeping, dude."

"No, it's fine. Lemme write mine," he groans, curling up over his knees. It's a tight fit with how tall he is and how low my ceiling sinks, but he squishes himself smaller with crossed legs.

I stand and bring him my laptop before he has to get off my bunk. "Thanks. Okay, gimme a few minutes."

Few minutes? Literally took me an hour and a half. Wouldn't be surprised if it really does only take him ten minutes to crank out two hundred perfect words.

—

I only feel a little better that it takes him thirty minutes to write his. He gives a satisfied huff and I turn away from my homework desk and push my art history book aside. "Alrighty, c'mon up, Scott," he says, patting the bunk by his crossed knees.

This is all so surreal. Being in the same room as After, touching the same books and desks and laptop and breathing the same air. Dramatic, I know, but it's been so long. I keep hearing his words from our last talk. He forgave me a long time ago. So why am I the one making this so damn awkward? Maybe he hasn't noticed—

"Bro, you're staring at me like I told you to drop your drawers. I'm just saying come sit up here," he scoffs.

Okay, never mind, he's noticed. I grimace and climb up the five steps on my bunk ladder and sit a healthy distance from him with my legs to my chest, chin lowered.

"Okie doke." Love that he still says okie doke. "Let me read mine first if you don't mind."

"Go right ahead," I tell him. After nods and situates the Mac in his hands before he gets started.

"So you say you're a dreamer. You believe in everything wonderful in the world—in fact, you believe in the world itself.

Who showed you, taught you, to think so open-mindedly? Who encouraged you along your journey and told you that they believe in your potential, just as much as you believe so full-heartedly in each and every star that hangs over your head?

The sky is wide, vast and vibrant and never-ending, and every galaxy painted in that arched ceiling is just for you, and I'll tell you why.

For every yes you were told when you were little, for every encouraging hand hold and every smile, and every time your parent was there, telling you that you could try and try again after you've fallen off your bike—that's what made you a dreamer. Someone else said you could, so many others said you would, and you never had any reason to doubt them. Build your ladder to the stars on their shoulders; they'll lift you up forever."

This is why I'm a dumbass for letting him go first.

And *this* is why he's the writer, and not me.

After inhales so deep his shoulders raise to his ears, the top of his head brushes my low ceiling, and he sighs with a smile, meeting my stare. "Felt good to write again. It's been awhile. I've been asking Erica if I could look into directing some things, writing a script here or there, but…hasn't come through yet. Obviously."

You're fucking spectacular. That's what I want to say. You're extraordinary. You deserve every galaxy you could possibly want. You should be the one sitting in this dorm room with your friends and healthy decisions and getting the degree you talked about as a kid, becoming the writer you dreamt of being. "That uh…was that two hundred words?" I ask. He chuckles and squeezes an eye shut.

"Not quite. I tapped out early."

"Huh…"

"Alrighty, now you read yours—"

"Wait."

After blinks at me. His eyes bounce from mine to my mouth as I tear into my lower lip. "I didn't think you still did that," he says quietly.

I can't keep his stare, so I look to the faded, chipped paint of my wall. "I don't want to read mine."

I should've put on some music, or a fan. It's dead silent in this concrete box of a dorm. "Um…okay. Can I read it then?"

"Out loud?" I whisper.

"Is that okay?"

No. Never. "Fine."

He clicks around for a second before he pulls up mine. "Oh, you hit over two hundred words, good job." After clears his throat, and I wish nothing more than to disappear into the woodwork of my bunk.

"Why wish to be tall, they say, when you're taller than most? Why wish to be smart, they ask, when you're wiser than some? Why would you ever want to be anything more than what you already are?

Could it be, because those that tell you you're perfect, you're perfect, they're full of brittle glass? Every promise. Sharp. Every assurance that you, yes you and you alone, are enough. A mirage. It's fragile and short-lived. Their affirmations are flames. You are the butterfly. The moth. The foolish little flea to be stepped on by someone taller, used by someone wiser.

You wish for stars? You? Who tried once and failed? Who tried twice? You believe a third swing, a third attempt—a third breath of air is allotted to you? You who let them down before? So much rides on you. Why think you can be more? Drown. Drown in their shallow expectations.

Stay small, they mean. Stay small enough to be destroyed by their boots. Stay ignorant, they mean. Stay foolish enough to be manipulated. Everyone wants to reach for the stars, until they discover there's no air in space. Stay on the ground. Stay safe, stay safe. Stay a dreamer. But not too much. Not more than they can handle."

I want to cry. I think I might be crying. I know I'm sobbing inside, breaking apart bit by bit as the quiet lingers between us.

After clears his throat. "I uh…"

Nothing he could say would make this any better. I failed the fake assignment; I know I did. I picked up on things here and there; his sentences are run-ons, they're longer and beautiful and full of descriptions. Mine are staccato, repetitive, angry and sharp, sharp, sharp.

I want to cut off my fingers and toes, if only to free myself from the promise I made to him. I can't do this. I can't let him see just how different I am from him.

"Is there a cafeteria?" he asks.

"What?" I grunt, trying to casually wipe his jean jacket sleeve over my wet chin and turn my head away.

"I'm starving. I assume y'all have a place you gather for sustenance."

"We got a food court, yeah."

"Can we get dinner?" I don't mean to glare at him, but it's cemented on my face when I look back at After. If he notices the lingering streaks of tears on my cheeks, he doesn't say anything. "Would you mind? I haven't eaten since breakfast," he adds.

"Uh. Yeah, sure, fine," I nod. He saves both our writing samples, closes my laptop, and hops off my bunk without needing the ladder. I crawl off like a college kid, and not someone used to doing their own stunts.

With tense muscles and shaking knees, I stagger as soon as my bare feet hit the cold floor. His hand steadies me by my elbow, and I shrug it off before my brain can tell my body not to. "Put your hat back on, Captain America, it'll keep you undercover."

"Does that make you Bucky?" After asks, slipping into his shoes. "Or maybe Sam Wilson."

"It makes me Peggy Carter cause she's the hottest of them all," I blurt out. He laughs, high and giddy, and despite still feeling crushed inside, it has me smiling when we leave my dorm.

Chapter 11

He didn't ask about my little poem. Not what it meant, not where the hell it came from. We got hours old pizza, soggy salads, and lemon scones from the cafeteria and ate them outside while we discussed the contrasts in our style. After pointed out the obvious: sentence length.

Was one of the reasons I got so much sass from the English teachers all through my last two years at James Bowie. "You need to *elongate* your thoughts, Scott." "You need to be more *descriptive*, Scott Everett." "You're not *listening*, Scotty."

Never listened. Didn't listen in my Intro to Fiction class, spring of my sophomore year at JU, either. Was the one time I got a B+ on a mid-term.

Was the one time I didn't go see Bevett and Grandpa for my birthday weekend in April, too, and I refused to write poetry or fiction for a grade ever since. Writing for a paycheck is another thing. (I think.)

After and I agreed that I'll try a new writing exercise. He asked me to pay attention to how often I'm breathing. (After compared it to the times he forgets to breathe when doing squats—boy, like I know what *that* even feels like.) Do I get anxious and start to hyperventilate as I format my thoughts? Do I hold my breath on accident?

I told him for every punctuation, I'm inhaling or exhaling. And, when I write like I usually do, it means I start to breathe faster and faster until I'm seeing spots and emotions start driving the Scotty train.

He also suggested I lay off the coffees late at night. I laughed in his face.

Meanwhile, After writes like water.

He puts out one long sentence all at once, broken up by the occasional comma, and that's the ocean reaching up along the coast to your toes, just within an inch of reach, offering you a reprieve—then it retreats with another long, lovely thought.

Teachers at James Bowie might've not liked it much either, no more than my chop-chop sentences. But Jackie Silversmith loves it, and that's what's most important right now.

Dozen other things I'll need to change of course, including taking emotion out of what I'm writing—especially if it's meant to just be summaries for someone else's work, and talking about my boo-hoo self will just muddy it up—but we think sentence length is a good start.

Before he left, he asked me to email him both our little scraps. I sent him mine with gritted teeth, then promptly wiped it from my laptop. I printed his out and pinned it above my desk.

———

It's Wednesday when I get lunch with Charlotte. She only knows about After helping me with my writing, and that him and I are talking a little more.

A fun little fib by omission: I'm yet to tell her about what I'm doing for After in exchange. Honestly, I'm hardly thinking about it. Fake dating? Acting in front of people and pretending we not only get along, but we're head over heels for each other? It's fine, I'm fine, I'm chilling. It's not that big of a deal to me, as long as it doesn't interfere with school.

I'd say as long as it doesn't screw up my mental health, too, but let's face it, that ship has long since sailed and sunk in the harbor.

Charlotte's squinting at me over her chicken salad, chewing with purpose. "You're tense," she says.

"Always," I reply, tearing my grilled cheese to bits.

"More so than usual. What's wrong?" She holds up a long fingernail. Black on top, blood red underneath like a Christian Louboutin heel. "Don't you dare say 'school', buddy boy, I know for a fact that you're taking the lamest courses offered here aside from basket weaving."

"There's nothing wrong with basket weaving," cuts in Mei, coming over with her own lunch: a disaster of burger and sushi and some sort of pasta all over her plate. She smiles and stoops to kiss Charlotte. "Hi, dove."

"Hiya, teach," Charlotte replies, pushing a seat out for her fiancée. "You only say that cause you're the TA, and every sad little freshie who's struggling to get through the semester knows if they bring you a handmade basket full of your favorite chocolates, you'll give them an A."

"I'm a simple woman," Mei grins, dipping her long neck into her shoulders. Even sitting down, she's a full foot taller than Charlotte, and I smirk at their differences. Charlotte with the aggressive, smudgy eyeshadow and triple pierced ears, rocking cut off shorts that show her trillions of thigh tattoos.

Next to Mei, who's bringing back the shoulder pads with her wide-leg polka dot romper that makes her look twice as long as she actually is, red eyeliner pointed to perfection around her black eyes. I'm smiling at her in response, until Charlotte kicks me in the toe and gets my attention with a plotting scowl.

"Tell us. You've got your grumpy face on. I haven't seen you so weird and pinchy looking since high school."

"This is just my face."

"What happened with After?"

"After what?" Mei asks.

"After—he's a friend from Lubbock," Charlotte explains. Mei blinks, tilts her head. If she hadn't gotten her Mia Farrow haircut in January, her long black ponytail would've ended up in the bizarre penne and soy sauce combo on her plate. Charlotte sucks on a tooth and waves Mei closer.

First she kisses her rosy cheek. Then she whispers something behind her hand. Mei's eyes shoot massive and she squawks, "You never told me you know goddamn *David Después!*"

"For fucks sake," I laugh, hand at my chest as twenty heads turn and stare at us all at once. Charlotte glares and play swats Mei's shoulder pad. "Well, that's out there now."

"Long story short, babe, Scotty and I know After from high school. I mean, Scott knew him since they were little—that's beside the point—" She rounds on me again and points a nail. "You! What happened—last we talked, you said he came over and helped you write. Though I'm still angry you didn't tell me when he was here, we could've hung out!"

"I could've drooled over him," Mei adds with sincere hurt.

I snort at them both and shake my head. "He showed up out of the blue. I mean, I knew we'd get together at some point—maybe that day—it doesn't matter—it's fine, everything's fine. He's helping me with my writing, I just had to agree to—" *Toooo* keep my mouth shut.

Charlotte's interest is piqued tenfold. "You have to what?"

"To…be a good student?"

"Bullshit."

"Agreed," pipes in Mei, munching on penne, still clearly confused about the nickname 'After' while being supportive of her stubborn-ass fiancée. "What did you say you'd do?"

I sigh and push my destroyed grilled cheese aside, and the ladies both do the same with their trays of food, taking up 'tell me the deets' stances with arms crossed on the table, blinking brown and blue eyes at me.

"Okay. So we're doing my favor—don't ask, Mei, just know it's a serious thing from when we were kids—and he said he'd do it, he'd help me write like him. But. He wanted something in return. He asked me to be his cover, to help…him…" Technically, After never said I could tell others that he's gay. But he also didn't say *not* to tell them. If he's coming out of the closet, this is gonna happen. Literally, that's part of people knowing he's—

"After is gay."

Mei's face goes 'huh?' then it goes 'oh...' then it's 'yeah, I could see that'.

Meanwhile, Charlotte just goes, "Yeah, I knew that."

"The hell you did!"

"I sure did, bud. He told me a year ago. We got drunk in Fresno for my birthday."

I slump. "You told me you were out of town for your birthday."

Charlotte slumps, too. "Umm. I mean, I was, sort of. Fresno is *technically* not in LA. I didn't invite you because I knew things between y'all were still awkward."

Well, that just makes me feel like shit. I go for my grilled cheese just to pick at something other than my knuckles. "So anyway, people have been pushing at him to keep it on the down low. He's asked me to be his easy way to come out without having to actually commit to a boyfriend. Like, show that he's with a dude. Not necessarily one he likes."

"How?" Charlotte asks. "Like Facebook official?"

"What's Facebook official," stage-whispers Mei. Charlotte waves a hand at her.

"Go on a few fake dates, have a fake romance, fake argument and breakup, and people will leave him alone and stop harassing him about girlfriends. They'll get the idea, and he can go on to date people he wants to date. If. He wants to date. Ever," I add for literally no reason.

Mei and Charlotte look at each other, tinkling of Mei's long earrings as they hit her shoulder pads the only sound in the now empty cafeteria. "That's...a lot to unpack," says Mei, lifting her tea, cup already lined in lipstick stains.

"You're his reverse frontal," Charlotte adds. Mei snorts on iced tea.

"I *highly* doubt that means what you think it means," I snicker.

"Okay, yes, I didn't mean frontal, I meant front—shut up, Mei, oh my God—really. You're his back door—oh my *God*, shut *up*, Scotty!"

I burst as Mei shrieks a laugh. "I get what you're saying, but holy shit—"

"You're doing him a *huge* favor here, seriously," Charlotte says, holding her hands up to the side of her face to block Mei from her view, who's now turning red with giggles. "I hope you know that. He's been bad, dude, really bad lately, and on New Year's, he went off the deep end. It got so messed up with the magazines and I was worried he'd…"

She mutters into silence, looking to the table. Mei stops chuckling and takes Charlotte's hand in hers.

I want to ask. But the more I know about After and everything he's gone through, the more I'm scared he'll want to know about me. Better we keep this surface level with easy things like…

I know his favorite color is cool, dark gray, but he especially loves burnt orange in the fall. I know his favorite song is a tie between Springsteen by Eric Church and Long Live by Taylor Swift. I know he likes his dressing on the side and orders his iced coffee with light ice and that he talks in Spanish in his sleep.

I know he sleepwalks, too, ending up outside sometimes, and that's the reason I started staying in his bed when I slept over at his house, to keep him from wandering down the street. I know he'd sell his soul for Whataburger to bring back their chorizo taquitos. I know how he sounds when he comes.

I know his biggest fear when he was fourteen was someone shooting his dad and brand-new stepdad for being gay, just like how his uncle on his mom's side was murdered, and he wouldn't find out about it until he went to visit Pedro and Vernon and found them dead in their home in Spain.

See? All surface level.

I don't need to know every single dark secret, even if I think I might already. All but some, it seems, as Charlotte never finishes her salad, or her sentence about New Year's.

Mei follows me on Instagram.

First, it takes her the rest of the week just to figure out how to *make* an Instagram. And a Twitter, and a Pinterest for some random reason.

She proceeds to follow me on all three, commenting on my photos on Instagram one by one, and I start giggling so bad I have to leave my Functional Pottery class. Cause she's like a mom, saying 'be safe' and 'so cute' and using an insane amount of exclamation points and :D :D :D *~*~* nonsense.

My heart gets all fluttery, imagining her and Charlotte at their wedding in August. I wonder if After will get an invite to the bridal party later this month. I bet he will. Maybe he'll take that as one of his five things, and I'll be Scott free, pun intended, before I have to even think about flying to Spain.

Just as I calm my face down and get ready to go back to my third attempt at painting a mug without breaking it, After posts something, a photo of a dorm.

Him: working hard. Me: hardly working :P but I got the best view! @ScottEBoscoe @JethroUniversity #mybfisababe #JU #writerlife #boyfriendstealsmyclothes

It's me. At my desk, typing in my signature 'in the zone' pose; one foot up on my swivel chair, arms still decked out in his jean jacket as they reach around my leg for my keyboard. My face is lit up by my screen, and so is my glare of concentration. The angle is from my bunk, where he was supposedly sleeping.

I bite my tongue, thumb hovering over the heart under the image. Instead, I hit the paper airplane, sending it to him via direct message.

@ScottEBoscoe: TF is this? You hoarding stalker pics now? When did you take this?

He leaves me on read until I get back to my dorm after my pottery class ends, newly finished mug with a crummy bluebonnet painted on it in my hand. (Cause I'm a basic Texas bitch, don't come at me.)

@DavidDespués: u looked so serious

That answers nothing.

@DavidDespués: idk, u sat like that for so long without a word. I got tired of watching so I took a pic before I passed out

Watching me? That most *definitely* answers nothing, and on top of that, it asks a shit ton more.

@ScottEBoscoe: So you just held onto it for a week?

Again, left on read, until I'm crawling under my covers with my white noise machine on, along with some music. If I had a TV, I'd have that on, too. Can't sleep in such a deadly silent room.

@DavidDespués: first, I put it as my locked phone background. Then I held onto it for a week

Right, that would make sense; if someone noticed his locked phone screen, they'd see a picture of his pretend boyfriend on it. People have freaked out over less, like if Tom Hiddleston got paparazzied holding a white cat, and some random celebrity also just *happened* to have a white cat, too.

I should do the same, I guess.

But that would mean rifling through the photo album I have of him to find the best one and, yeah, I'm not about to spend hours doing that again.

Chapter 12

I'm just out of my last Thursday class before spring break, dragging my feet to get back to my dorm, when someone whistles at me. Not like a wolf whistle. Not like a two finger in mouth whistle like Charlotte can do. Like a straight up weenie whistle.

I turn with a glare of more WTF than anything, and I squint out at the parking lot.

There's a squat woman standing in front of a bumblebee yellow truck that's twice her size, and I hope to God it's hers cause that would be hilarious.

With my best Quasimodo impression of hunched back and not giving a shit about my posture anymore, I turn in a semi-circle, then stare back at her. I point at my chest.

She points at me and nods a head covered in hot pink cotton candy hair, and I wander over to her.

First thing I notice: she's got the smallest mouth on a human being I've ever seen, unless you're, like, three years old.

Second thing: she has at least seven piercings on her face, not including her ears. "Uh...hi?" I ask with a raised ET finger.

"Hi! Yvonne James." She juts a petite hand out to me and wiggles stubby digits with stubbier fingernails. I shake it with a growing frown, until the name comes back to me as she says, "I'm meant to be dressing you up for the End of Heaven premiere donation gala."

"That's a lot longer of a title than I remember," I reply, continuing to look her over as my confusion molds into curiosity.

So, we got pink hair tied into two pom-poms on her head, plus a ruffled Renaissance shirt that would make Labyrinth star David Bowie jealous, paired with neon blue and orange plaid tapered pants, and the most hideous pair of black Doc Martens I've ever seen.

She's definitely a fashion designer. "How old are you?" I ask like an asshole.

"A million years old," she says.

Her tiny mouth spreads into her best attempt at a Cheshire grin, and she goes—yes, hell yes, she turns and goes straight for the highlighter yellow pick-up truck! I half expect a ladder to drop out of the driver's side for her. "Hop in, toots, it's fashion time!"

"It's Thursday," I blurt, walking to the passenger door anyway. "I haven't eaten dinner."

"I got food." She hoists herself into her truck, giving a satisfied *humf* as soon as she's ass to seat.

I scramble to get in despite my longer limbs, and I close the door, leaning my elbow to it. "I haven't showered."

"You can shower at my place, if you want."

"Your studio has a shower?"

"My studio is my apartment." Yvonne pats her patch-covered knees with a shy smile. "Is it…I mean, is it okay? That we go now? I want to get your measurements and try some looks out before I'm swarmed with another event, and the gala is coming up in early April, so…"

With a hand through my hair to push bangs from my face, I give a nod. "Yeah, it's fine. I'll take you up on food though, for sure."

When she nods back, her pom-pom hair bounces around. I'm tempted to touch one.

"Perfect! David said you'd be down for yummy food, told me to lead with that in case you didn't want to come—he's meeting us there, by the way, so no worries about missing out on your boy."

'He's not my boy' is halfway out of my mouth, when I clamp my lips closed and buckle up my seatbelt. "Right. Yay. Um, yay boys. And yummy food."

"And yummy boys," she cackles. I like her cackle.

—

Her flat is just as short and stout as she is and I love it, already imagining After having to stoop as he clomps around her place. I'm almost disappointed when we walk in and the ceilings are all arched, doorways an average seven feet high.

He's in the kitchen, standing by the island covered in fashion mags and a nearly empty pizza box, and he looks up as Yvonne announces our arrival by screaming, "I brought the boy-toy!"

After laughs and accepts a low-five, handing her a plate of jalapeno and sausage covered pizza. His smile is more rigid when it lands on me, but he passes me the last slices he'd been plating for himself. "Sorry I couldn't be the one to pick you up."

"It's okay," I shrug, stealing a paper towel and stuffing it between my fingers and the paper plate. "How've you been?"

He shrugs, too. Haven't talked to him in a few days, not since he posted that photo of me on his Instagram.

My follower count keeps going up, by the way; I've picked up the daily habit of deleting hate messages and threats on my life every morning from angry, jealous fans.

I haven't told him about that yet, and I doubt I will. It's not really his business, and they all repeat the same bullshit anyway. How I'm stealing After's attention, lying about how long I've known him.

I tried to answer the first fifty by explaining our long history (leaving out key details, obvi) but I gave up when it was clear no one cared.

However, the moment someone comes at me with, "Does he know about Gabriel Avant and the cop from El Paso," *then* I'm gonna start throwing hands.

"You look tired," I tell After, following a jabbering Yvonne into her living room turned fashion studio; she's got multiple ten-foot-tall mirrors leaning haphazardly on all sorts of surfaces for a full 360 effect, a carpeted stool sitting in the center.

"I am. Been thinking about some stuff, and work is getting rough. Mom's pushing for me to do more before the fundraiser on Saturday, when she knows I've got a thousand things going on." He sighs, and I offer him the slices of pizza. He stares at them like they're speaking at him in Russian.

"Go on, take it, you look like you need some sustenance."

"I'm…" His nose twitches, and his tongue darts to the corner of his mouth. I lift the plate an inch higher, higher, toward his chin, until he finally smiles and takes it from me. "What about you?"

"I'll forage for something else." I step away from him and set my backpack on Yvonne's sofa, hidden under layers of blouses and dresses. Forage=success, she's got an opened bag of Dove chocolates on her coffee table, yaaaas. "Alright, what can I do?" I ask Yvonne, three candies in before I remember to breathe.

"Strip!" comes a squeak from behind a rack of dazzling fabrics, sequins and shimmery shirts catching light through her floor to ceiling windows. Her face appears between two pairs of pin-striped pants. "Not you, darling, not yet. I need to finalize David's first."

After wordlessly sets the pizza down with a lingering forlorn stare. He's already barefoot, so he pulls his t-shirt off his shoulders, setting it aside. He sends me a look. He sends me three looks, none of the same. "What?" I yawn, wadding up more Dove wrappers.

"I'm um…" His thumbs go for the waistband of his sweatpants, and he clears his throat.

Pausing my assault on another chocolate, I snort and cock my head. "Oh, egad, After, must I avert my maiden eyes?" I clap a hand over my face and drawl, "By Gods, don't tempt me, concubine, dare I say, Delilah of dudes—"

"Shut up, Scott—"

"T'would hate to see—forgive me—an ankle! A wrist! Scarlett letter, strumpet, my poor virgin sensibilities—"

I get a face full of sweatpants, making me choke on my chocolate. "Oh, you nasty—don't throw your drawers at me!" Balling them up, I chuck them full force at the back of his head, knocking him forward. Yvonne appears from behind her Narnia of clothes and wafts her hands at me.

"Don't you dare harm my muse," she chides, massaging his arm. She comes to his bicep.

"Yvonne, you keep your apartment at thirty degrees, can you please put me in some clothes and stop groping me?" He turns his back to me and starts to pull on pants she's working on, and I go for his abandoned pizza slices on the coffee table by my knee.

I gave my best effort to not pay attention to his rise in Hollywood. Didn't open up many, if any, of the magazines he was in, didn't glance twice at the pictures Bevett would cut out and pin up on her friend and family board.

He hasn't asked me yet, but I can only imagine how he'll either think it's hilarious or infuriating that I haven't seen any of his movies, not even the one we're going to the gala for. It's the third of a trilogy he started years ago. I'm gonna have to rent them on Amazon and speed watch them over break or I'll be a lost little noob at the viewing party.

All that to say, I haven't thought much about how he's physically changed since I last saw him. He wasn't skinny when we were younger, not like me. He never outgrew the baby fat in his face as long as I knew him. His edges were softer and rounder when we were teens.

He's all solid now, tight. I can see where there are knots in his shoulders from stress, and I kind of take back what I said about him not being jacked like Tom Hardy. He's sculpted, clearly he's put a lot of hard work into his diet and exercise; I can only imagine the strenuous workouts he's had to do for filming to keep in shape.

But when he smiles and laughs at Yvonne, his cheeks still push to his eyes just like before.

His muscle-lined shoulders shift as he shrugs into a button up, bare toes curling on the carpeted stool Yvonne's got him perched on. With his back to me, I notice his reflection in one of the many mirrors, and I recognize a look on his face from our younger years. She keeps talking over him, and he continues to let her, smiling like he doesn't mind. His slowly lowering eyes tell me he minds a little.

We were eleven at a picnic in September for another classmate's birthday. All the other kids had already finished their crustless sandwiches and greasy Doritos, and After was struggling to eat fast enough as they got up one by one to run around with kites and water guns.

"Why do you eat so fast?" I asked him, drinking a Hi-C between bites of a Hostess cupcake. He blinked at me with panicked eyes, cheeks full of homemade quesadilla. "You can slow down, you're gonna choke."

He swallowed and looked at his hands. They were shaking. "If I don't finish eating in time, everyone will leave me. Including you," he added, darting a look to my nearly empty plastic bag of cupcake.

I frowned and followed his stare, then shrugged, finishing off the last bite. "Well, *I* won't leave you," I mumbled around my food. He slowed down then. Yeah, we got left behind by the others, but I never walked off while he was eating, even if I was already done.

Then we're sixteen, and we've got a new friend Charlotte added to our gang, and she's brought five other friends with her to make that gang a posse. They loved to talk, interrupting one another, their own stories even, to take the conversation somewhere else. They loved to cut right over After, too, and he'd stand there with his mouth open, last of his words clinging to his tongue.

I'd always stare at him. And tell him, "Keep talking," and I'd ask, "What were you saying?" and when Charlotte would ramble on with her new friends that were never really ours, I'd wait for him to finish his sentence, just like I'd wait for him to finish his food.

In Yvonne's living room, I stand with the second slice of pizza uneaten, and I walk over to him while she's off getting more pins from her sewing kit. He looks exhausted. I offer him some pizza.

"If I get grease on this shirt, she'll skin me alive," he smirks, raising his wrists, white sleeves frilly and hanging over his knuckles. I lift the last slice, and he bends at the waist to reach, craning his neck.

"Tell me about your day," I say, feeding him another bite as he inhaled the first. After scowls and very clearly doesn't get my question. "You said you've been thinking. What about?"

"I'm not sure you want to know," he mutters, taking a third bite.

"Of course I do."

"It's about you and our deal."

I swallow and jalapeno stings up my throat. "Okay. What about?"

After finishes off the pizza and lets me dab at his chin with the paper towel. He straightens and turns to where Yvonne disappeared to. She's muttering to herself about the severity of choosing the right nail polish for After and me.

"Just that. How's it going?" he asks. "The writing. When do you want to do the next session?"

God, I *never* want to hear him read my writing out loud again. "It's going okay. Slow work, trying to write like that, not break things up with my—" I slice the empty, crumb-covered paper plate in the air repeatedly to signify my choppy style, and he rewards my goofiness with a light smile. "I gotta flow. I'm not good with flow."

"Maybe you should try another exercise. Time yourself to—"

Yvonne comes bursting back in with a fitful sigh, so loud it makes After jump. From the sound of it, she's not saying anything note-worthy, rambling about what shoes she wants me to wear, what to do about makeup, that she'll have to change the jacket she was planning on donning, because another designer beat her to it and, "Why *don't* I just wear one of my own? So silly, hadn't even thought of that…"

After glances down, taps his bare toes to the stool, then starts to look back toward the mirrors. "Time myself to do what?" I ask him.

He sends me a doubletake. "Oh. Um. Yeah, just see how long you can write without pausing for ten seconds at a time. No punctuation, no breaks."

"That doesn't seem like a long time," I snort. He grins that After grin that squishes at his eyes.

"You *say* that. It's like planks. Try it and tell me afterward how much you wanted to shoot yourself in the foot while you did it."

"Maybe you can be there, to watch me shoot myself in the foot?" I shrug.

After stretches his shoulders back in his nice shirt and checks his toes again. I hold an unwrapped Dove chocolate in my flat palm. He takes it with two fingers. "Yeah. We can do another writing session. After the fundraiser?" he suggests.

"Sounds good." Another chocolate, two more fingers.

"I'll text you to let you know when I'm showing up this time."

"Wear your Jethro hoodie. Excuse me, *my* hoodie." I scoff when those two fingers pinch at me, and I get a chuckle and present a third chocolate.

Chapter 13

Last fundraiser I went to was something for Bevett's junior high; a silent auction for local animals in need. I left with a stuffed German Shepherd I donated way too much money for. It still sits in her room on her dresser as the grump pup. She hugs him when she misses me, so she says. I'm pretty sure she beats the stuffing out of it when she's mad at me, too.

Last fundraiser I went to with After was when we were at Navy Glenn Elementary, and it was run by the local firefighters. His dad, still married to his mom at the time, had After pose on the fire truck wearing the clunky helmet and jacket that went to his calves. After's mom was right up there by him, with an equally silly grin. I stood by and watched, cause I was seven and tired and eight months without a mom.

He said he'd pick me up from campus. I was expecting a fancy car, but subtle, like one of Grandpa Mitch's Caddies. Something flashy, but chill. Something that says, 'someone important is in this car,' but also says, 'you don't need to know who, move along'.

I get *none* of that.

After shows up to Jethro in an atrocious, ostentatious, cherry red Ferrari convertible.

"I won't do it," I tell him, standing at his driver's side on the curb by Jones Hall, glaring with crossed arms. I keep having to shift my feet, finding myself pouting with my toes pointed in like a literal child. He continues to grin, elbow crooked over the open side, eyes no doubt mischievous as fuck behind his Aviators.

"What's wrong with the car?" he asks. He tries to act sincere, but he starts laughing at his own words before he's finished talking. "I figure it's like this—I mean, it was kind of your idea, Scott—"

"The hell it was!"

"It *was*! You called me Captain America. What does he do when he's incognito? Hat, shifty hoodie." He never did give me back my hoodie. Asshole. "What does he do all the other times? He dons his white, his blue, and…" After waves a hand along the sleek car with a wicked smile. "His *red*."

"So you're planning to just Clark Kent it up each time you come to campus to help me write and hope no one notices you're the same person in the stupid, flashy sports cars?"

"That, or you can come hang out at my place, up to you."

"I'd rather only step foot in your home on one single occasion, if I can help it."

Rude, and unfair Scott, the fuck? "You're a pompous ass. Way to rub it in, dude," I add with a grunt. Way to celebrate his accomplishments.

His poem still lingers in my skull; I keep seeing a mirage of white paper and black letters every time I blink. This is his big dream realized; he's reached the stars. Even after I destroyed his chances at Jethro, his chances at Jethro with *me*, he went and found himself a new star to capture. And it's just so much shinier than mine.

After's smile twitches at the corner. He sighs and unfolds from his car, slamming the door shut. His gray wool coat billows as he hops up the curb. Lifting his Aviators, he bends down close to me.

"Listen, man. What's this really about? Cause we're gonna be late, and I'd rather have this out right here than at the fundraiser. You're doing me a favor, and I'm doing one for you, but it won't work if we're not honest to each other."

"I *am* being honest; I *hate* the car—"

"It's not about the car and you know it," he snarks, knife-handing at me. "Face it, dude, something's twisted up in your head.

So what is it? Don't let us stall out at the starting line cause you won't get your shit figured out."

I scowl and stand up on my toes in a weak attempt to meet his eye, raising my own hands up between our faces just to make him take a step back. "*You* face it, After. Honest or not, this won't work at all. You're on a whole 'nother level than I am. You're *People's* Hottest Hits and sexy sports cars—you're in a freaking *cobalt* blue suit. Do you even know what color that is? Dude, I'm straight up wearing fucking J.Crew." I flap my hands at my pea coat hanging open to my knees, turtleneck over a button up.

"I'm in my *nice* Converse, and they're only nice cause they're not *grass-stained*. I don't have the confidence and the suave, I don't have the perfect grins and still-squeaky brown Oxfords. I don't know how to be fancy. I *like* my basic, minimalistic life and riding my bike—but man, if being around you doesn't just make me hate myself a bit—" And we're just gonna nip the rest of that straight in the bud, thank you very much.

After's face scrunches. He scowls, squints, purses his lips. Then he starts snicker. He's laugh—he's laughing at me. "Stop, why are you laughing?"

"You're just—you're exactly like you were when we were little, Scott," he chuckles, shaking his head.

"No I'm not, I've grown."

After sighs and puts his glasses back on, peering at me through them down his nose. His hands are in my hair, fixing, probably improving, the cowlick that goes wild over my right eyebrow no matter how much product I put in it.

"I meant more like, you're the same in all the good ways. I'd go with you in your J.Crew, or in jeans and a t-shirt, or in freakin' Armani. Shit, you could wear that doofy tux you used to break out every year, from ninth to eleventh grade homecoming, and you'd still look great. You always look great," he says.

I don't know what to make of that, so I just frown. "You don't need to change—I mean, literally. And metaphorically."

I *have* changed. Grandpa Mitch said so. Said I'd gotten better, progressed. After hasn't been here, he doesn't know what he's talking about.

I shift my weight and glance once behind him. "I...*like* the car."

"I know you do. C'mon, get in."

"We didn't work through the shit," I reply.

"We'll work it out eventually." I can't see his eyes, but he looks up and around us. "Plus, we've gathered some lurkers, so...at least that plan is working. Getting seen together in close proximity."

"Could be that we're just two idiots arguing by a Ferrari," I retort, stepping away for the passenger side. He slaps my ass.

I spin and punch him in the arm. "Why did you do that!" I hiss, flopping into the car. Smells like fresh leather, iced coffee and After. What a weird mix.

"Cause now they saw two idiots arguing by a Ferrari, but those idiots could be *more* than friends," he says. I bet he just winked at me behind his glasses. I'm smirking despite how furious I am. "Buckle up, B—Scott."

That sounded like the beginning of 'Bo'. Glad he stopped himself, unlike when he was partially asleep in my dorm. I don't want that nickname to come back.

—

My shivering got After's attention despite my best efforts, and he pulled over to put the top of the convertible up for me. He got overheated, but he didn't complain, telling me I could crank the heat up as much as I wanted. I kept my hands in my lap. He might've thought I was cold, but I knew it was a panic attack coming on, one I was hardly keeping at bay.

So, I get *talking* about fake dating, planning to go on outings together—shit, even the slap on the ass didn't bother me that much. No different than what I used to do to him. But back then, it would be out of play, being stupid, calling him 'buttercup' when he'd go get me another soda at my request.

Now it's meant to show fake affection, and that turns it sour in my head as I realize we're about to go out in public and have to like. Act. Flaunt it. I am *not* fine. I am *not* chilling.

It's hard enough pretending to be friends again, let alone lovers. I mean, that's what this is, right? We're *pretending* friendship, he's *pretending* that he's forgiven me.

And we're gonna pretend around hundreds of people, including his mom and agent, who I find out is gonna be there the moment After curses under his breath when he spots a sleek, black Porsche.

He sighs as we park in the already super full, grassy field next to a gargantuan country club. It's pink brick and white stone. It's Legally Blonde if it was a building. "Of course Erica's made an appearance," he grunts. "I'm gonna be sick."

I'm gonna be sick.

"Hey." I startle into the door, and I wish we had the top down again; this car is too damn confining. After pushes his sunglasses up into his hair and leans over the armrest. He gives a light smile, unbuckles my seatbelt, and I'm surprised I don't fling myself into the atmosphere as soon as I'm free. "You good?"

"Humgud."

"Was that English?"

"M...mmmaybe."

"Dude—"

I scramble to unlock the door, toss my legs out of the car, and projectile vomit right at the front tire. "Oh shit—" He leaps out of his side, and I'm prepared for, 'don't you get it on the car, boy', when he appears under my eyes, stooping by my knee and pushing me back by my shoulder. "Scott, do I need to take you home?"

"What? No, no—"

"Are you sure? You don't look so good, man."

"I'm..." Not cut out for this. Not important enough for this. A fraud. A fraud. A fraud. "I'm okay." After frowns and tilts his head. His hands clasp around mine where they're currently trembling between my legs. He stands, pulling me gently, until I'm out of the car. I have to lean on the back door, and my knees shake and knock together.

"Do we need to go through the shit?" he whispers. Why are his hands still around my fingers? Is this part of the fake boyfriend thing? Would it be too much to ask for this to be a genuine friendship thing? Probably.

"No, I'm fine. Bad salad or something." He's not convinced. I don't like how his hands release my fingers and go for my wrists under the cuffs of my jacket. "What're you doing?"

"Checking your pulse."

"Why?"

"Cause if it's faster than 200 beats per minute, then you're having a panic attack. Do you feel any twinging in your chest?"

"How do you know that?"

"I do my own stunts, man."

"So...?"

"So, I have panic attacks."

"Oh, word?"

He doesn't need to stand right in front of me to do this, he can check my pulse with two fingers while keeping me at arm's length. "Answer the question, any twinging?"

"Um. A little, but nothing more than usual."

"Usual is zero twinging."

"Whatever."

"Lightheaded?"

"Not so much anymore." Lies.

"Pain?"

"No, no pain."

"Okay, that's good." He looks to my wrists, thinks. A minute passes, but it feels like a year with him too close. Only friends stand this close, and we're not friends.

"Okay. You're pushing it, but it seems to be slowing down. You thinking nice, calming thoughts? Don't think about big crowds or lots of attention or—"

"Nope, not helping bro."

"Sorry." He drops my wrists. "What're you thinking about?"

"My mom." Yikes. I suck in my breath but it's too late to drag the word back in.

After's face lowers into my view. "What about her?"

"I'm like. H-h-hella underdressed here," I tell him, turtling into my turtleneck. "And. My mom. She'd be underdressed sometimes, too. She'd wear straight leg jeans and her boots everywhere. T-shirts that hid her stomach. But. My mom had a scarf. And when she wore it, she looked like a queen."

I mime 'scarf', but it just looks like I'm Britney Spears with an anaconda around my neck. Noticing that my fingers are twitching interdependently, I clench them into fists and shove them into my pockets.

"This scarf had her favorite colors mixed in with mine. All sunrises and blues. She used to let me borrow it when we went to the movies, if I got too cold. Would wrap me up in it like a blanket. Lost it on a trip to Galveston, though. Someone stole it right out of her bag in the lockers at the beach. Mom was upset at first, but then she smiled and shrugged and said someone needed it more than she did, and it was just the scarf's time to move on."

Wow, golly Scott, any *other* story times we wanna share right now? No? Oh, thank God. "Anywhoo. Y'know. Panic attack equates..." awkward shimmy-shrug, "scarves."

After's smiling at me, and I bite my lip like a badger and smile back. I think I must look like there's something wrong with me, cause he clears his throat and stares at the castle-sized club behind the field. "That's the most I've ever heard you talk about her."

"True," is all I say back.

After nods in silence and puts his sunglasses back over his eyes. He beeps his car locked, puts the keys in his coat pocket, and pulls out a piece of gum like a freaking wizard, passing it to me.

Then he extends a hand. I squint at it, fiddling with gum wrapper. He wiggles his fingers. "You cool with this part?"

"Oh—right." I take his surprisingly sweaty hand, and we fumble with finger placement for a second before we decide on him being on the outside, leading me. "What about the um…" I don't dare turn to look at the damage I did to the Ferrari that costs more than my entire life.

"That's the least of my concerns right now," he replies. "It might get bright, lots of flashy cameras. Just smile, okay?"

Easy enough. I nod and follow along at his side. We make it to the end of the grass, over a cobble-stone path, and I'm starting to get my breathing back to normal.

At least, I was, until we turn the corner, and we're greeted by a monstrously loud, two-hundred-person garden party, and every eye turns to us.

Chapter 14

What're the rules around throwing up on celebrity guests? None? Blame it on the tequila I won't be drinking, or the mimosas I won't be drinking? Blame it on the cream cheese and cucumber sandwiches, says After. Think I can do that.

Glad he warned me about the flashing lights. There are dozens of black cameras pointed at us as we walk—or more, as After glides, and I trip—through the party entrance. He smiles, tosses up his token peace sign, and I keep darting looks around with probably a glare plastered on my face despite his one direction to smile.

Last time I had this many eyes on me, Grandpa Mitch was getting moved up in the ranks, and his party was full of stuffy white men with gray beards who all looked like they could be named Floyd Williams.

Guests are laughing and shrill, there's a live band playing on one side of the garden, and a twelve-foot-tall white party tent is filled to the brim with folks dressed from Target's best to Prada. (I feel a little better now, love you, J.Crew.)

I'd be lying if I said I didn't immediately want to run away and explore what looks like a hedge maze to my left. Maybe if this all turns to shit, I can white rabbit this madness and dart off, and they'll never find me.

"Scotty!" I jump at my name and accidentally swallow my gum, and After laughs.

His mom is just as much a disaster as I remember; her vibrant, tan face is covered in butterflies painted by her eyes and cheeks, black hair curled and gorgeous down her back.

She's gotten some gray by her temples, but it looks like she might've tried dying it hot pink to match her tiered dress that makes her poof out like a pastry.

"Hi, Ms. Florence," I smile. I barely have time to unlace my fingers from After's hand before she's colliding into me with a hug, knocking the wind out of me.

"Holy mackerel, honey! Gosh, how long has it been!" she chuckles, leaning back on blocky heels. Her hands go for my face, and I start to tear up at her familiar, motherly smile. She 'awe's at me and wipes at my lashes before kissing my cheek. "Don't you start, you'll make me cry, and I *just* got my makeup fixed after I burst into tears earlier!"

"Why were you crying earlier?" After asks, accepting a hug from her. His eyes keep darting to me, and I look away to scratch at my cheek in an attempt to wipe at my face without him noticing. Hasn't worked yet, but I'm still practicing.

"Cause the band started playing Brett Young when I *know* I requested *no* country music!"

"Why no country music? Other than the obvious," I ask, getting a snort out of After.

"It's all Pedro ever played that last year in our marriage—hearing it gives me a headache and I'd much rather *not* be thinking about him today when I'm having so much fun," she scoffs, adding with a disgruntled grumble, "he didn't even *like* country music until *Vernon* showed him—"

After clears his throat and takes my hand again. "When do the festivities start?"

"Festivities?" I ask, latching onto his conversation shift. She claps her hands with a grin. She clearly attempted to paint her nails but chewed most of the black polish off.

"We're having a scavenger hunt in the maze in about fifteen," she announces. "First to find the pink flamingo wins!"

The band picks up a chaotic Demi Lovato song, and the three of us duck our heads more to hear each other. "Wins what?" I ask.

"The Ferrari we drove," After says. My eyes bug and I think of the vomit-splattered tire. He winks at me. "Just kidding. They win tickets to Mom's Easter event in the spring. Biggest party in LA. How much did you make in donations last year?"

Ms. Florence pretends to think long and hard about it. "Oh golly, well…it had so, *so* many zeroes, I just can't remember…"

"Who are y'all donating to?" I ask. A server walks past us wearing a suit made of pastel peach and mint, and I accept a drink without knowing what's in it. One sniff tells me it's rum and coke. I hand it to After, and he downs it. Hope he doesn't go overboard; I don't feel like maneuvering a Ferrari through LA to get back to Jethro.

"This year it's to curing breast cancer," his mom answers. She squeezes both our shoulders and sighs, grinning. "So! Boscoe and DD, oldest friends, back at it again, right?" she says with a wink so much like her son's. "Plenty of pretty ladies to take home today, boys, I'll tell y'all that! Hang out by the champagne bar long enough, Scotty, the gals will swoon over that scarred, chiseled jaw of yours."

Guess she wasn't as easy to fool as After thought she'd be. He fidgets, silent. I swallow, silent. Someone calls her name, and with barely a, 'talk to you later', she's off, rushing through the crowds as an argument erupts over who gets to bid on the butterfly garden set.

"Guess um…we'll need to take it up a notch. Or something. For her to get it," After says to himself. I attempt to agree, but I kind of just stand there frozen for a second.

First messed up thought: I didn't expect her to be so friendly toward me; I thought she'd be in full Momma bear mode, knowing what I did to her son by stealing his college essay and crushing his heart. I'm wondering if he never told her, then I'm wondering why the hell not?

Second, probably more messed up thought...Ms. Florence is a whirlwind of affection and laughter and snacks and hugs. I used to have to remind myself that she wasn't my mom, especially when she'd wake me up with chocolate chip pancakes after staying at his house.

But as much as I love and respect her, I'm thinking...would After have to try so hard to get her to understand that he's gay, and to love him for being gay, if he realized that about himself while being away at college? Living in a dorm, in an apartment, having privacy from August to November. Goes home for Thanksgiving and surprise, there he is with his committed boyfriend, bringing in the casseroles and pecan pies.

Instead, he had her there for all the twists and turns and God knows what. Present, but not supporting. Loving, but not understanding. With him every step of the way and standing in his way.

After releases my hand and nudges my arm. "You okay?" he asks. He's staring at me too sternly.

Don't know why, I'm fine. I tell him that, I'm fine.

"I'm worried." Well, so much for that.

His face softens and he leads me by my elbow to a quieter part of the nearby rose hedges. "What're you worried about?"

Honesty. He wanted honesty. "Am I the reason you didn't apply for other colleges?" Read: Did I really derail your life as much as it feels like I did?

"I applied to other colleges," he replies. He crosses his arms, and I do the same just to protect myself. "I applied to four, a couple acting schools. And I got accepted to each of them. But I just didn't want to go anymore."

"Why not?"

"I went out on a limb and did a little thirty second ad thing for one of Mom's friends. It got noticed by someone on YouTube, who told someone else about the plays I did at James Bowie, who showed Erica Yates my CV. Four months later, I signed a contract for ten years with her representing me."

"Then it got bad?"

"Didn't start that way. Was real nice and shiny, felt like I was living a dream. Indie films. Music videos. I'm still most proud of my early movies." He stares at his Oxfords in the grass. I inch backward with my Converse. "Then uh, well things got more legit. Got the house, the extra bodyguard. Traveled all over. Met some…people. Got my tattoo."

"Are you going to add to it?"

He looks up and around, raises a hand and covers his eyes, searching for something. "I might. Haven't decided yet."

"Did it hurt?"

After's lip twitches and he fixes his coat collar, popping it Sherlock Holmes style. "A bit, near my elbow especially, and between my knuckles."

"What's it all mean—"

His sigh is hard and sharp. "Scott. To put—to put this nicely. Um. I don't think I want to tell you yet."

Why does that sound like, 'you don't deserve to know'? I thought he'd forgiven me. Not that I'd forgiven myself. But he's still staring, and that stare turns into a scowl, and that scowl turns into…

I want to slither into the hedge maze and disappear. There's that look of disappointment I hoped to never see on his face, directed at me.

An air horn honks out, and we both leap, turning in a circle as a crowd starts to gather by us at the entrance of the hedge. I look back at After and take a wide step away, not sure when I started standing so close.

"May the hunt begin!" Ms. Florence screams over a mic. "First to find the flamingo is the victor!" We separate even more as the guests whoop and laugh, rushing between us. He watches me over heads of excited participants. I glare at my feet.

Chapter 15

We're split up by the time everyone stops galloping through the entrance of the maze. Either that or he walked off on purpose. I wouldn't blame him if that's the case.

I wander left, thinking I might've heard a rule once that said if you keep left you won't get lost. Or maybe it was keep left every two turns, then alternate going right. I'm gonna be the dude that starts moving in a big ol' square, just watch.

Turning the next corner, I bump into another party goer, and we both laugh and bounce backward.

"Sorry, didn't see you," he chuckles, helping me right myself from where I nearly fell through a bush. One look at the guy tells me he's either a model or a Greek god, or both, so I ain't even mad about getting thrown into the shrubbery.

"No worries, I'm easy to miss," I reply, picking a leaf off his jacket. I realize it's attached, then I realize his baby blue suit is covered in leaves and flowers. "You just blend right in, don't you?" I smirk up at him.

He shrugs and smiles at me with a dimple in his chin. "Oh, for sure. I like to hide in the bushes and squawk out at the drunkards, just to laugh at them telling their more sober friends that someone's screaming in the maze."

"What a hobby."

"It's my way of life. But—" He squints at my hair and pulls an actual leaf from my head, handing it down to me. "What you said. You're not easy to miss."

I snort and twirl the leaf stem between my fingers before letting it fall. "Well, thanks, I think?"

"You came with David, right? I'm Jacob Nolan, great to meet you…?"

I accept his handshake and stand taller, though this guy towers over even After's 6' height. "Scott Everett Boscoe."

"Not Judge Norman's grandson?" Jacob asks, quirking a blond brow.

"The same." Please, God, don't tell me one of your relatives or lovers is in jail because of Grandpa Mitch. "I should really—"

"To tell you the truth, I wasn't really listening when Florence announced the rules. What are we looking for?"

He turns his body to stand at my side, and with a forced, polite smile, I head down another path. "A pink flamingo, supposedly."

"Is it large? Small? Yard-sized?"

"You're asking questions I have zero answers to," I chuckle.

"Fair enough. Here's a question you can answer: do you go by Scott Everett? Like Mary Jane or Susie B? Or is it just Scott."

"Call me whatever you like," I shrug.

"Whatever *I* like, huh?" I glance at him when he's not looking. Except he's already looking, blue eyes serpentine. I try to give another smile. He hums and stares ahead.

We both groan when we hit a dead end, and we do an about face, trying a new direction. "How do you know Af—David?" I ask. Ech, that tasted weird. *Tasted.* That was *definitely* the wrong word to describe how his name felt in my mouth.

"We met through a mutual friend, Nicholas. Then David worked with me on a set a couple years ago. He'd never been to Portland—where I'm from—so I showed him the ropes. Celebrated his twenty-first. I took him to all the places I got trashed in when I was his age."

I eye Jacob as he checks another path, not able to tell just how long ago that was. The lines down his cheeks tell me he might be in his mid-thirties, but he smiles and walks like he's as old as After and me. "That was awfully nice of you. Were you director on the set?"

Jacob chuckles and sends me a look, and my creep-o senses go off. "Ah, uh…not exactly. We were co-stars. Wasn't anything that got…aired. For the public." Red alert, red alert, what the fuck does that mean?

"Was it an indie film? Anything I might've seen?"

"Judging by your turtleneck and sneakers, I highly doubt it, Scott Everett." He grins and it's less young and more ageless, in an immortal, no cares in the world kind of way. "Although. It's always the quiet, shy-dressed ones that surprise you, isn't it? So maybe you might've seen it. Depending on what connections you have on the deep, wide web."

I stop as Jacob keeps walking, and my jaw hangs open.

Porn. He means porn. He *has* to mean porn—oh sweet bouncing baby Jesus, was After in a *porno*?

Also, *rude*, I did cocaine off a male stripper's happy trail when I was eighteen, so shut up about 'quiet ones'. Shy-dressed my ass, for all he knows I could be wearing a leather chest harness and nipple clamps underneath this turtleneck and discount bin button up. (Not that I would. You'd see those through the knit.)

"You coming?" Jacob asks, poking his head around a hedge.

"Uh—yeah, sorry," I reply, catching up. I'm on high guard around this guy now but I can't help but be curious. If there's porn of After floating around the Internet, why hasn't his agent taken it down? Paid who she had to pay, as much as necessary, to keep her precious straight boy clean?

I mean shit, how fast do other celebrities' sex tapes get leaked? Is it a sex tape if he did it for money? What does After have on this guy that's keeping him from dropping that bomb on Tumblr? Imagine, dozens of gifs of After, sweaty and naked and plunging his—okay, yeah, the turtleneck was a mistake.

I'm probably being weird for no reason. Jacob's full of it and has nothing special up his sleeve at all. I sternly tell myself that, as we round another corner and hit a dead end.

I'm mid-turn when Jacob grabs my hand, and lighting shoots up into my ears. Abort mission, abort mission, flee Scotty, oh shit—

"You've been quiet since I mentioned my work with David." Jacob smiles, moving to block my path and tilt his head down to me. "Did I make you nervous?"

"No, why?" Wow, I sound a lot more confident than I feel.

"Y'know, I've been looking for another guy or two for my next film."

"Don't really have the time for that; busy."

"Busy with…work? What do you do? Whatever it is, I'd pay you double," he adds, hand trailing up my forearm to my elbow.

"Student." Fuck, shouldn't have said that. But it was either that, or my dumbass brain was about to have me blurt out, 'cop in training'. Seeing as he's currently groping my bicep, he's gonna know that's a fat lie.

"Oh, cute," he breathes. "Prep school? Do you have a uniform?" How old does he think I am?

"Um. For special events. Tie and everything." I'm choking on saliva I can't seem to swallow.

"Tie…that's adorable. I bet you can restrain all *sorts* of things with that tie."

Jacob's lashes flutter as he looks around my face, and I hate that my knees are Jell-O, and I hate, *hate*, that I'm finding this somewhat of a turn on. I know I could scream loud enough to get this guy to back off if needed. The hedges are thick, but not so much that no one would hear me—I'm literally outside, and there's, like, hundreds of people here. I'm not in. *Immediate*…danger…

And the last guy who looked at me like this, he was tall and handsome, too, and he held me afterward, high and drunk and weightless.

I'm not high, I don't drink anymore, and I don't smell anything on Jacob's breath but spearmint. I can't help it when I chew on my lip. Jacob's eyes zero in on the movement, and his finger loops into the collar of my turtleneck.

"Your pulse is going crazy," he murmurs.

Probably cause I'm having a panic attack, I think, holding in a mix of a smile and a whimper. My brain screams run; my heart says just one kiss after five years of being touch-starved out of our mind wouldn't hurt.

A hand claps on Jacob's shoulder. He turns to face After, jacket looped over his arm, Aviators perched in his hair. His hazel stare is locked right on me. He looks angrier than I've ever seen. My stomach drops to the grass and shrivels.

Chapter 16

"There you are, baby boy," Jacob muses, stepping away from me. *Baby boy?* I think my body just did a visible cringe shudder dance. Oh God, absolutely *not*.

"Here I am," replies After. He blinks, and that flash of murder disappears. He smiles and accepts a kiss on his cheek, hand on Jacob's elbow. "Seems you found my date."

"We were just talking about you," says Jacob, keeping his hands to himself now. "He's awfully jumpy, isn't he?"

"He's full of surprises, trust me," After chuckles, circling behind me. He places his hand on my shoulder, but it doesn't stop there. It snakes across my collarbone and rests on my opposite shoulder, until my throat is warmed by his muscled forearm. I'm not even here. I'm just a thing to these two larger than life men with fancy suits, secret sex lives and shiny snarls.

"You've been a difficult rabbit to catch these days," says Jacob. "I've been wanting to talk to you." The arm against my trachea flexes. "Heard you might be in Nashville this spring. For Nicholas's show?"

After's words steam right past my ear. "I might be."

"Very nice. We can chat about that later, yeah?"

"Sure. Later."

Jacob dips his head and walks off without another glance at me. As soon as he steps past the next corner, After jolts away from me, and I'm suddenly cold even with my turtleneck.

"How the fuck did you end up talking alone to Jacob Nolan?" he snaps.

"Huh?" I'm still tingling from hands on my arms and my throat and I'm still hella confused about what it's doing to my heart.

I bring fingers to the pulse under my jaw. It's beating out the typical message, nice and rhythmic. 'How-are you-still-alive?' Yep, I'm good.

His anger turns to concern. "What's wrong with you—"

"What's wrong with *Jacob?*" I ask over him.

After's eye twitches and he juts his chin, standing straight and looking over my head. "He's one of the reasons Erica's apprehensive about me coming out."

"What does he have to do with it?"

"He's got…something. On me. She's concerned more people are gonna want me for stuff like that, and I'll lose what rep I have about being a family friendly star." He walks on, and I follow with wobbly legs.

"We're literally going to the premiere of an R-rated movie you're in."

"R-rated cause of gore and language."

"And sex—"

"Not…*gay* sex."

"If I see Erica, I'm slapping a 'homophobic' sticker on her face."

He falters and chuckles, rigid shoulders relaxing. "Yeah, well. Anyway—he's not gonna release the…video tapes. To anyone else. I don't think—he's not that kinda guy."

"Video tapes—you sound like American Psycho. You can just say 'porn', I get it."

He trips and his brows shoot up his forehead. Is he blushing? Didn't think After still blushed.

"I—well, it wasn't—I didn't—"

"Was it consensual? He said he got you drunk, or trashed, something along those lines."

"Yeah, it was…wow. Thanks for asking," he says. "Not even Erica asked me that when she found out."

"Forget the sticker, if I find her, I'm gonna falcon punch her." After throws his head back with a laugh, and his arm comes around my shoulders.

I very subtly, very sneakily, try to wiggle out of it, pretending I need to fix my jacket collar.

I'm neither subtle nor sneaky, cause he clears his throat and walks so far away from me his opposite shoulder scrapes along the hedge. "Sorry I freaked out over Jacob. He's uh…well, he's easy to talk to, and it's easy to get talked into things with him."

"Were you worried your fake boyfriend would be fake unfaithful to you?"

Oh, wow, *that* was a hot button. After's nostrils flare. His jaw flexes so hard I swear I can hear his teeth grind. "Anyway. If you wanted to find him when we're through with all this, after we do the breakup shit in May, you can. And y'all can talk or…whatever."

"Nah, gave me a weird vibe," I mutter. Weird isn't the word I'd use, but I don't think After would appreciate me rambling about my kinks and desperation these days.

"Why didn't you walk away from him then? Or call out for me—I was looking for you."

Cause I was weak, excited, curious, lonely. Said it yourself, After, when you saw my dorm. So lonely. "I could've taken him."

After releases a sigh. "Yeah, sure."

We turn another corner, and there's a hot pink flamingo ornament hanging on a bush. He walks right up to it and plucks it off the leaves, presenting it to me with a silly flourish. "Thank you very much," I nod, giving him a short bow before tucking it into my pocket.

"Back to the tent?" he asks, reaching for my hand. I take it and let him lead me to the entrance. Until it's evident he has no clue where he's going, so we just barrel through a thinner hedge and run for the club, leaving a Scott and After sized hole in the foliage.

We pass the flamingo off to a lady in her eighties. She has a nose ring and had dyed her white hair a soft lavender. She pinches at After's bicep under his layers and totters off, giggling and swinging the flamingo from a finger adorned with a bright jade ring.

A thought forms and floats to the surface, and I almost blurt it out, except it would ruin the pleasant-ish day we've been having. But I imagine that my mom would've been like that, had she lived to be that old. I could see her dying her gray hair blue or something and rocking glittery makeup she got from Claire's. I could see her loving After to bits, too.

He clears his throat, and I look to where he's staring at the parking lot. A tall, tan woman with sheeny black hair is coming straight toward us in a bloodred pantsuit, magically walking in stilettos and not sinking on the grassy turf. "Erica Yates," After mutters.

"I gathered by the way you just crushed my hand in your fist."

"Sorry. Um. Don't falcon punch her."

"No promises." I stand at my tallest and don't come near her chin. She gives me a single, pointed glance with eyes bluer than the sky, sends them down to our clasped hands, then slaps a smile on for After. Stepping forward, she kisses his cheek as he kisses hers, and she straightens with a hand on her hip. She's drop dead gorgeous.

"Well hello, honey, so nice to see you here," she says, white teeth glistening behind ruby lipstick. "Your mom said you hadn't RSVP'd last time we talked."

"I don't usually RSVP to her events; keeps her on her toes," he chuckles. "Erica, I'd like you to meet—"

"Ah! The Insta-famous Scott E. Boscoe, right?" She extends her hand and I shake it, momentarily thinking her skin would be ice cold for some ridiculous reason. Maybe it's the vampire aesthetic she's got going on with her red and black. "How do you two know each other?"

"I've told you before, Erica," After sighs.

"Tell me again, y'know I have too many things going on to remember silly things like that," she snorts. Never before have I seen someone live up to their bad reputation so fast.

"Fine, only cause I love the story," he replies. Good grief, you big fake sap, since when? After pulls me closer by my hand and sends me a look he must have practiced, cause it's both sweet and fragile as hell. "We grew up together in Lubbock, met at seven years old in the cafeteria. We bonded when we smashed faces playing football," he adds, tapping his brow. "We've been close ever since."

Her stare lingers at the scar on my jaw, and she cocks her head. "But you're just now dating. Slow cookers, hmm?"

"Something like that. Rekindled friendship recently, got some things…straightened out."

"No pun intended," I pipe in. His smile that time is more real, and he laughs.

"Right, yeah—"

"That's *super* cute," she grins. Crest Whitestrips should be afraid of her. "So y'all are BFFs, yeah? Just *meant to be*, huh?"

Erica blinks, turns her attention to After, and just like with Jacob, I've managed to disappear all over again. "I still hate how things turned out with Sasha, David, but maybe you can give her another chance? I'm sure rebounds are gonna happen, but—"

"Scott's not a rebound," After frowns. He brings me closer a second time, and if he does it a third, I'm gonna end up standing on his foot. "Sasha didn't work out because I'm gay, Erica, you know this. It's not gonna happen; I could give her five chances or a thousand and it wouldn't make a difference."

"I'm thinking of your *future*, David, you don't need to get mad at me," she says, putting a hand on his shoulder. Her nails massage his arm; they pop him and he starts to fizzle. "I'm on your side, remember? I don't want your heart broken all over again by some kid you grew up with and have never talked to me about until right this second."

My brain is sending a signal to the muscles in my leg, readying to swing my foot back and kick her right in the pant-suit clad vagina, when her phone rings, and she slips it out of her pocket. In a swift move, she kisses After's cheek, says something in his ear, and walks off with a sharp, "This is Yates!"

"What an absolutely vicious woman," I snap. After's hand in mine twitches. I look back to him; he's shrunk a few inches since we started talking to Erica. "What did she say to you?"

"When?" he mumbles, rubbing his eye. I step in front of him, grimace, and lick my thumb, wiping at the lipstick she left on his cheek, red like a fresh welt.

"When—just now, she whispered something to you." He stares at me. "After? What did she say?"

"She said. Remember what we talked about…"

"And what have you talked about?"

He looks to his shoes, his toes turned in, enough to make him seem so small. "Um. My uncle. The one who died in Nebraska. She doesn't want me to end up gay and…dead like him." I spin on my heel and launch, and he releases my hand and goes for my shoulder. "Don't, Scott—"

"I'm gonna kill her—"

"Scotty." I try to soften my face before I look at him. He puts the Ferrari keys in my hand and closes his fingers around mine. "I have to uh…come back up here. Talk to Mom. And some of the guests for a bit. But I want to take you home, you've got homework."

"It can wait, I'm not leaving you—"

"No, it's fine. I don't want to force you to stay out any longer. But, going back to JU…can you drive?"

Like hell do I wanna try to drive a Ferrari on a Saturday in LA. But he looks beat to shit after one single conversation with Erica. And he's been with her for *years*? "Yeah, fine."

We're nearly to the car when he squeezes my hand twice. "She was wrong, by the way."

"About which part? Cause I'd say 99.89%." He opens the door for me and hooks his fingers over the window.

"About. Me not ever talking to her about you. I have. All the time. I told her everything." That makes me feel 99.89% worse.

Chapter 17

"Yvonne is never allowed to dress me again; I don't care what I said about being a willing Barbie Doll." I shift my phone in my hand and kick off my sneakers by my bunk, groaning into a stretch. "I didn't think it would be that bad when we got started, but she texted me the updates she's been making—she'd deck me out in ivory and sequined chaps just to go to Trader Joe's."

Charlotte's laugh shrieks over the line as I chuck my mail on my desk. "If you're referring to that photo you sent me where the mannequin look like Panic! At the Disco meets Game of Thrones, I'd pay big money to see you in that."

"You'd be wasting your cash, woman. I'm never going out in that in public besides to this over-the-top gala. Though I might wear the outfit to Cindie's, see if they give me a discount on sexy lingerie to go with my golden lace—"

My phone vibrates in my hand, and I glare at After's filtered puppy-eared face lighting up my screen. "After's calling me."

"Oooh, boyfriend trouble?"

"Hardy har, enjoy your spring break, I'll see you Saturday—"

"Tell him he's invited to the bridal shower!"

"Yes, fine, love you."

"Love you, sugar tits!"

"You're trash," I smile, hanging up as she squeaks at me. "Hey, After—"

"You at home?"

"I'm in my dorm."

"That's what I meant—" A fast, agitated knock, and I thump over to open my door. There's After, looking like a very pissed off Nordstrom advert in a casual version of his fundraiser outfit. One hand holds his phone like a brick he's gonna smash through something (preferably not my face), and the other fist is locked around a magazine.

"If this is what roaches see in your house, you with a death grip on a rolled-up mag, face full of fury, I fear for them all."

He snorts through his nose. "Not funny."

"What happened to you texting me before you waltz up here again?"

"No time," he grunts, shoving the magazine at me as he stalks in. I toss my phone back on my desk and look at the cover.

"It's you—"

"It's me and *another girl*," he sneers, pacing in the room. He swings his leg back like he wants to kick my hamper, but then it's like his brain says no, idiot, we don't kick other peoples' shit, cause he trips at the last second and topples into my bunk. Has no problem slapping my bunk, though.

I squeeze an eye shut and stare at the magazine, tilting it left and right. After in a dark purple hoodie or jacket, outside somewhere with green awnings, leaning close to a pretty brunette with her back to the camera. "So…?"

He spins on me, fists tight at his sides, ready for takeoff. I'm sure I'm meant to be intimidated but I'm too fucking tired.

Over the weekend, Bevett mentioned in the slightest of passing to Mitch that After and I were talking again for the first time in years; saying that he was finicky about that is a very sad understatement.

Grandpa kept me on the phone well after midnight, berating me for bonding with 'that boy' again (AKA, After) because he was worried we were reminiscing over our 'past mistakes' (AKA, everything stupid I did in El Paso, even though After wasn't part of any of that) and therefore, by reuniting my childhood friend, I am, 'sending all my hard work down the toilet for the sick, twisted sake of craving attention'. (AKA…yeah, no, that's it, no AKA needed, that's what he said and meant.)

I proceeded to get no sleep, debating if now would be a good time to flee the country, except I promised Bevett I'd be visiting the rest of my spring break. In an attempt to chill out, I tried After's newest writing exercise; typing without pause until I got my thoughts in order.

Wrote for three minutes straight without a single mark of punctuation, reread it and deleted it, cause it made my dorm feel more like a concrete coffin.

Then I got a grade back for an exam in art history that was *much* lower than I was expecting, was gifted a parking ticket for my goddamn bicycle chained to a post I've used since day *one* while I was just checking my mail, and *now* I've got a cranky celeb hulking around in my room like he owns the place.

He makes enough money *to* own the place, but that's beside the point. "Are you an idiot, or do you just play one on TV?" he spits.

Now I'm grinning and give even less fucks than I did a couple seconds ago. "I'm not on TV, you are, so *you* tell *me*."

He inhales a gulp of stale college air, then drops to my desk chair, crossing his arms.

"D'aw, are you gwumpy? Do you need a sippy cup? Maybe a nap-nap?"

"Go fuck yourself with a toilet brush, Scott."

"The handle or the brush part? Cause one sounds a lot more fun than the other," I reply, opening up the magazine to the page about this mystery girl and After. He mutters something obscene, but I'm too busy reading for it to register.

"*David Después was seen leaving Starbucks*—why is it always *Starbucks* with you? Don't you have female encounters at other high-priced coffee establishments?"

"I like the lime refreshers, so fucking sue me," he grumps, chin in his hand as he scrolls through my laptop. Lucky for me, I save anything incriminating to my phone, so I doubt he'll find something good. I read on.

"*...Seen leaving Starbucks with potential new side hustle Hanna Markowsky, star of television horror and drama series, As it Comes Knocking. Erica Yates says the two met at David's mother's fundraiser at the*—first off, ew Erica. But also, if *you* met her, then *I* met her, and I don't remember seeing her, unless it was when you went back."

He splays his legs out and slouches, wrinkling his tapered blazer. When he looks at me, it's a lot less angry, and more flattened. "No, I never saw her at the fundraiser. Never met her before at all."

"How about you tell me what happened, because this—" I hold up the magazine and jab a finger at the circled picture of him potentially kissing her. "*This* looks like y'all met ages ago."

After blinks at me in silence for a few seconds. "Do you believe me, when I say we hadn't met before Starbucks?"

"Of course I do."

"Thank you," he sighs, drooping his head back against my chair. "Cause Mom doesn't. And she felt the unhelpful urge to say something unpleasant."

"What'd she say?"

"She got the article before I did—that's how I even knew about it. Told me Hanna's a nice girl, don't be a Playboy and ruin her, don't get her pregnant..." he blinks up at the ceiling and adds under his breath, "told me to get tested first. Said 'who knows what you got from those'...whatever."

I'm sorry. *Those*? After, how many fucking 'video tapes' did you make? I pull at my collar and clear my throat, and I think we're both turning a similar shade of red cause he coughs and leans over his knees.

"Anyway uh. I met her at Starbucks, straight up. She was buying behind me. I offered to get her stuff since I heard her on the phone with her aunt, telling her she only had a twenty and it wasn't enough for their lunch. We left at the same time, I was helping her carry her to-go trays out, and a leaf—I *swear*, Scott, a fucking leaf—flew into her hair. Her hands were full, I got it out for her, and snap." He mimes taking a picture and nods to the magazine in my hand.

"They got the perfect angle. She walked off after that, I didn't even know her past her first name, not until the article showed up. I found her on fucking IMDB. She doesn't have my number, I don't have hers, so it's not like we can talk about it. Mom said Hanna and her aunt were guests at the fundraiser, but I had no idea. Then Erica strung up some shit and the tabloids just felt like slapping two-and-two together."

His face drops into his hands and he slumps. "That was a lot of talking…"

I sit in the other chair and wheel over. "So, what can we do to fix it?"

"Get Starbucks." I laugh and he kicks my shin with his boot toe. "No, really. Or do something, we need more than just this." He holds his phone out and shows me a photo of us at the fundraiser.

At the time it was taken, someone was shooting pictures, and he saw them angle the camera near us. He brought our linked hands up to his face and kissed his own fingers over my knuckles. By the photo, it looks like he's kissing my hand. He timed it perfectly, just like they did with him and Hanna. "I thought it would be a good start. But this got, like, no attention," he huffs.

I snort at that statement, watching the likes and comments still pouring in days after the event. "Meanwhile this stupid shit got printed in *Us Weekly*. There's another article in there about Sasha and how she's doing after our split."

He mocks with air quotes, "She's a 'strong woman' and she's 'moving on' and I don't 'know what I've missed out on by dumping her'."

My lip curls. The more I hear about this Sasha, the more she gives me Missy Davis vibes from high school, and I'm not about that. "Alright, so let's go get some coffee. And what about after?"

"I'll figure it out."

Chapter 18

He is so impossibly fidgety.

Imagine a pack of rats, wearing a nice cotton shirt under a tailored navy blazer paired with dark jeans, but all the rats have fleas and are hyped up on sugar, and one may or may not have powdered cocaine it's getting all over the others, and there are also badgers in the fancy cowboy boots.

That's After.

He keeps scratching at his arms, rubbing his neck, pulling at a loose string on his jacket, pushing his Aviators into his hair just to perch them on his nose again. He promised we're on our way to get coffee, but I'm not sure he needs to even *smell* caffeine with how jittery he is.

"What the heck is your problem?" I ask when he pulls his hands from his pockets for the hundredth time to wipe at his face, disrupting his glasses until they're hanging on by an inch around his ears.

"I'm fine, what's *your* problem?" he grunts, scowling at his reflection as we pass by a closed bakery; he's walking so fast I've had to hop-skip every few steps to keep up.

"You're like a crack addict, what's going on?"

"How would you know what a crack addict looks like? Precious Scott Everett, safe and spoiled in his grandpa's fancy colonial castle…"

Oh whaddup, since when did this get personal? Homeboy today is *not* the day to test me.

"Nope." I stop before we get to the next intersection and cross my arms, and he does a triple take so fast he nearly sends his head spinning around his shoulders. "You tell me right now what's going on or I go home."

"*Nothing* is *going on!*"

I arch a brow at him. An older lady across the street scowls disapprovingly, hurrying along with a little kid holding her hand. When someone on the other side of the crosswalk looks up from their phone and takes out an ear bud, it registers across his face just how loud he shrieked at me. His whole face scrunches until he resembles Bevett when she was seven and thought she could get her way by punching me in the 'nads for six months straight. "After. What is wrong?"

He sways, boot heel thump-thumping on concrete as he wanders back toward me. "I just. I had an idea. On how to move this up a notch."

"Move what up a notch?"

"The *fake* dating with the *very* real homosexual," he says. Maybe he's trying to pat his chest to signify himself, but it just looks like he's attempting to calm down the rats racing around in his mansuit torso.

"Are you going to tell me what it is, or do I have to just guess things out loud?" I ask, afraid he's about to pop a blood vessel in his eye at any moment. "Do I get a lifeline? A hint?"

"I guess I…I thought. If they're so hellbent on catching me *kissing* people, then…I mean…maybe we should. Y'know."

He's going to jump out of his skin any second, so I take the leap and blurt the damn word out for him. "Kiss?" Then I shiver and cover it by fixing my button-up collar. "Sure, fine with me," I shrug, putting my hands in my pockets.

His eyes squeeze into a squint. "What?" he asks, making maybe the most hilarious and ugliest face I've ever seen him make in all the years I've known him.

"What, what?" I ask with another smooth criminal shrug.

"We've—cause we've...I mean..." His face turns as pink as Yvonne's hair and he looks to his boots.

I stare at my shoes, too, in case the Earth is about to crack open and swallow us whole. Don't think I'd mind that. I may have said it super nonchalantly, but the offer made my throat close up instantly.

"I'm...still..." He looks up and around, and his stare lingers on something past my head. "Someone's got their phone raised."

"Cool, and?"

"And...and another—okay, awesome, this is gonna work." He squares his shoulders, sniffs, and the manly man is back. "I think I've got it. And it's not like I'm gonna *actually* kiss you."

"If you need to, it's cool, I can—"

"I'm *not* gonna kiss you," he snaps. He'd have shouted it if we were alone. My jaw clacks shut. "I'm not. I don't want to kiss you."

Duly noted, thank you for clearing that up with a knife to my chest. "Okay."

"I just need them to *think* I am. They're behind you, they'll just see me come in. E-even if they come up behind me, it'll be a good shot, it'll work, I can make this work."

It makes my skin itch that he's thought so much of this out. "Alright, fine."

After nods and turns on his smile. "Okay, I'm gonna walk over toward you," he says. I start to smile back, until I see his eyes dart over my head once, twice, and I remember he's not smiling for me. "You good?"

"Good, yeah," I reply, struggling to remain chill. He's much better at this than me. Obviously, paid actor.

He pretends to be bashful, checking out his boots as he shuffles closer. "Don't freak out," he says quietly.

His brow quirks at the click of another camera behind him, but he doesn't turn toward it. We're surrounded.

"I'm not freaking out," I mutter. Another step. He tilts his head and moves one hand out of his pocket. I can sense he's seconds away from raising said hand, but I can't look away from him.

"You totally are, stop."

Seventeen, in his Jeep, in his lap. Now is *not* the time, brain. "I am *not* freaking out."

After chuckles at some joke I must've made, smiling half toward the direction of a camera. I can see it now: 'David's new beau Boscoe, funny *and* cute.' Ugh, vomit. "Your eyes are doing a ping pong match in your skull."

"Oh my God, shut up and just do what you need to do—"

The next wide step, the next time he meets my stare, he's inches from me. My breath catches. I hold it. Then I release it shaky out my nose.

"I'm gonna put my hand on your face," he explains.

"Fine." Seventeen. In my backyard. Against the elm tree. A cold finger slices up my spine as a bead of sweat races down.

"And I'm gonna lean real close."

"Sure, whatever."

His hand goes to my cheek. It's. Not what I was expecting. Haven't noticed the callouses on his palm against my own. Now I feel them scrape slow along my face.

His fingers land near my ear. His thumb crosses my lips. "I'm gonna bring my mouth to my thumb. Not your mouth. Okay?"

Reasonable enough. Get another weird vibe that he seems so practiced at this. Maybe kissing scenes in his shows. That dumb thing guys do when they're kids, when they put their hand over their friends mouths and kiss the backs of their knuckles just to laugh and say, 'no homo'. Did other kids do that? Just me? Just young and sexually confused me, who never actually did it to the one person he wouldn't have minded kissing? Probably.

Who was After's first guy kiss? Was it Jacob? Did they kiss in the porno? Did Jacob's dimple rub against After's chin, those blue eyes staring into hazel like I am right now?

After cranes his neck down and his lashes start to close, but not all the way. Up so close, for the first time in ages, I find the glint of green in his eyes.

And what looks like frustration. Hopefully not at me. Cameras shutter like a symphony and he tenses. All that confidence to get here and he can't do it.

Weird vibe turns to pity for him. He'd rather be doing a thousand other things right now than pretending some kind of love story, especially with me. Worst fake boyfriend ever.

Without much thought to it, I stand on my toes, put my hand to the back of his neck, and force his mouth to come down and meet his thumb on my lips. I make one more dumb decision and close my eyes.

After gasps. It's soft, quiet, but it's unmistakable.

Dropping back onto my heels, I take his hand from my face and lead him purposefully past where I know all the paps are. I lick my lower lip. I bite my lower lip. One of the paparazzi wolf whistles, and I laugh and shoot a bright grin their way. I can fake it too, y'know.

Chapter 19

Charlotte's bridal shower is tomorrow on Saturday. Mei's family lives in Pasadena, which is closer to Mitch's house than Jethro. So unfortunately, that's where I am right now, ending my week off hunched over my desk, attempting to write.

Less unfortunately is the fact that I got to hang around with Bevett all spring break, too, since they matched up this year, and Mitch has been out of town the last two days, and tomorrow's going to be a blast with Charlotte, Mei, their bridesmaids and—

Bevett launches off my bed. "Doorbell!" she shrieks, as if I hadn't heard it ding-dong through the house. She skips out of my room and lets out a *whoop!* as she slides down the banister, something Mitch prohibits her from doing, so naturally she does it any time he's not home. There's more screaming, laughing, and a deep voice that has me tilting my ear toward my door.

"Who is it, Bevvy?" I shout, glaring at my work and shaking my head at the jumbled mess. A week ago, Jackie sent me the first book she'd like summarized, requesting I at least attempt to finish the job by the end of my break.

I'm just now working on it. And I want to die.

"Bev?" I try again, sitting back in my chair and willing my laptop to set on fire.

"Yo."

I turn to After in my doorway, wearing joggers and a baseball tee, cap on backward, always. Looking like Academy chic.

I'm in shorts I've worn four days in a row. I get the urge to mad-dash toss my dirty laundry into the hamper, especially the three pairs of boxers I know for a fact are still strewn about near my dresser.

Unable to do any of that subtly, I just slooowly close my laptop to hide the screen and turn to fully face him like a Bond villain in my chair. "Hello."

"You watching porn?" My horrified face makes him smirk. "I'm joking."

This dude near tore my face off after our fake kiss not five days ago. As soon as we rounded the next corner away from people, he had yanked his hand out of mine, clawed at his mouth like I *actually* kissed him *and* had the black plague, then abandoned me to find my own way home in LA. I didn't even get a Starbucks like he said we would.

So screw this guy. "I'm not watching porn," I scoff.

"Writing it then? A lil E.L. James?"

"Get out." He cranes his neck back, squinting at me with a look of amusement. "Why are you here?" I ask, crossing arms and legs into a protective pretzel.

"Cause you told me Charlotte and Mei's party is tomorrow."

"Why are you *here* right *now*?"

"Cause I brought you food?" After lifts a plate of something purple, covered in plastic wrap.

"What…" I walk over, scowling between him and this mystery offering.

He laughs when I gasp and rip the plate from his hands. "No! No, you made—you made Spanish bread!"

"With yam, you said you liked the yam—"

"Oh, I love the yam! What the—" I tear the plastic wrap off and plop onto my bed, chomping into a piece with a heavy groan. "God, it's *disgusting*, I *love* it," I sob. "Why bring such a glorious gift?"

After leans on the doorway, hands retreating into his pockets. "Cause I was…I mean I was a total dick to you about the whole. Kiss thing. This is an apology."

"Y'all *kissed*!" screams Bevett, lurking in the hallway. I only hear a shrill squeak as After darts away, returning with her in a headlock, making me laugh and choke on densely packed bread.

"*Yes* we kissed, we *are* dating, you little snoop," he grins, shaking her around as she squeals and fights to be free. "What're you up to, miss? Do you think being fifteen now means you get to be nosy in everyone's business?"

"Only when it comes to my two favorite dorks, obviously," she giggles, giving a loud grunt as she gets out from under his arm, thumping into the opposite wall in the hallway.

Her head appears at my threshold again, eyes straight on the plate in my hands. I hardly have to lift it an inch for her to race for me, falling onto my bed and Kirby-ing an entire roll herself.

"C'mon, let me show you around," I tell After, just to get away from Bevett and her insatiable curiosity.

—

I'm a little shaken by how easy it was for him to lie like that. We're *dating*. We're *boyfriends*. I don't think he ever told Bevett a lie as long as he's known her. (He was, in fact, the one to accidentally reveal the falsities of Santa Clause, and deal with the tears afterward, too.)

I mean I think I get it; she's super popular on social media for someone so young. She's bound to get a lot of attention when it comes out that her brother is dating Giddings and Chance Harris and Lancelot. (His upcoming movie, as I found out from her, is another dramatic retelling of Lancelot and Guinevere's love story. At least he's not playing King Arthur; I don't think I'd survive two hours of people going on and on about how he's the *chosen one*.)

Speaking of that…

We're on the second floor now, and he's poking his head into Bevett's room with a smirk, commenting on how it's perfect for her; every wall is covered in Fleetwood Mac and The Last Unicorn posters, two things she wasn't even alive to experience for the first-time years ago.

He looks back to me and smiles, and I must look like I'm either about to die or pass serious gas, cause he squints at me with apprehension "What's wrong with you?"

"I haven't seen any of your movies," I honk. "I meant to watch them a week ago, and I have no excuse other than I'm a lazy dingus who has no time-keeping skills."

His brows shoot up. He actually grins. "Really?" I nod too fast and he laughs, walking on without me. "Okay, so?"

"So, I'm gonna be lost as shit at the movie premiere," I reply, catching up to him with one big step. He shrugs. "Why are you not more upset about this?"

"Why am I not upset you didn't force yourself to watch some of my home videos?" he scoffs.

"You said you were most proud of your earlier movies—that was the first two for this series, wasn't it?"

After's smile fades. "Yeah. True, I guess." He drops his head back and walks with his eyes closed for a few feet. "What were you working on when I came in?"

"Jackie sent me the first book she wants me to cover."

"What's the book?"

"Some chaotic sci-fi horror shit. Zombie dragons."

"Bad ass."

"Amazing to read, difficult to summarize. I need to send her something that resembles real work by the end of spring break."

"When is that?"

"Sunday."

"When did she send it to you?"

"…Sunday. Last week."

"You're a disaster."

"I'm well aware."

"Okay, I got an idea," he says, clapping his hands together. "Let's do your writing, crap something out. Then to celebrate, we can watch the movies—not to sound super conceited, but they *are* pretty good—and we can make dinner or something before to snack on. Sound like a plan?"

"How long are you wanting to stay? It's like an hour back to LA on a Friday evening."

After rubs his neck as we get to the stairs closest to my room. "Um. I mean…I saw some rooms."

"Are you inviting yourself over?" I laugh. He scratches his nose with a wince-smile, and I laugh harder and nudge him in the ribs. "Of course, we got rooms out the wazoo, you can stay the night no problem."

He nudges me back, and by the time I walk through my threshold, all the Spanish bread is gone. I seek vengeance on Bevett.

—

Then I seek vengeance on After. I got better with my sentence structure, sure, but I still have a plethora of feelings behind the summary and not enough facts. He tears me a new one every time it feels like I'm going backward one attempt after the other. I write the narrative with too much emotion; I tug at too many heartstrings.

"It's a dramatic book! Horror aside, there's romance and heartache! Heartstrings to tug!" I shout in defense after he's scrapped my sixth revision.

"It's not your dramatic book, nor your heartstrings—stop tugging and let the book speak for itself!" he yells back.

"Stop saying 'tug', it sounds pornographic."

"*You* sound pornographic."

"What does that even mean?"

"It means you sound like a brat, whining and moaning over something that you can do with your eyes closed!"

"What does *that* even *mean*!"

It continues like that well into the evening, until it gets to the point where I'm on the floor with my knees bent up near my face like a spider, poking at my laptop between my feet. After's on my bed with his brow smooshed to his crossed arms. He begs me again to just let him read what I've written, since I've been typing away in dead silence for an hour straight.

"Fine. Fine, read it, fine." I almost toss my laptop at his head, but he rolls off my bed and lands on the floor with a thud that has me laughing and relaxing my tight neck muscles for the first time all afternoon. He smirks at me and plants himself on his elbows, face lit up by my screen.

He reads it once. I watch his eyes hit the end, then return to the top, and he reads it two more times. After peeks at me over the laptop and smiles. "Better, dude. So much better."

I groan and uncoil, dropping to my back and kicking my feet up on my bed. After pushes my laptop aside and inches closer to me on his elbows as I close my eyes. "That should *not* have been that difficult. I don't get why I struggled with that so much."

He chuckles and warm air puffs over my nose. I blink up at him staring down at me. He's close enough that I could kiss him on the chin if I wanted to. "You've got a lot of heart Scott, that's all. You're having to literally cut a piece of yourself out to write like this. How do you get through the nonfiction essays in your classes?"

"I don't know. Those are easier sometimes. I do the research; I answer the prompt. When it comes to talking about things I'm passionate about—I've read this book twice, dude, it's phenomenal—it's hard for me to not want to gush about it, y'know? I want it to do well. I know it's not mine, I doubt I'll ever write a book to be honest—"

"Why not?" he asks. I sputter through my lips like it's obvious why not, cause it *is* obvious why not, and I tilt my head to him more. Now I'm close enough I could kiss his nose. If I wanted to. "You could have a book of poems. Like Atticus, The Truth About Magic. I think you'd like their work; they make me cry sometimes."

He shifts his arms and his hand lands in my hair. Fingers trace wild bangs from my forehead. His thumb runs along my hairline. I've frozen solid.

"I don't think I have any of their books…"

"I'll get one for you," he whispers.

I bite my lip. He watches me bite my lip.

After smiles and my pulse is in my ears. "Why're you smiling?"

"Because Bevett is in the doorway holding her phone up to us," he replies.

Flash. I tilt my head back, glaring at her upside down. Bevett grins. "Posting this one as 'old fart lovebirds who talk about poems'. Or something equally stupid."

After smirks and pushes up off his elbows, while my pounding heart slams into the hardwood and shatters into oblivion. "If you were any sneakier without the freaking flash on, you mighta gotten a kiss cam."

"Really?" she gasps. *Really?*

"No," he snorts. I'd like to disintegrate, please. "Let's make burritos and watch me be sweaty and dumb with a sword in HD!"

Chapter 20

We stayed up too late. By too late, I mean well after four. We watched the first movie, then the second, listened to Bevett go on and on about what she thinks is going to happen in the third installment, since they've already taken a different approach to the well-known myth and it's anyone's guess.

After had no problem discussing it with her. I got agitated, glaring at her Tumblr on her laptop and the countless renditions of a shirtless scene where Lancelot is working as a blacksmith before he becomes a knight for Arthur. They just *had* to keep zooming in on After's sweat and soot-riddled pecs and deep divots in his back. Please, we get it, guy's a hunk with rippling surfer hair and rippling…everything else…who falls for a married woman—can we move on?

It's romantic, crooned Bevett, watching the scene where Lancelot meets Guinevere for the first time; her riding in on horseback, wearing oversized men's clothing to blend in since her stuffy husband Arthur wouldn't let his queen out of the castle for fear of her fragile feminine safety.

I was over it the moment they showed her being *clumsy* and *endearing*. Gave me flashbacks to Bella Swan, straight up. (Whether I'm a secret Twi-hard or not, you will never know.)

But the fight scenes were spectacular; watching After in action, knowing he did his own stunts and practiced for hours daily. Bevett didn't believe him, so he grabbed unwilling me and made me stand opposite him with the fireplace poker, while he took the shovel and showed off some skills. I admit, by the end, I was grinning.

Then, when we went to the kitchen to reheat burrito makings and do round three of too much Tex-Mex (Cali-style—a weak imitation, at best), I asked him to pass me the Mexican blend cheese in the cheese drawer.

He replied with full confidence, "I *am* your Mexican blend." That startled such a big cackle out of me that I lost control of my burrito, and it ended up scattered across the tile, which had us both joining it on the floor with our faces in our arms trying to muffle our wheezing laughter to no avail.

By two in the morning, we moved on from watching his movies and behind the scenes, to screaming over Ali Wong.

My face ached from so much smiling that I started to forget about the whole 'hand in hair only cause there's a camera on me' thing, and started to remember what it was like before things got weird. Before it felt like I got booted from main character in my own life to sidekick, to potentially villain in someone else's story.

The bad guy doesn't get to be sad over being used when so much of his horrible, chaotic plot is his fault. I don't have a place in Lancelot's story anymore.

However, for a brief moment, with After and Bevett and laughing like we were young again, it was like none of the pain had happened yet.

But *then*, when Bevett went to bed (passed out on the sofa in the movie room) and I walked After to one of our guest rooms, he hugged me.

Hugged me. Tight. Out of the blue.

His arms around my neck, hands pressed to my shoulder blades while mine flopped around in confusion before they landed on his lower back. This wasn't hand holding or caressing fingers in hair or fake kisses for someone watching. A hug should've meant next to nothing after that.

But it made me tear up, and my 'goodnight' was too whispered out of shock. I ran for my life, sleeping in my window seat nook for fear of him finding me in my room. Not that he would seek me out. In my room. In the dead of night. Not that I wanted him to.

—

We rode together to Mei's mom's house, and I think we're standing a satisfactory 'fake boyfriend' distance from each other on opposite sides of the porch with a healthy three feet between us.

Thank goodness the lovebirds let us know (literally half an hour ago) that this was a pool party, so we could have time to get him swim shorts. (Literally stopped at Walmart on the way here. Gave the poor check out guy a heart attack when he recognized who was standing in front of him trying to buy Tabasco patterned trunks.)

Mei opens the door first in a white and green striped one-piece swimsuit with a dainty wrap around her waist. She sees After. Her eyes get larger than I've ever seen, and before either of us can say a word, she slams the door in our faces.

There's a sound like a mouse inhaling helium then having the life choked out of it on the other side. After stifles a snicker behind his fist, but it makes me giggle, and by the time Charlotte opens the door in a black bikini with jean shorts unbuttoned, we're both in stitches.

"Hi, hotties," Charlotte huffs, tucking wet hair behind her ears and grinning. "Please don't mind my fiancée who's fainted on the floor. She didn't believe me when I said you'd be coming over, After."

He walks in first, gets a hug, and looks around the door like he might actually see Mei passed out on the ground. There's a rush of green and white, and After's getting a hug from Mei who's lost all celebrity freak out and has gone into full 'hi new best friend' mode.

"You are so welcome, Aft-Daf-Dafter!" she squeals, hopping back and planting her hands on his shoulders. He looks more startled that she's meeting him eye to eye than anything else.

I abandon them to follow Charlotte through the house into the backyard where the rest of the party is by the pool. Chairs are all occupied, people sunning themselves in the shallow end, music blaring Niki Minaj.

It's all girls. Bikinis, tankinis, bathing suits, cleavage, high cuts at the hips, freckles on pierced noses, cute, round rolls and hip bones and squishy knees and dazzling brown skin and pink cheeks and glossy tans.

I'm in *heaven*.

It's. *Allllll* girls.

And they scream bloody murder the moment Mei appears at the French back doors, shouting at the top of her lungs with her arm looped through After's, "Look, ladies! We've got *strippers*!"

His face turns as red as the Tabasco bottles on his shorts, and I just laugh.

"I'm sure After here would make an excellent stripper," smirks Charlotte, coming to stand at my side. She eyes me up and down, then hums.

"But this one. Too much bone on him, too scrawny, not enough meat. I don't think he'd be good for stripping." She pats my ass with a look of pity.

I scare the dickens out of her when I lift her easily with an arm behind her back, one under her bent knees, and chuck her straight into the deep end while Mei guffaws.

Charlotte comes up sputtering and bright pink, and I point at her, 'how's *that* for scrawny!' ready to launch out of my mouth, when a bull smashes into my back, and I go flying into the water a foot away from her.

By the time I surface, I'm gasping and glaring at whatever the hell just John Cena'd me into the pool, and there's After, grinning maniacally.

"My *phone*! Was *in* my *pocket*! Asshole!" I yell, slapping water at his face with every exclamation.

"I'll buy you a new one," he laughs, grabbing me and dragging me toward him. I chuck my useless phone, wallet and keys into the grass by the pool chairs and cling to him like a cat on a log, nails digging into his shoulders just to keep afloat. Then there's Mei, cannonballing in after us, creating an incredible splash for someone so lithe.

A new beat takes over the Spotify station (CharMei's Lady List, Charlotte said it was called) and I don't even have to guess who it is, cause After gasps like he was the one choking on water, and his fist shoots into the air, other arm hooked tight to my waist. "It's my girl T Swift!" he shrieks at an octave I didn't know he could reach.

I'm thrown aside and he's out of the pool and shirtless by the time the lyrics of Shake it Off pick up, and then he's singing and pulling girl after girl out of the pool to join him, shaking his ass like he thinks he's Magic Mike. And glory hallelujah, did I say I was in heaven before? I am now.

Elbows leaned back on the white brick side of the pool behind me, I have the best seat, watching them dance along with After in wet bathing suits that are not *nearly* as supportive in the upper area as some of these gals seem to think. Even After's muscled chest has *quite* the bounce to it. Fucking *marvelous*.

He gives a wicked grin and crooks a finger at me, and I roll my eyes and join the others, getting yanked into the chaos. He starts to sensually go for the buttons of my soaked chambray, when he discovers my shirt has faux pearl snaps. The joy that crosses over his face when he just rips it open has me laughing until my abs hurt, and Charlotte and Mei whistle and swing their towels in the air.

We surpass stripper expectations. We gyrate like we're in ninth grade again at our first homecoming, and I'm quite proud and impressed by my own sexy and yet totally not dancing skills. After breaks a pool chair. I won't say how, but it had to do with his hips. It's glorious.

—

"Never have I ever had sex in an office over real estate plans," Claire says.

Everyone glances around at each other. Megan groans and takes a shot, and Claire gives a brace face grin like she knew that one would get her. "You can't purposefully choose things you know I've done, that's not fair," Megan grumbles, tossing black, still wet hair over her shoulder. "Besides, if we're being picky here, Ms. 'A hot air balloon is not the same as dirigible'—"

"It's not," Claire giggles.

"Then it wasn't real estate plans, it was documents for a lender, to *get* the plans."

Claire pretends to inspect a pink nail, then leans back on her elbows, closing her eyes and tilting her face to the sun. "Tomato, potato. Your turn, Megamoo."

Megamoo scoffs at the nickname then hums, tapping at her chin and looking around at us. "Never have I ever…kissed a boy!"

There's a group wide groan and Megan cackles. "Yes! Lesbian powers, activate!"

"Unfair," Charlotte whines, taking a swig of her beer while Mei agrees with her martini. Nearly every girl here raise their drinks, too.

I glance at After beside me, sitting on the side of the pool, long legs kicking in the shallow end. He sighs and lifts his cup in submission before taking a drink.

Yeah, saw that one coming. Cross-legged on the step by his thigh, submerged to my chest, I squint into my cup of soda and debate taking a drink. Technically, I *should*.

I mean shit, I took the drink when they asked the more embarrassing ones, like who's peed in a public pool (not this pool, obviously) who's thrown up mid roller coaster, who's been that person at Starbucks who's asked for a hot latte then a cup of ice like it makes any difference. (I made After take two drinks with me for that one, since he's admitted to doing it at least four times.)

But…no one here knows I've kissed a guy before. Done more with a guy before. And I'm not sure why, but I feel a need to keep that a secret.

Charlotte's staring at me from her perch on the blue outdoor table. I shrug and smirk. She squints, face diabolical and shadowed under the wide umbrella. Alright, *almost* no one knows…

"It's my turn," she pipes in. Oh fudge.

Instantly I regret the day I was emotionally weak, when I first saw her again at Jethro orientation and was so overwhelmed with recognizing someone from home that I told her about Gabriel.

"Says who?" I ask.

"Says me, bride, and future bride," she adds, nodding to Mei in the chair by her side, feet kicked up in Charlotte's lap.

Mei grins behind horn-rimmed sunglasses and lifts her martini like, 'listen to my stubborn wifey, boy'. "Alright..." Charlotte sings, tapping lime green nails against her beer bottle. "Never have I ever..."

Hoe, don't do it.

"Never have I ever driven the entirety of Texas, from El Paso to Louisiana—" After laughs at her in triumph— "Or! From Dalhart to McAllen! North to south, bitches!"

After and I both curse her out, but mine is more like, 'fuck, thank you God' and I gladly take a drink of my soda.

Illana hops onto her knees on a pool chair, orange hair perfectly fluffy and dried now. "Can I go next?"

"Sure, just don't say anything insane," Vanessa says for us, laying out on a towel, bare back to the sun since she took her bikini top off ten minutes ago.

"Never have I ever done cocaine!" Illana peeps.

I snort on my coke. Wow, bad phrasing.

Megan shouts again. "I *told* you not to purposefully target me!"

"I wasn't," Illana pouts.

Charlotte giggles and Megan and Claire both take a shot while Vanessa flips Illana off and takes one, too. Oh goodie, at least I'm among company. I keep my cup in my lap.

"Scotty, you've lived a dull life; your cup is still almost full," Claire points out.

I shrug and take a sip just to get her off my back. "Or he's been lying," Megan scoffs. I take a longer chug and it fizzles in my throat.

"I'm just not feeling the soda." I get to my feet with shaky pool legs. "I'm gonna um…grab a water—y'all want anything?"

There's a chorus of no thank yous, and I rush inside, wet steps slipping on kitchen tiles as I wrap a towel around my waist.

The moment I'm alone, Imagine Dragons muffled under Claire's turn as she shouts, "Never have I ever cheated on someone!" I grunt and drop my forehead to the cold countertop.

Chapter 21

"You're red as a tomato," says After behind me.

I don't fully lift my cheek from the marble counter when I peek at him. He half closes the French doors on his way inside and lifts his cup. "Came in for more rum and coke."

I don't bother to ask if he drank at Claire's last question. That's not fair, and technically not true. Though it aches like it should be.

"You gonna be good to drive us home?"

"Yeah, I'm fine. I only get really drunk on vodka these days. Plus the rum Charlotte got is shit."

"I wouldn't know."

"You don't drink rum anymore?"

"I don't drink at all. Not for years," I reply, lifting my head with a crick in my neck.

"Why not?"

"Can you grab the sunscreen for me?"

He looks at me funny for my fast deflection but wanders toward the bag we brought to grab the lotion. I take the tube and reapply it to my cheeks, nose, and down my arms.

"Your back is starting to burn, want some there, too?" he asks after he takes a sip of his refilled drink.

"Yeah, sure," I sigh, passing the bottle over my shoulder. It's freezing the moment it hits my skin, and I suck air through my teeth at the instant relief. His hand flattens along my lower back. I feel those calluses again and think I could get used to them.

I'm just beginning to overthink *that* thought, when a single finger starts moving around between my shoulders. "You're drawing a dick, aren't you?"

I can hear the smile in After's voice when he replies, "Maybe. Maybe not. You like dicks."

"Not all the time."

"Only on days that end in Y?"

I laugh and tilt my ear to him. "I mean I don't only like guys, After."

He pauses. A finger pokes into my rib. "You're *not* gay?" In a split second, I realize we never talked about his sexuality when we were teenagers. Which means we never talked about mine. "But you…I mean. In high school…"

In high school, I nearly lost my mind to you, After, but I'm not about to bring that up now. I take the sunscreen from him and set it back in the bag, readying myself to go to the backyard. "It's cool, bro—"

His fingers close around my wrist, pulling me back. "Let's…I mean. Can we talk? About it? I'd like to talk to you about it." He's still got some lotion on his hands. Rubbing my palms against his, I take my sunscreen coated fingers and wipe them around his face. He closes his eyes and lets me, too.

"What do you want to talk about?" I ask, layering on his nose.

"What do you call it? Are you bi? Like Nicholas, he's bisexual."

"Your friend?"

"Yeah."

"No, I'm not bisexual."

"Are you pansexual? I don't know anyone—I mean, I might, I just never asked. Are you pan?"

"Not pansexual. The word is abrosexual."

After's brows go up, and so do mine when he laughs. "That sounds fancy! Like abracadabra. What's it mean?"

I drop a fist to the sofa by my hip, leaning on it. "To me, it means my sexuality changes. It's fluid, not all the time though. I don't stay one way or another. I just love people based on...well, everything else. There are days I feel more asexual, too, like I go months without really ever having an attraction to anyone at all. Days I like men. Sometimes I like women, sometimes both, neither, all in between—" I wave my hand around. "I'm not making sense."

"You're making sense," he says, nodding. "No, it's. It's cool. I think I get it."

"When did you know you were gay?" I ask, hoping we can change the subject away from me.

After hums and walks around the sofa to flop down, perching his sunburnt feet on the coffee table. Music and laughter picks up outside, and he stares at the windows to the pool. "Okay, don't laugh."

I lay my towel down and sit on the other end of the sofa. "I'm gonna laugh."

"I know you are. Honestly, it took me until a couple years ago to be more solid about it. But when I was younger and I first read—not saw—but read the Hunger Games. That's when I started to be like, wait a minute, I'm not thinking about pretty Katniss like the other kids in our class."

He sighs and drops his head back to the cushions with his eyes closed. "Peeta had my heart, man. Blond, gorgeous, brave. Lover not a fighter. Then they made the movie, and—" After snorts and sends me a pitiful look. "They go and cast handsome motherfucker Josh Hutcherson. I wanted to die."

"No wonder you dragged me to see it so many times," I chuckle. "Why'd you never tell me?"

After fiddles with his leather necklace and shrugs. Always, so much unsaid in his shrugs. "When did you first know you were...what was it, abrosexual?"

"Good job, yeah." He beams at me and I sink into the pillows, staring at the blank TV.

I know it was him. I know the first time I felt different, it was because of him.

At seven years old, when I saw this kid eating lunch alone, I thought he had such a pretty, soft face. I knew what pretty meant. My mom was pretty before she got sick. She'd say horses were pretty with their long eyelashes, and After's were just as long.

In my little child heart, that was all that mattered, even if he told me to go away the moment I introduced myself.

I just can't say any of that out loud. I don't think I ever will.

"Does abrosexual have a flag?" he asks, when my silence hangs too heavy.

I nod and go for my pocket, then glare at him. He grins and dips his neck into his shoulders. "Sorry…"

"You better not have been joking about buying me a new phone. I'll need a new everything that was in my wallet, too. You're lucky I didn't have a car key that got ruined."

He scoffs, pulling his phone out of our bag. "A car key would still be fine. Maybe."

"A push start wouldn't."

"Like *you* could afford a push start."

"As your fake boyfriend, who may now have, like, five bruised ribs because of you, you better buy me a push start car."

He laughs and gets off the sofa. I'm about to stand, thinking we might be moving back for the kitchen, when he lands right next to me, sharing my towel-covered cushion. "How do you spell it?" he huffs, snuggling in and pulling up Google.

I type it for him, and the flag pops up. All sea foam and teal, white and shades of rose and pink. "Oh…wow," he whispers.

"Isn't it nice?"

"It looks like a watermelon."

"I like watermelon."

"I know you do. There's only ever been the rainbow flag for gays. Don't get me wrong, I like it, but—"

"Oh, no, y'all have a flag," I tell him. "For men who love men, there's a flag." His big eyes dart to the phone in my hand. "Wanna see it?" He chews a thumb nail and nods, and I start another search.

Green and white light up the page, with ombre hues of sky blue and mint and cobalt like his suit at the fundraiser.

"I like that they both have that light green," he sighs. His chin moves against my shoulder. When did he put his chin on my shoulder?

"We'd match," I reply.

He hums and it's right in my ear. His wet hair tickles my temple. "We can get t-shirts, or bandannas or something snazzy. For pride in June. LA has an amazing pride parade. I've been dying to go with Charlotte for years."

That's a bold assumption. Thinking we'll still be talking in June after our oncoming fake breakup. Thinking we'll be anything in June other than ships that have passed one too many times in the night, captains reaching out to one another in failing earnest.

After takes his phone back, makes us take a selfie, and he leans over his knees as he posts it, chuckling when his friend Harry likes it in seconds and comments that I'm out of After's league. He's saying something about going back outside, asking me when I'm gonna wanna leave since I start my first day on Monday and he wants to make sure he's got time to get me a new phone. I look away from his face and stare instead at his bare arm covered in art.

I can't take my attention away from the swan tattooed near his bicep, drawn to the haunted look in its eye. Serene, peaceful. It's gorgeous. And for some reason, it makes me sick.

"What's your tattoo mean, After?" I ask. It's been a few days; maybe he'll tell me at this point. Maybe I've earned the right to know now.

He glances at me past his shoulder, and a wave of cold air washes over me as he reaches away to set his phone back in our bag. "You don't have to explain it if you don't want to," I add.

"It's fine, I want to." He faces me on the sofa and flexes his arm straight. First he taps at the flowers around the swan's neck.

"Gazania. From Spain. They grow in my dad's yard," he says. "Funny enough, the flowers took the longest. But the whole thing needed three sessions. Spoke to ten different artists before I found one online in Washington. Flew to Seattle to get it."

"It's incredible. And...hard to look at."

"What do you mean? I paid good money for this," he laughs.

"No, sorry, I just, I don't know if I get it. Or if there's anything to get. Flowers from your dad's home." After nods and runs his hand down his arm. "Swan...being choked? Cut off? Why a swan?"

He grows quiet, and his thumb rubs across the crown over the swan's head. "You've heard the story of the ugly duckling," he begins. I give a hesitant nod.

"What they don't tell you in that story is what happens once the ugly duckling realizes he's a swan. When the boy is seen as beautiful just cause he fits social standards. When he loses the baby face and gets taller. Nearly drives himself insane to gain muscle and trim the fat by any means necessary to fit into the aesthetic and expected. No one cares about the depression or the eating disorders or what happens after the happy ending."

Cute and handsome and sexy and flesh and bone and muscle. Articles never talk about his heart. About the kid who would stop his Jeep on the side of the road to help turtles cross into the ravines. Who'd give his best friend's little sister the perfect slice of cake on his own birthday.

"What about after?" I whisper. He sniffs. Doesn't sound like his usual cover to mask his emotions. After's eyes when they meet mine are a thousand miles away.

"Everyone wants something from him; they tell him they know what's best. They're older, wiser, they know what he needs to succeed and live a fulfilled, happy life. The swan gets pulled and pushed and shaped to look better, be better, get sex appeal. They crown it with admiration, shower it with flowers, but it's all a lie. And eventually the beautiful swan just...takes it. Accepts that he's gonna be hurt. By his family, his mentors."

"By his friends," I choke. Could be pool water slipping down my cheek to my chin, but I doubt it.

After looks up at me. Each swallow just shoves acid and fear down, it never gets rid of it entirely. "I'm...Jesus, After, I'm so, so sorry for what I did."

He shakes his head. "I already forgave you—"

"But I never said it. How could you forgive me if you never got an apology?"

"Because I had to. I couldn't wait, and I didn't want to beg for one. I had to keep going, and the only way to do that was to get past it on my own, with or without your sorry."

His hand lands on my forearm. "But thanks for saying it anyway, Scott. I appreciate it." My knuckles are sore from keeping my hands balled into fists in my lap. I try to relax my fingers one at a time, let the blood flow back into my digits. "And thank you for talking to me. For not leaving me again."

Again. Always the again. I nod and bow my head like his swan.

Chapter 22

This has been the spring of firsts, and they remind me of other firsts.

That makes no sense. Hold on, head empty, just repressed emotions at this point. Bottle screwed shut too tight, let me think.

My first fundraiser as After's 'boyfriend' had me not so pleasantly reminiscing to the last time we were at a fundraiser together. My first 'kiss' with After reminded me of my first attempts at kissing on playgrounds.

It's Monday, first day at my new job. And I'm thinking about a particularly hot summer day in El Paso when I started working at Chili's.

I was eighteen and eager to prove myself. My employment began with a little orientation; got to know the chefs, the servers. I'd be a host, in charge of seating people, the first smiling face customers would see, and the last face, too, as they tottered along full of fries and onion rings, grabbing a mint as they go.

I could do that. For seven bucks an hour and a thirty-minute lunch break including free sodas, riding my bike to and from work to exercise off those sodas, I could totally do that.

First shift was good. Came home excited, rejuvenated, with a few extra chest hairs. I mean it wasn't a great gig, but shit, it was mine, it was an adult responsibility. I was finally a big, money-making *man*.

Bevett and I celebrated with a dance party in the living room, despite how tired I was from being on my feet in sensible black shoes for eight hours.

Fourth shift was okay; had my first experience with a rude customer who tossed a used toothpick at my face. Manager Pete patted me on the back and said at least I got that outta the way early on. I said thanks, I guess.

By the tenth shift first week of July, I'd earned my first paycheck. $443 after taxes, cause those exist as I was painfully reminded.

Pete said, 'sign that shit, and you put it in a bank account, kiddo. Save up for a good college'. I said yes sir, and I signed that shit with a crappy ballpoint pen and greasy fingers.

Bevett and I laid out on the driveway, holding the check up to the late afternoon sun like it was a golden ticket. "Big number," she said, nodding and getting popsicle all over her chin.

I smiled and nodded, too. Then a shadow came over us, and there was Devon, grinning with her hands on her hips. "Hiya, babies, how y'all doing?"

"Scotty got paid," Bevett smiled, tapping her empty popsicle stick near my check, still hovering in the air.

Devon's blue eyes sparkled. "Oh, right on! Can I see?" she asked, wiggling patriotic nails at my check. I handed it off to her and she whistled. "Oh, baby, fantastic, congrats! How you liking the job?"

"It's good," I had said. "They like me. Pete says I'm a good host."

"Course you are, they're lucky to have you," she chuckled. My ears warmed, and I sat up on my elbows in awe when she threw in one last special compliment. "You're smart and friendly, just like your momma."

Since that was one of the rare moments she mentioned Mom, I got swept up in it immediately. Poking, prodding, asking questions, what'd she mean, what else could she tell me.

Never noticed she pocketed my check. The one I'd already signed.

When she did the same with the next one, and the one after that, I wanted to believe that it made sense. She was giving us room and board, her and Kendra were our guardians—mostly Bevett's, I told myself; I was older than eighteen by a few months at that point. Her job as caretaker was buying us groceries, gas for driving us to school, field trips for Bevett. Made sense that I, the adult, paid my dues when I could.

By September, I started cashing in half my checks at Walmart and hiding the rest, telling Devon they cut down my pay cause of tips or something. She didn't question the logic of Chili's.

By November, with Gabriel's help, I blew through whatever I had saved up.

By December, I was without a job or safe room and board, and I was without Devon and Kendra's trust. Even though they'd never earned my trust to begin with. Not since they sold Mom's ring.

———

As excited as I was back in February for this job and that offer phone call, I don't want to be here.

Mona's first to greet me as soon as I hit the Silversmith publishing floor. She's instant grin and sunshine, with yellow eyeliner and a hot pink romper under a cropped jacket, black locs held up by a tie-dyed braided headband.

I'm in slacks and a polo. Like a dweeb.

She takes in my dweeb-ness and laughs. "Now I know, I *know*, I told you to dress chill here, Scott."

"I don't listen, you'll learn this soon enough," I reply, stepping out of the elevator.

"Untuck your shirt at least, you look like you rode your bike here and are about to ask if I have time to talk about our Lord and savior."

"I mean, do you? I took an Uber today, but I can leave and come back on my bike if it you're looking for the whole effect."

She laughs again and I smile. In another world where I wasn't toeing the line of a lie, I think we could be friends. As we walk toward my cubicle, she tells me all about how my first submission is doing, the one I sweated over Saturday night and turned in half awake without any more fucks to give.

It's all great news to her, but in my head it's distinctively split up good and bad.

The good is I've started to get paid already for my salary work as a publicist assistant for Jackie. "Check your inbox on Friday for some juicy zeroes," says Mona.

The bad news is, Jackie liked how I did the summary that After helped me with, so much so that she inhaled it before breakfast on Sunday. She only had to make a couple changes, but otherwise it went straight to the next step and it's getting good attention.

I can only imagine After's response when I tell him. I'm sure he'll be pleased. Pleased I'm out here stealing his voice all over again like Ursula and the little mermaid. Sing for me, After, let me just rip that right out of your heart and make it my own.

Damn, my head hurts. And it's only ten in the morning.

"Oh yeah!" Mona spins on her pointy gold heels and I stumble back, blinking rapidly from the wind she's created with her braids. "I forgot to tell you; your boy came by!"

"My boy?" I mutter, hopping to match her sudden rushing steps. So glad I wore Keds; pretty sure I'll be walking twenty k steps a day just to keep up with her lopes. In her heels, she's taller than After. "You mean my bof—my boffren—"

"Don't strain yourself," she laughs, coming to stop at a cubicle on the end.

I look between the little square and her supposed office that's 'nearby'. She said it was down another hall and through a labyrinth and maybe on the moon. This place is gigantic, not a damn thing is nearby. "Yes, Scott, your boyfriend David. Also? Fuck you."

I stutter. "Excuse me?"

"I cannot *believe* you didn't tell anyone you were dating a celebri-tee! He waltzed in here and sucked all the air out of the office.

Then he just waved like, 'hello, tis I, your dream man, no biggie'. I was *appalled*."

"When...when did he come by?"

"About twenty minutes before you, actually! He startled Taylor downstairs enough—our receptionist, brow piercing, blue hair—that she just let him go straight up and mosey on in without giving us any warning. He brought you a gift!" she adds, flourishing her hand toward my desk.

I pull my eyes from her and look to a perfectly wrapped rectangle with a glittery yellow bow that extends past the edges of the box itself.

"Oh."

"Don't sound too enthused."

"No—sorry, I'm just. Confused," I laugh, setting my backpack down by a filing cabinet.

I'm trying to politely figure out how to ask Mona for space when she pops her lips. "Oookay, I'm gonna..." She dances backward, thumbing the hall behind her. "I'm going to make coffee; would you like some?"

"Sure, thank you."

"Alrighty, come find me when you're settled and we'll get started on the next project! Since you did your work for Jackie already, you're all mine, Mr. Assistant!"

She saunters off, and I sit in my desk chair, fingers tapping on the armrests.

My gut tells me it's a phone.

Furthermore, it tells me After only made a big show of coming to my work before I got here to 'surprise me' with a shiny new phone as a ploy for his fake boyfriend shit. This isn't him just paying me back. He could've sent me the phone in the mail. By fucking messenger pigeon, on the back of the pony express. This was to get all eyes on him at my new workplace.

So tempted to just chuck it in the garbage and get a used Nokia or something.

I don't, though, I bend of course, using a convenient letter opener on my desk to nudge, nudge, nudge at the plastic sticker keeping the bow attached. Bow ends up on a stapler, next to the mason jar of pens. Sure thought of everything, didn't they?

Maybe he's making a big deal about it as an early birthday gift. I mean, I do turn twenty-three on Saturday. Haven't spent my birthday together since I turned seventeen. I don't count my eighteenth. I think the gala is on Friday, so we have all day on my birthday to do something fun, if he wants. Cause I want to.

I'm taking too long opening the gift. With a mumbled apology at the wrapping paper like it's sentient, I tear into it.

He'd taken my old phone with him after he dropped me off at home on Saturday evening, along with its waterlogged SIM card. Said he'd get it worked out for me.

And boy, fucking *howdy*. Did he deliver.

In the box is a shiny, glossy, glistening, glorious gold iPhone 12. Oh baby, she is *sexy*. I think I moan.

"Lord save me," I grumble, shaking my head. There's a flicker of disappointment that there's not a handwritten note or anything in the box that says, 'sorry I nearly broke your ribs chucking you into the pool,' or, 'happy early birthday, loser,' or something.

I hold the side button, ready to turn it on and get it charged, but it's already got a full battery. And a background photo.

I'm gonna kill him.

After's face grins back at me in full HD glory. It's a picture of him, one I took on the dock behind his mom's lake house. Which means he not only discovered my folder of old photos of him, but he looked through it to find one from *seven freaking years ago*.

I unlock my phone (gotta change my passcode before he fucks with it again) and there's another photo of us. It's him, me and Bevett after one of his musicals at James Bowie; he still has on his makeup and costume. He was cute Background Dancer #3 in Fiddler on the Roof.

I'm smirking but I'm not amused, and I get a little tingle in my chest. It itches, burns. Like the moment Devon greeted me after a twelve-hour shift with her hand out for my check before she'd even said, 'hello'.

This phone is mine, but it's not. *Mine.*

I go to our text thread. After, you piece of shit.

[Me] 10:21: you're an asshole.

He replies immediately, and now I am a little amused, thinking there's a chance he was sitting by his phone, waiting for me to get to work to find the gift and see the changes he did to his stupid name.

[Sexiest Man Alive] 10:21: what did I do!

[Me] 10:22: you have infiltrated this brand-new phone. You changed your name, went through my photos. It's you everywhere, and it's filthy.

[Sexiest Man Alive] 10:24: Did u already find the smut stash I left for u in the files??

[Sexiest Man Alive] 10:35: u looked for it didn't u?

[Me] 10:40: no, go away, I'm working.

[Sexiest Man Alive] 10:43: Does this mean I ain't gotta go to work? Are u the bread winner now? My sugar daddy? The bringer of the bacon?

[Sexiest Man Alive] 10:52: u angry at me, straight up?

[Me] 10:57: no.

[Me] 10:59: thank you for the phone, it's very thoughtful.

[After] 11:00: ur welcome!

Chapter 23

I'd rather be anywhere than on my way to a final fitting for a gala I don't want to go to anymore.

A gala, might I add, that's taking place on April third.

He had a week. A goddamn week—no! He had all the way back in *February* to tell me the actual date of this thing and not just saying it was in early April.

No one told me it was *on* my *birthday*.

"I swear I thought I told you it was on Saturday," After grumbles, turning us onto Yvonne's street. He left the Ferrari at home this time; we're in the same beat-up GMC Canyon truck he used to drive us to Charlotte and Mei's party.

"Nope, everyone kept saying 'early April'. Plenty of things are in early April..."

"Like today, April Fool's."

"Is this all an elaborate April Fool's prank?" I ask. "That would be both incredibly intricate and horribly upsetting."

"And also a cleverer web than I could possibly ever weave, by the way," he scoffs. "There's also World Autism Day, it's not just about you."

You big, ugly jerk face. "Sure, After, it's definitely not just about me. There's National Peanut Butter and Jelly Day, Ferret Day, National Find a Rainbow Day—"

"Those aren't real—"

"For the last twenty-three years, it has *also* been one Scott Everett Boscoe's birthday."

"Do you *really* care?" he sighs, parking us outside Yvonne's.

The only way to end this argument and not have it again is to say no and mean it. "No, I don't care," I tell him. And *mean* it, Scott.

We can celebrate another time sounds like a lie, when would that be? I don't mind that this is the first birthday I'm spending with you in years, since you were busy screwing someone else on my eighteenth. That's not only a lie, but it's also super fucked up, so we're just gonna keep that one to ourselves. I send him a smile. "It's fine, I swear."

There, easy, bland. And acceptable, as After gives a loose shrug and nods and drops out of his truck. I take a few seconds longer to control my face before I get out, too.

—

Yvonne's finished outfit for me is absurd, itchy like nothing else, and it makes me a thousand times more irritable. Also, there's no food for me this time around.

So by the time After and I get done at her place well after midnight, I'm crabby as all hell, scratching my back against my car seat like a bear on a tree, and I'm *hangry*. Which is the *worst*.

"How're you getting to the gala?" he asks, tapping fingers at his chin. I'm just cranky enough that I want to grab his wrist and swat him in the face with his own hand.

"I'm picking up a rental tomorrow afternoon."

"Cool. I don't think we'll be able to ride together."

I didn't ask to, so whatever.

"Do you remember the first time we got all dressed up for an event?" he asks me out of nowhere.

I have to keep squeezing my eyes shut; every time they're open, they follow the streetlights, and it's making me need to pass out.

"Um. Yeah, maybe. There was a little hoedown dance or something at Navy Glenn?"

After laughs, taking a right turn at the light. "No, actually. Think back, super far. We were uh…shit. Maybe, like, nine?"

"Nine…"

"We had a fake wedding in my backyard."

"Who were you marrying?"

"You, dumbass."

I have to open my eyes then. "What?"

"You don't remember? I had a poison ivy bouquet, got a mega rash. I wore Mom's apron as a dress cause it had frills on it. Dad's got a photo of us in his house after the flower toss. Was the moment they realized I'd been parading around with poison ivy, cause Mom caught the bouquet."

I hate that I don't remember that. What did I wear? Was I in a tiny suit? Did I roll my pants up to the ankle cause they were too big, shuffling around in my dad's dress shoes?

There's a phantom weight in my hand, and I think—yeah, that sounds right. I think I might've put Mom's ring on his finger. Back before Devon sold it. There was a green stone on it, emerald for her birth month. "'Matches your eyes'," I whisper to myself, old words familiar.

"'But only in some light'," he finishes, like he's nestled and comfortable in my thoughts.

Why the hell would he bring something like that up? You don't talk about this shit with your frenemies. Those things you used to do when you liked each other and loved each other in ways you didn't totally understand. You don't bring it up after all that trust has been broken. If we made any vows that day, I'm sure I've destroyed them by now.

I'm tired enough to stop blaming just myself at this moment. My usual song and dance for the last four years, talking like it's all my fault, it doesn't fit. He broke those vows, too, and unlike me, he hasn't apologized for them.

After turns onto a street that's not the way to school. "Where are you kidnapping me?" I grumble, nails fighting to reach an itchy patch on my left shoulder. His hand makes me jump, but I lean into it when he hits the spot for me.

"You'll see."

"Don't like that."

"It's fine, you'll like it, I promise."

That gives me flashbacks to dark, lonely parking lots and I'm not okay with that. "After, where are you taking me?" I ask, pulling out of his reach.

He looks back at me with concern and sits on his hand. "I was gonna take you to get food, Scotty. Do you not want food? Maybe some DQ?"

I'd sell my soul for a dip cone. "Fine, yeah."

He smiles, nods, and there in the distance like a beacon is blessed Dairy Queen.

—

We toss two servings of large fries into the bag and park it between us back in my dorm. I inhaled my small dip cone without a single incident of brain freeze ("Cause you have no brain to freeze," said After. Then he got brain freeze. I laughed at him) and he also gifted me a dilly bar cause I'm a five-year-old.

Legs crossed against the wall, laying on our backs, we're shoulder to shoulder on my bed. He's looking at some of my writings printed out, papers lit up only by me screwing around on my phone. "This is getting really good," After says, shoving six fries in his mouth at once.

"Thanks. She sent me the next book."

"What's this one about?"

"Shit, something next level bizarre—portals, rainbow crystal knives, talking caves. I think Mona said she cried when she read it, so I'm in for some angst."

"I wanna read it after you; send me the PDF."

"No way, rich boy, you gotta buy the book." He sticks his tongue out in response. "I'm going to have to work on this one between the gala and Tennessee. When is that again? Don't you dare say early or late anything, you give me a damn date."

"Not until the end of the month, like the thirtieth. You got time."

I pinch at the bridge of my nose, getting dreaded brain freeze from the dilly bar. After makes a noise of surprise. "Whasit?" I groan.

"This is...this *reads* like me, but I don't remember writing it."

I squint at the paper in his hand and waft my popsicle at him. "Cause you didn't. That one was all me."

"All you—you mean you wrote this one without needing help?"

My hum answers him as I bite off a massive chunk of chocolate shell. "Wow," he chuckles.

I can see the pride all over his face. He tilts his head to look at me with a grin. I'm not proud of me. I think he can see that all over my face, too.

After lowers the papers to his chest. "Can I read some of your older work?"

"You've read some of my older work already," I tell him, finishing off my ice cream and chewing on the stick.

"I mean. I read the stuff you were working on to write like me. But it's been years since I've read *you*."

"Why do you want to read that stuff?" I ask. To make fun of me, I think.

"I like how you wrote. It's punching."

"Fine. Fine, sure." I switch off Instagram on my perfect-condition phone (it's not, I dropped it on my concrete floor before I'd gotten a case; there's already a crack in the corner) and I pull up some older work.

"It's saved on your phone?"

"Easier and quicker to wipe it. If someone got their hands on my laptop and I wasn't there to delete all my work, I'd be fucked."

"Um...why?"

"Just in case. It's LA, you never know." I'm speaking from experience, but he doesn't need to know that I've already timed myself to see how fast I can move to destroy every single thing saved on my phone, if it's ever confiscated by my grandfather again.

I pass it over and he gets cozy on my mattress, chomping fries as he reads. He offers me more, but as hungry as I am I can't eat, knowing he's sitting there reading my work. Only the real juicy shit is kept under an additional passcode. I gave him the boring crap. Mostly. I think. It's been awhile since I perused my own writing file.

After chuckles at times, hums at others. He sends his eyes my way, but I'm too busy counting the lumps of popcorn texture on my ceiling. "I like this one," he says after a good ten minutes have passed.

"Which one?" My voice is hoarse. I think I fell asleep with my eyes open, cause they're twitching and dry now.

"Want me to read it out loud?"

"Fine."

"You always say 'fine'—are you sure it's okay?"

"I don't *always* say 'fine'," I grunt, scowling at him, then my phone. There's not a lot of text on the screen; looks like he likes one of the shorter ones. Not sure how I feel about that. "You're welcome to read it out loud if you want to."

After stares at me, then nods. He adjusts his legs crossed at the ankle and clears his throat.

"For her. The one whose name means farmer. The daughter of a man made of stone. Her with the blue eyes. Like ice, like the sky. With the sharp nose and face, chiseled from porcelain.

For her, I'd boil the seas, if she were to say she wanted to walk the ocean floor. For her, I'd build an ivory tower to the universe, so she can become one with the twilight she admires.

For me. Let me stand in the face of fury, iron, steel. Let me kneel with arms outstretched, be swallowed by flame. To accept every lance and spear in my ribs. Rip me apart piece by piece. Take the stars from my grasp. Take the breath from my lungs. Give it all to her. Let her live.

For her, I'd kill thousands. For her, I'd die a thousand times. Let her roam in the gold fields, a sunset cloaking her shoulders. Let her live. Let her live."

Dull silence other than the white noise machine on my desk.

"So…your mom," he says first. I hum, fingers massaging my sore throat. "Why don't you talk about her?"

"What's there to talk about?"

He hands me back my phone. It's open to a folder of poems titled 'To Momma'. There are at least a hundred there.

"You tell me," he replies. Tears slip down into my hair. I lock my phone and we're engulfed in the dark.

Chapter 24

Every eye is on me as I go up the carpeted steps toward the theater entrance. I can't see a damn thing from the camera flashes, steps guided by instinct alone, praying I don't trip. Thank God there are random pauses of flat land, places for celebrities to stop and pose for pictures. I just take the moments to rest my poor thighs from doing a thousand lunges going up these stairs. I feel bad for anyone wearing heels higher than two inches tonight.

Yvonne texted me yesterday before work once I'd picked up the rental car, asking me to be at her place bright and early and before the miserable ass crack of dawn this morning. When I showed up, she offered me coffee and my weight in donut holes, and I took them willingly, eased into comfortable mocha and glazed bliss.

Until she sat me down and looked at me all firm and serious with her little pinched mouth and upturned nose.

"I've changed my mind," she'd said. "I'm starting you over. As of right now. No eyeliner, no glitter, nothing."

"What happened to the insane red, sparkle get up?" I'd asked.

When I had my fitting Thursday night, my shoulders were plastered in gold, almost armor-like; admittedly, I was glad we'd be changing it up, even if it was last minute. I was afraid I'd be causing lens flares left and right, potentially even setting something on fire.

Yvonne shook her head, lower lip coming over her upper lip in thought. She looked like a teeny bulldog. I smirked, still half-in bed, still whole-delirious with coffee.

"It's just not. *You.* I know it's meant to be a big ridiculous show—and I stand by the decisions I've made for David, he must...um...exude—pr-protrude—" frantic waving of her hand—"something! He must shine on his own like a giant ball of flashy gas! That's not up for discussion."

She sounded so professional and slightly manic that I had started to wake up then, even if I was trying not to laugh at 'flashy gas'. "Alrighty. Well, what can I do?"

Then Yvonne smiled so sweetly that I had a sudden urge to introduce her to Charlotte and Mei and even Bevett. "I need you to be you. Just you."

So here I am, me, being me, incredibly overwhelmed and horribly underdressed.

Gowns are miles long and adorned with every pearl and gemstone on the planet, heels are ankle-breaking high with ruby soles, suits are everything from functional dragon wings that expand out, to someone strutting their stuff in a hot pink, iridescent three-piece.

And I'm...in intro to luxury.

I'm in velour. Fucking *velvet.*

My tux is near black, but in the right lights—and trust me, there are lights everywhere—it looks more like a cool, dark gray, secret floral pattern blending into the fabric of my cropped jacket. To top it off, she's choked me out with a triangular turquoise and silver bolo tie. I didn't even know they still made bolo ties.

The moment I had the whole getup on, tailored to perfection with just a couple hours to go, I sent a picture of it to Charlotte, and she replied, no doubt all-capsing via voice to text, "**IF YOU DON'T WEAR THAT TO MY WEDDING I AM DISOWNING YOU**". Yvonne cackled and turned rosy with satisfaction.

Each time someone behind the red roping calls out and asks who dressed me, I have to bite my tongue and not answer with, 'madwoman who's got a kink for causing humiliation, Yvonne James'. Just replying, "Yvonne," gets ripples of gasps and awe.

I think she said she'd be running around in yellow and white houndstooth suit with foot-tall dragon horns in her pink hair. I wouldn't put it past her.

I'm nearly to another solid level, chewing on my lip like it's my last meal, when screams build up behind me.

Then it's After hour.

I look over my shoulder, grateful that he's taken the spotlight off me. Before anything else, I notice the crease deep between his thick brows.

He's taking the stairs two at a time, of course, hunky gazelle. There's something glinting around his forehead, but with the amount of cameras flashing, I'm not sure what it is.

After's arms flex in his black suit, decked out in glittery sequins sewn into the shape of wings that go down past his elbows. With every calculated step, his shoulders sway, reflecting the light. He's wearing a golden cape. It catches some unseen breeze, and without missing a beat, he grabs it and holds it in one hand. He turns to wave at someone behind the velvet rope, and that's when I see the gold band circling his head.

The *drama*.

I'm assuming it was Yvonne that did his makeup; she gave him shining blue wingtip eyeliner, the points almost reaching his hairline. Jealous, she said I wouldn't get any makeup. She only painted my nails white, his black.

"Hi," I say to him when he gets closer.

"Hey," he replies.

You look so regal, I think. "You look like a twat." I take a half step to move on toward the last set of stairs. After looks up at me with that wrinkled brow and I smirk. "I'm teasing, obviously, you look great."

"Thank you," he mutters, continuing up.

But then he does a doubletake and he stops, one foot on the step. There's that realization flooding his face again.

Or. I mean some sort of emotion is flying through his eyes, but I'm not sure what it is.

"What?" I ask, when he's stared with his mouth open for longer than necessary.

I run my tongue over my teeth and fiddle with a pearly cufflink. I knew I shouldn't have accepted the salad Yvonne offered me while she hemmed my pants. All the photos of me will have a big green spinach leaf protruding from my face, I guarantee it. "Is it that bad? Do I look ridiculous?"

"No. No, sorry. You're just…"

He closes his mouth without finishing his sentence, which just makes my fancy suit more stifling.

"It's not J.Crew, that's for sure," I try to laugh, not sure why he's scowling at me.

Now I *really* wish Yvonne had given me a more fantastical outfit. At least I would've blended in more.

"Nope…it's certainly not." He blinks, squares his shoulders, and reaches my level, all glittery black on matte black on glossy black. I thought his boots were black, too, but they're a dark red. The white fluttery cuffs from his blouse poke out over his hands under his suit sleeves. His jacket dips low past his sternum and cuts high to his abs at the same time, a single button in the center keeping it together.

"Cover up, you harlot, there are children present." I pretend to hide his midriff in an attempt to get him to chill the hell out and stop frowning at me like he's trying to set my brain on fire.

That finally gets a smile out of him, and he laughs and looks to his outfit. "It's a bit colder than I imagined—what happened to the red and gold? The outfit you had on the other day; Yvonne had finished it."

I shrug. "She called me in at, like, five this morning, I was there until two hours ago. She'd changed her mind, and this—" I gesture to my get up and adjust my tie— "was what she came up with instead."

He remains too quiet. I shift my weight. "After, be honest, am I underdressed? She wouldn't even let me wear makeup—"

"Because you don't need any," he cuts in. His nostrils flare as he inhales like he's catching his breath.

He lifts a finger and trails it from a gathering of flowers at my arm to the ones centered on my chest, until he's correcting my already perfectly positioned lapel. A wave of cameras flash all at once in response. After ignores them, looking only at me. "And. I'm glad she didn't put you in the red and gold. This is…more you."

"That's what she said." After's brow twitches and he smirks. "That's not—Yvonne *literally* said that." I don't like how close he's leaning toward me. I squint at him and retaliate with, "Whoever did your makeup gave you too much blush; you're pink as a cherry." He swats at my finger poking his cheek.

"Whatever—are you wearing red bottoms, too?"

"Are you asking about my underpants? Good sir, you haven't even bought me dinner yet."

After barks a laugh and nudges me in the arm to get us to walk out of the way of the other celebrities. "Red bottoms—Louboutins. Lemme see…" He pulls me by my elbow to lean on him, and I lift my foot as he does the same. Sure enough, both our shoes are bright red.

"Hold on." After pulls out his phone and snaps a photo of the bottoms of our boots. Quick to load up Instagram, he adds the photo and types with his tongue between this teeth.

Matching with bae at the @EndofHeavenpremiere. Who wore it better? Him, it's a trick question, any other answer is wrong. @Yvonne @ScottEBoscoe #newboyfriends #oldfriends

I smile and fidget at 'old friends'. "There, done," he grins, putting his phone away. Adjusting the gold band around his forehead, he shakes out his shoulders and tosses his cape behind him, presenting me his arm. "Shall we?"

Chapter 25

So, I regret comparing Greta Hashfield to a Mary Sue. She's like a flower garden personified; green clover eyes, natural hair a dark red that looks like fire with all the lights overhead, and she stands with her toes pointed out like a ballerina duck.

Her voice has a bit of a scratch to it, cracking at random times, and before I could ask her why, she said it was because her little sister punched her in the throat when they were younger. I haven't decided if that's a lie or not.

To top it all off, the first thing out of her mouth when she met me was, in total croak-mode, "Scott! I stalked you on Twitter for an hour! Remember me? @GreatestHashbrowns?"

The best part? I totally remember her. Two nights ago on Twitter, After and I got in a heated discussion over Digimon versus Pokémon, and she went through and liked all my posts, talking about how Digimon was superior because the critters could hold a conversation. We gave it our all, but Greta and I were most definitely on the losing side of that argument.

She's not exaggerating, either; she bounced around with us for over an hour. I thought nothing of it and assumed she was just a fan; her account was all Red Irish Setters and log cabins with only fifty followers. (Who all had the same green eyes and red hair, by the way, so I'm assuming her club was mostly family members.)

Her actual celebrity account numbers in the low millions, very close to After's follower count, and is run by her agent, so she told me.

"Morpheus doesn't like when I talk about things like puppies and hiking and Japanese TV shows," she sighs, taking another sip of her spiked lemonade while we wait for After, who's in the concessions line. Celebrities, dressed to the nine thousands, and they still have to wait in a queue for popcorn and pretzels. Preposterous.

"Why do I get the feeling most famous people have a lot less control over their personal lives and social medias than I previously thought?" I ask with a squint. "His name is *Morpheus*; you'd think he'd be a total bad ass who loves a good stupid post about whether waffles are better than pancakes."

She purses green lips and slurps her drink. "First, waffles—"

"How dare you—"

"Second, I've had an agent since my first acting gig at eight years old. They keep tabs on everything, down to what I eat and what I wear out in public. I can't leave my house in yoga pants unless they're Lululemon and the logo is in plain sight *and* we have a marketing deal with them at the time. The craziest thing I ever did was run away from Morpheus and my moms for a day."

"Where did you go?" I ask, smirking at After moving up in line with an awkward Cha Cha Slide shuffle.

Greta snorts, grinning around her straw. "The mall a mile away from my hotel. Stayed all day, played every arcade game they had. Hid in the stuffed animal claw game until they closed, then I got back out and ran around in my underwear."

"How old were you?" I chuckle. She looks over my head and her cheeks tinge a furious bright red, all that Irish blood she talked about earlier coming to the surface.

"Tell him, David, how old were we?"

I tilt my head back and look at After upside down, standing behind me with our snacks. "I was twenty," he says first. "To be fair, she was only nineteen, so she gets a teenage pass."

"You both ran around in your underpants just three years ago in the middle of an LA mall?" I laugh back at Greta.

"Wasn't in LA. We were in Shreveport for filming," he explains, resting his chin on my shoulder.

"Where did you hide while she was in the machine?"

He smiles like he's a kid again and feeds me a bite of pretzel, holding a napkin under it to keep butter and cheese from dripping onto my expensive coat. I feel a little giddy, wrapped up in nice clothes and his thick arms, talking to him and someone I can totally see as being my friend in other circumstances. I mean shit, even under these circumstances. She already follows me on every social media platform. That's as good as getting her number.

"I hid in the air vents," he replies. I choke on pretzel.

—

Greta, After and I goof off for another few minutes before we wander into the gargantuan theater. "Do you think Meryl Streep is somewhere in here?" I ask, gawking at the expansive auditorium, seats filling up with glinting high fashion and mustard covered hot dogs.

"Why would Meryl Streep be here?" After asks ahead of me, going up the stairs in search for a good row.

"Cause you're a movie star, and so is she."

"Bro, if I knew Ms. Streep, I'd most *definitely* be sitting by her, and not you."

"Rude," I grumble, letting him drag me along by my hand to some seats in the middle. He promptly kicks his Louboutin boots up on the chair in front of us and laughs when I make a desperate attempt to do the same but can't reach.

The lights dim, the conversation shushes (all but ours, cause we've always been those punk kids who whisper during movies) and music starts up. No commercials. That feels almost alien, and we're launched right into the story. Movie two left off with Guinevere getting kidnapped by Mordred or some shit, and I'm preparing for an overdone, beefy bro rescues the damsel plot.

But half an hour in, I'm sitting there with my jaw dropped, cause it turns into this incredible woman versus warmongering mage fight, showing off Guinevere and her underestimated intelligence and craft, getting the best of Mordred despite how much he throws at her.

She rides a motherfucking dragon and burns his castle down, rescuing Morgana in the tower. (I can't tell you how insane this trilogy is. Like, just take everything you know about King Arthur, toss a few dragons and some of the most intricate costumes ever made into a blender, and hit 'feminism puree'.)

Guinevere and Morgana fly back to the battle, hoping they get there in time before Merlin (yes, *Merlin* is the villain, like what the hell) attacks Arthur and his knights with his army of the dead. Holy shit. I have to take off my coat cause I'm sweating straight through the velvet.

Greta gives a celebratory woot! behind us the moment her character Guinevere lands on the field with the dragon, like, 'Sup bitches, I'm here for the war'.

I turn and smile at her a few rows behind us, and she shimmies her chest at me in her low-cut dress, which has me cackling and getting shushed by After. I shush him with a slap to his cheek and get a hand upside my head in response.

We get to the sex scene, but honestly? I don't mind it.

Really, I think I get it. Here Lancelot is, and Guinevere, and Arthur sees them staring at each other after they didn't think they'd see one another again, and he just…steps back. He sees the love they have, sees the fact that they might not live another dawn after tomorrow. He puts a hand to Lancelot's arm, kisses his cheek, sends Guinevere one last look and then just leaves.

I get flashbacks of benches and fences and heartache that make me sweat through my nice pants, too, but I can't really rip those off to cool down.

Lancelot and Guinevere fall into each other. His hands shake, he's clumsy, she's gorgeous and covered in dirt and bruises, and it's beautiful. The music covers most of the sounds of passion, but my ears pick up on After's moans—

I should say—I mean—Lancelot's.

After leans on our armrest, and his sequin wings scratch against my forearm. "Y'know, Greta—she told me she's a lesbian halfway through filming the first movie."

I look at him in the sexy sepia lighting just to not stare at Lancelot's face when they keep doing inconvenient close-ups. Except the hero is sitting right next to me and he smells like expensive nostalgia and I'm suddenly regretting that pretzel. "Seriously?"

"And asexual. She said she only signed on for the trilogy cause she was told there wouldn't be any intimate shit like this. I was her first onscreen, like…everything. So, we had some rough times…"

"Oh my God, dude, that sucks."

"We got super drunk after and cried about it a bit—" Someone hisses at him from a few rows back, and After scoffs, turning in his seat to chuck some popcorn at them.

There's a ripple of laughter and I hear Greta's scratchy voice shriek, "Down in front!"

"It's my fucking movie, I can talk if I want!" He gets clocked in the head with a wadded-up hotdog wrapper.

Things pick up fast after that. There's hope in the army, they've got a dragon, they've got Morgana, there seems to be a shift in powerful sides.

But I get a sinking weight in my gut that Arthur, the one and only king, is gonna end up dead. I mean, he just sacrificed his heart to make his lover happy; I imagine he'll jump in front of someone to save them, too, thinking he has nothing left to live for.

The battle nearly gives me a heart attack. My fingernails dig into something soft, and it takes After squeezing my wrist a couple times for me to realize it's his hand I'm clinging to. The dragon gives it his all, Merlin is a madman, and the CGI—legit, if this doesn't win awards I'm gonna riot.

There's Arthur. I can see the inevitable coming, see the smile on his face as he looks at Lancelot like, we can do this. We can win this. We'll all be okay. I've seen enough Game of Thrones, y'all, you ain't gonna live through this, king dude.

Lancelot grins back and raises his sword. The music cuts out—a heavy breeze is the only sound, along with the tinkling of a wind chime that used to hang outside Lancelot's blacksmith shop.

He falls to a knee, and the camera pans back to an arrow in his chest. Lancelot collapses, dead.

Camera flashes to Arthur's face. The tears on his muddied cheeks. The scream that echoes out of existence, ripped from Guinevere just a few feet away.

The battle rages on. The survivors fight to live through the war.

He's dead. And life goes on.

Oh my God.

After never fucking told me he *dies* in his *own series*.

I'm…distraught. And I'm crying. I'm never watching any of his movies again.

He's staring at me; I can sense it. I turn and meet his eye and don't bother wiping the tears from my cheeks. After leans his head back against his headrest, and there's an ache for something all over his face.

You asshole. Bring him back. Bring this amazing character back, the one you let me get used to and grow to love in just a few short weeks. The one who fought so hard for love and won it, had a person waiting for him to survive.

Bevett's gonna lose her freaking mind.

'I'm sorry,' After mouths, thumb running circles on my fingers.

'Fuck you,' I mouth back. He grins and I hate him.

I don't give a shit about the rest of the movie cause breathtaking Lancelot with his handsome, smiling hazel eyes isn't there. But it must end, and it must be superb, because there's a rushing wave of thunder swallowing all those in the auditorium. It's applause. For him.

The lights are on for a mere second before we're flooded by a spotlight. Everyone stands to him, to the other stars in our row, to Greta a few seats back, to the musical director and the costume designer.

Guests are smiling and cheering in their glossy clothes, some have no fucks left to give and are tossing popcorn in the air like regular people who enjoyed a movie.

I start to pull my hand from his so I can lean out of the light. After's fingers grip mine. "Please don't leave me," he says as we stand together. He grins, waving to the masses. He's shaking. To prove I'm not going anywhere, I hook my arm in his and press tight to his side. I'll fight the storm with you, After, don't worry.

Chapter 26

As soon as we're out of the theater and back in the lobby, he either gets rushed off in a swarm of people, or he runs off to find safety. Both make sense.

Greta says she hasn't seen him. I bump into Ms. Florence—she gives me a big hug and plants a pink-lipped kiss on my cheek—but she hasn't seen him either. I'm tempted to ask Erica who's supposedly floating around, but like hell am I alerting her that After's missing. Eventually, I figure out just where to look for him.

At his dad and stepdad's wedding, After hid under the table closest to the coat closets. He hadn't hit a big growth spurt yet, and he could fit underneath, covered by tablecloth. I found him there with his knees to his face, and he whispered so small, even at fourteen, that everything was too loud and there were too many people. We played two truths and a lie until the reception ended and we heard our parents calling our names.

I don't find him under a table, but I find him in an empty hallway near a coat closet, arms curled around his bare abdomen. He's taken off his gold cape, wearing it over one shoulder now.

"Here you are," I smile, coming up to his side. He flickers a startled look to me and scratches the back of his neck with a shiver. Goosebumps cover his abs down to his waistband. "You okay?"

After shrugs and twirls a gaudy turquoise and gold ring around his middle finger. "Thought I could hide until Greta was allowed to go. She said she'd DD for us so we can go bar hopping."

"Why don't we leave now? Get some food somewhere—after we change, of course, or Yvonne would bury us alive out back—meet up with Greta later."

"I kind of have to pretend to stick around and be present. Erica said—"

"Nope, she's a four-letter word, you speak her name and you summon the devil. Try again."

He chuckles to his shoes. "Okay. Fine, let me go say bye to Mom and we can sneak out."

"I'll go with you?" I offer, reaching for him. He snatches my hand up and lets me lead him back into the fray.

"Greta wants to show me a bar off 99 and Monroe. We can do shots, wanna do shots with me?"

"I don't drink, remember?"

"Right…right." He fiddles with the cape over his shoulder then squints at me. "Why not again?"

Let me list thy ways. "I just don't, dude, why are you pushing it?"

"Cause I thought you'd want to let loose. You can leave your car here, Greta's driving. She said she'd drive us."

I really hate how he gets when he does shots. But I'd rather keep an eye on him tonight, seeing as he seems to be shivering, yet there's sweat on his brow. "Sure, fine, I'll go."

"Fine," he snorts, rolling his eyes. Has he already started drinking, or is he just being rude? He takes his hand from mine and rubs at his arm, cracks his knuckles.

Before we make it to the lobby, he starts wandering for the front doors. "What's going on?" I ask, following. If he still had his cape attached to his jacket, I'd have stepped on it to get him to stop.

His voice is lower and sharper when he replies. "I'm *stressed*, Scott."

"I can see that. What's stressing you out right now?"

"All sorts of shit. Movie. Party. Noise. You."

"Me, what about me?"

"Our deal." He glances at me and shoves the glass doors aside, not waiting for the bellhop to open them for him. "More than that. Um. My essay."

I straighten my shoulders and pick at a velvet flower on my jacket over my chest. "What about it."

"Just…sometimes, around you, some uh. Feelings. Come back up. Tastes like acid."

He's quiet then. Cars honk, taxis roll along, picking up celebrities to go out or go home. I reach into my pocket and loop a finger into my car key ring, and an old thought starts to tangle itself more and more into my brain. "Hey, After…"

"Yeah," he sighs, checking me once. His hand goes for something in his own pocket. I tell myself it's not a flask.

"Have you….*really* forgiven me?"

His brow knits, and he stares off at the line of taxis. "Yeah." With a rough scratch to the back of his head, he clears his throat. "Gonna go piss before Greta gets here. And um. Say 'bye' to Mom. Stay—stay here, I guess," he mutters, stomping back into the theater.

I wait for half an hour. He doesn't come back. So I go for my car around the block.

And I get a call from Greta twenty minutes later. "Hey, Scott. Um. I'm with David, we're at a bar, it's ten minutes from the theater."

"Okay, and?" I huff, sitting at a stop light.

"And um…I mean. You might wanna come here, Scotty. He'd emptied his flask by the time I picked him up." Of course he had a flask. "I think he needs help."

"Why do you think that?"

"Cause he's drinking straight vodka."

The light turns green. "Send me the address."

—

Not so much a bar as a fucking hardcore dance club. There are round tables with plush blue couch seats, and every pole on said table is occupied by some scantily clad dancer.

I find After easy enough; taller than the others, bushed brows poking up over other peoples' heads. The strobe lights give me an instant headache, and the moment he claps his eyes on me, I nod at him. He cocks his head to the dance floor, and I go to sit at the bar, hoping he'll come to me instead.

He does seconds later, loudly with drunk gusto.

"*Why* don't you drink anymore?" he glares, dropping a heavy arm to the bar.

I give him a once over: jacket gone, white shirt on underneath unbuttoned, showing off his entire torso covered in what looks like glitter and alcohol, but it also shines weird in the strobe light like jizz, so who fucking knows.

Makeup smeared to his ears; his neck is covered in an array of lipstick marks. He lost his crown; it'll probably appear on eBay tomorrow for thousands of dollars. Lost his cape, too, but I don't blame him for that; it was a choking hazard waiting to happen.

But he *reeks* like vodka. That's the major thing I take away from just those five words he slur-shouted at me. "Cause I don't like what it does to me," I say back, reply on repeat always around this stupid subject.

His lip curls and he lurks closer. "What does it do to you?"

"Turns me into an asshole with loose morals."

"Turns you into a loose asshole?" he snickers. "You used to be fun when we got drunk on Dad's—" classy burp— "Dad's tequila."

"I used to be a jerk, same as you. We got in fist fights when we drank together, After, don't you remember?"

"I remember. 'Member the make ups," he sighs. "Kiss and make up?" By kiss and make up, he means Scott apologizes, even if he's the one that got his face punched by a sloshed After. No thanks.

My ears burn at his tipsy proximity and I push him back, getting God knows what on my hand from his chest. I wipe my palm on my pant leg and send a mental apology to Yvonne.

"You're being a dick, more so than usual, how much have you had?" He lifts a bottle in his fist. An empty bottle. "Dude—"

"It's fine, it was free."

"It's *not* fine and I bet you it wasn't free—where's your damn wallet—" I make him spin and pad at his pockets. No phone, no keys, no wallet. "Jesus, how're you buying your drinks? How're you gonna pay for a way home?"

"I'll get a ride somehow," he snips back.

"From whom? Greta, your supposed DD, is drunk as sin; I passed her on my way over here. Let me drive you home—"

"No, go away, you're bringing me down."

"If I go without you, I'm not coming back." He blinks like I just screamed in his face, and he stares at the bottle in his hand with a frown of, 'Where did you come from'.

After licks his lips, blinks a few more times, and even over the music, I can hear a sharp hitch in his next inhale.

"Hey..." I put my hand on his tattooed forearm, sleeves rolled up and probably destroyed. Yvonne's gonna kill him when she sees this mess. "Why don't we go outside for a bit?"

He leans toward me again, though I think it's just cause he can't stand upright anymore. "Outside..."

"Fresh air, some quiet, how's that sound?"

After clunks the bottle to the counter and presses the heel of his palm into his eye, further smearing his blue makeup. "Um. Okay."

"Okay c'mon, let's go."

It's cooler outside, even if it's still seventy-five degrees. But the noise is muted, the music less thumping. Once he drops onto the stairs behind the bar in the alley, After's head falls between his knees. If he throws up on those shoes, Yvonne's gonna eat him.

"You okay, man?" I ask, sitting a step above him on the stairs.

"I'm so tired, Scotty…"

I rub my hand between his drenched shoulder blades. "I can't imagine. Why don't I take you home?"

"Don't wanna go home yet."

"That's fine. We can go to my dorm if you want. Get you a shower, order some pizza—" He lurches away from me and throws up where the brick wall meets concrete. "Okie doke, no pizza."

"I think I'm getting sick."

"I think you're drunk as fuck."

"I…okay yeah, I agree to that."

"Maybe no more drinking for a while, yeah?"

"I agree to that, too."

He cleans his chin with his shoulder. "Dude. How does it feel to be a walking dead man?"

After scowls, eyelids drooping in separate intervals. "What do you mean?"

"You just wiped popcorn kernel and vodka vomit on a shirt that cost three grand. Yvonne will rip your gonads off and put them in her oatmeal."

He cracks a smile and tries to lean toward me, but his arm slips off his knee and his head thunks into my shoulder. That's gonna bruise, fucking ow. I pull him to my chest and his arms come around my waist. When my fingers brush into his hair, he inhales so deep it lifts me half an inch off the step, and his head tucks under my chin. "You do feel too warm. Maybe you are getting sick."

"I'm okay now…" He mumbles. "Just don't stop what you're doing."

"Praying you don't blow chunks on me?"

His chuckle vibrates into my ribs. "Your fingers. They're nice in my hair. Keep doing that. Stay here with me."

"Is there a 'please' in there somewhere?" I ask before biting my cheek. But he was a jerk just a few minutes ago, he doesn't get to be all boo-hoo now.

After leans away from my chest and looks at me with hunched shoulders and puffy, red eyes. His messy eyeliner makes his face seem bruised and shadowed.

"Please, Scott. Don't leave me. You're like...*way* more than I deserve. You're a...what is it—a sunflower. Gold. And taller. Than I could *ever* be. You're so full of life. And you let me hide. I can hide under you, under your leaves."

Well, shit, I'm not even drinking and now *I'm* gonna be all boo-hoo. Where the hell did that come from? I'm torn between reminding him he's got a few inches on me, and being like, can I quote you on that later when you're sober. "After, are you—"

"*Ther*e you are!" Click-click of heels, plumes of fabulous smoke, and there's Erica, looking stunning as ever in a strapless opalescent dress, holding the hem off the dirty concrete.

"Jesus, David, I've been looking everywhere for you! You just darted off, right before the party even started to come...come here with..." Her eyes fall to me. Hello, yes, I'm here too, how did you miss me on your red-carpet strut from the curb?

"Sorry, Erica. I needed. Needed space," After mutters. His arms circling my waist pull back until he's folding them around himself, knees up by his chest, attempting to ball his large form small enough to fit on a single step.

"'Space'? David, the party was for *you*, it was to honor you and the rest of the cast—do you even know how much effort everyone put into tonight?"

"I know, I'm sorry I left."

Erica huffs, squares her sharp shoulders, and flicks on her smile like a too bright bulb in this dimly lit alleyway. "It's fine. No worries, Davy, why don't we head back? We can clean you up, get some good shots of you with Greta—where *is* Greta?—forget it, not my circus, not my monkey. Y'know Sasha came to support you, too, by the way."

"I don't wanna see her," he sighs, remaining seated. "If I go back I'm hanging out with my date."

"Your *date*," she grunts. Her eyes dart to me. I wave a hand for some stupid reason. "Well. Fine, he can come too. But I need photos of you with the cast."

"No photos Erica, please, my head's killing me; I just want to hang with Scotty. Please let that be enough, I'm so tired—"

"*I'm* tired, David," she snaps over him. "Tired of this—whatever the hell you're doing with your life, with your friend here. It doesn't make any sense; you're tearing up things we've worked on for years. The paperwork I'm having to go through alone—now *that's* a headache!"

"What paperwork? I'm *gay*, Erica, I have a *boyfriend*. What paperwork are you having to deal with?" he shoots back. At least he sounds more sober now, but he still hasn't gotten up, pressed to my side. "What, you gotta—gotta change my relationship status online? Does that require signatures and NDAs?"

"You can't come out as gay right now, David, it's not good timing."

"Not good timing to just be myself? It's the 21st century—"

"And this is a country of hate crime! Do I have to remind you that people are killed daily in cold blood for being homosexual?" she shouts, waving her hands. After sinks. "You really want that? Your family already lost a loved one because of prejudice—do you really want to destroy your mother's life by making her bury another gay relative? Must I remind you of what happened to your uncle?"

Oh absolutely fucking not.

He's shivering against me. I swear I can hear his heart threatening to shatter.

"You crossed a line."

At my words, After looks to me, crying quietly. Erica stares at me and scoffs. "I'm not sure you need to be part of this conversation, Scott."

"I'm not sure you need to be part of his life," I reply. "You don't get to project your fear and your own opinions on him just because of what you think might potentially happen."

"I'm only trying to help him."

"You're not. You're not trying to keep him safe. You're trying to keep him caged. If he had come to you and said this was who he was, help him keep it under wraps for now, help him stay in his shell a little longer, that's different. But he's come to you repeatedly, asking you to help him get out there, help him speak his piece. He could do so many amazing things with his big name and his sexuality, he could help thousands, and you're hiding him for your own purposes."

"They're not *my* purposes, he has a face to maintain."

"Forget all that. Would you try to help him if all he really wanted to do was have peace in his life? To—to breathe?"

"He doesn't *get* to sit back and 'have peace'."

"Why the hell not? He's a human, isn't he? He's not a fucking machine, Erica."

"You have no idea the kind of conversations that go on behind closed doors in Hollywood. They're already saying shit about him because of what happened at New Year's, and it's been hell keeping all *that* at bay. It's not just the drinking, now he's ruining his figure by eating excessively and going off his workout plan."

Without even looking at him, she points at him like he's a dog at her feet. "Do you even care that his clothes tonight had to be *altered*? Twice. Because of *you*. He's an actor, he can't have fun like average people. You're not helping him, you're just as bad an influence as that guy Jacob. *I'm* the only one on David's side."

What a complete harpy. "Oh, are you? Then what have you done to actually help him?" I stand up and put myself in front of him. He can be angry at me for butting in later, right now I'm desperate to protect my friend. "At all, with any of it? Or are you too ashamed to admit some of those problems are your own damn fault?"

Her cheeks tinge darker and she juts her chin higher than my head. "If he comes out as gay to the world, people will want things from him," she deflects. Fine, I'll play that game, I'll tear your flimsy argument apart.

"How is that any different from right now?"

"It'll change his entire name; his line of work will get cut to splinters. They'll cast him in LGBT movies, shows, horrible romances where one of the gay guys *always* dies. He won't have the same reach as he did before."

I actually laugh at that, which seems to piss her off. "So? He'll have a different reach. Do you think there's only a tiny fraction of people out there who are gay? Who are ace? Lesbian? Bi? Pan—or abro like me?

"Do you think we huddle together over trash fires and accept whatever scraps of LGBT representation we can get, while TV shows like the ones *you back* queer bait us? We're *everywhere*. To have someone who's not only Hispanic, but also gay, standing up and speaking out—imagine the impact that will have on generations. And you want to dampen that?"

"I don't want to *dampen* it, I'm—he will—" Her phone rings in her hand. She squints at it desperately and shakes her fist before sending an exasperated look behind me. "I have to…it'll change everything. David, you don't get it. You thought it was bad before? You're choosing to make this difficult. The hate you're going to receive, the threats on your life…"

There's only silence in the alley. I turn and watch After, his head lowered. He sighs, gets up, and goes down the last two steps to stand next to me. I don't think she can tell, but he's leaning most of his weight on me. "I got used to the threats on my life when I played a brown Lancelot, Erica. I think I can get used to the ones around me being gay."

Her jaw goes taut and she answers her phone, sending me one last glare before walking back to her car by the curb.

Neither of us say anything. After doesn't look at me as he yanks the bar door back open, claims of not drinking again thrown out the window. And I go home on my own.

Chapter 27

So I admit, leaving was probably not the best thing I could've done. But I was over it.

I drove past the gala again, took a peek inside, debated walking through the fancy doors, calming my suit and face down and hoping I was recognizable as After's date. Maybe, I thought, I could do some damage control before rumors started to spread about him getting blitzed out of his mind at a local gay club, which are bound to add more fuel to the fires Erica has already been fighting.

Obviously, I didn't go in.

I got a phonecall from Bevett on Saturday for my birthday, had to return it Sunday afternoon since I didn't have a moment alone the entire gala day. She said her gift for me hadn't come in yet, but as soon as it does, she'll meet me in town for coffee or something.

Charlotte and Mei left a very pitchy voicemail, screeching Happy Birthday as they drank birthday cake shots in my honor, which sounded like a mistake waiting to happen. The second voicemail I got fifteen minutes later confirmed that I was right.

Nothing from Grandpa Mitch on the day of, but he did call me after work Monday and said I looked handsome in my suit; someone from his office has a teenage daughter obsessed with everything After, and eventually Mitch saw photos of me in the getup.

I stuttered a thank you, then immediately called Yvonne to apologize for the state I left her nice tux in. She said mine was a lot more manageable than After's. His ended up in the garbage. And as irritated at him as I was, that concerned me.

So I sent him a text Monday night. Something easy, asking if he was doing okay. No response.

It's Tuesday now. I'm back in my dorm after classes, feeling closer to sixty-three years old than twenty-three. Taking a break from homework, I push off from my desk and check the social media circuit. Some action gifs on Tumblr, since someone at the gala was a sneaky shit and posted clips of the movie on the Internet. But no messages from After on Twitter or text.

Instagram though, there's a little note by my DMs.

@DavidDespués: Hey u there

Sent three minutes ago.

@ScottEBoscoe: Hi, yeah, how're you doing?

@DavidDespués: I'm okay. Think I did get sick.

Getting drunk off your ass in a germ-flu-yuck-infested club will do that to ya.

@ScottEBoscoe: Do you need anything? I can bring you some food, or meds. If Charlotte's going into town I can bum a ride easy enough.

@DavidDespués: No thx. Erica has me on a cleanse. New diet. Protein shakes, broccoli, chicken, and rice. Wants me in good shape for Nicholas's episode. Gained like 2 pounds and that's a no-no.

@ScottEBoscoe: Please make sure you're drinking water and eating fruit. Or something. I'm sorry if DQ and I were a bad influence.

@DavidDespués: ur not bad anything. And I got fruit

@ScottEBoscoe: Fruit smoothies don't count. Eat an orange. Or three.

@DavidDespués: ur a good friend, Scotty

I get up and pace around my dorm while we talk back and forth. He seems okay, a little clipped, randomly saying he's so glad we're talking again. He mentions three times that he appreciates how nice I'm being, not sure why.

I start to sense that concern again, like I did about how destroyed his suit was. But I don't ask him what else happened that night. I don't really need to know.

We move off Instagram, and he texts me some things that people are saying about us from the gala. He shows me his favorite first: some girl from Twitter commented on a picture of me and David eating pretzels in line with Greta, "**Is this a make-a-wish thing? Who tf is this gangly asshole stealing David?**"

I laugh and ask if I stole him or if she's delirious. He sends me a winky smiley face, along with half a dozen magazine articles and photos of me looking much more suave than I felt at the time. The captions all describe me as being mysterious. Really I was just squinty and agitated, but I'll take it.

"**Boscoe bringing back bolo ties at the End of Heaven premiere,**" says one. I won't deny that I went and bought one off Amazon that has a yellow rose on it the moment I woke up Sunday. Fits in nicely to my small box of miscellaneous.

Another says, "**David's mystery guest Scott Boscoe stole the show—all eyes were on him even as he stood next to stars like Greta Hashfield. Although the new and old flames hit it off like regular BFFs—**" heck yeah, we did, angel of a human being—"**how does DD feel about his ex and current fling talking? Dirty secrets about the never-single hunk himself and more on page eleven.**" There was not more on page eleven.

"**Who needs glitter and glam when you have cheekbones and legs for days like Scott Everett?**" Okay, um thank you, *Us Weekly*, whatever did I do to deserve that?

I start laughing when Buzzfeed immediately creates "**Top ten things hidden within Scott Everett Boscoe's outfit at the gala. Not as subtle as you'd think! Number six will shock you!**" Number six is the fact that my socks were Yvonne's orange polka dot ones, cause the others were too thick for my boots. They'd been hidden within my Louboutins; I have no idea how someone found that tidbit out.

Y'know, I bet Greta told them; when I showed her, she started giggling so hard she nearly snorted spiked slushie all over her $10,000 gown, shouting at anyone within ear shot. Like I wanted to try to stop her, I loved the sound of her laugh.

People's spread gets the loudest cackle out of me. "**Yvonne James knew exactly what she was doing when she sent Scott Boscoe off to the red carpet without a touch of makeup or unnecessary razz. The brightest thing about him all night was the proud smile he was sending best friend since childhood, David Después.**"

When he sends me that one, I text After back with, "**Hey, hey, we're gal pal level! We gotta up our game. I'll start doing yoga :D.**"

He never replies. And another week goes by.

—

I'm not totally awake, I don't think. I've been coasting in and out of consciousness, touching the edges of sleep just to get pulled back by more stress. I have class tomorrow, early, but my mind is moving too fast around other things.

School, After, Silversmith, After…Mitch.

Apparently my, 'you looked distinguished in your suit, Scott, very handsome,' was short lived. Pics got posted of me leaving the gay club, appearing irritable and disheveled. Just happened to be the same corner After and a tall, blond, blue-eyed man were seen leaving, half naked and all over each other.

Jacob. I knew just by Mitch's description over the phone when he called me around dinner. That explains some things I guess…

Grandpa's call turned into a three-hour long barrage of insults real dang quick the moment I told him what I did that night wasn't his business.

Bevett called me right after he did, and that alone had me wanting to sink into the Earth. She asked if I was okay, I said fine. She asked if I was really okay. Like. *Really*. Cause the hair looked bad, the blood red in my eyes looked worse, and the glare I was giving the person who flashed their camera at me all looked. Familiar.

I took a minute longer before I echoed my first reply. And when we hung up an hour ago, I knew she wasn't convinced.

Shit's already popping up online about After and my 'first fight'. At least our relationship is gaining traction, but it doesn't look good that I left the club going one way, and After walked off in the other direction with another man. One Twitter thread started off with, "**Domestic squabble leaves David Despúes seeking out mentor Jacob Nolan for support. Quote by Erica Yates about Scott Boscoe's true intentions in link below.**" My new phone got another crack in it after I read that.

I haven't stopped checking my apps for something, anything, from After, and each time I get zilch. I'm assuming if he was dead I'd have heard about it by now.

What if he *was* dead? What would I do then? I think if he had died before we started to connect again, I'd be upset over all the what-ifs and words unsaid, but I'd get over it. Probably.

Now that it feels like we could've gotten another slim chance at friendship, if something were to happen—

There's a clink against my window. I sit up on my elbow and squint into the dark. Another thunk, followed by a hiss. Is a cat launching pebbles at my window?

I kick my legs out from under my blanket and crawl down my ladder, grabbing a boot—not an ideal weapon of choice, but it's what I got—and I peek through my slanted blinds.

The scream that comes out of me is super unfortunate and I swear to never recreate that in all my remaining years. "After!" First voice crack. "What the fuck!" Another squeak as I claw at the string of my blinds and yank them up. "*What* are you *doing here*!"

"You texted me," he slurs, leaning both his hands on my first-floor windowsill. His shirt looks two sizes too small and is covered in something ungodly. So much for the health cleanse. That didn't last long.

"A *week* ago—"

"You're not doing yoga," he grumbles, bending at the knees as his brows go up, checking into my dorm. I look at my bare legs in my boxers. "Why no yoga?"

"Because it's two AM on a Monday?"

He nods so many times his whole torso droops. Did he just fall asleep standing up? His head snaps back up with a snort. Oh, Lancelot, how far you've fallen. "*Have* you? Been doing yoga?"

"Do I *look* like I do *any* exercise?"

"You bike, you got those weird, nice, muscular biker legs. Where's your bike?"

Was there a compliment in there somewhere? "Chained up outside."

"You said you'd do yoga—"

"Oh my God—"

"Lemme in, it's hot and humid and icky."

"Good, you can sweat the liquor store you drank out of your system."

"Piss off and let me in!" Buddy boy ain't got no room to be sassy right now.

"*You* piss off. What the hell are you doing here anyway? Why are you throwing rocks at my window like a boozy John Cusack? I'm on the first floor, you could've knocked." Or, I don't know, used your damn phone like a normal person?

"I *did* knock, you didn't hear me," he grunts. "I threw, like, *three* rocks before I got you here—third one ricocheted into my *face*, by the way."

"Serves you right." I tug the string of my blinds all the way and unlock my window. Before I lift it five inches, he's got his tongue between his teeth and he's dismantling the screen, shoving it into my dorm room. "Stop, stop it, you're—that's school prop-er-ty!"

"Move, Scott Ev-er-ett," he mocks, diving his shoulders into my window. I move and don't bother to try to catch him as he comes careening into my dorm, smacking his ass onto the concrete and near bludgeoning his skull on my desk chair leg. "Son of a biscuit!"

He smells like a Walmart dumpster if it wore expired Calvin Klein cologne. What the hell is this person on my floor? I do not know this man. "How drunk are you," I spit, slapping my window closed and locking it. He rubs the back of his head and glares at me. "After. Tell me or I lock you outside."

"I'll break in." He's got a finger knuckle-deep in his ear, and I'm fairly certain his eyes are going in separate directions.

"I'll call the cops on you." Like hell I will, not with my record. "What are you doing here, drunk as sin on the floor of my dorm on a school night?"

"There was a party off campus…"

"And you were at this party of college kids *why*?"

"I met a couple of 'em."

"How?"

"Online. When I posted pictures of JU last month."

"So you met some strangers online and thought it would be a good idea to frolic over there alone—"

"Wasn't alone, I'm not a *baby*." Sure sound like a baby, my dude. "I was with Jacob."

My eye roll is so strong it could reverse the Earth's axis. "Wonderful, that makes this *so* much better. How do you still have a functioning liver?"

"I…I take vitamins."

"After, you said you were eating healthy and stuff. That you weren't going to drink for a while. Awhile usually means longer than nine days." I cross my arms, refusing to help him up. Lies, I reach down and take his hand, pulling him to his feet. "What's going on, what happened?"

"Can we talk?" he mumbles, running a finger under his nose. His weight sags against my shoulder.

"Shower first," I huff, struggling to keep us both on our feet. "You're wasted and disgusting."

"You don't have a shower here," he sniffs, using his whole hand to rub his nose again. I shove a paper towel from my desk over his face.

"No, there's a community one, you can use that."

"What about after?"

I lean him against my bunk and go for my dresser, debating which sleep shirt and pants I'm willing to potentially part with. "What about it?"

"Can I...stay?" he whispers behind me as I pull on a sweatshirt.

"This isn't going to be your 'seen leaving my place' thing, is it?" I sigh, putting a t-shirt, sweatpants and clean boxers in his hands.

"Dunno—you want me to wear your underwear?" he giggles.

"Seeing as my eyes sting with onion stench, a cloud of Hollister and fucking *Fireball* of all things, yes, you gotta change. And you can stay here after. Like hell am I letting you bumble about in the dark like this."

He repeats 'bumble' with a snicker, and I loop his arm around my neck, snatch up the toiletries bag I keep by the door, and drag him to the communal showers.

—

After gets cozy in my spare bunk, hair wet and fresh from my shampoo. The second his head hits the pillow, his eyes start to close. I stand by the side of the bed and shake him awake; I need answers. "Why were you at a college party just a block away with Jacob?"

He stares at me with one eye open. "Um. He called me. Said he was nearby, asked if I wanted to meet somewhere."

"There are a dozen hotels a street away, y'all could've met up at one of those."

"Didn't want to. Hotels with him scare me. But I was uh—I was nearby, too. Was debating um...anywhoo, it got weird. Party got dumb. Jacob got. I got. Aw, geez—" He ducks his head into the pillow and belches, and I get flashbacks to just minutes ago when he was throwing up in the shower. "I ran for it. Hopped the fence. Knew you'd let me stay if I came over."

"You couldn't have known that."

"I did though. You're my friend."

"Friends don't do this, After," I reply, gesturing a hand between us. "They don't show up rude, drunk and demanding after a failed hookup."

He raises his head from the pillow. "They don't steal each other's work, break one another's trust, and leave them without answers, either."

Well, damn.

Not like there's anything I can say to that. Would make more sense to cut my chest open and let him read it all right then and there on my heart.

I start to step back. "I'm sorry," he rushes out. "I didn't mean that—"

"No, it's…it's fine. You're right."

His hand goes for mine before it can leave the mattress. "Scotty, please, I didn't mean it." He scoots closer, sucks my hand in toward his chest until my fingers come to his collarbone under his t-shirt. "I…I *have* forgiven you. I know I have. But I still wanna know why, so. So maybe I haven't, all the way. Or I wouldn't care so much."

There's my answer to that nagging question. I nod and look to my toes, to the window. Debate launching out of it and running into the night. "Right."

"So…why? It's not because of what I texted you that December, right?"

Sounds like he *does* remember that very one-sided conversation. Good to know I'm not the only one lugging around guilt. "No, it's not, After. I'll tell you one day, I promise. Just not tonight."

He accepts it, thankfully, and lets out a heavy sigh, curling around my forearm. "Hey, Bo…"

Hate it. Hate it, hate it. "Yeah."

"I never told you. Happy birthday. M'glad I spent it with you."

By the time I gain enough courage to look at him, he's asleep, lips parted and brow relaxed. I have to pry my entire arm out of his grip just to go lay down on my own bunk.

Chapter 28

By definition, a booty call is when you ring up a fling or a hookup or whatever, have them show up to your place late at night, and you fool around until they run off and leave you to wake up alone.

Somehow, I ended up on the other end of a booty call, one I did not initiate.

Didn't call up drunk After, didn't fool around with him (found out he was nearly part of some kind of college orgy, though. Now's not the time, but I'm sure we'll cover it later) and then he bounced before sunrise while I was still asleep. As expected, I didn't get my shirt or pants back. Not too broken up about the boxers—but with my hoodie, he's got a whole Scotty outfit.

Last week was, well, a week, as they say. I was batting off students Tuesday through Thursday as they asked if the TikToks they saw of After dancing with people at a college party just down the street were legit or not. I never saw the videos so I just shrugged the questions off.

That's where I draw the line—hey, better late than never to figure out where my boundaries are, right?—I refuse to get a fucking TikTok.

Since he's been coming to campus for writing days and feeling the need to post photos of me every damn time, I've become the beacon of After knowledge. Straight up one of the main reasons I didn't want to do this fake shit: attention. I do not like it, no matter what Mitch says.

Friday was the quietest day all week because, lo and behold, I have no Friday classes, and therefore didn't have to leave my dorm except to squirrel food away. Never before did I think I'd appreciate the silence and lack of roommate.

Now it's Monday, and it's pouring rain, torrential, complete with thunder that shakes the office of Silversmith, and clouds that make the entire floor near pitch black. The relaxed easiness of the office allows for us to make our own schedules, and many of us checked the weather this morning and went oh hell naw, gonna rain and storm all day? I'm workin' at home.

Me, the moron, didn't think to check the weather. Hence why me, the moron, is still stuck at work.

Mona went home an hour ago before it started to come down so bad; she had to pick up her kid from school. Jackie Zoomed into our meeting on her Lay-Z-Boy with curlers in her bangs and a cat in her lap.

Every time the motion detector lights went off, I had to reach up and flail to get them back on again. I gave up twenty minutes ago; been using the little lamp on my desk that Mona re-gifted me for my birthday. It's hot pink with fringe. It didn't suit her office aesthetic, either.

Either I bike back to JU now and pray I don't drown in the three hours it takes me to commute (got a ride here from Charlotte. When I asked her if she'd take me back, she just replied with, "**Look outside. Ask me again if I'm driving in that**"), or I'm here all night until the sunshine returns tomorrow around ten AM. See, *now* I check the weather.

The elevator dings and I hardly look up. Oliver was the last to leave, and he seems to never remember his keys on the first trip down to the parking lot. I think he secretly likes the stomach-dropping, rollercoaster feeling of the elevator, and it's the only adrenaline he gets besides chasing his dachshunds around the block when they escape. (Only reason I know that is from the one day he showed up drenched in sweat. Thought he was red-faced and grinning cause he won the lottery or got laid or something. Nope, dachshunds.)

I pull on the fray of my shorts at my knee and squint when the overheads detect motion and buzz back on. "Hey, Oliver, they're by the Nespresso," I shout, switching which foot I've got propped on my seat.

"Well, thank ya kindly, Scotty," comes a voice that's most definitely a fifteen-year-old girl's and not Oliver's Irish baritone.

I smile and pivot in my seat, checking around my cubicle. Bevett beams at me as she trots down the path, looking too freaking adorable in a lime green, iridescent raincoat and rubber duckie goulashes. I wanna squeeze her.

I get up and squeeze her. "What're you doing here, weary traveler!" I laugh, squishing her cheeks in my hands.

"I came to rescue you; I brought an oom-bralla!" she announces, shaking a collapsible umbrella at me and getting water everywhere. She giggles as I shriek and cover my laptop. "It's my Kermit one."

"Spectacular—you came all the way here for me? Did you walk?"

"No, Grandpa dropped me off! He had to go back into work for something and he let me catch a ride into town."

"That was nice of him," I reply, packing up my backpack. "Though I don't think you wanna hang out here until he's done with whatever it is he's doing."

"No, but we can get an Uber back to the house and you can stay with me until the rain lets up."

"You planned everything," I smile. She smiles back, but her face does this little squint thing, mouth going tight and small like Yvonne. "You okay, pooch?"

"Yeah!" Wow, squeaky much? "I got uh—I got a gift for you; can I give it to you now?"

"Sure, but are you really okay—" She's already pulling her floral backpack around from behind her, and she drops to a crouch.

"Now," she says. Her voice cracks. Something's off and I don't like it. "This is your belated birthday gift."

"Bevvy, you didn't need to get me anything," I remind her. She swats me in the knee and points for me to sit back in my seat.

"It came from the UK, took a while—I straight up ordered it in, like, January, too. But it's from Etsy, and it was the only one I could find that I really, really liked, and I mean I might've got it wrong but I was going off of descriptions you've given me so…well. I hope you like it." Bevett gives me one last look, inhale shaky, and she lifts something folded in brown paper from her backpack. "Happy birthday, Scotty."

I bend over my knees to kiss her on the head and take the gift, pulling at the string of twine that wraps around the paper.

It falls open, and colors upon colors wash across my lap in a wave. Deep blues and glints of silver. Indigo paisley, lavender and fuchsia, bursts of bright, sunrise orange. Navy tassels. A Pashmina scarf. Just like Mom's.

I think I mean to gasp, or sigh. Or say wow, or gosh, or holy shit. I should tell her thank you.

I don't have a strong enough grasp on my emotions to do any of that. Off my seat, I'm on my knees and hugging her, gorgeous scarf held between us, fabric so cool and soft against my hot cheek. Bevett crushes me hard, and I hate that I cry into her shoulder, but there's nothing I can do to stop it.

"I did good?" comes her tiny voice.

That gets me to laugh. "You did phenomenal. Oh, man…"

"I couldn't find what I was looking for until at Christmas, when you said it was like the carpet from Aladdin."

"This is gorgeous, Bevett," I sniff, running it under my chin. She sits up on her knees and takes it from my hands, wrapping it around my neck. My chuckling turns into weepy hiccups. "Goes with— with my outfit, yeah?"

She giggles and wipes at her tears before she runs her thumbs under my eyes. "Perfectly, matches your dirty black Keds and ripped jean shorts."

"I wanna take you out. Can I treat you to some tea?"

"Tea sounds nice," she sighs. But now that she's crying happy tears, the floodgates are open, and there's nothing to stop whatever she's been holding onto. She thumps back down on her heels, head hung low. "I gotta talk to you, grump."

"Tea—let's get tea and cookies, you need cookies. There's a Starbucks right around the corner, we can walk under the awnings to get there." I help her up to her feet, hug her once more, and tuck the ends of the scarf into my hoodie collar for safe keeping.

We pass Oliver at the elevators, and he compliments her Kermit umbrella, complete with a 'hi ho!' in the green frog's voice. It gets her to smile, and I make a mental note to buy him a retractable key ring as thanks.

—

We've devoured one full chocolate chip cookie between us. Got a snickerdoodle half eaten on the table next to refilled teas. Sugar cookie is prepared to launch just in case. And Bevett's finally ready to unscrew the cap on her bottled emotions and really let me know what's going on.

"I can't keep going with NJHS," she huffs, rubbing her fingers into her temples and looking much more stressed than a fifteen-year-old should.

"That's okay, Bevett, what's wrong with that?" I ask, taking a small bite of cookie. She sniffles and rakes her hands through her curls, and since they're slightly damp and the humidity is at a horrid 65% today, her hair floofs to new Mia Thermopolis levels.

"Because, when I told Grandpa I got accepted into it back in February, he was over the moon. He was so proud of me; I'd never seen him so happy except for maybe when my painting got best in show at rodeo art in fourth grade."

"Okay, and?" I feel an explosion coming. I push the cookie toward her.

You could find her shaky lip and big, brown eyes next to 'pitiful' in the dictionary. "And, if I told him now that I'm struggling just to keep an A- in English AP—it's English, it's direct and indirect objects—why are we talking about *objects* in

English?—he'll be so mad at me. I can't step down now, I don't want that look of disappointment on his face like how he looks at y—"

My brows lift when her mouth clamps shut. Then there's that explosion I was expecting, except it's less teary and more absolute distraught, and there go all our napkins to wipe at her drippy nose. "Hey, pooch—"

"I'm s-s-sorry, I'm sorry, I didn't mean it! Scotty, I didn't mean—please—"

"Hey, hey." I scoot my chair around the table and bring her against my chest, cheek on her wet hair. "You're okay, we're okay, no one's upset at you." She continues to whimper little no, no, no's to herself, and I rock her side to side, hand circling her back.

There's a tap on my arm and we both look up.

The way Bevett darts away from me and starts furiously wiping at her face with crinkly raincoat sleeves, one would think it was Mitch who'd suddenly appeared.

Nope, definitely not Mitch, but I don't lose my glare, either.

"Um…hi," says After. If it wasn't for the tattoo under his rolled-up sleeve, I really might've thought he was just another dude; his eyes are bloodshot and sunken, line between his brows cutting deep. He extends his hand again, full of napkins.

"Thanks," I grunt, turning back to Bevett. I clean up her cheeks with the softer napkins, pushing her sharp sleeve cuffs away from her eyes.

Why. Why? *Why* is he *here*, always at a Starbucks? Is he in partnership with them? Every time he goes to one and there's some sort of dramatic, Real Housewives moment, do they get a thousand dollars? Do they use his face on the painted sugar cookies?

"I'm gonna—bathroom," Bevett mumbles, getting up.

She darts around After, rushes for the toilets, and he glances back at me. I'm still glaring. He blinks so fast it's like he's taking pictures and his lashes are the shutter, and he looks to his boots, half-hidden under soaked jean hems.

"There are almost four million people in LA," he says. "How do I keep bumping into you?" Bumping into *me*? Says the dude who cropped up outta nowhere drunk at my dorm, furious at my dorm, at my house. (Maybe drunk, who knows with him.)

"Beats me. I only wish I had this kind of celebrity magnetism around someone better. Like Keanu Reeves. Or Zendaya."

"I thought I was just gonna have to see you, like, five times. But I feel like this just keeps going whether we schedule anything or not," he adds. He kinda sounds mad about it. I know I am.

"You can turn right around and leave."

He pouts and lifts a bright green iced drink, shaking it once. "I had to get my refresher."

"Aren't those supposed to be some sort of 'pick me up'? You look like shit."

"Maybe I need four more," he hums around his straw.

I can't disagree with his statement (not about the refresher); I was thinking five weekends tops where I'd have to be around him, aside from anytime we met for my writing—which, hopefully, won't be that many more times. But now I'm like…LA suddenly feels smaller than ever. When does this end?

Bevett comes back, looking fresher-faced but still tired. This time, she smiles at After, and he pulls her under his arm to keep her tight to him. He's allowed a pass right now as long as she's smiling. "It's stopped raining. Y'all wanna go for a walk?" he asks mostly her, squishing her against his ribs.

She rubs at an eye and nods, and I get her backpack and umbrella before she has to pick them up. Then After's taking them from me, and as soon as he's opened the door for us and I've unchained my bike, he links his hand with mine and I'm forced to push my bike onehanded.

So desperately I wanna just yank my hand from him, take Bevvy's shit and speed off with her on the handlebars. But she's got her arm hooked through his other elbow while he drinks his refresher. He's parked himself front and center. Prime for paparazzi photos.

Chapter 29

Park is nice, I admit. Bevett has a Crayola watercolor set in her backpack along with a small notebook of thicker paper. After offers her a couple of ice cubes, and once she's found a bench to get settled on, she's using the melting ice and watercolors to paint the trees.

"You really had no idea we were in there?" I ask him as he comes back to stand by me. He looks over his shoulder to her on the bench with my bike in the grass by her feet.

"No, no clue," he replies, hand going into his pocket. "Just wanted to get out of the house, took a walk."

"How far do you live from Grizzly Street? I thought most of the big celeb houses were super far."

"They are."

"Have you eaten? I've got extra cookie in my pocket for Bev, but I'm sure she'd share."

"No. Thank you."

So chatty. Tempted to just up and ask what the hell last Monday was, but that means I'd have to show that I care, and I like being secretive, too.

We walk the concrete track beside the trees, circling a soccer field. I fix my hood over my head when it starts to sprinkle again. Bevett makes no move to leave, so neither do I. After, however, has no hood or jacket or anything.

"Want my hoodie?" I ask him. "I can get her umbrella for myself."

"No, I don't mind it, thanks." He does a doubletake to me, then snorts, looking me over like he's just now seeing what I'm wearing. "You're dressed like a toddler—you went to work like this?"

"Mona wore Nike shorts and cowboy boots yesterday. Jackie was straight up in Grinch pajama bottoms. In April. Trust me that my shorts and Keds are not nearly as appalling as you think."

I start to walk around the short track as he continues to stare at me. "What is this uh…what's this hoodie anyway? I thought you only had JU ones," he adds, pointing toward the screen-printed logo on the front.

I look at my baggie jacket; it's one of Mom's, from my box. "I did. I had two. One is now Bevett's. It's drenched in so much Hilary Duff perfume; I'd never get that washed out."

"Where's the other one?" he asks, reaching over my head to raise a low hanging branch before I smack into it. Perfectly capable of moving it myself, plus it would've gone right over my head, anyway. The look on his face when he brings his hand back to himself makes me think that occurred to him a little too late.

"The other is still with you," I tell him.

"Ah." After brings the straw of his drink back up, even though he's only got ice left. "Well, you still have my jean jacket…"

Weak argument. "I can give it back to you."

"Nah. Doesn't work with my wardrobe. Kinda like your scarf."

I grin at that and peek down into my jacket for the Pashmina, cozy and tucked in close to my chest. "Bevett gave it to me today as a belated birthday gift. It's like my mom's, the one I told you about." He tilts his head to see more of it, and I pull some from my hoodie, laying the colors out flat and letting the muted sun catch the silver threading.

"It's like you described," he whispers. "Sunrises and blues."

Another low hanging branch. He doesn't lift this one for me and I duck under it. Not enough though, and it almost tugs my hood off my head. My fingers are at the front to fix it back into place, when

After pulls it over my forehead first. I look up at him, he looks at me. I squint. He scowls.

"You're being weird," I say, in case he hasn't noticed.

"Am not."

"Are, too."

"*You're* weird."

"Sure, After."

"Scott, I just—"

I stop walking, and he takes two more steps before he stops, too. "I just want to say thanks. For last Monday." He turns back to me, then looks straight over my head. "You didn't have to do all that, and you did. So thank you." Finally, his eyes flick down to mine. "I appreciate it."

I shrug further into my jacket. Not too cold out today, but the wind is torture on my bare legs, making my knees shake and— dammit, now I'm shivering all over. (Yes, I have *full* control over my nervous system.) (No, I'm *not* nervous, thank you very much.)

"Well, sure. Highlight of my life: washing semen off your back while you sat on the community shower floor, buck naked."

After's jaw dropping silently tells me he most definitely doesn't remember that. Probably doesn't remember throwing up on the tile, either, let alone bringing up old scars again in my dorm.

Cleaning the vomit wasn't the worst part. Did the same thing when we tried his dad's tequila for the first time and didn't know that, if you *can't* taste the liquor with the mixer by the third drink, you're totes fucked.

But when he woke me up again in my bunk, more sober around four AM and crying and wouldn't calm down until I opened up my blankets and let him curl against me—*that* was bad.

Through snot and tears, he told me he didn't just run off and hop the fence like he said. He was late to the party, and Jacob was already there, talking to some guys. After tried to join the conversation but Jacob ignored him and After didn't know why.

One guy was nice, funny. Brown eyes, serving chips and salsa. They shared Chex-Mix, which tipsy After found super fun and rebellious cause he's been on that strict diet since the gala. The two goofed around with water balloons. "We had such a good time," he sobbed to me.

Then in came Jacob and some of those dudes from earlier, and Jacob offered After a drink. And another. After's strong, tall. But pretty soon, he was trashed, and outnumbered, and none of those dudes were nearly as drunk as him.

One thing led to another and he kind of regained consciousness face down on someone's bed, shirtless with his jeans undone. (Oh look, the insane college orgy I mentioned, we're back to that.) When someone brought out condoms, and there was heat on his back, hands on his shoulders and voices he didn't recognize, After started to panic.

There was an argument, and Browneyes-Chex-Mix was like, fuck no, this isn't cool, he's drunk and not answering us when we've asked if he's okay. When Jacob shrugged him off, that guy left, and I guess to super sloshed After, the guy looked like me. That's when he ran; to follow him.

After stumbled around on campus before he found himself at the steps of Jones Hall, and he somehow knew his way to me, thinking he was chasing some white rabbit Scotty.

I don't think bringing any of that up would help him now, not when he looks so sick and upset.

Also, I'd feel inclined to commiserate like, hey bro, it's cool, I've hallucinated you, too. But I was hyped up on a shit ton of weed at the time. So no worries, it don't mean no thang, haha...*eesh*.

I keep walking and pat him on the arm as I pass. "You're good, dude, it's fine." There's a long sigh, and he follows behind. His boots are too loud on the concrete path, so I move us off the sidewalk. We cross through the empty, dewy soccer field to muffle our steps. "Tempted to sell the towel you used on eBay, though."

He coughs. "You could. Wouldn't blame you. Think the shirt I showed up in wasn't even mine."

"That explains the Hollister smell." After nods and wipes under his nose with his wrist. I offer him a napkin; he gives me a quiet thanks.

"You don't look so good, man," I continue, checking him in my peripheral. "Couple weeks ago you said you might have gotten sick."

"Yeah, I dunno. Feel gross."

"Do you usually feel like this after you drink that much?"

He winces at me. "Yeah, but I get over it. Just need a few days to dry out."

"Maybe a few days without Jacob, huh? More than a week?"

"I mean...might be starting that over."

My head falls back with a groan. "Do *not* tell me you saw him again after that party."

"I needed a ride somewhere, he offered. I bought him a drink to thank him—"

"After, you're gonna kill yourself," I snap, turning on him.

He rolls his eyes. I don't give a shit when my hand flies and slaps into his chest, knocking him back an inch. There's a bit more life in his face when he snarls at me.

"You have *got* to stop if you want to stay alive until you're twenty-four—no, if you want to live until your next fucking birthday in May."

"It's not like I'm doing hard drugs man, knock it off, I'm fine."

You fucking moron. "So you'll just repeat Monday until it kills you? What're you gonna do if I'm not there to pick you up off the floor, or give you a safe place to sleep, or—"

"You didn't have to do any of that shit."

"*Didn't* I?"

"I said I was sorry for Monday."

"Actually, y'know what, you never said you were sorry." He stutters and frowns, but he can't argue with that. "Apologize or don't, drink yourself to death, whatever. I don't really care. But your mom cares, and your dads. Greta cares. You have thousands upon thousands of people who love you and care about you. Geez, After, even Erica cares in her own screwed up way—"

"They're fans. They don't know me, none of them know me at all," he snaps. "And Erica only cares about my net worth and how much it's gonna fluff up her resume."

Okay, fair. I try to cut in and his lip curls into a look of agony. "Y'know, I actually broke and called her? Didn't wanna tell Mom about JU but—but I thought Erica, she might be on my side. Might talk me through this, might be the f-friend she claims. Instead, she flat out said I had it coming. I was almost—they nearly—holy fuck, Scott—" He shudders, eyes flicking to the rain clouds. "She told me I *had it coming.*"

Haven't heard him sound so beaten since his dad moved to Spain. I wonder if hugging him right now would be a bad idea. But he looks shot to hell, and when he brings up his melted drink, the ice rattles in the cup with his trembling hand.

"After, I'm sorry." His eyes drop back to me. They're a gray I've never seen. I take a short step toward him, then another. "Can I say something?"

"You can say anything."

I don't think that's true. Can't tell him about the wrath I felt in my gut, in my dorm, hearing him tell me about Jacob and the others. When he told me why hotel rooms with Jacob scare him. Can't tell him how much it hurt when I woke up to an empty bed.

Can't tell him that, as much as I lie about it, I'd care if he was gone.

So I turn and look at Bevett, and he follows my stare. She's in full artistic hunch with her watercolor paper balanced on her knees, not a tear on her cheek anymore. And, like all the times I called him when we were younger, asking him to come over and help with Bev, just to be around him for five minutes or five hours, I use her as a crutch. As my shield.

"She loves you. She has since you were the first person she went to when she learned how to walk, since your name was her third word, before she ever said mine. You helped me raise her when Dad and Cassidy were at work. When it got too much for me to handle as a teenager, you YouTubed how to change a diaper, how to bring a toddler's fever down, and you'd do the laundry I was supposed to do. You let me sleep while you took care of her."

"You fell asleep watching Up so many times you couldn't hear the music without yawning," he whispers with a small smile.

"And I'd wake up to you with barrettes in your hair," I smile back. His eyes pink and I offer him another napkin for his runny nose. "You're important, man. She believes in you, she always has, whether you remember any of that or not."

Hate that look of defeat and exhaustion on his face. "Why?" he asks. I can almost see the humid, thick air as it gets pulled into his mouth. "What's there to believe in?"

"I can't begin to guess what's going on in your head, or what you've dealt with since you left Texas. If it's more of what happened at Jethro, I'm so fucking sorry, and you never have to tell me the rest of it. Just know that the day you leave too soon, she will miss you with a heavy heart. Don't make it too soon."

After watches Bevett long after I've finished my rant. I'm about to keep walking when his hand lands on my forearm. It goes down to my wrist, my sleeve cuff, and his fingernails trace the lines on my palm. "Hey, Scott."

When I link my fingers with his, it's for support, to be an anchor. He squeezes my hand like a lifeline. "What can I do to help you, After?"

"We need to…can we. We can do the sleepover thing. You can come over," he sighs, circling his thumb around my knuckles.

"Whatever you need."

"This weekend?"

"Sure." After nods, releases my hand, and goes for Bevett. He sits on one side of her, leans his cheek to the top of her head. I join them, sitting on her other side. Thought she was painting the trees.

There are washes of tans and browns, but they form into a face with thick brows and hazel eyes, little dots of freckles made with the stem of a leaf. He kisses her hair, and I hear the faintest whisper of, "I love you, goose," come from him. I look off to the park and let my hand rest on his arm along the back of the bench.

Chapter 30

Slumber party night. Also known as, get as much amp up as possible across social media, posting on every site, under every account, that I'll be going to stay at my boyfriend's place in LA, all night, with a big ol' bag packed of who knows what. (It's my phone charger and hoodie and sleep clothes, that's what. Kinky, I know.)

I post a picture of my #ootd (outfit of the day; trust me, I had no idea what it meant either until blessed Bevvy told me) in the full-length mirror that hangs on the inside of my weak excuse of a dorm closet. Basic, but chic as I could muster; black Chelsea boots, obvi, black skinny jeans ripped casually at the knee, and a dark gray shirt I tucked and untucked sixteen times until I got that Tan France 'French tuck' perfected.

Bevett taught me all the right things for posing: Don't look at my own face in the mirror, look at my phone. One foot bent behind me, head tilted so my cowlick fluffs just right, brow raised but not too excited. Like, yeah, no biggie, just going to sleep over at my super-hot celeb boyfriend's house. Hand in the pocket, she said. Only because I'm notoriously that doofus who does a thumbs up no matter the situation.

Caption (I admit I didn't think of this, Charlotte did): **Hope the weather in central LA is better than here at @JethroUniversity. Didn't have enough room in my bag to pack my new @BananaRepublic jean jacket—stolen from @DavidDespués. And no, babe, you're not getting it back. #boyfriendsclothes #boyfriendprobs #boyfriendfashion**

I stopped her when she wanted me to add another six 'boyfriend' hashtags. I think they get the idea.

After's friend Harry followed me after I got home from the gala (**@NotHarryStyles**), and he's first to comment that he likes my boots, joking that they look roughly child sized. I reply that I am indeed the size of a child.

Harry laughs and sends a DM, asking me to take photos of the house so he knows where to look for all the good shit he can steal and sell when he visits Cali next.

I get a dumb grin when one comment says, "**Why do all the super cute ones have to like boys? :(**"

Then there's another that totally makes my entire year: "**#loveislove #representationmatters #abrosexual**."

Wasn't sure my little watermelon striped pin was visible on my bag strap over my shoulder, but the fact that someone commented on it makes me jump up and down in my room and punch a fist in the air, promptly cracking my back like an old man in the process.

One name comments and I suddenly get a new follower. "**@SashaNewFierce: Love your boots! You guys have fun! ^_^**"

First off…who uses emojis like that? I don't know anyone outside, like, DeviantArt that does that.

Second off…I'm now stalking Sasha Newman's Instagram, and my smile is extra ridiculous cause the magazine articles don't do her any favors. At. All.

Her posts are workouts and smoothies and Black Lives Matter rallies and feminism posters and 'this cat meme is a mood' and 'we need to check our privilege and use our reach in a way that helps others' and…girl, hi? You're kind of amazing?

I'm trying to tell myself this is legit Sasha and not another Morpheus who takes over Greta's Instagram, making it all aesthetic hot girl shit, when I know she really just wants to post pictures of puppies and cabins.

After likes her comment (why do I feel like that little act had him freaking out for three minutes before he just went for it?) and adds his own sassy jab to the post. "**That's okay, I still got ur #JU hoodie. Text me when ur on ur way! C u soon, babe ;)**" Clever bastard. It gets a thousand likes in a minute.

—

I pull my bike into my dorm and lock up for the night, afraid my rise to stardom will include someone stealing it, and I'd rather not get arrested again when I hunt said thief down.

After didn't want to pick me up; he said he wants me to appear at the front gates like a long-lost lover.

By the time I roll up, my look has gone from styled to disgruntled. The multiple people flocking his property, flashing cameras at me, and *slamming* their *hands* on my *motherfucking rental*, have me debating, again, getting arrested.

The gates open and there are two men in black cargo pants and black shirts and black sunglasses waving me in, pushing screaming fans back. Someone shouts my name, and I have to fight the urge to turn my head, slinking up the long stretch of gravel to his…

His…

Remember when snarky After said something along the lines of me living in Gramps fancy castle mansion?

Homeboy had *no* room to talk.

This colonial, deep red brick, rugged but handsome *Southern Living* dreamhouse has four floors. Straight. Up.

An outdoor pool—an *indoor* pool I can see from here (wondered why he told me to pack swim trunks), there's an open four-car garage (hi, Ferrari! Miss you), and a garden the size of six of my dorm rooms covers the front lawn.

He's on the porch between two white columns with twining ivy, hands in his pockets, looking chill and boring and yet I'm sure everything he's wearing cost hundreds of dollars. Light wash bootcut jeans, white v-neck shirt half-tucked into the waistband. (That French tuck, man.) Hair? Perfectly tousled. Mine? A disaster.

Something on his face glints in the sun when he tilts his head to me. He's got light brown framed glasses on his nose. Didn't think he still wore readers; it's been years since I've seen those.

After sends the adoring fans at the gate a wave and a smile, and he makes a big show of opening my door, helping me out. I've got, 'whaddup, loser,' on the tip of my tongue when he kisses me? On the forehead? Like, excuse me?

My first words sound like, "Hgneh…hi," after that.

He chuckles and loops an arm around my neck, leading me to the trunk of the car. "Rental?"

I nod. "Same one from the gala; I found glitter from my tux in the driver's seat. I think at this point they might just let me own it."

"I can buy it for you, if you want," he says, taking my bag from the trunk.

"I'll just take the Ferrari." I get a laugh and another kiss on my temple for that.

I don't like this. It's all for the cameras. Just like his fingers in my hair at my house, the handholding in public. I'm regretting not wearing his jean jacket, cause at least that would've given me another layer of armor. And I could give it back and not feel like I owe him anything.

We walk into the house after he salutes the people lining his property one more time, and he closes the door behind us.

Smells like vanilla and lavender. Looks like Pottery Barn threw up in here. John Denver is playing somewhere upstairs. And I don't really register any of it cause my shoulders remain cloaked in his arm. And his face remains close to mine. Even with the door closed and all the cameras off. "Uh…hi," I mumble again, craning my neck up to him.

He smiles and lightly bumps his hip to mine. "Hey. What do you wanna do first?"

"Nap." He laughs at me. "Sorry, that's super lame—"

"No, Scotty, you can take a little nap. It's ten AM on a Friday, places are just now opening up anyway. Can you stay awake long enough for me to show you around a little?" he asks, turning us to face the gargantuan, echoey front hall.

I slip off my boots and nudge them to sit by the doorway, and I scratch at my nose and play like I'm stretching my arms out, before letting one rest around the back of his waist. "I'll do my best to not snooze during the tour."

After beams and takes me down a hall with floor to ceiling windows chasing us on the west. Tile flooring shines with white and tan grout, long strips of Persian rugs muffle our steps, and the ceilings are all arched twice my height.

On the first floor alone, we pass two separate spiral staircases, a bathroom with a jacuzzi tub, multiple closed doors—

"What do you hide in all those locked rooms, Bluebeard?" I step out from his arm and linger by one that's wide open. Tallest ceiling and windows in the house so far, room naked without a single scrap of furniture. White, presidential walls are speckled with landscapes and oil portraits with golden frames. The space itself feels like a painting.

"They're not locked, feel free to explore. I really only use the first floor's west wing; got a gym, a few closets. I haven't even unpacked shit in the library and I've been here for years," he explains, continuing without me.

"You've got a library? Where?"

"Honestly no idea. I think it's in the east…? That sounds right." He checks back at me and smirks. "I need a mall map."

"And a food court."

"I got a food court."

"You're lying."

"Tell that to the Whataburger I've got waiting for you in the kitchen."

I gasp and yank at his arm. His cackle tells me he's full of shit, and I smack him in the shoulder. "You can't play with my emotions like that!"

He takes my flailing hands and links his elbow through mine. "We can stop at Whataburger on our drive through Texas to get to Tennessee, I promise."

"Why are we *driving* to Tennessee, why not flying?"

I don't get an answer, but that's okay, cause the room we stop at is superb. And it's really only superb because it's nothing like the rest of the house.

This is absolutely After's room; how I thought he ever had a hand in decorating the rest of his house, I have no idea.

First and foremost, I'm shocked that I can actually see the carpet; After's bedroom when we were younger always had his entire closet strewn about. I can only imagine how long it took him to clean before I got here.

The walls are covered in posters, from Deadpool to Resident Evil and a ton of other games we used to play. Many of said games sit in a squatty shelf that a TV is perched on. His bedsheets are dark gray, mattress might be a queen, there's a sectional sofa in the other corner of the room. A light brown desk is covered in papers and an open laptop, there are books on a lone window seat, and—

"Oh my God," I whisper.

"Don't move, he can smell fear," After teases.

My squeal sounds like Bevett's when she sees kittens, and I clamp a hand over my mouth in an attempt to muffle it.

There's a sleeping German Shepherd on a large doggy bed, coat a sleek, shiny onyx with two white socks on his front paws. "Is this...*the* Chicken?" I ask with an unintentional, dramatic wave to my voice.

Chicken's ear twitches our way, and he stretches lazily, slinking out of his dog bed. He looks up to After and pants into a smile. Sees me. And he goes *bonkers*.

He's both much larger and lankier than I was expecting, and much, *much* faster, as I hardly have time to let go of After's arm before I've got puppy snoot right in my grill, front paws landing on my shoulders.

"Oh—oh geez—hi! Hi, Chicky!" I laugh, dodging slobbery kisses left and right. After makes no move to help me, merely walking in to toss my bag on the sofa. "How old—egh! How old is he?"

"He's two, he goes with me almost anywhere," After chuckles, coming back to pat Chicken's scruffy neck, adorned with a yellow bandanna. He lifts him by his ribs and plants a noisy kiss between the pup's ears, and Chicken's eyes close in delight.

"I adore him with my whole heart. He's going with us to Tennessee; I've never been away from him for longer than a couple days before."

"He's wonderful—you're wonderful!" I tell Chicken, laughing at After holding him up under his elbows and making him shimmy.

"Still want a nap?" After asks, squishing his face to the side of Chicken's until he gets a tongue up his nose.

"Honestly…yes, but only so I'm not a total drag all day long."

"No, that's fine with us."

"Can he…" I link my fingers and bring my hands to under my chin in a silent plea, and After grins. "Would he hang out with me for my nap?"

"He hangs out wherever I am, so totally."

Wait, what does that mean? "Are you—did you need to rest, too?"

After shrugs and drops Chicken, who starts circling me like a soft, black shark. "I could use a nap, yeah. Been rushing around since, like, sunrise."

"Doing what?" I ask, heading for the sofa.

"Was mega cleaning." I knew it, spotless floor and the zesty smell of at least four cans of lemon air freshener gave him away. "Wanted it to look nice—hold up, Scott—"

"I'm only here for a day—"

"Stop, Scotty, take the bed, it's fine." I do a weird this-way-or-that dance in the center of his room, pulled toward his mattress with my fingers looped in Chicken's bandanna, and pulled to the couch, cause that's where I figured I'd be staying. That or one of the many guest rooms.

Then I'm getting shoved in the back toward the bed, and I crawl in willingly and get cozy. Yeah sure, it's not a waterbed and true the sheets might be from Walmart probably but—dayum. This *mattress*.

I melt. In snuggly comforter, in warmth, in smell of After all over this bed. I melt and pass out in seconds to the sound of his voice talking softly to Chicken about the fun things we'll do when we're all well rested.

—

Delirious and woozy with sleep, my eye flutters open to someone drawing the blinds before the sunlight can cross over my face. I murmur a thanks, I think; might just be a grumble.

The bed dips behind me. I reach back for Chicken, for long body, sleek coat of fur covering warm ribs. I get warm ribs alright, through thin t-shirt. And I get a thick arm draped over my waist. Chicken's laying on my feet. I'm trapped in…shit, I don't know what this is. Puppy pile.

I whisper the first name that comes to mind. "David?"

His fingers slide between me and the mattress, anchoring me to him. "Hi…is it okay I'm here?"

I refuse to breathe in case he shatters and I'm left alone. So I just grip his wrist and hold him closer in reply.

Chapter 31

We wake up from our nap an hour later and don't talk about the spooning. I should say, *I* don't talk about it.

After rambles about it, pattering around his kitchen as we divvy up food. "Figured it was okay. You were shaking—I keep my house kinda cold—not as cold as Yvonne's though—*was* it okay? You didn't say anything. I mean you'll be on the sofa tonight, so don't get used to my bed—the bed. I was tired, I don't like the sofa, so I mean...and it's *my* bed...so..."

He got our lunch order after naps. In an attempt at healthy solidarity, I ordered my Dairy Queen chicken strips without fries. Already I feel myself wasting away, but don't fret, I'll be strong. "It's fine, dude, no biggie," I reply to his mishmash of statements, putting ketchup on my paper plate. (It *is* a biggie, but I'm not gonna even go there.)

After huffs and plops on a bar stool across from me. He scowls at his salad. I reach a fork over and pile up a couple bites for myself. "Salad's good," I tell him.

He gives me a little smile in reply. "Okay—food, yay, alright lemme tell you the itinerary."

"Ooh, did Sasha and Greta and Jolene get itineraries the first time they stayed the night at your place?"

He holds up three fingers, taps them one at a time. "Sasha, no, cause she only stayed over once and I pretended I had to leave when in reality I hid in a room on the fourth floor until she went home."

"Super classy."

"Totes. Greta, yes, repeatedly. We were dating eight months and were in three movies together; if I didn't write us a schedule, we would have never gotten shit done."

"I can imagine."

"Jolene…no itinerary. But she stayed over the most nights. We had a lot of sex, in most of the rooms of this house." Hoookay, just blurt *that* right out there. "To be honest—" please don't, you've been over honest already— "I don't go back into some of those rooms just cause of. That."

"But it was…" I wave a hand in a slow circle like that will get him to know what I'm saying without me having to ask. "I mean. You didn't want that, I get it. But it was—"

"Was consensual, yeah, I agreed to it each time. Even when I was drunk, I was aware of my actions. Not like at the. At Jethro. No, I get what you mean." After smiles and forks up romaine and spinach. I don't manage a smile; I think we both have a very different understanding of the word 'consensual', but now's not the time to discuss something as potentially traumatic as that. "I like that you ask me that. Thanks, man."

I hand him half a chicken strip as a 'you're welcome' and he takes a sip of my cream soda, too. He hiccups, burps, and he groans and holds a fist to his chest while I laugh at his disgusted face. "Oh Jesus, I burp like my grandma used to—"

I gasp, fork midway to his salad again. "Meemee's dead? When?"

"Oh—no, she's not dead, she's still very much alive and being unfortunately racist in Dallas."

"Damn, poor Dallas."

"Straight up—okay, see, we're already distracted, we need the shed-yule."

"Tell me the shed-yule then, good sir." He drums his fingers on the counter and splays his hands out in the air like that 'picture this' thing he does. Under different circumstances than the first time in February, his squint of concentration makes me grin.

"First: we nap. Check. Next, we eat. After this, I wanna show you the property."

"Oh, goodie, parade me about for those drooling at the sidelines, desperate to get into the pearly gates?"

"You got it," he smirks. "No, actually, I've got a shooting range further out; I thought you'd enjoy going and blasting some cans."

My eyes round and I laugh so loud it echoes off the marble counters. "Yes! I'd love that! It's been forever since I went to a gun range. Last time was…it was with Dad. Sixteen."

His smile squishes his cheeks up and he accepts a small spoonful of Reese's Blizzard. "I figured you'd like that. It's hot, so we can swim after for a minute if you want. Then maybe some video games before dinner—I wanted to order from this place nearby."

"What they got?" I grunt around a much larger spoonful.

"Tex-mex."

"Naturally."

"And I mean I'd—I usually make pina coladas when I order from there, but I can make something else. Maybe virgin ones—I can YouTube how to do it."

I slow my reach for an additional brownie Blizzard. (They're mini size I swear, I already took one for the team by not ordering fries.) "You were being serious? About backing off for a bit with your drinking? For how long?"

"Long as I need to, to feel better. Got a lot of bad shit to undo." His face reddens, and so do his eyes. He leans back in his seat, raps his knuckles on the counter, then slides off his stool, walking over to a two-doored, dark wood cabinet next to his pantry. I spin on my stool and watch him, continuing to devour DQ ice cream.

When he swings the doors open, I fumble my spoon. Four, three-foot long rows of bottles upon bottles, green and brown and clear and opaque. The top shelf is so tall he'd have to use a ladder—oh snap, he legit has a rolling ladder like at a bar, tucked into one side of the cabinet.

He turns to me, and I don't think I look nearly as calm as I mean to, cause he hangs his head. "Yeah."

"For uh…for how long?" I repeat.

"Got a little—" he sucks on a tooth— "little out of hand last summer. Mid movies, dating, other stuff. Then New Year's sent me down a month long spiral, so…"

That's three times someone's mentioned shit happening this past New Year's. He shifts his weight over and over, and each time has his toes pointing in more.

I hop off my stool and join his side, feeding him a bite of ice cream. "Okay, here's what we're gonna do. You go get everything we need for shootin' and tootin'."

He snickers. "You're barreling your way through two Blizzards; we've got the tootin' covered."

"You have no idea—and I'll take care of the…" frantic hand wiggle, "this."

"What're you gonna do with it?"

"I'm gonna hunt down those two beefcakes that let me in and ask them to help me."

"Thor and Angus?"

I scream, and he laughs at me, catching my ice cream before I launch it. "No *way* are those their names!"

"They're husbands."

"Stop it!"

"They are! They're usually in the billiard room, furthest door down the east wing. Go right, listen for Enya," he chuckles. But his chuckle sounds more like a giggle cause I haven't stopped giggling either and I'm starting to think us shooting when we can't stop laughing is already a bad idea.

—

Thor and Angus, who are indeed husbands from Montana and Utah respectfully, are without a doubt two of the most hilarious people I've ever met. They pass no judgement on After, but they don't hold back on their little sarcastic jabs either as we tear through his alcohol pantry.

By the time After finds us in the kitchen, Thor's 6'5" self is doubled over in breathless giggles, and Angus has his face against the counter, hiding his hiccupping in burly, tattoo covered arms, laugh hissing through the gap in his teeth like a tea kettle.

I'm on the floor, gasping and setting us off all over again every time I go, "So as I was saying…"

"I leave y'all alone for half an hour," After smirks, leaning over me. "Did you get any work done?"

"Don't you dare make fun until you take a gander at your glorious new storage space," I pant, flailing a hand toward the closed doors.

His steps recede with an unconvinced mmmhmm. There's a curse on his inhale, and another on his exhale. "Oh, wow…"

"Come help me up," I groan, stretching my fingers. His hands grasp mine and yank, and I'm on my feet with a yelp, held to his chest. "What do you think?"

Five seconds pass with him just staring at me. Another five, and Thor and Angus clear their throats and take the remaining bags full of empty liquor bottles out to the recycling bins. Five more seconds. "So—"

"U-um. Yeah. Shooting?" he smiles, rushing away from me so fast I stumble forward.

———

I'd love to say that all his excellent stunt work has made him a horrible shot. And that he's never practiced in all his time living in this fancy big house with an acreage that allows him to have a shaded, woodsy gun range without worrying about bothering neighbors.

But this is After. And he's a magician at everything.

Thor and Angus join us for a few rounds. After seems so small and young, standing between these men who reapply sunscreen to his nose and make sure he gets water and hand him apple slices.

I'm starting to feel like they might be the fatherly stand in that he's been seeking, since his dad and stepdad moved to Spain. He lets them stand close, help him aim, and he leans his head on Thor's muscled shoulder while he waits his turn to shoot. Without the opaque shades, Thor's got muted blue eyes surrounded by smile lines in his dark brown face, and he has dimples which are just the *cutest* thing. (Yes, I called ex-wrestler and state champion Thor cute, shut up.)

Angus has one blind eye, the other as brown as mine, pale skin covered in freckles. He looks like a movie character with his white, glass eye and neck tattoos. I'm told he has a sweet tooth like no other, too.

"How long have Thor and Angus worked for you?" I ask as we go through the trees toward the house, pulling my shirt away from my chest to cool off.

"They've been here since around the time I signed with Erica. They actually met because of her," After tells me with a wipe of his arm across his sweaty forehead. He slings the rifle up to rest on his shoulder, stepping carefully over a log.

"Thor was my guy first; Mom hired him when I turned nineteen and started getting gigs. Angus came on as extra safety when I got my first big role, where I wasn't just a background character. Suddenly, cause I had an agent and I was being taken more seriously by movie producers, I was also noticed hardcore by fans."

He grimaces at me and shakes his head. "I actually had my house broken into a few times. Once while Mom was staying the night in the master suite. They thought that's where I slept, scared her half to death. Had to get a restraining order, more security. Whole lotta nonsense…"

"Sorry dude, that sounds stressful."

He huffs through his nose but gives a bright smile to Angus coming up to my side, taking my handgun for me. Thor appears next to After and relieves him of the rifle, and we watch them walk off, close side by side.

"Without them, I'd be here alone all the time," he sighs, continuing down the path to the porch. "It's a big, unnecessary house."

I laugh as we go up the steps to the back patio. Dude's got an entire hibachi grill out here next to a full tiki bar. Most definitely unnecessary. "Yeah, sure is. You could get something smaller."

"I've thought about it," he replies. "Maybe somewhere in Texas. Like San Marcos, or Austin."

"That could be nice. Why don't you invite more friends over? Like Charlotte? Greta?"

He pinches the corner of his mouth and leans against the railing around his porch. "Greta tends to be introverted—which is fine—but she has days where she just wants to be by herself. And Charlotte. She's great, and we've talked often since she moved to Cali. But…" He scratches at his chin, tracing his toe in a circle on the light wood of the patio. "Y'know in February, when I thought I was meeting up with her?"

"And got the delightful surprise of me instead?"

He snorts and nods. "Yeah. Um. I was actually practicing smiling that whole way up the sidewalk. Parked extra far away so I had time to kind of put on a happy, healthy face."

"What, why?" If you can be hurting and open around anyone, it's Cat-Cat. I know that from experience.

"I'd been on a bad…ride. Hadn't seen anyone in weeks, had hardly left the house except to film and get alcohol—or get bullshit photos taken with Sasha. It's absurd, but I got this thought in my head that, if Charlotte saw just how low I was, she'd…I dunno. Call you, tell you she was worried. Then you could either choose to, like, find me, help me, or turn your back on me. Both outcomes were terrifying. But then seeing you for the first time in years, right as I was thinking about you—"

His eyes flash to mine as his words halt. I nod in hopes that he'll continue with whatever this admission is. Seeing me sent him off the deep end, seeing me made him hopeful. Seeing me made him want to punch something. We're healing here, I'll take anything.

But this is real life, not the Hallmark channel. And sometimes lingering questions are all we're gonna get.

After stares off at the trees on his property. "Guess there's a benefit to this house. Sometimes."

"What's the benefit?" I ask, taking a short step to stand in front of him in hopes that he'll look at me, and not the vast acreage behind me.

"Lots of rooms. Lots of places to hide. Every once in a while, I'll leave my phone in one of the rooms I don't use, as far away from me as possible. I turn off all the music, no TV, and I sit in that art room with Chicken. When I do that, it feels like every single person in the entire world has disappeared, and I wouldn't know who was still alive until I left my house." He lowers his gaze, and he looks right through me.

"I imagine I'd walk to Texas then, back home. I'd stand in the desert at Lubbock, look out at the flat land. I'd turn left, and it would be no one. And I'd turn right; not a soul would come find me. Sometimes I think I'd be okay with that. And…with no one left to miss me, I could fade. And it would be okay."

I kick myself for not realizing that, as brave as he is, the hero needs a rescue sometimes, too. Maybe, if I was braver myself, I'd say we could run and escape the dragons and expectations together. Or better yet, turn and face them head on, side by side.

"I'd know you were gone," I tell him. After's eyes focus on mine, and they slide down to my smile. "I'd find you."

We're both gross and smelly. And it might be a mistake. But I bring my arms around his neck and hug him. He crushes my waist like I'm a balloon about to go off into the atmosphere, and he's my last chance to stay on the ground. His face presses into my neck, and I stand on my toes as he squeezes me.

Then we go and jump in the pool with all our clothes on.

Chapter 32

We get off schedule as soon as we hit the water. I know he said next we would be playing video games and we'd only swim 'for a minute' after shooting. But we chase each other around in the pool for an hour, just to get out and go mess around in the indoor one next. That one's got a diving board. I make it my life's mission to try and break it.

Once Chicken hears the commotion, he flings his wiry body into the deep end, and all bets are off for After's itinerary.

Instead, we switch to mine. Operation: chaos.

First is dance party. We don't bother showering after we get out of the pool. We start running around the halls, sliding down every banister we can find, recreating the Risky Business scene—y'know, *the* scene—with sunburnt feet and torn at the cuff sweat shorts.

Next is wrestling match. After waits until he's thrown me to the couch three times before he tells me he bench presses my weight as his warmup. However, I manage to catch him off guard when I swing one of my 'nice, muscular legs' and take him out at the knees. (At least then he sees my red cheeks and maniacal grin as a victory smile, and not me losing my cool over being *lifted* and *body slammed* by a sweaty, clingy, sexy superstar.)

He gets it in his head that, since I was strong enough to pick up Charlotte and chuck her into the pool, I'm strong enough to give him a piggy-back ride. I agree full-heartedly. And I get rug burn on my shins when his weight crashes us to the ground.

That sets us off on a Barenaked Ladies binge, listening to One Week a million times and shrieking out the line about rug-burned knees.

We try again with the piggy-back ride. I land face first this time.

He's upside down on one of the sofas in the first floor living room, legs kicked up over the back cushions, head near mine as I sit on the floor and check the wet paper towels I've got on my shins. Mother hens Thangus (my ship name for them, isn't it great?) tried to get me antibiotic and band-aids, but I waved them off. (Still, I *was* thoroughly tempted when Thor mentioned they were Spider-Man themed.)

"Did I tell you your friend Harry started following me on Instagram?" I mention, tossing Chicken's rubber chicken leg with probably a lot less enthusiasm than he'd like. I'm too distracted scrolling through the PlayStation Store on one of After's PS4s, trying to find something we can play.

"No, you didn't. Y'all talking?" he asks, readers slipping down his nose toward his forehead.

"Yeah a bit—he's funny. We got into a debate over Lord of the Rings versus Star Wars. He asked for my number so we could move off Instagram. The moment I gave it to him, he called me and shouted that Lord of the Rings was superior. I couldn't breathe for two minutes cause I was so thrown off by his thick southern accent."

"You gave him your number?" After mutters. I snort and squint at him in my peripheral while he pretends to ignore me, reading an Atticus poems book. Biggest dispute in cinematic history and *that's* what he takes out of what I said?

"Yeah, I did—"

"Eh, I wouldn't have…"

"Why not? He seems like a good guy." Not like Jacob, I nearly add. I thought he and Harry and Nicholas were all good buds? If not, why the hell are we driving cross country for them?

After scoffs and makes a noise of disgust when Chicken comes trotting back with his toy and shakes his wet self all over us.

He snatches the chicken leg and chucks it as hard as possible down a different hall. "I mean he's okay. He smokes sometimes."

"Cigarettes?" I ask the alcoholic. *Recovering*, Scott, be nice.

"Weed. And he drives over the speed limit. And..." If I had glasses, I'd be peering at After over the frames right now. He sniffs and pushes his back toward his nose. "Well, like, sometimes he'll wear his sneakers without socks—"

"And you eat spicy food with your mouth open, what's your point?"

"We should do an Instagram live," After grunts, tossing his book aside.

I just laugh and wipe at my face. "Sure, how do we do that?"

"I'll show you." He takes his phone out of his pocket (we did end up showering and changing just so we're not pulling a Chicken and getting chlorinated water everywhere) and he opens up Instagram. "It's easy, it's fun. Usually I schedule these so people know when I'm gonna pop up but...I mean fuck it."

"Fuck it," I echo, angling my head to get in frame as he titles it 'Slumber Party' and turns on the live show. Instantly, viewers start appearing, hearts flooding in at the corner, exploding like confetti cannons. OMG emojis pepper the screen, and hundreds of people ask WTF is going on; I get dizzy trying to keep up with the comment stream.

"Say hi, Scotty!" After grins, waving at the phone. I chuckle and take it from him, holding it so he's the one upside down. He doesn't like that, so he sits correctly on the sofa and pulls me to join him.

"Hi, y'all!" I give a wave, and After thumbs his glasses up his nose like a nerd.

I laugh at the rush of people freaking out over them as soon as they notice, frames blending into his bronze skin. "Did no one know you wear readers like an old lady?"

"Apparently not—here—" He takes them off, cleans them on my shirt, and turns to me, sliding them over my ears. "There, you can borrow them."

"Ah yes, me and my 20/20 vision thank you." I squint at him through the slight blur and look at my face in the screen. "How do I look?"

After stares at my profile before inspecting me in the live video. He hums, tilts his head. "Like a dork."

"Perfect, optimum dorkage achieved. Alrighty, now what do we do?" I ask, going through and pinning random comments and changing filters.

"Okay, so first off—wait, stop—Scott, stop—" He laughs and covers the camera, blacking out the screen. "You don't just go through and poke buttons, bro. You ask questions, they answer. Vice versa, answer some stuff they ask."

"That one just asked if I'm the big spoon or little spoon."

"And the answer is…?" he smirks, putting his arm on the back of the sofa behind my shoulders.

I start to grin and my sunburn ruthlessly heats up my face. "Uncover the camera, they'll think we're making out."

"We *are* making out," says After as he moves his hand.

We hang out on live for another hour, answering questions about his new movie, how it was finishing up filming in New Mexico for the next project. Some people ask what we've done today, ask how we're doing. Many, I'm surprised, ask about me.

He lets me answer them, too, until it's obvious I'm getting more attention than he is. When **@NotHarryStyles** pops up and says hi and he's excited to meet me in person, After tries to steal his phone back.

I hop up from the sofa and run with it. "Hi, Harry! I'm excited too. Whadya got, y'all, I've got a five second head start," I laugh, darting to another corner and taking stairs two at a time, Chicken right at my heels.

The comments erupt and I can hardly keep up with the questions, people asking for shots of the house, how's my school going, do we ever visit Texas— "Yes! Hopefully, Af—um, he says we'll stop at El Paso—I mean—y'all are gonna have me spilling secrets I don't know I'm supposed to keep!"

I snatch at Chicken's bandanna and we hunker down in a random closet, both panting and squishing to fit in frame. I try to answer questions while puppy kisses attack my face. "Let's just say—oh, gross Chicky—let's say I'm excited for Whataburger again!"

"**Are you excited to be in El Paso again?**" someone asks, oh so innocently. Then it's an onslaught of, "**Come see us in El Paso! Come hang out with us! Visit Lubbock! Odessa! Are your parents in El Paso? What's in El Paso?**" and my tiny closet becomes too tiny and closeted.

After's shadow appears under the door, and without a clue how to answer their questions (without shrieking cause that's all I suddenly feel like doing) I slide his phone underneath the door.

He says his goodbyes, his love y'all's. Then there's a heavy sigh and, "What happened?"

Oh, nothing, they just sweetly asked if I was looking forward to being back in the city where my life fell to shit. "Um. One asked if I've ever done a sixty-nine—"

"Dude, oh my fucking God—"

"I said duh, and a thirty-eight." What's a thirty-eight, Scott?

"Some of my followers are *kids*, Scott," he snaps. Oh shit that's his angry voice; he thinks I'm being serious.

I roll my eyes and reach for the door handle, peeking out and up at him standing with his fists on his hips, glaring at me. "I'm just joking—"

"You *cannot* say those things on the Internet, Scott Everett, I'm dead serious."

"Nothing happened, I swear! I got nervous and didn't know how to end it. Can't I get nervous?"

His eye twitches. Chicken does that thing dogs do where they start off laying down, then begin to drag themselves forward with just their front paws until their back legs are all kicked out. Finally

After sighs into a smile, wiping his face down with one hand. "Okay, yeah sorry."

"What the hell was that? I feel like I just got in trouble for spray painting a dick near a playground." He helps me stand, and I pass him back his glasses, seeing his deflated face unblurred now.

"Sorry, sorry…it's just. That's one thing Erica cautioned me on, and I wish I listened to her at the time. Some people take advantage of you in this situation. You're friendly and smiling, and you want to have a good time. You start to be honest, too honest, and people will use that against you."

He holds up his phone and gives me an 'I'm not angry, I'm disappointed' face, and it makes me wrinkle my nose.

"Whatever you say here can be permanent. Doesn't matter that it was live and supposedly goes away right after. People record. Things. Whether you know it or not."

"Like sex tapes."

After's lips crease into such a tight line they turn white, and he sniffs, walking away from me down the hall. "I'm sorry I shouldn't have brought it up," I say as I follow after him.

"It's fine. They were consensual to make. Just not really…to share."

"If I see Jacob again—"

"You gonna falcon punch him?"

"I'm gonna drop kick him."

After releases a tense laugh and lets me push his shoulder. "Please don't. I already never want to see him again, I don't want a lawsuit mixed into this. So don't do too much to get attention on you—like. Try to keep this stupid thing around me. I know that sounds selfish, but I need you to be careful." He slouches going back down the stairs. Looking to the living room, he leads us to his room instead.

"Y'know, even after this whole fake dating thing ends, you'll still be known as the dude who dated a celebrity, and people will still want things from you. They'll dig old shit up on you and try to get you to say something about it in hopes of getting a good story. Or a good picture of you. Erica once said pictures sell better than stories, and videos sell better than pictures."

Shit, After, where the hell did all that come from?

"Why didn't you say all this before we shook on it?"

"I didn't really care about it then."

And now? I'd ask, but I doubt I'd get an answer. So I try another one that's been chewing at me, especially now that he hasn't met my eye as long as I've been staring at him. "Hey, After?"

"Yeah."

"What was Jacob doing at the club after the gala?"

He scratches at the back of his head. "I called him on Greta's phone. When I went back inside after Erica came by."

"Then you went home with him. Even though you just said you never want to see him again." After nods to his feet. "Why?"

"I don't know."

I think you do, man. And I think of Yvonne, saying his suit went straight to the trash. "Did y'all have sex?"

We get to his room. I'm close enough I can see a bead of sweat, or shower water from his hair, slip into his shirt collar. "Yes."

Cool. So. That's kinda different from finding out he was nearly assaulted at a college frat party.

Who knew being fake cheated on would hurt so fucking much? Didn't realize I'd stopped walking until he turns around to face me frozen in the doorway. He comes back with a lowered gaze. "Can I explain?" he whispers.

"You can try." I move past his hand before it can reach my shoulder, and I sit on the sofa. Chicken hops up by me, and After paces in a circle, touching at Chicken's ears every time he passes us.

"I—okay, so you walked out. And that's fine, I was being a dick. But I got a weird pit in my stomach. So I called him, cause he filled it before, and filled—filled me. And before New Year's, there was a time when it was nice." There's that dreaded New Year's again.

"I was cared for by someone older, wiser. He's thirty-seven. We met when I had just turned twenty-one—"

"Then he sent you on a bender," I mumble. He's tracing a finger up and down his tattooed arm, staring off at the windows.

"He's all I had though. I needed someone. I mean months ago at the fundraiser, we hashed it out over him sharing the sex tape—he only leaked it to a couple of friends cause he got crabby I was ignoring him. It's why I went back that day, not to talk to my mom. Really he's why Sasha didn't want me to go in the first place; she knew he'd be there." Okay, *there's* a lie I didn't know he was holding onto.

"But he said he regrets it. And he's sworn everyone else to silence; Erica only knows it was recorded; she doesn't know it got shared. And he said he was sorry we got our picture taken leaving the club—*and* he apologized for the frat party thing, he wasn't really gonna let those guys mess with me or…y'know…take it too far…"

He sounds like he's trying to convince himself more than me. "Did Jacob apologize for the trauma? For the night of sleep you lost because you were sobbing hysterically into my shirt for hours?"

Low blow, Scott. Maybe it had to be said but. Not like that.

After takes off his glasses and sits on the floor, leaning his back to his bed, and he does this thing. He's done it since we were little and he was stressed. He rubs his fists into his eyes, pushes his fingers against his brows. He did it so much after his parents' divorce that he got headaches. Trying to white out the world, he'd say, so when I look at it again, it doesn't make me so upset.

Did it at the gala. At my dorm. In my bed. When he stares at me, his eyes are beyond bloodshot.

"After you left the club without saying anything, it sent me back to when you left me alone in Texas without a goodbye, so—"

"For fucks sake—I *did* say goodbye!" Chicken jolts at my raised voice, and After balks, startled.

He leans over his knees with wide eyes, like seeing me better will help him understand my words. "What? What do you mean?"

"In Texas. In Lubbock. I *swear* I did. I rode a damn greyhound eight hours to your house the night before I flew out to Cali. I had my—my box. I asked you to hold onto it for me, all my old books and journals and a couple of hoodies, things I wanted you to keep safe for me."

"No you didn't—when was this?"

"In December, after Christmas senior year. It was midnight, I knocked on your window so hard I thought I'd break it, but you sleep through anything when you want to. You pulled me in, took the box from my hands and set it aside, started talking at me in Spanish like you do. You told me not to worry about it. Said we'd talk in the morning."

He's looking at me like he truly doesn't remember. I hope he doesn't hate me for this. Or call me a liar. Cause I think about that night too often for it to be fake.

"Dude I…you brought me into your bed with you and asked me to stay. You kept saying you were sorry for something. I held you until you went back to sleep. I…" Broke that one stupid rule and kissed your cheek, kissed your forehead, your hands, told you I loved you right then and there and have meant it ever since. "I took my box and I left."

His lip trembles. I want to take it between mine. That's too much. All of this is too much.

"So. Yeah, I said goodbye. And. Anyway." I stand and walk over to him and reach down. "Sorry I brought up Jacob. We don't need to talk about that anymore. I'm getting pretty hungry; can we do dinner? And um. Did you still want to play video games?"

After's brow scrunches just to relax in waves. He stares at my palm for so long I think he's counting every crease and scar in my skin. Then he takes my hand. We order the Tex-Mex; I hardly taste it. We play video games and blast music and stay up late like old times.

And by old times, I mean we sit with a wide space between our bean bags, pretending that an intense bubble of *something* isn't lingering in the air around us the entire night.

Chapter 33

There's a block of new texts on my phone when my alarm goes off on Thursday at six AM, reminding me to pack my toothbrush for the sixteenth time otherwise I'll forget like I always do on every road trip ever.

Squinting at the bright screen, I unlock my phone and pull up my messages. Every single text is from After's old number.

[After] 01:15: Hey Scott u awake?

[After] 01:18: I'm assuming if u were ud have answered me by now. Seeing as ur always attached to ur phone

[After] 01:23: no? no go? okay so it's like leaving a voicemail. A text voicemail

[After] 01:24: no, I'm not drunk, BTW. Haven't had anything since u stayed over. I can tell u the headaches have just now started to go away. So that's been fun. Longest sober run I've ever had. Huzzah that's fucked up. baby steps

[After] 01:26: not why I'm bothering u. Not that me texting my friend is a bother. Which we are, by the way. Friends. But I've been thinking, when u stayed over, what u told me about ur last night in Texas and ur box

[After] 01:29: I really hope this isn't the moment u wake up and go 'new phone, who dis?'. If u did I'd just go and launch myself off the 4th floor balcony into the trees

[After] 01:30: whatever here goes nothing fuck it

[After] 01:40: man I'm so sorry. I'm sorry Scotty. I didn't know u said goodbye, I'd honestly been holding onto that for awhile, I even dreamt about u that night, or I thought it was a dream, I remember u being there with me, but then I woke up the next morning and just saw that msg from u saying u were boarding ur plane to Cali. Then I sent u that horrible txt then regretted it but couldn't take it back and I hate, hate that it was the first thing u read the moment u landed

[After] 01:45: or maybe u didn't read it at all, and that's why u started talking to me so easily in February when I reached back out again and why u were the one to apologize for no fucking reason. I never said I was sorry for that txt. I still haven't

[After] 01:48: Scotty please I'm so sorry. I'm sorry I sent it to u and that I said those things. I didn't mean them at all, I swear I say things I don't mean cause I get scared and I don't know why. I mean I probably know why fuck

[After] 01:52: I should sleep. I've been up for 30 hrs straight with work and Erica over stupid gala night pictures. I guess someone had a camera inside the club and she's trying to pay ppl off to keep them from the press. Please don't look for them, Scotty. I'm asking a lot from u right now but please. Can we pretend the night ended with u finding me hiding by the closet, just like I knew u would? And it picked back up again when I saw u at Starbucks

[After] 01:55: always fucking Starbucks. I'll c u soon Scotty. Night

Alright, After. I'd like to pretend that you said all this to me in person. That you were brave and apologized for that text you sent me after Christmas, the year my life was spinning out of control.

I'd love to think you mean all of this, too. As much as I meant my apology to you. And that we can stop hurting each other over and over, and I can stop apologizing for things I didn't do just to hold onto our friendship. And you can stop saying heartfelt things via modern technology where I can't see your face or hear your voice.

None of that could possibly translate well in a text, and I don't want to share my feelings through black and white anymore.

Instead, because I can't help myself, and I'm grappling tight to After showing me his heart on his sleeve and praying it's sincere, I reply with the best cheek I can muster.

[Me] 06:14: New phone, who dis?
[After] 06:15: I hate u

―

After's in my Jethro hoodie. "Wanna hear my theory?"

I drop my second suitcase to the tile of his entry hall with a grunt and stretch my back. "What's your theory?"

"My theory is, I think you planned your semester schedule in January just for this trip."

"The hell you mean? We weren't talking in January."

"I mean you *sensed* that on *this* particular weekend in late April, you'd be going to Tennessee, and therefore would have the chance to visit Dollywood. A place you told me about when you were eight, by the way." He puts his hands in my Jethro hoodie pocket.

I smirk at his wagging brows. "Yes, you're entirely correct, I knew all this would happen." Boy, howdy, if I did, I'd have done a *whole* lotta shit differently. "Did you ever hear back from Erica about the publicity for the weekend?"

He pulls the hood (my hoodie, Jethro hoodie, FYI) over his ears and nods with a yawn. "Yeah, she said to make sure I'm in as many photos and posts and hoo-ha as possible. Show me doing my thang, getting back into acting—it's not like I left, I *just* finished a project two months ago—but she says shots of me being a good boy on my best behavior can only help me out."

"Best behavior meaning…?"

"No drinking, no shenanigans, no Jacob or bad company. If I'm in a club, it better be seltzer in my hand or nothing. But that won't be a problem," he grins. I grin back. "Think you packed enough?" he jabs, poking his boot toe toward my larger suitcase.

"One of these is full of dildos."

"Oh, well, at least you won't be bored."

"If something starts to vibrate on the drive over, it may be one, or all of them, going off at once. Tell me again why we're not taking your super snazzy private jet?"

He picks up both my suitcases without even a straining grunt and walks toward the garage with them. Did I mention he's just casually wearing my Jethro U hoodie?

Maybe I forgot to mention that I, in turn, am wearing his jean jacket with the sleeves rolled to my wrists. No big deal.

"Probably cause I don't have a super snazzy private jet?"

"Lies, your Bat Cave has everything." I don't bother to open the laundry room door for him until he looks back and squints at me.

"Harry left one of his trucks here back in December," he says, once he's through the door I'm holding open, while wearing his jean jacket—okay, I'll stop. "I said I'd drive it when I come visit for his show."

"So why am *I* being dragged along for this? Thirty hours in a car?"

"It's not thirty hours straight."

"Of course not, since neither are we."

"We're—" He snickers and sends me a nose-wrinkling grin. "Funny. There's a hotel stop or two in the middle."

"Will you be okay with a hotel room?"

"I'm fine since it's you."

My glee feels absurd and I fight to click back into teasing mode. "This is torture. I'd rather fly alone than get stuck in a car with you for thirty hours."

"I'm hurt, I thought you liked me?"

"More lies." He chuckles and drops one suitcase to open the cab of a truck sitting near the back of the cavern-sized garage. Dark blue Fsomethingorother-fifty. I have no clue. It's big and dumb with its lifted wheels and long bench front seat and looks like a fugly giant next to my, yes *my*, Ferrari.

"Did you get your homework all finished? I don't want you getting carsick trying to read on the way there."

I hoist up my second suitcase and shove it in behind the first, making sure there's room for Chicken. After's only got one bag, but it's a me-sized duffel, so he's not allowed to tease. "I don't get carsick."

"Now who's lying? Too bad we're not staying longer in Texas; we could've made time to visit Buc-ee's, gotten you some beaver nuggies—don't think we'll be close to the one that's in Tennessee." After goes and clicks a keypad on the wall, and the garage doors rattle open, letting in early morning light.

He turns, finding me scowling. "Don't ever say nuggies again."

His smile is Jokeresque. "*Nnnnnnnuggies.*"

"Stop that."

"No, but really—"

"I don't even *like* the beaver nuggets—"

"No, no, I meant like. Staying in Texas longer. Since we're leaving a day earlier than I'd planned, we can maybe think about stopping for a little bit. See your aunt Devon and Kendra? I bet they'd make time to see you."

I have exactly four seconds to not look like I've just sucked on a lemon coated in Sriracha and skunk. "Eh—uh—n…I mean. They're probably s-super busy with. Work." Don't even know what they do for work these days. Don't care.

"Damn, okay. That's too bad," he says.

I shine a smile and shrug. "Sure is, ain't it?" Okay, tone down the ho-hum, gosh diddly-darn attitude, Scott. I slouch and shrug again and it seems to do the trick, cause he nods and leads us back into the house.

In the kitchen, I send a mental thank you to Thangus when we find two Venti coffees hanging out on the counter for us. After's has a bushy-browed face with a scar drawn on it. Mine has a big ol' smiley face with little stars around it that I just know After is jealous of. I bet Thor drew these; I can see him being a secret artist.

"How did you worm your way out of your class today?" After asks, stealing a sip of my coffee. "Don't get me wrong, I'm glad we're able to leave a day early."

I take my coffee back just to hold onto something, still reeling from the reminder that we'll be in the same city as my aunt and her wife for...well, hopefully no longer than the time it takes us to pass through El Paso. Unless we stop at the Whataburger there. I'll take that chance.

"I didn't worm out of anything. Mr. Kastle loves me and gave me a free pass since I made a bomb ass queso plate with a bowl attached in the center. I'm a pottery god."

"Alright there, Swayze."

"Where's my son, where's Chicken?"

"Say his name louder, he'll come running."

I gulp in air and After laughs before I've even shrieked it into the house. The 'n' is still echoing when there's a collision of four clumsy paws thundering around the floors above us, then down three sets of stairs, and I'm kneeling with my arms open by the time Chicken speeds toward me like a slobbering bullet.

Chapter 34

We're on the road twenty minutes later, barely beating the rush hour of people going off to work this morning. Chicken's got his head in between us for the first hour of the drive until we stop for donuts, then he's attempting to get into my lap as he goes for my sausage and jalapeno croissants.

The moment we hit open highway, we queue up After's road trip playlist. It starts with a blast of R.E.M. and It's The End of The World. Neither of us knew the speedy lyrics when we were younger, and we don't know them now. Most of our jumbled, laugh-singing ends in us screaming out in frustration and high-fiving when we make it to the chorus at the same time.

It's no surprise to anyone that, six hours in, we're ready to kill each other.

How we ever thought we could be roommates is beyond me.

I'll start small: After's gas is toxic. He eats the same things I do, drinks the same things, but something horrific goes on in his gut that makes whatever's cookin' in there ten thousand times worse.

When it's my turn to drive, I do so with my window down, even as he's shouting at me to roll it up cause it's too loud. I just shriek at him that I refuse to be trapped in a sealed, metal box with that stench, not until he stops smelling like something died, got resurrected, ate a raccoon with halitosis, then died again.

Then it's an argument over who gets to steer and who has to navigate the bulk of the trip.

We both want to drive as long as it means the driver picks the music, and both of us are shit at reading maps, too, so it's a never-ending cycle of paper-scissors-rock and a fight over the aux cord. We compromise on a mutual love for Violent Femmes and Josh Ritter, but the next time he plays Wagon Wheel, I'm choking him with said aux cord.

Next is Chicken.

I adore this dog. He's a delight, an angel. He also is the only one of the three of us who has to pee every couple hours or less. He has the bladder of…I dunno. A very, very small mammal.

By hour nine, I'm losing my mind, and After is either laughing at me out of spite, or he's kicked into his nervous reflex. The reflex is, coincidentally, also laughter. (Made for some interesting arguments in the past, I can assure you.) Seeing me on the edge of explosion when we're in the middle of the desert with no witnesses would make *anyone* nervous.

"Dude, you keep doing that, your face is gonna get stuck," he chuckles, standing on the side of the road with Chicken while I hold my hands to my temples and pull my eyes tight in an attempt to get rid of a building headache.

"It can only be an improvement to my looks, I'm sure," I grunt in reply. Chicken comes prancing over to me, back feet kicking up dirt. "You ready, babe? Wanna drive another ten minutes before ya gotta tinkle?"

"Don't do that," says After, coming back to the truck to join us.

"Do what, say tinkle? You have your nuggies, I get to say tinkle."

"No—don't call him 'babe'."

"Why not? Does he prefer lover boy? Honeybunch? Shnookums?" After rolls his eyes and opens the back cab door for Chicken to hop in. "What about handsome, incredible, best pupper ever?" I coo, fluffing up his face and big ears, getting a wet kiss on my own ear in response.

"Just don't—don't do the baby names. It's weird."

"They're not *baby* names, they're endearing pet names—he's literally a *pet*. With a *name*."

After snorts and opens the door for me next. "Thanks, *babe*," I grin, grabbing the oh-shit handle to hoist myself in. He stomps around the front of the truck and flops in, crossing his arms. His fingers tap along his bicep before he starts up the truck.

It's another thirty minutes before he says anything else to me. "I don't. Mind it."

"Mind what?" I ask, looking up from my phone. (And yes, getting a little carsick.) Post I made about the road trip this morning has already blown up to new levels; even Greta's reposted it. (Sorry, I suppose I have Morpheus, king of her social medias, to thank for that.)

"The names."

"For Chicken?"

"For me." After sends me a fast look. "In public. We did it on your post before you stayed the night, got lots of attention. So. In public."

"Public. Right."

Wonder if he'd mind me trying one or two or thirty out on him in the meantime. I won't push it. Might push Chicken out of the truck, though, cause he's already whining and needing to potty again.

———

I'm nearly dozing when After pokes me in the face. "Wake me up when we hit Dollywood," I yawn, stealing his hand and wrapping my arm around his wrist so he doesn't jab me in the cheek again.

He laughs and it's fluttery and light and makes me smile. "Dude, look where we are, look at the oasis I've brought you to."

I stretch and squint out his window. Hallelujah. Angels singing. The great. Big. Orange. W.

"Oh, my heavens," I sigh, leaning far over the folded down armrest to put my chin on his shoulder. "You are a godsend."

"You're welcome, be blessed."

I grin at him when he tilts his head toward mine. "Thanks sweetie."

After squeezes an eye shut and scrunches his nose. "Eh, no. Try again."

"What about cutie?"

"Ain't feelin' it."

"Hm…honey?"

He smirks and turns us toward Whataburger nirvana as the light flashes a yield green. "Sure. I like that one."

They let us bring Chicken inside since it's just us this late on a Thursday night in a smallish town. After keeps checking his phone, but I hardly care cause I've eaten a kids grilled cheese, a grilled chicken barbecue sandwich, and I'm on my second container of fries.

"I think I'm gonna pull a Chick and go to the bathroom again," he sighs, getting up with his phone.

"Do what you must, leave me here forever, I'll be fine," I reply with a lazy hand wave, taking another sip of vanilla shake. He smiles and pats me on the shoulder, wandering off toward the restrooms, and I feed Chicken half a chicken strip. "Your namesake, son, enjoy," I smirk, scratching him between the ears.

After gets back a minute later, maybe ten minutes later, I have no concept of time, lost in southern fast-food bliss. He shakes his head at the now three empty fry boxes. "Did you get *more*?"

"Guilty. Sherry—little lady behind the register—she somehow remembered me from high school, when I'd bring Bevvy here to do homework. She said if I keep eating like this, she won't have anything to worry about tonight with closing, so she's happy to keep feeding me. I told her it was only seven PM and I've got your credit card, line that shit up. She laughed."

"You're not gonna fit in any of the clothes you packed," he chuckles, crossing his arms on the table. His eyes dart over my head. "You'll have to buy new pants."

"Which means I'll have to buy a new suitcase cause my awesome new wardrobe won't fit in my other two, oh noooo," I pretend to sob, making him laugh again as I grin.

"Is this seat taken?"

I look up, still grinning, and I freeze. My smile's stuck on my face. It's not for her, though. It's never gonna be for her ever again.

Devon smiles at me. Sharp nose like mine, blue eyes like Mitch and Mom, blonde hair pulled in a braid over her shoulder. Aunt Devon. With Kendra right behind. She's cut her hair like Farrah Fawcett, even though that was way, way before Kendra's time.

I turn to stare at After, in case this is an illusion and I'm losing my mind. He beams and wiggles happy jazz hands. "Surprise! Family reunion!"

I'm gonna hurl vanilla milkshake.

Chapter 35

Devon makes like she's going to sit by me, but I jump up and stumble, fast food slushing in my gut and ready to explode. She mistakes me getting to my feet as an invitation to hug me. She smells like desert and Japanese Cherry Blossom from Bath & Bodyworks. It does nothing to mask the marijuana clinging to her tank top, hidden in the strands of her braid shoved into my face.

It's only been four years since I've seen them, but some madness in my brain told me they should look older, more mature now, not the party-girls I knew them to be when I was trying to raise my little sister on my own. Devon's in Daisy Dukes. Kendra's in overalls that make her look closer to my age than thirty-two.

"So good to see you, babies! Shit, it's been too long!" Devon laughs, stepping away and putting her hands on my face. I'm sinking, pulled into a hug from Kendra next. I hold my breath.

Chicken's up and excitedly making friends, and After's standing and smiling and getting hugs, too. I'm the only one cracking inside.

He sits back down, and I go to sit on his side of the booth too aggressively and too fast, slamming my hip into his. The truck keys in his pocket jab into my thigh, and I scoot an inch away from him to keep him from noticing that I'm vibrating off the plastic seat.

Devon and Kendra sit across from us; they descend on our food, even as Kendra sets down their own plastic orange number for when their meals are ready.

"How y'all been? How's the drive—what time did y'all leave LA?" Devon asks, taking a handful of fries.

"We left later than intended, but it's fine, been switching off and on," After answers, crossing his elbows on the table and nodding his head to me.

"Oh, fuck, hope you're the one driving the most—this one here would get himself lost going to Walgreens down the road," Kendra snorts, winking at me. Why? I share no humor with you, woman.

"No, it's been good," After says. My jaw is popping from grating my teeth repeatedly, chewing at nothing. If I'm not careful, I'm gonna bite off my own tongue. "This one here—" he reaches under the table, and Chicken's thick tail thwaps against my shin—"he's the one we have to keep stopping for."

Devon laughs and peeks under the table, too. She comes back up with an arched brow and a smirk. "So…I gotta ask." You really don't, please don't. "We follow you on Instagram, Davy—hate that we can never find *your* page, Scott; not sure what that's about—but we saw those pictures of y'all at the gala and JU—"

"Saw your livestream," Kendra adds, going straight for my shake. My hands remain in my lap, fists tight to keep from clawing at my knuckles. "It was so good to hear your voice again, Scotty!"

"Then David texted us a few hours ago when y'all stopped for gas," Devon continues with a nod, "said it wasn't part of the plan, but would we wanna meet for dinner, and we said—"

"Yes, of course!" she sings along with Kendra. After chuckles and shifts his body in the booth. When his knee taps mine, I wonder if he can tell how much I'm shaking. He sends me an unreadable look, so maybe.

"Anyway—we wondered about all the photos and shit. But it looks like y'all are actually a couple now, huh? Legit?" Devon smiles, twirling her silver wedding band around.

"Legit, legit," After echoes. "We're going to Spain for my birthday next month—"

"Oh, fuck! Birthday—your birthday, Scotty!" Kendra gasps, hands flying to her face. "Oh, baby, we totally forgot."

"It's next month," Devon frowns. Kendra smacks her on the arm. "Isn't it? In May?"

"Mine's in May," After laughs. "His was April third."

I haven't said a word to either of them this entire time. Just, y'know, as a reminder. Don't have shit to say to them.

"April third, oh damn, how did we forget," Devon groans, rubbing her face with her elbows on the table. "I should remember that…that day. That time of the year a little better. I'm sorry, sugar."

See, here, I get where After was coming from. Right now I despise pet names. "It's fine," I croak. I want my milkshake. It's sitting in front of Kendra. "We had the gala that day anyway. Was a big uh. Celebration. Was fun."

After's thigh presses to mine. Now I know he feels me shaking, cause my knee is going haywire.

Kendra puffs air through her lips; her smile is tight and sends lines up to her eyes from too much sun and not enough sunscreen. "Well, happy birthday! Belated!"

"You got a good gift anyway, I feel less bad," Devon snorts.

"What gift?" After asks.

Kendra and Devon share a look and snicker. "I mean, hel-looooo," Kendra chuckles, gesturing a hand at him. "He only talked about you nonstop the entire time he was with us."

I try to cut in and it comes out a gasp. "Guys—"

"Does this finally mean you're done playing whatever the fuck you were?" Devon asks. Her foot taps my boot toe and I shrink my long legs back as far away from her as possible.

"What does—playing what—what does that mean?" I stutter.

"Your whole uh…shit, what did he call it?" Devon mutters to Kendra, scratching under her nose.

"Sexually…sexually fluid?" Kendra offers. My heart sinks.

"I wasn't playing abrosexual. I *am* abrosexual."

Devon rolls her eyes. "The fuck you are. What even is that, what does sexually fluid even mean, Scott? It sounds like a sex term—like—"

"Like fluids," Kendra chuckles. "Are you fluidly active? Sexually?"

"Are you *moistly* gay?" Devon chimes in.

"Oh, my God, like *mostly*, cause he's—"

"—He's not straight! I didn't even mean to do that!"

Devon laughs. Kendra laughs.

I don't. After's hand comes around my fist under the table. He doesn't laugh either.

"Y'all this isn't…it's not a joke, guys." I swallow and try to clear my throat. After offers me his peach tea.

"How can we *not* joke about it?" Kendra says with a shake of her stupid fluffed hair. "See, this, you and David, you're both gay. This is easy. You're making it difficult on purpose."

"I'm not, and I'm *not* gay. I'm just me, I'm just trying to love the way that makes sense to me."

"Well, your way of love doesn't exist, Scott," Devon scoffs. She kicks her leg up over her knee and hits me in the shin. "You can't live like that and expect to be loved the way you want."

"Yes I can, how dare you," I snap, gripping tight to After's hand. His thumb runs circles around my knuckles. "I'm not just gay, I've never been just gay—would you care if I was bi? Or pansexual?"

"Obviously, cause it's the same thing as your sexy fluid shit."

"It's *not* the same."

"It's either, or," Kendra frowns. "If you're gay and fucking around with a girl, then it doesn't make you some sort of magical in between."

Devon sits back and puts an arm across the bench behind Kendra's shoulders. "Why can't you just be like everyone else? Why are you wanting to be something that's different and isn't even real?"

Orange and white cuts across my peripheral, spiraling in on me in this mad house. It's just barbecue sauce and root beer and prejudice invading my senses, and I keep getting whiffs of weed radiating off them.

It's like I never left their home with the yellow shag carpet and the green and brown striped sofas always covered in bodies of their drunk friends. After all these years, the arguments we used to have that ended in us shouting and slamming doors—I've grown. I've changed—progressed. I thought they might have gotten better, too. I thought they'd get it.

I know it's not as old a term as gay or lesbian or bisexual even, but I mean it's the 21st century. If I can't be safe in LGBT, where the hell am I supposed to go?

"Y'all…I don't understand why you won't accept that this is what I am. It's always been me; I've never been set on one thing."

Devon sneers at me, and if I could knock this booth seat over and run, I would.

What did you do to Gabriel? she screamed at me, eighteen and shaking and hunched over, half-naked on their living room floor. Kendra had started to clean the cuts left behind from the handcuffs, until I told them what happened. Then they both stood over me, shouting, towel meant to warm me still held in Devon's fist.

What did you fuck up this time? You've ruined this. You're ruined.

"Of course not," she steams with a face that looks like her father's. "You, Scott Everett, get to put yourself in a *separate* circle that gives you all *sorts* of permissions. You're scared of commitment and that's why you think you get to change your mind whenever you want. That's unfaithful. You're not special, Scott, you don't get to make your own rules. You're gay or you're not."

"I'm *not always*—"

"Then you're straight!" Kendra yells, "and you're leading on poor David all over again!"

"Hey y'all," After says, raising a single hand.

Kendra and Devon are instant eyes on him. You could charge a lightbulb with the sudden electricity forming between the three of them. "I'm sorry to cut this short. We um…y'all, I think they called your number for food. And um. We gotta get going," he smiles.

"Right." Devon blinks fast and looks back to me. "Right…"

Kendra sinks in her seat, all taste for argument lost. There's a soft clearing of a throat at the register, and Sherry's tiny voice speaks up. "Ladies? Number fourteen?"

Devon slides out first, looking down at me as Kendra goes to get their food. I don't meet her eye. "We'll talk later, right? I think we should talk about this. We're just trying to help. We want y'all's relationship to last, baby. It won't last if you fight who you are."

I don't hug her when I stand, and I don't wait for Kendra to come back. I gather up our trash one-handed, my fingers still locked in After's, and we take the plastic trays to the bins.

And as much as I'm trying to be fast and walk strong and stand firm, he's the one leading us out the door. Pulling me to safety with Chicken guarding my other side.

After opens the passenger door for me, waits for me to get my legs in, to buckle up. His hand goes to my knee. His eyes go to mine.

I can feel it bubbling, can practically see the apology rising up his throat. I have to look away from him, and I reach for the door and force him to take a step back. "Don't, After. Let's just keep going."

Chapter 36

Vance Joy is blaring. And you know you got a headache if the soothing, chill voice of Vance sounds like it's blaring. "Can you...can you turn it down a bit?"

After's hand slaps at the radio in a rush to knock the volume lower. "Sorry."

"It's fine."

"Sorry, Scotty—"

"Jesus, After, please. It's all fine, all of it. I'm fine."

He echoes my 'fine' under his breath. "It's not uh. Not too late, for me to go up three-seventy-five, hit up sixty-two."

"Why would you do that, that takes us northeast," I sniff, rubbing fingers into my temple.

"Toward Lubbock, Scotty. If you wanted to, I dunno. Visit Flemings Park."

My heart can't take this. I sit on my hands to keep from clawing at my seatbelt and unlocking the door so I can launch myself into the desert. "No."

"I mean, I really don't mind; Harry and Nicholas can wait, if you wanted to see where y'all spread their—"

"I'm good man, thanks."

He whispers my 'good' softer than he said my 'fine'. "Scotty. Please...talk to me." I'm seconds away from shrinking into myself and shooting off into all directions.

"If there was. Anyone. Any place. I'd want to visit," I start, sentences shaky as it's taking every effort to not scream at him. "Then it would be Mom."

"We can totally do that, it's not too far off the trip—"

"But I don't know where she's buried, After."

He looks at me for a dangerously long time for someone who should be paying attention to the road. "Devon didn't tell you?"

"No. Even though I asked and asked." I refuse to unscrew the bottle, but I let a little leak out, staring out at the passing landscape of dark purple and sepia. Flat and endless and dead.

"I scoured findagrave.com for hours when I was younger. I did it every year on the day she died in March, right before my birthday." Because I was destined to lose my loved ones days around my wretched birthday.

"Never found her under her name, her married name, her middle name instead of her first, her birthday. I bet the records were somewhere in the house before all that got swept up and sold. But Mitch never talked about her. Doesn't have a single photo of her in the house. And Devon only talked about Mom on special occasions. When she wanted something. As soon as I learned that, I stopped asking about Mom."

"What about Tyler? Didn't y'all visit her?"

"Maybe we did at one point, when I was little. Dad didn't talk about her that much after he met Cassidy. Last day we talked about her was the day he told me he'd be asking Cassidy to marry him. Last thing he said was. Was…"

It was by a fireplace. I was in Christmas themed flannel pajamas. I don't even know if it was Christmas. Dad smelt like his cologne and coffee. I didn't ask any questions as we talked about Cassidy then Mom. I don't even know if I got the chance to ask questions.

My face stings, itches. I want to peel it off. "I dunno, man. No damn clue. I was nine. No clue." After takes a breath, and I talk over him again before he can say anything, especially if it's another apology.

"Please don't bury me. In a month, in ten years, in a hundred. If you're alive and I'm not, don't let anyone put me in the ground. I don't wanna be a stone that grows moldy and cold, with dying flowers and an inscription that gets filled up with moss. I don't want to make my remaining loved ones have to visit a slab of concrete to keep it clean."

Maybe that was too intense for a road trip with friends who are still getting to know each other again. I don't care. After speaks up an hour later, passing through Odessa as I'm fading off into a tense sleep. "Where do you want your ashes spread, Scotty?"

Silly Scott would say something like, chuck me across the parking lot of a Whataburger, or turn me into moth balls so I can destroy Mitch's nice winter coats.

I'm not up for silly right now. So I don't answer.

—

By the time my eyes open, the sky is still a dark indigo, but sparse light is coming from the east ahead of us. Orange illuminates everything in the truck, and After's tan face and white shirt are in flames. He sees I'm awake and sends me a small smile.

"Hi. Stopped to get gas about four hours ago—you slept right through it."

"How long have you been driving? It's…" I deliriously squint at the time on the console, then out the windshield, "is that the fucking *sunrise*?"

"Yeah and like uh…eight. Hours—"

"Seriously? Why didn't you wake me up, I could've driven."

"Don't worry about it. I grabbed you a Milky Way, Midnight, of course," he says, reaching for a bag by my knee.

He presents me a candy bar, and as soon as I take it, he hands me a second one. Then a third. I crack a smile, and I chuckle when he gestures to a second bag on the floor by my feet. Chocolate milk, 20 oz. Who sells chocolate milk this size? I'm a child, appeased solely by chocolate, it seems.

"Dang, eight hours all night. I didn't think I was that tired. Where are we?" I ask, opening a candy bar.

"Just passed through Emmet, Arkansas—I'm sure it's no surprise that it took all night just to drive through Texas."

"Not surprised," I mumble around Milky Way. I hold the bar up to him, and he accepts a bite without taking his eyes off the road. "You need a pee break? Want to switch?"

I crane my cramped neck and turn around in my seat to check on Chicken, snoozing across the cab. "What about you, darling?" I whisper. His tail thumps once, eyes still closed.

After shakes his head and waves a hand at me. "Nah, I like driving. And he was actually really good during the night." He chugs a gulp of Monster, silver can. Don't even know what flavor that is. "Plus, as long as I'm driving, I'm picking the music," he winks, changing to the next song and cranking the volume up a click now that I'm awake.

Springsteen by Eric Church comes over the radio. I'd know those opening piano notes anywhere. I look over at After, already singing along. He grins at me, one hand on the wheel, the other tapping the rhythm out on his knee.

I *hate* this song.

It brings too many things back. Who knows how many times he's played it while I was passed out. He looped it every day when it first came out in 2011; wore the disc out on his dad's Sony CD player, carried in his backpack when we'd wander to the grocery store to get Eggos and Red Bulls.

We walked close just to keep from yanking the ear bud cord away from each other. Sometimes his fingers would brush mine. I'd move my hands into my pockets whenever that happened.

After's singing gets louder. There's a touch of vibrato to his voice. It's not perfect, not even on key probably. But it's him. I can feel how much he's trying not to look at me now. I'm still so out of it that I can't tell the difference between dreaming and current events and memories.

We were seventeen when I last heard this song, or at least when I last paid attention to it. In the silence, in his room at the end of spring break. The first almost. No hands on faces, no kissing.

Was the rule he came up with. I remember that I didn't understand the need for the rule. I liked him. I thought he liked me. But I'd do anything he wanted, just to keep him around. His mom knocked on the door and startled us apart, letting us know my dad was there to pick me up after staying the night.

After that, there was his old Jeep, trapped in a parking lot in late March rain. Where we almost, almost. I'd ended up in his lap that time. Wasn't anything more than friction and heavy breathing and fogged up windows, his slick forehead pressed to mine. Long as we didn't kiss, we could chalk it up to just being guys. Friends did this all the time. We told ourselves they did. Cop came prowling into the parking lot of the school we took shelter in, and we drove off before either of us could finish that almost.

Then, his back against the elm tree in my backyard after a regular Monday night family dinner. Where we almost, almost, almost, then he did. His cheek hot against mine. But no kissing, no lips on him no matter how badly I wanted that, no hands on necks or faces. Just fingers gripping hips, palm seeking him outside his jeans, until I said screw it and dove into the waistband of his boxers. Pressure, heat. Fast and sticky when his whispering turned to muffled moaning. He bit my shoulder when he came.

He ran out of my yard without looking back, even as I begged him to stay, cause the porch lights came on and Dad appeared in the back yard, confused as to why I was standing outside alone at midnight.

A week later on my eighteenth birthday, I went over to After's house after dinner, with my heart in my throat leaping into my hands. Hands that's still tingled from touching him days before. We hadn't really seen each other recently at school, he kept skipping lunch—I assumed he was busy with the spring musical. I didn't mind. I was happy to go find him. Meet him in the middle, or. Leave my safety net and meet him entirely on his side.

Found his mom's car still gone and thought, no one can stop us this time.

Found him in his backyard with Missy Davis in his lap.

He had no problem kissing her, putting hands on her face. He never saw me watching them fuck on the bench by the fence. Never saw me leave.

Never sent me a 'happy birthday' text either. Last text I had from him around that time was him begging me to call him the night he heard my parents had died. I didn't call him until the day before the funeral, and we didn't talk about those almosts.

So I doubt he thought about any of it. I hadn't.

I'd forced myself not to think about it.

Cause I broke it like a fledgling in my fist. Ripped it apart and left it to bleed on the ground the day I tore his heart out, all the way in California, where I couldn't see his beautiful tears in person.

I'm crying now. My head throbs, and Devon and Kendra's sick words play like a loop in my brain as I wake up more.

That's unfaithful.

Why are you wanting to be someone different?

Your way of love doesn't exist.

You're not special.

The music turns down, or off, I can't tell. Long fingers reach for my fist coiled tight on my knee. After's thumb strokes circles on my knuckles until my hand loosens. Then he takes it, pulls it back to his side. His thigh is warm through his jeans.

"We'll need to stop somewhere for a nap I think," he whispers, so soft, like he thinks he might shatter me if he's too loud. He doesn't mention my tears.

"I can drive if you're tired," I reply. My throat is sore. I sound like I've been screaming.

After shakes his head and sends me a long look on the open road before staring forward again. "I want you to rest, for real, not in a car. You deserve something peaceful. I'll get you someplace safe."

Too much. I can't tell him I'd be fine bunking in the bed of this truck, out in the middle of a wide field and wider sky. Sleep with our heads on his duffel and Chicken in between, puppy piled together under an arched ceiling full of fading stars as the sun rises.

All I can do is curl forward with a long, cracking groan, my arm bent at an awkward angle from my fingers still in his. First attempt at breathing makes me cough. My second has me choking on tears. We lurch to the side of the road and stop moving immediately, and Chicken's whine of distress in the backseat sends my hysteria into hyperdrive.

After lifts the armrest up from between us, unbuckles us both, and pulls me across the bench seat. In seconds, my forehead is against his neck, and I'm releasing body-wracking sobs into his collarbone.

After's arms are strong around me, and he holds me with care. Aftercare. Isn't that a sex term? For BDSM maybe. Why do I know that? Why am I thinking that?

Why am I thinking that my life would be so much easier if I stayed here, in the middle of nowhere, Arkansas? Away from everyone who's ever promised me safety and security just to rip it from my hands when I can't be who they want.

All but After. He'd be allowed to stay in my scraggly, desolate country hut. As long as he runs his fingers through my hair like this. Doesn't feel the need to say anything, just like this.

Chapter 37

It ended with the hug.

We got to a motel a couple hours later; all they had was a room with two twin beds. "People will think we're fighting if they find out," After had laughed. I tried to smile, but it didn't register on my face. And we slept separately.

I mean, I don't know why I thought we'd do that differently. In private we don't snuggle, he doesn't hold me, we don't walk with his arm around my shoulders and mine behind his waist. Except for when we do.

We get to Nashville by five-ish on Friday. The second I park us outside a small house with a vast acreage and what looks like a shed with a couple donkeys, After lets out a large sigh. I start to think we should've stayed in that little motel room a bit longer, let him sleep for a couple more hours.

"You gonna be okay?" I ask.

He snorts and squints at me. "Are you?"

"Eh, jury's out."

"Been out for, like, twelve years."

"Sounds right."

After nods and looks to the windshield, and as tired as he seems, he starts to smile. A large dude with carrot-colored short hair struts toward us down the gravel drive, through the wooden post gate, doing a silly walk as he goes.

He pauses, mimes that he's got a fishing line, that he's baiting it, and he tosses it, reeling us in. After snickers, and neither of us move.

The guy looks put out, pretends to dig his heels in, and gives a yank. "Nicholas," After says with a chuckle as the man shouts, words muffled. Though it sounds something like 'get yer ass over here'.

Another dude that's a straight up carbon copy of the first guy if you made him four inches taller jogs out from around the back of the house. He grabs the imaginary fishing rod and starts to pull, too. I recognize this guy's crooked grin from his Instagram. "And Harry," After adds.

"I guessed that," I laugh, getting out first.

"I got one, I got one!" the shorter (still gigantic) one screams. "Harry, brother, you owe me a fifty! C'mon over here, catch of the day, pose with me," he laughs, deep and bellowing, looking like a freckly teddy bear. He drops a thick arm around my neck and we both grin for his brother Harry to take our photo. "I'm Nicholas," he says, presenting his paw.

"Hi, Scott Everett—"

"Scott! The Scott Everett *Bossss*coe!" Harry laughs, squeezing the life out of poor After as soon as he's out of the truck. Harry darts for me next, and I'm expecting a handshake, but I'm glad I get a squishy hug instead. "So good to meet you in person!"

"You too, Harry, nice to see you—don't forget prodigal son, Chicken," I add as Chicken trots over like he's the true star of the show. He's in heaven; getting ear scratches from hands all over, tongue lolling.

Harry grins all lopsided and pats a hard hand on my shoulder. "Y'all are just in time, Momma's finished cooking the biscuits and gravy!"

"Of course there's biscuits and gravy," I smirk. "Are our bags okay in the truck?"

"Ain't no one here gonna steal from you," Nicholas nods sagely.

"I've got my laptop; I don't want it to overheat—" But then there's After at my side with my backpack already looped over his shoulder.

"Got you covered, babe," he smiles. Oh. Oh, we're just—okay, yeah, back in action.

"T-thanks," I mutter. His arm around my shoulders directs me along behind big red one and two, Chicken leading the parade into the house.

—

The spectacular momma of Harry and Nicholas is named Rosamine, and she's the personification of a strawberry if you made it swear like a sailor and gave it a smoker's laugh. I started giggling five minutes in, thinking of a particular episode of SpongeBob I watched as a kid, where every bad word was replaced by a dolphin noise. If you did that to her, she'd sound like SeaWorld on steroids.

I'm near tears when she breaks out the Bluebell and fresh brownies. (Both cause I'm holding in laughter like a painful fart, and it's blessed Bluebell, that goes unsaid.) "Now y'all (dolphin squawk) better not even (dolphin chirp) be thinkin' 'bout (dolphins) cause I just (more dolphins) and I'd be (dolphins screaming until she takes a breath again)."

"Yes, Momma," Harry and Nicholas reply in unison, digging into the dessert and shoveling it onto our plates.

"So when y'all wanna get me started on the episode?" After asks, declining a massive scoop of ice cream. He takes bites of mine instead.

That country drawl of his makes me smirk around my food; the longer the both of us are around other southerners, the more our accents are starting to come out. By the end of the weekend, you'll catch us spouting 'yeehaw' and 'y'all have a good 'un'.

"Tomorrow, bright and early," says Harry.

"Got a friend coming in to help out on set, he might be here soon if he gets a rental in time," Nicholas adds, going for his Corona. Harry looks at his brother, and an odd expression passes over the twins' faces.

I glance at After to see if he noticed; the way he's got his soda paused at his lip with a frown of confusion says he saw it, too.

Nicholas clears his throat and rolls large shoulders, ignoring Harry who's still staring at him. "Anyway. Tonight we'll go over a few things, show y'all to your hotel. Might go out dancing first if y'all wanna tag along and ain't too tired."

"Not too tired," I shrug. "What kinda dancing?"

"Line dancing, lil honky-tonk downtown," Harry answers, boot heel tapping to the floor. "Though the last time we went there, they played oldies for three hours straight so…there's always the other option, I guess."

"What's the other option?" After asks once he's taken another bite of my ice cream.

Nicholas grins. "We'll talk outside," he chuckles as Momma Rosamine comes back over with another round of root beers.

"Hey, babe…"

"Your boy's out fucking cold."

"It was the gravy."

"What'd you put in there, chloroform?"

"Gives it flavor."

"Momma's special recipe."

"Your momma's a fucking assassin—" The truck bed shakes, and I'm jolted alert at the sudden appearance of After on his hands over me.

"Whomst?" I grunt. He laughs, and Harry and Nicholas chuckle on the outside of the truck.

"You just passed the fuck out, man, we were only talking for an hour," After smiles. He puts a hand to my cheek. "Love that you were the one talking shit about not being 'too tired'."

"Blame Chicken," I grumble, stretching my arms above my head. He smirks and looks to Chicken, curled up tight to my ribs, playing little spoon.

"You wanna go dancing?" After whispers. I can still hear Harry and Nicholas talking nearby. My eyes keep darting to where they are outside the truck. And After's so damn close.

"Yeah. Um. Yeah, let's…we can go dancing—you wanna go dancing? H-honey?"

After laughs and sits on his heels as I lean on my elbow. "Don't force it, Scotty. And yeah, I'd love to—"

"Hey, hey, hey!" Nicholas shouts. *"Now* the party's here! Just in time, too!"

I glance over the lip of the truck at a car pulling in, blinded by the headlights. "Who is it?" I yawn, letting After help me stand in the bed. I lean too much on him, but he doesn't seem to mind. In fact, startingly, he crushes me like a lifejacket. "After—"

"Hiya boys," chuckles Jacob, closing his Tesla car door. He walks over to us with a bright smile, back lit by the Tennessee sun. "Nick, I heard you shout 'party' from inside my rental. Where are we going?"

Chapter 38

Well, this is a setback.

After and all his acting glory oh, so smoothly asked Harry what the ever-loving fuck Jacob was doing here. Apparently Nicholas invited him; said the two were talking and screwing around every once in a while the last couple of months.

I could see the mental math playing across After's face, as he tried to figure out if Jacob and Nicholas were fucking the night of the gala, when Jacob took After home (they were indeed fooling in a bed and breakfast three days prior in Dallas) or the night of the college party. (Not shockingly, Jacob and Nicholas were going at it just the week before in Malibu. Oh, and the week after.)

Nicholas, who had no clue, or knows and doesn't care, wanted to invite Jacob to chill and help out on set since he'd be in the area. Who the hell is 'in the area' in Nashville? Besides everyone who lives in Nashville, I mean. I smell a set up. Or a hookup. And I don't like either.

But After. Maaaan, is he *good*. Too good; he's all smiles and flirtatious winks, letting Jacob stand close and lean on him, like I, hello, fake boyfriend, am not even here. (Surprised Nicholas wasn't knocking out After and/or Jacob the first time Jacob kissed After's cheek like it was no biggie. That made me cringe. And After's grin made me cringe *and* want to knock him out.)

We're waiting to go into the dance hall after an awkward carpool into town. It started to sprinkle the moment we parked, and now that we've been in line for over thirty minutes, it's gotten heavier off and on.

Guys in the back don't seem to care that they're getting drenched through their Wrangler button-ups, but I can't stop shivering. No one seems to notice the cold shoulder I'm getting now but Harry.

A light nudge of his tree arm sends me tripping sideways. "You uh…you good, Scott?" Harry asks, flicking the brim of his trucker hat up.

"Yeah, fine, why?" I ask, pretending to inspect the Edison lights strung overhead. Every time the doors of the club open, there's a rush of yelling and thumping music, and it resets my heart rate to go higher and higher.

"I mean…" Harry scratches at orange stubble and glances behind us to where Jacob, Nicholas and After are all talking with their heads bent. Cigarette smoke puffs out from one or all three of them; I can already smell it clinging to the wet air. "There's a ton of history brewing over there."

"I'm sure. History tends to stay in the past though, doesn't it?" I lie through my teeth, digging my boot toe into the concrete.

"Right. Tends to." I check Harry while he's looking away.

But then he catches me and sends me a big smile that has me smiling and relaxing a bit. I mean if anything, he's been nice since I met him online, and he seems just the same in person. (What a relief, right? Someone's exactly who they claim to be when you meet them face to face? Unheard of.) I can see us talking and hanging out if the other three want to be stupid all night.

"Doesn't matter to me, cause at least I got you. You DD'd, and I don't drink. We can laugh at the dumbasses together."

He doesn't hide a blush very well. I know Nicholas is bi, but I'm wondering if Harry might not be straight. Didn't mean it as a come on, but he chuckles and dips his head so his hat shadows the flush blooming around eyes. "Yeah that would uh. Sure. We can have fun…"

The rain picks up, and as I'm unrolling the sleeves of my Henley, he takes his hat off, securing it on my head. He's got hat hair, and it curls over his ears, making him look both twenty-five and fifteen at the same time. "I like your little wisps," I laugh, poking at the fluffs by his temples. He grimaces and tries to run fingers through his hair, but it only makes it worse.

Then there's a hand on my back, pushing me forward. "Our turn," After says, sharp in my ear, coming right between me and Harry.

I stumble and surge back against his hand, tossing a hard elbow at him with a glare. "The hell was that?" I shout as soon as we're inside after showing our IDs. He doesn't look at me, instead pulling me with a grip around my wrist to the side and out of the way as we wait for the others.

"Nothing, y'all weren't moving, and it was our turn," he replies, looking over my head at nothing.

"You're full of it—"

"Am not—"

"For the love of—" I grab his hand and snake us through the crowd toward the bathrooms where it's quieter. "You've been on edge since Jacob showed up—is that what this is? You're all crabby? Just ignore him."

He puffs up just to sputter. "I can't ignore him, he's—he's all over me! Even in front of Nicholas—"

"Yeah, I saw, and I don't see you telling him to back off, either," I cut in. "I was having a nice conversation with Harry—"

"You were having a *close* conversation," he scoffs at me. There's smoke on his breath, clouding right around my face. Oh honey, hell no, we ain't playing games anymore.

"You are *not* gonna turn this around on me. I get to have friends, dude, and to everyone else, it just looked like Harry and I were talking; you're the only one being weird about it. Meanwhile, you and Jacob are obvious as hell. If someone sees you making out with him in the middle of a bar, while I'm just twenty feet away, you're fucked. After everything Erica's supposedly doing to keep those gala pics on the downlow? You're gonna get what you want, you'll be gay all over magazines, but it will *not* look good, dude. It won't be received the way I think you want it to be."

His eyebrows knit so tight they become one angry caterpillar across his face, and I try to calm my own emotions, putting my hand on his arm. "I can talk to Jacob for you, if you want me to. Tell him to leave you alone."

After laughs; it's shaky and gets cut off by a cough. "You'd…you'd talk to him for me, just like that?"

"Yes, of course, if it helps you."

"He's twice your size."

Now *I* puff up, chest out, shoulders back. "I'm 5'10", bro, what do you think I am, a fucking Hobbit? I'm not some fragile little flower—if someone's messing with you and you need help, I've got your back no matter what."

"You say that, but I saw you when you met him at the fundraiser; you were under his spell, too. He's…he's hard to say no to, man, you don't get it," he sighs, frantic eyes bouncing all over my face.

I adjust the bill of Harry's hat so I can send him my strongest glare. I'm not under anyone's spell. Not now, not ever again. "I have no problem saying no, *and* piss off, to him or anyone else that's causing you problems. I came here with you; fake boyfriends aside, you're my friend, and I'd like us to have a good time. We can't do that if you're looking over your shoulder at someone you hate but also want to sleep with."

His cheeks flush, and it goes down his neck to his loosely buttoned black shirt. "Right…right. No, no I'm. I don't wanna do that. Not with him anymore."

"You stand by that? I'll hold you to it as strongly as I hold you to no more drinking."

Staring at the dance floor, After's quiet for a quick five seconds. I'm wondering how long it feels inside his head. "Yeah, I'm…yeah. I don't like the hangover I get after I'm around him."

"That's a good way to put it." He wriggles his nose and looks back at me with a small smile. "You're not drinking."

"Nope."

"And no Jacob."

It wasn't a question, and I'm glad he doesn't seem to think it was. "No, no sir."

"And no more cigarettes, okay? Even when we do that fake kiss shit and you're all up in my business, it still stinks."

He smirks and eyes me under his relaxed brow. "Yeah, sorry."

"I like your friends, man. Most of them. We can be civil and chill, yeah?"

He nods, and before he can say anything else, the DJ cuts over the music, shouting about having a celeb in the hizzy-house.

After's name is bellowed, air horns blast out, and the floor erupts into screams as eyes scan over to where we are, still huddled by the bathrooms. After straightens, flashes his grin, and takes my hand. "Wanna dance?" he asks, flipping Harry's hat around to sit backward on my head.

"You're leading," I scoff as he takes us away from our quiet corner.

"What, you don't wanna dance like we did at the last theater banquet I dragged you to?" he laughs, bobbing his head to Florida Georgia Line. After spins me around, floor slick and made for cowboy boots, and he presses me to him with an arm around my waist, holding our hands out.

"I broke your stupid toe at that banquet," I remind him, itching and self-conscious at the amount of people staring at us now.

After leads us in a fast, four-beat country song. As long as we keep doing this left-left-right-right thing, following the flow of dancers in a circle, I'll be good.

Two songs in, he shouts that he wants water, and I must look panicked as hell cause he laughs and turns me around, giving me a smack on my ass and sending me over to Harry. "Take care of my boy, Harry! I'll be right back."

Harry grins and snags my hand, anchoring me from one buoy to another. "You doing okay? Y'all look like you mighta worked it out, huh?"

"For now," I reply, watching After disappearing into the crowd.

Harry's so damn tall, I can't do the moves right, which just makes me blush with irritation and makes him laugh. "Don't worry bout it, we'll figure it out once they play something better than…than—who the *hell* is this?" he yells over heads at Nicholas.

Nicholas has his arms around Jacob from behind, and they turn and grin at us. I mean, Nicholas grins, Jacob's looking at me with both bedroom and snake eyes. "Blanco Brown, baby!" Nicholas screams.

Harry turns his attention back to me, laughing. "No—Scotty, not like that—work the hip action."

"I'm *trying*, I'm a white dude, I have no hip action!"

"Boy, so am I, you don't see me trippin' all over myself! He's literally singing the dance steps; how can you be getting this wrong?"

"Prepare to be amazed at just how bad I am at listening to directions!" He barks a laugh so deep it makes my chest thrum against his.

"Alright, finale, you ready?"

"Ready for—for what—no—" He's cackling at me like a freckled mad man, and I'm smiling and terrified at the same time. "Don't, Harry, don't you *dare* dip me—"

"I gotchya Scotty, don't worry!"

I claw at him as he throws me far out, both our arms extended and straight, and I get yanked back by my hand, spinning on my slippery boot toe. His fingers grab my shoulder, his arm hooks around my waist—

With an unattractive squawk, there I go, dipped so low that my last boot on the dance floor leaves the hardwood, and I'm supported only by his arm behind my back and his thigh under my ass. Sure, he got me, but I think my heart shot off through the roof of the club.

When he flings me back up, his hat flies off my head, and his laugh is so delightful as he sets me down, I can't help but laugh, too. "You're insane!"

"You're perfect! You did amazing!" He gives me back his hat, and we pick our shimmying up again.

Just as I get the hang of this new song and stop mouth breathing, the rhythm changes again, less country and more—what on Earth is this? It's panic-inducing drumbeats and my pulse is breaking my ribcage all over again. Think I would've preferred the old folks honky-tonk downtown.

"Hey," says a voice, low under the throbbing bass and right at the hairs of my neck. I look back to After and his smile inches from my face. He winks at Harry and hooks his chin over my shoulder. "Mind if I cut in?"

"Only a little," Harry chuckles. "Watch yourself with this one; Scotty here's got moves! You're liable to get left behind."

"Don't I fucking know it," laughs After. Harry squishes me in a hug in the middle of the packed floor before snagging another eager dance partner, then After's offering me his water bottle. "You doing okay, Bo? Got the hang of it?"

Was that him calling me Bo in *public*? Even if it is a loud dance hall and people are paying closer attention to how we look than what we're saying. I nod and chug the water, and he holds the back of my neck, rubbing his thumb behind my ear as the song gets wilder and the dancing around us turns from G rated boot scoot boogie to raunchy with a capital R.

"I know this one," he says, taking the empty bottle and crushing it into his back pocket. "JVLA. First time I heard it was on a TikTok a thousand years ago."

After moves his head along like he recognizes the lyrics, except it just sounds like someone mumbling right into the microphone. "Think this one's a remix." He crushes me tighter to him, rolls his body, and his mouth comes to my ear. His breath is way too warm. "This is the way to listen to it: turned all the way up, sweaty in a full room, with someone pressed *right* against you."

I fight to leave at least an inch between us for Jesus, but he keeps dragging his fingers up my waist. "What—what's it called, I don't know it," I reply.

He smiles against my ear. He doesn't have to shout the name, but he doesn't have to fucking whisper it like this, either. "It's called Such a Whore." That word makes my chest squeeze in on my lungs, but the way he said it sent my heart into my throat.

His hips press in, and he moves his hand from my waist to my lower back, splaying his fingers, covering every inch of my spine. "I got you, man, chill out. You're tense as hell."

I try to relax my back, but the muscles in my thighs are telling me the safest thing to do would be to run for the desert. As soon as I reach up and drape my arms over his shoulders, he chuckles and traces a fingernail from my elbow to my bicep, and I feel his lips on my jaw. My neck heats to a thousand degrees. "Better. You're doing so good, Bo. So damn good."

Okay so cool, cool. Cool.

We were just—like. *Just* talking about being friends here, having a chill, platonic night out. Pals being pals. Guys being dudes. This is…this is friends, dancing with friends, and y'know…and…

There goes his thigh between my legs.

This is absolutely *not* friendly dancing.

Oh, God, I'm *so* fucked.

Chapter 39

We got dropped off by Harry (Nicholas and Jacob bounced before we left the club, small blessings) and I kind of wish we'd thought to lug our suitcases to our hotel room before we went dancing, cause now I'm discovering sore muscles I didn't even know I had.

After gives a dramatic groan as he flops onto the bed and tucks his hands behind his neck. Chicken hops up and circles around (I think he might weigh three more pounds than when we left him at Rosamine's earlier), and he decides the best place to sleep is with one of his back paws digging straight into After's armpit. "Ow—fuck—back off, child!"

I smirk at their wrestling antics, until After's grin lands on me.

Then I'm thinking of his fingers on my waist, and my hips, and the one hand that got cozy in my back pocket, and the leg that pressed against me for a grueling twenty seconds, until I escaped for the bathroom and smothered my face with a cold, wet paper towel. Chya. Good times.

I'm still wearing Harry's hat. I glare at nothing and yank it off and run a hand through my hair. "You got hat hair," After yawns.

"I'm sure I do," I mutter, dropping the cap to the desk. I'm too wired to sleep, especially since super considerate Harry and Nicholas believed the boyfriends would want a hotel room with just one bed. I miss the two twins at the motel. (I don't.) No, I do. "I'm gonna be up for a bit, what're you gonna do?"

"Shower eventually," After sighs. I glance back to him on his phone. He's smirking at something.

"What?"

"Look how sexy we are," he chuckles, holding his phone out for me. I take a step and squint at the screen.

Nicholas posted a picture of us at the club when we were at the bar getting waters. Sweet biscuits, were we really standing that close? Supposedly sexy me is laughing at something—I blacked out after that first dirty-dancing session so I have no idea what. After's face is dipped down near mine and his handsome grin is outright obnoxious. To top it off, his *hands* are *all over* every square inch of my *goddamn ass*.

My butt cheek tingles. Fake, fake, fake, fake— "Oh, shit, someone in the comments just posted the title of a fanfiction they wrote of us," he snickers. "And there's—ohohoh! *Fanart* with it? Gonna look that shit up right nooooow…"

"Ah." He laughs at my very flat, single syllabic grunt. "Uh—speaking of writing—"

"Scotty, *please* tell me you're about to smut this shit up."

"No! No, no, I'm—I was gonna stay up and write, if it doesn't—won't bother you." I stagger as I try to reach for the desk chair and miss, taking a toppling step right. He sits up on his elbows and tilts his head, and Chicken mirrors him. "Would it, would it bug you? I forgot my headphones; I was planning to listen to music. I can go to the lobby—"

"Nah man, play your music, hang out in here. I'll shower in a minute." He snuggles back into the pillows, then giggles, pulling his knees up as his toes overlap. That's the pose of someone getting *real* into something on their phone.

"Dude."

"Mhmmm."

"Do not look up the fanfiction." He grins at me behind his phone. "Forget it…" I sit with a huff, every muscle clicking at me in rage, and I kick off my boots underneath the desk.

There's a rustle behind me, and I look back in time to see After sitting up to unbutton his shirt. The thick tendon in his neck shifts as he moves his shoulders back, shrugging off the button up. I was like, inches away from that tendon just an hour ago, standing on my toes to talk to him at the packed club.

He liked when I yanked on his leather necklace and brought him closer on the dance floor, too. Could tug on that for hours.

Oookay, and we're turning *around*, we're *turning*, we're crossing our *legs*—

"What's your favorite song?" After asks as soon as I've pulled up my email just to stare at something else.

"Why do you ask?"

"Cause I feel like we primarily listened to my music on the way here."

"Cause we did." No replies in my inbox yet from Jackie over my latest submission. I pout and go to Word, opening up a saved doc I'd been fiddling with.

"Why?" he asks.

"We like some of the same stuff."

"Yeah but like. You know my favorite songs. What're yours?"

I lean back in the swivel chair and rub under my eyes. "I dunno, man…I've got a few."

"Why've you never played them?"

"They're not your style."

"Try me."

When I spin around to face him, I'm scowling. Until I see him sitting forward with his arms around his knees, head tilted, eyes bright. I forgot that he's such a night owl when he's not drinking day by day; he gets jittery, energized, he could probably keep going until sunrise. I mean hell, he did just to get us here, driving eight hours straight.

"They're slow songs. Sometimes sad. Mellow lyrics; not a lot of fast singing, so I can focus on my writing."

"Like what? Play me the first one that pops into your head," he smiles. I pinch my mouth at the corner and look to my phone.

"Fine. But, again, no headphones, so maybe later—"

"I brought mine," he says, crawling to the edge of the bed to get to his bag. The muscles rippling in his back as he works to find his headphones look like soft sand dunes, pushed around by a desert wind.

Maybe I'll wait until he's asleep to do my writing…

He looks up to find me staring, and I stand with my phone, scrolling through songs. "Okay—here, hook up to my Bluetooth, but don't play this yet." I set my phone on the bedside table and go for the lamp, turning it off.

"Oh, goodie, your fav song requires mood lighting?" he chuckles.

"It does if you want to listen to it right, let me work." I crack the door of the bathroom, and the only light left is from the muted TV and the orange lamp on my desk. "You on my Bluetooth?"

"I am on your tooth of blue."

"This one is called If I Go, I'm Goin' by Gregory Alan Isakov."

"What a *distinguished* name."

"Right? Okay, hit play. And don't say anything, it's quiet."

"Okie doke," After sighs, pressing play. He gets settled, hands clasped across his stomach, ankles crossed, and I watch him smile and close his eyes.

I watch that smile fade. Watch his face relax, brow furrow, tighten, smooth out again. His eyes open and fixate on mine. I turn to the desk, staring over my laptop and memorizing the ancient wallpaper.

Six minutes pass, much longer than the song. Either it looped, or it started playing the next one. There's noise of comforter and sheets as he changes position. "Scott…"

"Yeah."

He's ten years old when he whispers, "Did Cassidy and Tyler know…you were abrosexual before they died?"

I scrunch my nose at him. After's sitting cross legged, hands in his lap with my phone balanced on his fingers. "Where'd that question come from?"

"Your song. Feels like you didn't, um…I mean the lyrics, just had me thinking…" He hums a little rift of the melody. I think he sounds nicer than I pretended during my meltdown in the truck.

"You take the bed," After sighs, dropping his earphones into his duffel and grabbing his toiletry bag and boxers. He shoots a glance my way as he hands me my phone back, but he doesn't look me in the eye. "I'll…I'll take the sofa." I don't try to tell him otherwise. "Though uh—can I shower? You need the bathroom?"

"Go for it," I shrug, clicking the desk lamp off. "I changed my mind on writing. I'm gonna sleep, if that's okay."

"Go for it," he echoes.

"Can you leave the—"

"I'll leave the TV on for you," he says. Finally, he looks at me and smiles. The bathroom door closes, and I'm swarmed by quiet dark, other than the blue glow of the Nature Channel.

Unfolding from the desk, I shimmy out of my jeans and shirt and chuck them at my suitcase by the sofa. I unmute the TV, keep the volume low, and curl up on the bed. Chicken heaves out a long sigh as he gets settled over my legs. I don't sleep.

—

After comes out of the bathroom along with a fog of men's shampoo and vanilla body wash. He putters around the room. He sniffles and lets out a shivery sigh.

The bed shifts next to me. There's a slow heat melting across the bedsheets towards me under the comforter, coming from After, still warm from his shower. His clean, fresh smell has my insomnia slipping away.

I missed him last night. When he slept in the other bed, just a few feet from me. Close enough I could see his face in the TV light, but far enough I couldn't touch him.

I'd be lying if I said I hadn't been thinking about him sleeping against me during that nap at his house, or how he curled around me in my bunk. Remembering the weight of his arm over my side, the press of his face to my hair.

In my dorm, I've started bundling my blankets up and putting them to the wall. Then I sleep against them with a hoodie sleeve draped across my ribs. It's, I mean…not what I want. But it's enough for now, I guess.

Right now, a safe distance from me, he mumbles a goodnight and faces the wall.

I turn my head and follow the silhouette of his form in the changing light, tempted to reach over and outline the curve of his ear with my fingertip, tracing the mountain of his shoulder.

I look up to the ceiling, blinking stinging eyes. "You awake, After?" The mattress moves again as he rolls over, and there's a light tap of his finger on the bend of my elbow.

"Yeah. You okay? Is this…is this okay? I know I said couch…"

"You're fine. But, to answer your question, no. They didn't know."

I sense him lift his head up from his pillow. "Why not?"

"Timing."

"What do you mean?"

"They were coming back from a date night. I said I'd watch Bevett. Dad called me on the way, asked if I wanted any Wendy's since I was still awake. I said yeah, but then I said I had something to tell them when they got home. He teased me, asked 'who's the father'."

After's chuckle is soft, and he shifts an inch toward me. "I replied 'about that', and Dad and Cassidy laughed. Then she said to text her my order since they were at the drive-thru, and Dad and her hung up with a final 'love you, grump'." I leave out the part where once we hung up, I started crying and almost called After next. Cause whatever happened with him and Missy, he was still my best friend, and figuring out your sexuality is fucking hard.

His finger at my elbow slinks down my arm, going for my hand. "Then the doorbell rang half an hour later. And it wasn't them. So. No. They never knew." I curl up on my other side and ball up as small as I can. His arm comes around my waist, bare chest on fire against my tight back, and I don't let him see my tears.

Don't get used to it, I tell my heart, even as he lulls me to sleep with just his voice, talking about how he looked up Dollywood, found all these things for us to do, places to see on our next trip to Nashville. Don't grow happy here. Stay solid, stay firm, stay on the ground. This is not what you think it is. It'll never be what you think it is.

Chapter 40

Stuffed full of free continental breakfast, we're waiting on Harry to let us know when he's here. Without a way around, we're kind of dependent on the others for the time being. We could get an Uber, or attempt to find a taxi or something, but After doesn't seem worried about a schedule.

If anything, he seems over the moon that we're not being sent from point A to B then W and Z. He's cool to coast until he's needed. After all, it's not his show, he's merely making a special appearance.

He's letting me use his headphones while I write. Still nothing from Jackie, but I last checked six hours ago before bed, so no surprise. After's been mumbling over his lines for the last hour and forty minutes, since before I went to the gym, got in a good cycling session, came back and showered. All before eight AM. The miracles of coffee. (And wanting to avoid a single, very small hotel room…)

With soft music pouring into my head, nestled in a pile of pillows and sprawled across the mattress, Chicken pressed to my hip, I'm in my own world.

By own world, I mean own torture chamber, glaring over nonsense I wrote this morning. I don't delete the stuff I don't like anymore, not since I recently discovered the strike-through feature on Word. (I did not put 'efficient with Word Suite' on my resume, FYI, didn't lie about that.)

Makes me feel legit. Just wish I found a way to make the cutting line a bright red, for that added 'failure, disappointment, catastrophe, see me after class,' vibe.

~~"I'm on a line. Been here for years. I walk the line because my life depends on it. Too far left and I get what I want. Too far right, I lose that hazel. Why don't I just go left? Because what I want doesn't want me. And there's no net to catch me on that side. No one's told me yet that the net on the right was set on fire years ago and was never mine to begin with. Teeter, totter, there I go. Flat and dead or burning bright."~~

Scott, buddy, we gotta seek some sort of therapy shit after all this is over.

"Hey, Scott," After says. There's *a thump, woosh, thump* in front of me, and I look over my laptop to him tossing Chicken's rubber chicken (complete with startled eyes and absurd little feet) up and down in the air as he lays on his back on the sofa.

"Yes, After," I reply, hitting CTRL+S obsessively, saving and saving for no reason at all in case I happen to accidentally delete the crap I've garbled out and hate. Never ending cycle, I swear.

"So, we got lots of attention with that post at the club last night."

"Uh, huh," I mutter. Did we? I haven't dared to check Instagram yet. Not if someone's out there writing porn about us. (I seriously don't want to read about me being a disappointing lay in fiction when the truth is just as bad, if not worse.) "How much attention?"

"It's trending—there's a video." My eyes shoot up to him again, and Chicken's tags rattle at my sudden movement.

"What? What video?"

He glances over at me. "Just us dancing. You can find it on Insta, we're a hashtag now. #EverettAfter." My skin boils. That's not a nickname others get to use. That's not—no, what the hell? His smile looks weird. Jagged. Eyes sharp on the squeaky toy he tosses up again.

"Someone got a picture of us leaving, too. That goodnight kiss we did," he adds. It just gets worse. Wasn't even a goodnight kiss;

we did that stupid thumb thing again, like we did when I left after the sleepover.

"Hadn't been the best angle since I saw the camera flashes a little late, but. I mean it worked, I guess. Might end up on *Us Weekly*, who knows."

"Not that I'm not enjoying this conversation, cause I am," I start. He laughs and even *that's* jagged somehow. "But...what're you getting at with all this?"

"How do you feel about smooching in public? Like, for real?" he asks, tossing the toy up. Chicken and I both watch as it comes back down, goes up again.

Well, that's not where I thought this was going. After pauses, hand in the air, holding the chicken, waiting on my answer. Shit, my answer, uh—

"For real, right...how do *you* feel about it?"

"Not against it. I ask cause they'll get tired of hand holding and cheek kisses after a while. Even Nicholas and Jacob were making out like the world was gonna end, and they're not even in the spotlight. We gotta up our game, I think."

"You were the one that said Kassie Clem could be having a feast on her girlfriend and people would still say she's straight."

"Those were most certainly *not* the words I used," he smirks, tossing the chicken.

"Would you want tongue?"

The chicken flies past his fingers and thwaps him in the eye, squeakily smacking off his forehead once more with an 'and a fuck you, too', before flying away, bouncing for the bathroom hall toward the door. Chicken leaps off the bed and runs for it, and I snort and cover my mouth at After rolling around and holding his eye. "*Tits*, dude!"

"You good? You only needed one eye, right?"

"You can't just ask something like that!"

"Why not? It's a genuine question."

"Have you ever even kissed someone before? I don't want your tongue jamming down my throat if you don't know what you're doing," he snaps, reclining on an elbow.

So *rude*. And…unnecessary. He glares at me and I realize again he's waiting on an answer. "Um. Oh. I mean. Yeah, once or—or twice—"

"That was *super* convincing," he scoffs, mumbling something else under his breath.

"What did you say?"

"Nothing—"

"Speak up, After, what did you just say?" He grits his jaw at me, glaring. My brain fills his silence with a thousand horrendous things. "Fine—"

"I said you're probably bad at it," he blurts. My face radiates, burning down my neck to my chest.

Asshole. "*Excuse* you, I was trying to help you out," I spit at him. He raises a brow in reply, and I jump off the bed, tossing my laptop at the pillows. "Get up."

"You're not serious—"

"Get up, or shut up, and you'll have to let the tabloids suffer with boring, Milquetoast PDA cheek kisses forever."

After rolls his eyes and stands, nudging Chicken's nose aside when he comes back with his toy. "Can you even reach me?" he snorts.

I glare at him. "I've kissed taller men than you."

His douchebag smirk falters. His eyes widen until they slit into a scowl. I like how irritated he looks. I'd say even jealous. For his fake boyfriend? Please. "Like who, Scott?"

"Who do you think?"

"Did you kiss Harry when y'all were dancing last night?"

"I'm not even going to dignify that with an answer."

"Fine, but you lied during Charlotte and Mei's game."

"Do you *really* care?"

"What else did you lie about?"

Now is not the time, nor the place. Y'know what, never is the time, and nowhere on Earth is the place, how about that? "Do I have permission to kiss you how I want?" I ask. "I need consent."

"My safe word is heliotrope."

"I'm not joking."

After's brow relaxes and he slides his hands into his pockets. Whatever inner jerk took over his brain a few seconds ago is long gone as he opens his mouth just to close it twice. "Uh. Full consent."

"Yes?"

He licks his lips. "Y-yeah, yes."

He's kissed dozens of women in movies and never meant it, never thought anything about it. I can do that, too. I can be numb.

Sure thing. Easy-peasy.

My hands come to his face and I pull him down to me. He gasps like he does every time we do that whole weird thumb-kiss thing. Never need to do that again if we get the hang of this fake make-out.

But that gasp turns into a deep, heavy inhale, then a choppy and erratic sigh that warms my face. His lips part an inch. The second his tongue is on my lower lip, I encourage it with my own, and a soft noise vibrates through our mouths. Don't think that was me.

The heat coming from his cheeks feels like a sunburn on mine. He tastes like the chocolate chip muffin I split with him at breakfast, strawberry yogurt, and hazelnut creamer from his coffee. With an all over bacon-ness. It's a *good* mix.

Sending a hand from his face up through his hair, I curl my fingers and pull at the strands just a little, barely a fraction of how much I really want to—I mean, how much I would if we were in a *legit* relationship—which we're *not*. Our teeth kind of awkwardly clack together and I'm seconds away from pulling back to apologize, but After leans into me and moans deeper and—okay, yeah, that noise just now was a bit of me, too.

He doesn't sound at all like when we were younger, that last night in my backyard, when I had my hand around him—

Keep it together, Scotty. I can fake this. I *am* faking this.

My body might be doing its own thing— taking a step into him and as it debates pushing him to the wall (or to the fucking mattress that's *right there*) thinking of how goddamn soft his lips are, how he seems to vibrate when I bite at the lower one just because I can, wondering what he'd do if I slinked a leg in between his like he did last night (for experiments sake)—

But my heart is totally faking this.

To prove it, just as his fingers tap at my arms, and I feel one hand start to flatten across my shoulder blade, I step away. He blinks fast, clamps his mouth closed and swallows so hard his throat bobs.

"Okay. Yeah." After scratches at his cheek, turns his whole body away from me. I sit causally back on the mattress and casually cross my legs and casually pull a pillow into my lap. "Yeah. You know what you're doing."

"Told you," I reply. After makes like he's going to sit down, but he grabs for Chicken's collar and leash on the desk. He mutters something about taking him out to go to the bathroom before we drop him off at Rosamine's, and he stumbles over his own feet on the way out.

I don't bother to go find them until Harry texts me, saying he's outside, ready to take us to his mom's house, then to the set for the rest of the day. I'm not looking forward to another awkward carpool ride.

Chapter 41

So there's opening the door to one fake kiss.

Then there's an onslaught of *endless* kissing. End. Less. Closed mouth, dive-bombing, rapid-fire pecks. My lips are chapped.

After's good at it, super slick. He does it when someone's got their phone pointed at us, when cameras haven't been cut just yet as he's coming off set. The behind the scenes for this episode are gonna be 74% us making out. *Fake* making out.

Someone shows up to interview Nicholas and get a tour around set. They ask him some questions about After and ask After some questions about me. He pulls me away from the snack table to smack a surprise, sharp kiss on me.

"What if I had food in my mouth," I scoff at him, still chewing donut cause I *did* have food in my mouth. He just laughs at me. I don't like that the first person I see once he walks off is Jacob, staring at After.

The kissing is his new tool, and I'm a tool, too. But it's working; there are photos popping up all over the Internet in just a few hours.

By noon, he gives me a wide smile when Buzzfeed posts a new article that simply says, "**David Después: Gay? Yes way!**" and it goes on and on with photos of us all the way from the fundraiser, talking about old signs, why didn't we see it before? All that jazz. After taps his phone screen in case I didn't see it the second he shoved it in my face.

"It's working, Scott, slowly but surely," he says breathlessly. I get a longer, heavier kiss. No camera around for that one.

I try not to overthink it (it being how I may not be necessary anymore now that his plan is succeeding) and do my best to relax on this vacation. He's pretty amazing at what he does, and I'm enjoying watching him in action doing his stunts. Nicholas's show is a detective drama, complete with fights in interrogation rooms and chase scenes. After's one of the antagonist's lackeys, and I can tell by the constant grin on his face that he's having the time of his life playing one evil mama jama.

His white tank top is a dirtied mess; there's perfected knife holes and fake blood on it, and anytime Nicholas calls one minute to action, After runs outside and rolls around in the desert dirt to get back to the appropriate filth. The makeup department loves him.

Hopping up from the ground after his horrific death at the hands of the good lady cop, he dusts his dark jeans off and jogs over to where I'm standing behind the cameras. The fake sunlight lamps they have around the set were giving me a headache, so Harry gave me sunglasses. Not only do I fit right in with the other stars, looking cool as hell wearing shades indoors, but now After can't see when I may or may not be checking him out.

"How'd that look?" he pants, wiping his forehead.

I find myself smiling at his thighs before I remember that's not where his face is, and I make sure I'm looking at his eyes before I slide the sunglasses into my hair. "Just as gnarly as the last three times she's pushed you from the prop semi." He laughs and accepts a towel from a passing assistant, draping it around his neck.

Like a good fake boyfriend, I pull him down by the towel circling his shoulders and give him a lil smackaroo right on the lips, no different than the ones he's been peppering me with all afternoon.

Only I can see the startled look of 'what the ever-loving fuck' all over his face, and I wonder if it's because I haven't initiated the kissing except for the very first one. I lick at my lips and paranoia seeps in, cause now he's uh…glaring? At me?

And yet, like the professional actor he is, it's gone in a blink, and he's laughing and rubbing his grossness all over my forehead.

Harry calls his name behind us and After turns, hooking an arm around my neck.

"Say cheese, y'all!" Harry barks, holding up his phone. After plants a kiss on my brow, and I smile. Starting to wonder if smiling is a nervous reflex for me, like how laughter is for After.

"Alright! Break for lunch for a bit, maybe four hours until we're working some sunset scenes outside," Harry says, nodding at us. "They might not be ready to pass out food just yet, but y'all can hang in the cafeteria for now."

"Ooh, little film studio has a food court," After teases, pushing me down the hall away from the set. "You hungry?" he asks, massaging my shoulders. I send him up a look, and he smiles at me. Whatever flickered across his face earlier is gone, I guess, though I'm on edge now, waiting for it to crop up again. Maybe he's just hangry. Maybe it's the chili fries I was munching on earlier...

"Starving," I reply, passing the expensive shades off to a random set assistant before I forget they're on my head and end up stealing them. "How much more do y'all have to do?"

"I think there's a motorcycle scene. I get to test out Nicholas's bike!"

"Please wear a helmet."

"Yes, Mom."

I smack him on the arm, and he slaps my ass as I walk ahead of him for the cafeteria double doors.

Inside, we get a booth and wait, leaning on one another as I fan him with a mini laminated menu we grabbed by the buffet. Until Jacob strolls in, and After's off me like I pinched him. Nicholas walks in next, and the two send us smiles as they come over.

"Can we join y'all? No food yet," Nicholas says, sitting.

"Go ahead," I reply, inch, inch, inching myself further away from After.

After snorts at Jacob, who's squishing between the table and Nicholas's chest, taking up his seat on the big man's thigh. "You two sure are awfully cozy," he says. Jacob shrugs and drops his temple to Nicholas's head.

"What's your point?" he asks with a dry chuckle. "You have your plaything, I have mine; mind your business." When he winks at me, I'm amazed by my inner strength when I *don't* flip him off.

Nicholas smirks and plants a wide hand on Jacob's ass. "Meanwhile, we could sell real estate on the acres between y'all." He juts his chin at me, then eyes After. "What happened? Just a few minutes ago, you were swappin' spit all over my damn set." No spit was ever swapped with our G rated kisses. (Not since the hotel, but I'm not gonna bring that up here.) "Are y'all fighting? Oh boy, that'll make an awkward flight home."

"We're flying home?" I ask After.

"In my super snazzy private plane," he replies with a wink.

"You said you didn't have one!"

"You claimed I have a *jet*. There's a difference."

"Bullshit," I scoff, crossing my arms. Thank God though, I'd rather fly over El Paso than ever drive through it again.

"Don't be mad at me, you'll like it. There's spacious leg room, snacks, champagne—oh, wait. No, I'll get us sparkling water," After smiles, his knee tapping mine under the table. I bump his back twice in a 'sounds good'.

"Why no strawberry champagne? You always had that when we flew," Jacob says.

I don't *mean* to glare at him, I swear I don't. But it's there, that glare, on my face, directed at Jacob. He smiles at me like blue-eyed dimple chin sunshine. "Do you not drink, Scott Everett?"

"No. And neither does he," I reply, nodding to After.

Jacob arches a brow, eyes sliding over to him. "*Don't* you? What about a literal hour ago. We had mimosas."

I turn to After. He's already shaking his head at me. "No, we didn't—"

"Yeah, we did, you popped the champagne—"

"And handed it to *you*, Jacob. I didn't have any." He says it to me, even if it's not directed at me. He's still shaking his head. "I just had the orange juice."

"You better hope you're telling the truth, Davy, Scott looks like he's gonna kill you," chuckles Nicholas.

"Oh David, did you make another promise you couldn't keep? No drinking?" Jacob clicks his tongue. I want to rip it out of his face. "Everyone here knows you won't last long with that."

After's ears are dark red. He's not shaking his head anymore, but his eyes continue to dart between mine.

He's not my boyfriend. He made no real promises to me. He just needs to keep the commitments he made to himself. No drinking, no Jacob; it's his life. Whether he drinks himself to death isn't my responsibility. It never was.

But I'd miss him terribly. "Not even a little?" I ask.

"Not even a little," he sighs.

"Good." With my hand on his cheek, I stretch across the acreage between us and kiss him.

It was simple to me. Small, like, good job, you did it. There were a lot of tempting things there and you took none of them, proud of you. Here's us giving the middle finger to your buds who think they can mock you for your addiction. Take that, magazines.

Certainly doesn't feel simple to After.

Good gracious, if there wasn't a table in front of us, I think he'd have pulled me into his lap just like Jacob and Nicholas and eaten me alive. His hands shoot straight into my hair, and he's sucking on my lip before I can even catch up to what's happening. Okay, yep, here, this is *totes* spit swapping, holy shit.

Then *whoosh*, he's a foot away from me, staring at me like *I* was the one jumping down his throat.

"Well, he did *something* right!" laughs Jacob, getting off Nicholas's knee. "I'm gonna see if they're serving lunch yet."

"Looks like Davy already got his lunch," Nicholas snickers, following Jacob. They're still chattering and glancing over their shoulders at us until they turn the next corner.

I look back to After, who's fixated on the table. Sooo that was a first I'm gonna pretend didn't happen for both our sakes. "Wanna go get some—"

"Don't kiss me again."

Slap number one.

"Um. Okay?"

"That was…yeah. Don't." He wipes the back of his hand across his lower lip, hard enough to make his chin turn red.

Slap number two.

"Okay, no problem. Did you um. I mean we can go back to the other—"

"We should probably think about how we want to do the public breakup."

Slap number three, *steeeeeerike*.

He won't look at me. I take on the role of doting…whatever this is at this point. Soon to be fake ex. "Sure, After. Whatever you want."

He slides out first and doesn't go toward the food. "C'mon."

"You mean, like, right now?"

"Yeah, c'mon." I stumble to get up and follow.

And my little stupid heart goes oh, oh, this could be not what we think! This could be him taking us somewhere secluded, so we can make up and make *out* for real and talk *feelings* (not that I, Scott Everett, would ever truly talk feelings) and we can—

Yeah, no chance.

Chapter 42

His shoulder slams into his dressing room door, and he smacks it closed behind me even louder. "Whoa, okay, are you alright?"

After scratches at the back of his head with an unconvincing yeahsurefine. "So I was thinking um. After S-Spain, Gibraltar—where my dad and stepdad live—have I told you about their house? Their hacienda—it's real nice, not too large, it's only, like, fifteen hundred square feet, but it hangs right over the beach, it's nice, they got a pool and it's, like, ten steps from the pool to the room we'll be staying in—it's super nice, it's, the tile—yeah the tile is uh—that orange you like. Like. Blue and, and, and nice paisley, your scarf—paisley."

Was I supposed to get anything from that? Weren't we going to talk breakups? He doesn't pace, he spins in a circle, so many times it makes me dizzy. "It sounds really...nice, After."

"Yeah. Yeah, anyway. Anyway—they cook a lot, lots of good food. And. I mean. We're just friends, so we can enjoy the vacay, y'know? Maybe write out a s-script...for after. For how we want the argument to go down when we get back. I admit I'm not sure where to start. We could—" He laughs with a look of panic and pain and stops his tight pirouettes. Staring at the ceiling, he adds quietly, "We could do the showdown at a S...a Starbucks. Or. Yeah. I dunno what to fight. About. With you."

His rambling wouldn't be so concerning if his knees and hands and everything weren't shaking so much. "What were you and

Sasha fighting over? Maybe we can get something from that," I suggest.

After's knees pause. He's still focused on the ceiling, locked in so hard that I kind of glance up there too, like, are we gonna find the answer to why he's acting so weird all of a sudden over one kiss, when he's been smooching me all day? Is it cause Jacob was there? What do you think, ceiling?

"Sasha claimed I cheated on her." Oh, yikes. I suck a rush of air in through my teeth. "I did. With Jacob. This past New Year's. Only Charlotte knew, cause it was her party."

Okie doke. Now *my* knees are doing a wobble dance. "Did it when I was with Jolene, too. Though she knew and didn't care; she was sleeping around behind my back first. Was after her and I had sex."

I'm getting second-hand embarrassment and we're the only two in the room. Do I say sorry? Do I say dude, buddy, you done fucked up?

Wait—is he trying to tell me something about how he wants our argument to go? I mean I already knew about the club and the college party…am I missing something?

After sits in his chair by the makeup table. He catches his reflection. His eyes dart away and he glares at everything but the multiple mirrors in the room, and me. "Hey…are you okay?" I ask, cause what else am I supposed to say?

"No. Not really."

"What's going on, man, talk to me." I chance a couple steps toward him, and his shoulder flinches away when I tap him with my fingers. I retreat my hand and put it in my pocket, leaning back on the other small table in the room covered in spare dark jeans and dirty tanks.

"I've got no room to talk," he says.

I'm seconds away from pretending to look around his dressing room and joke like, looks pretty spacious to me, when he peeks up at me and meets my eye. There are tears in his. "My text to you. I've never had any room to talk, and yet I've…"

"What text?"

"The one in December." When I shake my head, his face twists into what I'm gonna call absolute rage. After leaps up from his chair so fast momentum knocks it over, and then he's for real pacing. "The text, the text, the *fucking* text." He slaps a hand to his temple and I jump at the loud smack! His hand retreats again and swings, and I grab his wrist before he takes out his damn eye.

"*What* text, After—"

He yanks his wrist from me and screams in my face. "Jesus Christ, Scotty, the one where I called you a *whore*!"

The room is carpeted, the walls are covered in posters and mirrors and racks of clothes, and yet that word reverberates for a thousand years until it fades into dead silence. He holds his breath. Then he starts to hyperventilate.

"When I said I—I hated you for leaving me alone in Texas, when I said you were a slut and a faggot for fucking around with me then running off, when I called you trash and, and, and said you were a terrible friend—you never—you never forgave me!" he yells, jabbing a finger in my direction. "You didn't accept my apology."

I bite down my first thought of 'well, if you said it in person, I might've said 'I forgive you' to your face'. "It's like you said, dude, you forgave me years ago to get past it on your own, I had to do the same—"

"No, no, no, no, you couldn't have, no. This is…this is just. This was all a big fucking mistake. I never should've asked you of all people to do this fake shit with me."

I feel smaller than ever next to him as he rips off his dirtied tank and chucks it at the makeup table. "What do you mean, me of all people?"

"Do you straight up not remember the text? Did you d-delete it?"

"Yes? Cause I was staring at it every day for hours on end, making myself miserable when there were never any new messages from you. Not for months." He hisses a curse and dives for his pocket, pulling out his phone, and my throat closes. "No, After, what're you doing—"

"Showing you the text so you remember."

"Remember what?"

"Remember why you should hate me."

"I *don't* hate you—for God's sake, why're you doing this? I don't want to read it—"

"You have to know this is fake, Scott! This is all fucking fake. This? Us here? Doesn't mean anything." He waves his phone around, eyes wild and hair a mess. He needs a haircut. I need to breathe.

"I don't think we can ever be friends again like before," he says, words slurring—either that or I'm getting dizzy. "We broke too much shit and never apologized for it."

"You did apologize for your thing, man, and I apologized for mine. And…and we're friends, we *are* friends. You—I mean in Arkansas, you took care of me, you held me while I cried—"

"I just wanted you to calm down cause you were freaking me out and we had to keep driving—"

"And last night?" I croak.

His voice cracks. "You were keeping me awake."

"Fuck you." I'm not taking his lies anymore, not after weeks of being a punching bag he likes to caress when he feels like it. "Why am I here then?" I spit, stomping toward him and away from the wall I'd backed up to. "Why don't we just hash this out right in the open and get this stupid argument over with? You got what you wanted, press accepts that you're gay now, congrats, what's the point in me?"

He looks me up and down three times. I miss the minutes earlier when he was staring so hard at the ceiling; I don't like being in such an aggressive gaze. Boxed in. "I'm an idiot," he shudders out. "I thought we once had a—a mutual understanding. That we could get through this without bringing up…stuff. That happened years ago."

"You're right. You're an idiot, and so am I. Since February, I've just been cycling through that nightmare, day after day, remembering things I don't want to think about. Bullshit at your house, at mine, flashbacks to you and Missy."

"Missy was a stupid fling, why do you care about that?"

"Cause I keep seeing it seared into my mind—you fucking her in your backyard!"

He cranes his neck back and I realize I let slip that little detail I shouldn't know. "When I told you about her…I never mentioned it was in my backyard."

"No, you didn't have to. I was there. I saw y'all on the bench. On my birthday."

After steps away. Takes three steps toward me. I stand my ground, even as I feel the heat of his flushed skin through my t-shirt. "You—you never said. Scott, you never said—"

What I thought was guilt mutates across his face into something hideous. "This…*this* is why we would never work." He draws a weak hand between us. Except there's no space left, and the slight tap of his fingers to my chest sends sparks into my ears.

"We can't communicate. We just keep hurting each other and pretending we can fix it—but we can't fix what's in a thousand pieces. They're too sharp. And every time we pick up a new piece to try to glue it back, we just stab one another with them. I can't treat you the way you want to be treated."

You can't be loved like you want.

Wow, hey there Devon's voice, so glad you could join us here. "You're saying you can't treat me like a human being?" His lip twinges and I stand up taller.

"You don't see it, After. You treat me nice in private, but the moment we're out and about, especially around your ex, it's all systems go, and all those niceties you did so easily when it was just you and me turn sick and sour. It's 'let me do this kiss real quick' then you shove me away the moment backs are turned, ignoring me all over again until you feel like being sweet. It's…it's *nauseating*.

I can't keep doing this hard-set switch if you can't make up your mind how to act around me."

He glares at his phone just to break my eye contact. I watch his stare dart around. His shoulders sag. I wonder if he's already pulled up the text and is now reading it.

"I know this isn't what you want. I get that I'm just the easy out, so you don't have to put your heart out there and date someone right now."

He has nothing to say to that. I don't know why I thought he would; this isn't a friends to lovers story where this is the moment he confesses I *am* the one he wants. After stares once more at me, at his phone, then drops it to the table. "Read it. Or don't. But don't think we're anything besides friends, if that."

"I never thought otherwise," I sigh, taking a step back. "What are we doing moving forward? You said don't kiss you, are you going to initiate it? Am I just at your disposal? Or is it off the table. I need to know before I set you off again, because clearly just that is enough to send you snarling at me."

After brings both hands up to his face, exhaling hard into his palms. "I don't care anymore, it's not for us anyway."

And he's out the door, closing it behind him.

Don't want to read the text. Never wanted to read it in the first place. I remember the words, I think. Maybe I softened them these past few years; tried to make them less furious.

My eyes fall to his phone screen whether I want them to or not. It's not even a text thread. He took a *screenshot* of the damn thing and saved it to his *favorites*.

I lock his phone without reading it. When I type in a password or two, I can't get back in. Good.

Chapter 43

The guys are all going out again tonight, along with some of the actresses and stunt doubles. It's turned into a huge group, and they've been leaving the studio in waves of cars.

"You sure you won't be joining us?" Jacob asks me, rushing fingers through his perfect Ken doll hair before fixing his cowboy hat.

I send him up the best smile I can, though it's not much, not after the rest of the day spent with After avoiding me, and me avoiding him in turn. "No, I'm pretty beat. Think I'll just get a ride back to the hotel."

Jacob hums and scratches at his chin, and if I didn't know better, I'd say he actually looked concerned. "Shit, Scott Everett, I don't think any of us are going back that way first. We're driving straight to Leroy's on the other side of the city."

Of course, cause who in their right mind stops to change and shower after a long day of work, before going out for a night around town. "It's fine, I'll figure it out." He rubs his hand up and down my back with a grimace of sick pity. I miraculously resist the urge to pull a Pennywise and rip his arm off with my teeth.

Nicholas comes over, wags his brows at me, and takes Jacob by the shoulders, leading him off to join the exodus heading to the honkytonk. "Um…" I hardly tilt my ear to After's voice as he walks up to my side. "You coming along?"

"No."

"You got a ride back?"

"Don't worry about me."

I see his head lower in my peripheral, and I glance at him. Whatever anger was plastered all over his face the rest of the day, the glares he'd have only for me before he blinked back into smiles for everyone else—it's all gone. He looks beat to hell. The purple setting sun makes the bags under his eyes extra dark. "Be safe," I toss out, squinting ahead before he notices me staring.

He throws a surprised look my way, I can hear it in the way his breath hitches, and I shrug and pull my hands from my pockets to cross my arms. "You're my flight home tomorrow. Don't get killed."

"Right," he sighs with a heavy nod. "I'll um. I'll get Chicken. On the way back."

"Stay at Rosamine's if you have to. It's fine."

"I don't want you in our hotel alone," he says under his breath. I frown and look fully at him and find him staring. He opens his mouth—

Nicholas punches the horn of his truck, and with a clearing of this throat, After rushes away from my side donning a bright smile, waving to Jacob in the back seat with the door open and waiting.

Last of the tires crunch, last of the headlights dim, and I'm left behind with some directors, and other cast members muttering about to themselves as they discuss plans to go somewhere else.

Temp of the desert cooling into the seventies makes me shiver, and I glare at the lack of service on my phone. My neck heat ups and itches as I have to turn in circles with my hand raised, praying for a bar so I can schedule an Uber.

Thick steps click up next to me on the sidewalk. "You didn't go?" yawns Harry.

"Neither did you." I pinch the bridge of my nose and hold in a sigh. He nudges me with his elbow, but it doesn't knock me over like it did last night outside the club.

"Need a ride back?"

"Not if it's out of your way."

"I'll make it on the way," he replies. "I was gonna get food first, you hungry?"

"Are you drinking?" I ask, releasing that sigh with a shudder. Don't want to be around that, don't want to smell that, don't want to end up driving if he gets drunk.

I finally look up at him, squinting in the fading light. Harry smiles and tilts his head. "Don't think they serve drinks at IHOP. You know something I don't?"

"I mean who knows, it's Nashville, I wouldn't count it out." He chuckles but doesn't fall for it like I'd hoped.

"You okay? You seemed off all day after lunch."

Don't think he knows me enough to know when I seem anything but basic Scotty. "Fine. Just peeved at myself. Had no idea how long I was gonna stand out here until I gained the confidence to walk up to a stranger and ask for a ride. Or. Y'know. Uber."

"Ah…okay, yeah. So, here's some magic for you," he says, turning to face me, blocking out the rest of the dusk and darkening horizon. He shows nothing up his sleeves (his short sleeves), flourishes his hands, then says as he pulls out his phone, "I happen to have here, a phone. And you—by the grace of the Lord, there in your hand, is that—also! A phone—and if you press a button just so, and if the stars are aligned which I bet they are, then *your* phone could connect to *my* phone and—"

"I get it, I get it, I could've called you," I laugh over his horrible acting and gasp of astonishment.

"You can always call me. C'mon, let's get pancakes. You like pancakes, right?"

"Hell yeah."

—

On the drive to IHOP, we maneuver through so many conversation topics that I'm not even sure where we started.

Might've begun with what Harry did for college (engineering with a minor in film studies), but then it was where he'd be without his directing job (he said he'd nix the degrees and be a pediatrician of all things), and that turned into what he wanted to do with his life. ("Living the dream," he said.)

All in the fifteen minutes it takes to get us to the highway heading for IHOP. Like, what?

"Yeah, I dunno. Momma raised us cause Dad was always gone with work. I'm having the time of my life, for real, but I'm worried, if I ever have kids and a spouse, it'll be the same thing. I mean whoever they are, they'd never have to work; I'd make enough for all of us. They'd be able to raise the kids if they wanted, only have a job if they want one. But I'd hardly ever see them cause I'm always on the road."

"Sounds like it would be pretty difficult for you to put down roots," I reply.

"Yeah…I mean, I could create the perfect cabin for them somewhere in the east. But I wouldn't get to see them other than two, three mouths outta the year," he sighs, turning the wheel with one hand, armrest between us up.

He offered to have it down for me, but he seems to like to widen his knees a lot, taking up half the bench seat for himself by spreading across the front of the truck. And I don't mind keeping to my little passenger side lane.

"Have you been out of Nashville before?" I ask, crossing a leg over my knee and leaning into my window. "Other than Cali."

"Been to forty-seven states," he nods, tapping fingers on his leg. "All but Maine, North Dakota, and Florida."

"Don't blame you for Florida."

"Gators, man."

"Straight up."

He laughs as we roll up to another light. "Sorry if this got too deep for a first d-day out, y'know?"

I grin at him and his horrifically flushed face, brighter than the stoplight. "You nearly said 'date'."

He's a balloon, a squeaky, red balloon. "No, no, I didn't—"

"You totally did—do you think this is a date?" Harry shakes his head, eyes bugging and focused on the road. I can't stop smiling. "Harry, if you don't breathe in the next three seconds, you're gonna pass out."

He gulps and chokes on an inhale and I just laugh. "Well, shit, if this is a date, you're buying me brinner."

"I can buy," he nods, just as fast as he shook his head earlier.

Fake relationship with After aside, even if this was a date, Harry just told me he'd never be able to commit to us, not with a job front and center. He'd just be another island for me to bounce to. Or log cabin, apparently.

I frown at the dark windows and wave a hand at him as the light turns green. "No, stop, I'm joking. I don't want to leech off you, that's not nice."

He blinks and looks over at me, less embarrassed and more concerned. I think I preferred the embarrassed. "You're not leeching; you're my friend, I wanna buy you dinner."

"I'm an adult with a job for a reason, Harry, I can pay for my own fucking pancakes." Harry presses his mouth into a tight line, and I sigh and shrug. "Okay, sorry. I appreciate your generosity, thanks…been a long day. I'm um. My social tank is tapped out from so much…conversation. With everyone. It's not you."

"Is that why you didn't wanna go out with them tonight? Think they were gonna get dinner first, too, not go out dancing until later."

I grimace and rub my shoulder to my door. "Eh. I like some of them. But between you and me, Jacob's not my favorite." Harry snorts, and when I glance at him, he's nodding again. "What about you? You can still join them after IHOP."

"Eh," he echoes, making me smirk. "I saw them all day, and I don't drink. So when they get all uppity it kinda wears on my nerves. Don't mind it at house parties, cookouts, playing video games, all that. But there's something about how they are when they go out, y'know? Throw Jacob into the mix. Utter chaos."

"I get it, yeah. Why don't you drink?"

"I'm allergic to most liquors and nearly all beers," he explains.

"Oh, travesty. At least you're not allergic to something like chocolate," I chuckle. Harry makes a high whine as he winces and I gasp and grab his arm. "No! Are you? You sad man!"

"I love it, I'd die for it—"

"You literally would—"

He laughs. "Right, yeah—I haven't had it in years, not since a Hershey's bar sent me to the hospital."

"So depressing! Man, and I was gonna have chocolate chip pancakes."

"Nah, go for it, won't bother me none having it around. Just can't eat it."

"Oh, thank God, cause I wasn't about to change my mind and you'd be dead," I laugh. "Thanks for taking me out for food. Hadn't realized how hungry I was."

"Yeah of course. Did you not eat dinner when they were serving it a few hours ago? Think it was roadhouse catering or something," he says, getting us to the last light, IHOP on the corner.

"Didn't want to leave my reading hideaway to get any. Too many dramatic actors hovering around the buttered rolls for my taste."

Harry gives a long hum and accelerates us toward the parking lot. "Probably for the best. It wasn't a great day for anyone in our group, I don't think."

"What do you mean?"

He doesn't answer me until we park and he's easily stepping out of the truck I have to launch from. "Nothing really, just a couple arguments. Got a bit outta hand between Nicky and Jacob. They were being weird and rude about Davy, talking shit about what happened at lunch."

"What happened at lunch?" Other than After and I practicing our eventual blowout breakup a few weeks too soon, and doing it all too well.

I ready myself to catch up to Harry's long strides. He walks short steps for me and rubs at his neck.

"Just this and that," he mutters, face turning as red as the front doors.

"Hey, Harry?"

He gets to the door and opens it first. "Yeah."

"Don't ever play poker."

Harry dips his head with a laugh. "Yeah. Sure."

Chapter 44

It's weird, learning about someone new. I met Mei over a weekend her, Charlotte and I spent in Beverly Hills at a hotel, eating brunch for every meal (AKA endless mimosas for them, orange juice for me, and Nutella filled crepes all around) and I still learn more about her bit by bit to this day.

I like Mona, I think I wouldn't mind getting to know her more, seeing her seven-year-old son again. (Felix and I bonded very briefly over a mutual love for Pixar movies.)

Jackie still kind of freaks me out on occasion. But she drinks her coffee like I do, so there's that in common.

Know all there is to know about After, and I'm really not interested in learning anything else about him. Though he's still surprised me a couple times since February.

Guess he's changed how he likes his eggs and he curses more than he used to. And he's changed which side of the bed he'd rather sleep on. And violent video games bother him now, he'd rather play adventure ones with nice music.

Probably all flukes—not a lot of hidden things about him anymore, not when I've known him since we were teeny.

So, getting to know Harry and enjoying it isn't only fun, but it's a breath of fresh air; laughing to the point of tears while he tells me about his time in high school band with his twin Nicholas. (Who apparently Harry, and only Harry, calls 'Nicky'.)

He's vulnerable about his fears with Nicholas giving his heart out to the wrong people. He's soft when he talks about how he hasn't seen his dad in ten years. He embarrasses himself when he gets cranky about parking laws at the film studio. And he shows off his skills at playing the spoons; didn't even know that was a thing. He says he's killer at the fiddle, too.

"I don't believe you," I grin, breathless from continuing to choke on pancakes since his pouty, hand-flailing trivia about hating speed limits had me laughing too hard.

"Prepare to get a video at two in the morning in a week when I find my old one in Momma's attic, I'll prove it to you," he chuckles back, shoveling his last forkful of eggs into his mouth. "Hate that y'all gotta leave, man, this has been fun."

"It's cool, I'm sure ya boy will be around again sometime soon."

"He was saying September or something. What about you?"

"Visit Tennessee again?" I snort and raise my brows as I lift my orange juice. "Dude, I dunno. I'd love to. Didn't get to see Dollywood. But I doubt it."

Harry's fork lowers and he cranes his neck back. "Why not? Just come visit when he does—you'll be graduated by then, right?"

"Right, but. Don't um…don't know if him and I will still be together," I say honestly with a small shrug. That might've been the wrong thing to say, but isn't it true? Breakup in May, why would we still be talking months later?

Harry hums and rolls his shoulders back, leaning against our shared booth seat. "I didn't wanna say anything. The way he talks about you when you're not there, though…I'm not surprised."

Oh, straight up? Excuse me? "What—why?" Thought we were playing the lovebirds quite well up until this afternoon. What's he know that I don't?

There go those red, flaming cheeks again. He mumbles a sorryforgetitdon'tworryaboutit and goes for his apple juice. When he sees me still staring, he droops with a sigh.

"Was part of the argument Nicky and Jacob were having. Love my brother, but he's an idiot when it comes to men. Guess Jacob was saying he and Nicky weren't as serious as my bro thought, and Jacob was just biding his time until Davy was single again. Said he gives you and Davy another month before you break up."

Now I'm glaring, and I don't think Harry knows it's not at him, cause he shakes his head real fast. "No, sorry, I really shouldn't have said anything. I wasn't even there, Nicky told me Davy had said something after lunch about you and him, that y'all weren't gonna last…" His eyes squeeze shut and he makes a noise of death by oversharing.

"Sounds about right," I grunt, dropping my fork and crossing my arms. Harry groans and covers his hot pink face. I'd find him sweet right now if I wasn't so irritated. Like he said. Not surprised.

"It wasn't my place to say anything at all. Y'all can sort through your own business and I—shit, Nicky and Jacob, we need to butt out. Sorry, Scotty, I'm sorry—"

"Stop apologizing, please, it's fine." My eyes burn like hell and rubbing them isn't helping. Stupid Tennessee allergies. "Y'know, I'm pretty beat. If you're done, can you…can you drop me off at the hotel?"

Harry pushes fingers through his hair and gets up with our receipt. He whispers one more apology with a tap to my shoulder before he wanders off to pay, and I shove the rest of my pancakes into my mouth to keep from biting my tongue or crying.

—

Harry parks and gets out when I do. "Mind if I use the bathroom in y'all's room?"

"Fine, yeah, I got your hat anyway," I grumble, stomping off toward the automatic doors. If they opened a second later, I'd have slammed into them.

So, pretend boyfriend is already admitting that we won't be together long. Not sure why I'm upset about it; knew our 'love story' had a deadline when we got started. Doesn't feel nice that he's out there blurting that fact to people, especially to someone like Jacob, who apparently is just holding out in the shadows until After drops my ass.

Strap a clock to my chest, I guess. Another countdown until I'm not needed anymore and I get kicked out of the equation. Three for three with After, Mitch and Devon.

I push the hotel room door open with my shoulder, kick it wider for Harry behind me, and wag a limp hand to the bathroom. "Go for it. Take as long as you want."

"I just gotta piss and I'll be outta your hair."

"Could snort a line or jack off for all I care."

Harry trips at the doorway of the bathroom. "Um…okay."

Why'd I say that? After would laugh. Maybe. Harry doesn't get my kind of anger—I don't either. I haven't been mad like this since…Missy. No one saw my heartbreak then but the fly on my wall in Lubbock. Kept those tears of rage quiet and muffled in my pillow.

This is stupid. I'm so pissed off—*why* am I pissed off? He can fuck or not fuck whoever he wants. After can. Y'know what, so can Harry. They can all fuck off.

Harry comes back out a minute later, and I'm on the bed with his hat wrinkled in my fists, forehead shoved to my knuckles.

"I'm sorry, man, it's not you," I huff, standing and slouching over to him. "I know I don't keep my mouth shut very well when I'm embarrassed. But I don't usually blurt shit out like that."

"It's okay, Scotty. I worked fast, didn't even make a mess on the tile. Whether I'm talking about cocaine or jacking off, you'll never know."

I snort, then laugh and squint up at him. His nose wrinkles when he grins. "Funny…you've been blurting things all night. Are you a flustered blurter, too?"

"Is blurter a word?"

"It is now."

"Yeah, I've been known to blurt."

"Blurt something."

"I'm sorry about Davy. Jacob's an asshole. And I've wanted to kiss you since yesterday."

Wasn't ready for that last one. I kind of chuckle. Kind of cough. Mostly I think about the last smile I saw on After today, directed at Jacob as he went for the car to join him and Nicholas.

Not a single picture Harry and I took at IHOP was posted anywhere, not a single moment when he had his arm along the back of our booth seat was meant for someone else. I think, if I had held his hand, he'd have let me, and it would've been for us.

Harry has his back to the only light in the room, a sliver of white coming from the bathroom, so I can't see what his blush is doing. But I can feel it, roasting me standing a good foot away. I should say something. Anything. Now's the time to blurt and I'm speechless.

"You're allergic to chocolate," I manage to mumble.

Harry laughs and I realize his hat is still clenched in my hands. I set it on the desk and turn on the lamp, and his finger taps under my chin. His hand smells like Cinnamon Toast Crunch somehow, even though he had eggs and bacon at dinner. "Are you made of chocolate? If so, how have you not melted yet?"

"I had chocolate chip pancakes; I don't want you dead." I'm on my toes now.

"If you don't wanna kiss me, you coulda just said no," he replies, dipping his head toward mine.

"I'd like to kiss you, too."

He lets out what sounds like a sigh, another laugh, and a soft groan. "Probably shouldn't, though...don't think I could stop with just kissing you, Scotty. What about after?"

"What about him?" Harry looks confused at that. Less confused when I hook my finger into his shirt collar and bring him down a few more inches. "May I?"

I like how thick his southern accent is when he says, "You're sweet for askin'." Then his lips are on mine.

He breathes me in so deep, it's like I'm his only source of oxygen. And fuck, he's just cinnamon and apple juice and hot breakfasts in a log cabin somewhere in the east.

With a twist of our bodies, his arms wrap around me entirely and I'm overpowered and pressed to the wall. Sparks fizzle in my stomach, and I don't mean to but, oh man, I let out just a teeny bit of a moan cause good God he's *warm*.

His mouth falls away for only a second before he drops, takes my thighs, and *stands* and wraps my legs around him. "Oh—geez, Harry—"

"Yeah?"

"*Yes*."

The hit of my back to the wall knocks whatever air was left in my chest out of me, and I sound like I'm on a rollercoaster. I can't catch my breath, but I don't even care anymore, not with his hands on my legs, fingers spreading over the entirety of my hips.

A deep groan builds up low in his chest when I bite on his lip, and I peek at him through my lashes to see his eyes roll, his brow knitting hard. There's a bead of sweat on his temple, and when I drag my fingers across his jaw through his hair, when I tug at the root, I swear he's trying to crush me into the plaster. He pins me with just his chest, pulls back his hips, and lets them roll, and I finally get the rest of him.

Dear gracious, I get every *inch* of the rest of him, right between my legs against my dick. I open my mouth to choke out something stupid like, 'You're built like fucking lumberjack Adonis', but his lips cover mine as I just uselessly gasp instead. It's been so damn long since I felt someone else, touched someone who wanted me like this, who kissed me and meant it. Not like how After kissed me all day long.

This isn't After—I mean shit, hello, of course not.

Do I care? He's slept with Jacob at least once (admittedly) while we've been 'dating'. Did he ever think of our fake boyfriend loyalty any time he ran off behind my back?

A good person would continue to put someone's heart over their own, even if that someone else never bothered to do the same.

No...that's not just a good person. That's someone selfless.

Didn't realize I'd stopped kissing Harry. He moves his face back an inch to look at me through red lashes. "Are you okay?" He sounds like gravel, and I love that it's because of me.

I decide I'm not a good person, and I'm selfish as hell. So I reply with my voice shot to shit, too, "I want you to fuck me."

"*God*, Scotty, don't talk like that."

"Shut me up then."

Harry glares at me and it's the hottest thing. He goes straight for my neck with another lift of his hips, grinding us together like horny teens who snuck off in the middle of a high school dance. Every few seconds he laughs, makes me laugh, then he moans and starts kissing me again even as he's smiling.

He shifts me in his arms and I go up an inch higher than him, yanking at the back of his shirt. I'm tempted to just tear the damn thing off to see how far that blush of his goes when he's bright red in the face like this, freckles like poppies over ivory.

Gabriel had freckles like Harry, and his flush only went to his collarbone.

This isn't Gabriel.

Obviously, c'mon brain, keep up, the hell we doing here, rifling through old feelings? No, move on, let's go, pay attention to that sweet sound that comes out of Harry when I arch my chest into his and run my mouth up his neck.

"I gotta put you down, Scotty, sorry—" Where'd his southern accent go? Come back Harry, what's happening in my head?

"Am I too heavy?" I joke. Why do my eyes sting?

He laughs and kisses my cheek. "No. I could hold you for hours. But this is getting dangerous. You're too damn pretty." Well, golly, *that's* a compliment I've never received before. It sends me after him all over again.

I think my renowned zeal startles him, but only for a second. Then he's breathing even harder, holding me to the wall with one hand planted on my abdomen, the other gripping high up my thigh. Something hits the button on my jeans, and I think it's my shirt.

Until the something turns into fingers, turns into a square palm, and the first touch of his hand on my dick shoots fire into my gut and it's not good.

This is not a good heat. This is not Gabriel. But it might as well be, cause he's there in my brain, front and center.

This guy is twice the size of Gabriel in more ways than one. He's made me laugh all night, he's soft, he's round and kind. Gabriel was amazing and funny, too, but he was sharp elbows and jaw, dangerous eyes that he could make friendly when he wanted to. He called me 'sweetheart'; never used my name. He wouldn't be able to hold me up like this.

And though he held me after that first time, when I sobbed as I came down from my first intense high, he never held my hand.

Last time in his Jeep, in the parking lot, I don't even remember the moment the sex started. I only remember being naked and under him, when my brain started to fight back just a little.

No idea why. Maybe one last attempt to tell me this was all gonna get me killed. It ended with a flashlight shining through the window straight at us, and red and blue swirling behind the Jeep.

I suddenly don't want to do this and I don't know how to stop.

"Hey—Scotty—"

Don't cry, don't cry, *do not cry*— "Y-yeah?"

Harry's still looking thoroughly snogged, happy and horny, so at least he hasn't noticed my oncoming whatever-the-fuck attack. Slowing his breathing, he lowers me to the floor. "As much as I wanna throw you to the mattress and bend you in half—" oh, mercy, sweet southern boys do *not* talk like that— "I don't think we can do this here. Not with Davy coming back any second."

Leaving the hotel room now is a decision I'll never be able to take back. Just like lowering my nose to the dashboard and snorting that last line in Gabriel's Jeep before it all fell to shit.

"And…this has been fun, Harry, but. I'm not sure I can go with you anywhere else. I'm not sure I'm ready for w-whatever else."

Harry nods and tucks hair behind my ears. "How 'bout this. I'll wait in the hall for ten seconds. If you open the door, we'll go to my house. I'll make you breakfast in the morning." Every exhale he gives pushes into my chest. Already I feel his heartbeat calming. "And in the afternoon, I'll drive you to the airport for your flight after spending all day hanging out and doing whatever you wanna do."

He smiles with a lot more patience than I deserve. "Or. If ten seconds pass. If I hear you lock the door. Then no harm done. We'll still be friends." Harry brings in one final deep breath, then taps his forehead to mine. "That'll never change."

"You're okay with leaving it all up to me?" I ask, going for the back of his neck as he straightens out of my reach, my body like no, we can still do this, we can put on the content face and do it for him.

"I think it has to be all up to you, Scotty. I see this going either way." I nod to my feet and reach for his hat on the desk. "Why don't you keep that?"

"If this could go either way, I'm not sure I should," I reply, holding it between us.

He takes his hat and kisses me on the temple, once more on my lips, lingering there as my heart starts to crumble.

Then he steps back and grins so genuine and soft that I nearly make up my mind right then and there to go with him, if just to have someone hold me for a few hours.

"Ten seconds," he whispers.

"Ten seconds."

Harry puts his hat on and closes the door, and I rush up to it, hands on the wood. I count down.

I get to eight and my pulse pounds in my ears. I get to five and I bite my cheek, my lip, my knuckles, anything to keep from crying too loud. I get to one. I lock the door.

Slow boots depart down the carpeted hall, and I sink to the floor with my head in my hands. Don't bother to get up to turn on the TV to muffle my hiccups. I just press my face into the crook of my elbow. My phone goes off in my pocket.

[Harry] 21:44: Sweet dreams, Scotty. Thank you for talking to me tonight.

I either dodged a bullet or let something wonderful slip right through my fingers.

I almost text him and ask him to come back, let me explain. But he wouldn't get it. No one's ever gonna get it. Except you, Gabriel, cause you threw me off the deep end in the first place.

Can't even blame After for this one.

Chapter 45

That was definitely the door closing, Chicken's dog tags clinking, and it's definitely still dark outside, even with the blackout curtains open. Chicken hops up on the bed and circles into the perfect spot, and that's most *definitely* After thumping onto the bed right next to him to take off his boots, ass nearly crushing my foot. I pull it back slow, like I'm asleep (cause up to ten seconds ago, I was asleep) then I let his ass cheek have it and kick him *hard*.

He yelps. I have to bite my lip when he turns and goes, "Jesus, Chicken, that was rude..."

He's up and walking around, and I check him over my shoulder in the moving light from the TV, watch him take off his shirt, stretch. My eyes dart to the clock on his bedside table that says— you gotta be kidding me. "Dude."

After yelps again and it's a lot less funny. "Gracious sakes, Scotty—"

"You have woken me up at three. A. Em."

"Oh...is it really—"

Clawing out for my nightstand, I roll over and chuck crinkled burger wrapper from my second dinner at his head. (Love you IHOP, but you ain't enough to satiate me when I'm up until eleven freaking the hell out, and McDonald's DoorDash is a mere phonecall away.) After deflects my following assault of napkins, but he's too slow to smack aside the paper container full of pointy French fry crumbs. "Scott, stop—"

"What are you doing back here so *late*? And so loud? I was asleep."

"I'm surprised Chicken's thrashing didn't wake you."

"*I* kicked you, dipshit!" He pouts at me and I groan and cover my head in covers. "You're an asshole, After."

He gives the comforter an insistent yank, yank, yank, until it's back to my shoulder. "Scotty." Poke. "Scott Eeee." Poke, poke.

"Stop pawing at my cheek."

He chuckles a warm breath over my face. "Hey, c'mon, now that you're up I wanna talk to you."

"Go away. You were such a dick yesterday."

After hums and plants a knee on the bed. Like hell, bro, you're sleeping on the sofa. "I know, I'm sorry—"

"An ugly one, too. Veiny, bulbous, hideous fucking chode."

I hate his laugh, and I grab an extra pillow and shove it up at him. "Vivid—I was all those things, yes."

"I had to get a ride back here from Harry when you and the others felt oh so inclined to go get wasted again. You left poor Chicken at Rosamine's for hours—"

"He's happy, he's all fattened up, she said she fed him pancakes."

A stupid need to make him jealous creeps in, and I send him a side eye while he's hidden by pillow to the face. "Harry and I had pancakes, too, by the way. We had a good time. We got IHOP. And we made out, right in here, got real NC-17. I almost went with him, y'know; you wouldn't have seen me until our flight home."

After's sigh is muffled. "Harry's a good guy. Y'all would be really good together, if you want to keep talking to him."

That didn't have the effect I wanted at all, what happened to complaining about him smoking pot? (Which he doesn't, by the way, smoke it or eat it; poor lad is allergic to that, too. Worst night of his life, he said, chocolate weed brownie nearly sent him to Jesus.)

After takes my pillow and throws his other leg over my body, trapping the comforter under his knees on either side of me so I can't pull it over my head again.

"I'm sorry, hey," he whispers. He drops once, twice, makes the bed and me bounce around, then squishes me under his weight with his hands on my shoulder. "Please look at me?"

I refuse, so I stare at Chicken on his back with all his paws in the air, already conked out despite After's antics. "Why are you so energized? Did you chug six RedBulls again? Last time you did that, you put a hole in your mom's garage with your foot."

"I remember."

"Then your face. Then *my* face."

He laughs again. "I remember. I'm not hyped up on caffeine. I'm hyped up on *freedom*."

I snort and squint at his dopey grin out of the corner of my eye. He's gotta be seconds away from crashing on some sort of sugar high. "Do I want to ask?"

"Please ask me." He gives me big doe eyes and flutters his lashes. A smile threatens to slink across my face.

I shove my mouth into the pillows and groan, then relent and turn my head up to him. Our noses tap. He doesn't pull away. I physically can't pull away without dissolving into the mattress, which I'd gladly do right now if it put some space between us. "What…what kind of freedom?"

He rubs our noses together. Forget dissolving into the mattress, I want to set it on fire.

"I broke it off entirely with Jacob," he gleefully hisses. "Didn't just ghost him like I was planning. I talked to him, face to face, until I had to walk away cause he wasn't listening. I walked away, Scott. I said no!"

"You…wait, what?" There are two Afters from my crossed eyes, and both look super ecstatic.

"Yeah—yeah, it took me three hours. I told him I don't wanna do any of that anymore. No more parties, drinking, video shit. I told him to leave me alone, even suggested he leaves Nicholas alone cause he's a dick to him, too. Told Jacob he should just go back to Oregon, to his kids and wife—"

"His *what*!" I would've collided our heads together if After hadn't thought to dart back an inch at the last second. "After—bro, holy crap—"

"No, I know. Yeah, I know, and…" The glee is fizzling and now it's my fault for reacting like that. (Not like I could react any other way; I am indeed a human being who gets shocked by shit like secret wives and kids.)

"Hey, you're good, I'm just, that surprised me that's all, I'm sorry."

"No, hey, I'm sorry," he cuts in. I'm taking a breath to apologize again anyway when he gives a soft laugh and dips his head, short hair tickling over my nose. "For yesterday. None of it was fair to you. For so much, Scott, I'm sorry. I should've said my apologies to you in person a lifetime ago. You deserve that much."

I'm getting whiplash again.

It's like looking at someone completely different than the person who pushed me to the brink without blinking.

The TV flashes brighter, and that's when I see that he's not just happy, but exhausted. There are deep lines under his red eyes, the skin darker than just a few hours before. He sniffles and smiles again, and I get a pang of reality that this is straight up something to celebrate. Even if it looks like he's probably been crying nonstop.

I push Chicken away as he grumbles and argues, and I wrap my arms around After's neck and shoulders, rolling him with me to lay on my right side. He grumbles and argues, too, but only cause he's still in his jeans.

"Then get rid of them and go to sleep," I tell him. There's a clink of belt and a swish of denim, and after much wriggling, he's kicking under the covers with me, cold toes tapping at my shins as he shimmies down. There's a brief second where his lips trace at the hairs by my temple, and I think it's an accident.

But he does it again, and he doesn't separate himself from me, still laying on my arm under his neck, his falling over my abdomen. I'm a live wire hit by lightning, buzzing and electrified all over. My toes curl under the comforter, and his knee hooks around mine, and Chicken's got a new spot against my back. I'm hotdogged between the two of them. There's nowhere for me to run.

"C—uh…ya cozy?" I ask, scared to breathe as he's taken up his home with his face pushed into the crook of my neck. This is *not* a guy friend thing. This is also not a fake boyfriend thing, cause there's not a single fucking camera in here. (If there is, I apologize for my dancing in the shower yesterday morning, but also shame on you for peeping.)

"Comforted," he sighs. Good, hope *you* can sleep, bro, cause I ain't gonna get a wink now. "Scott…?"

"Yeah, man."

"Did you really make out with Harry?" I swear it sounds like he's smiling.

"Yeah."

"Why'd y'all stop?"

Oh, let's see. Cause the feel of another person's body against me, lips on my neck, and hands that weren't mine on my dick, sent me on a weepy spiral, questioning my own sanity, complete with late-night fast-food binge.

After's mouth is near my neck right now. His body is against mine. Why am I not losing my mind like I was with Harry? (Here I am, questioning my sanity again, hoo-boy.) "I'm supposed to be quote-dating-unquote *you*, After. Can't hookup with another dude in the hotel everyone knows we're staying in."

"You coulda gone with him. I wouldn't have been upset."

"I had no way to know that; you tried to convince me he was a horrible person cause he goes sockless sometimes…"

"Right…right, no. Harry's a really good guy. I was an idiot. So how was it?"

I smirk. "You want a play by play?" I'm shocked when he hums an 'mhm' in reply. "He picked me up."

"Goddamn. That's hot."

"Right? Threatened to bend me in half."

After scoffs, "Well shit, now *I* want to make out with Harry." I laugh, but then I imagine them both. Then I imagine them both and *me* and I'm like heyyy-*yup* his leg is a *little* too close to my crotch for my taste, let's think some holier thoughts before he notices a lil somethin' somethin' going on down there.

"Hey, Scotty?"

"Hma-huh?" So chill, much relaxed. Wow.

"Can I take you on a road trip tomorrow? I mean, I guess, later this morning?"

"Another one?"

"It's not far. Three and a half hours on the bike."

"The bike…?" I scowl and look down as he looks up, and my long nose pokes him in the eye. "What bike? Not Nicholas's bike?"

"Ow, holy crap, you fucking bird—yes, his bike, his motorcycle."

"Are you *out* of your *mind*!" My shout wakes up Chicken, and he kicks me in the hip with a wild paw. I grab his nose and shake him around until he's batting me off and gets grouchy and goes to lay on the sofa. "I saw you doing stunts on that bike last night—it's a death trap!"

"It's a Honda CB seven-fifty—"

"I swear, if you keep rattling letters and numbers off at me like you think I'll know what that means, I'm gonna punch you."

"But it's a classic."

"Crotch rocket."

After's frown breaks and he laughs right in my ear, shoving his face further into my neck until it tickles, then we're a mess of limbs, fighting each other under the covers. Nearly get a knee to my balls, and it takes me gripping his wrists and shoving him into the mattress for him to stop kicking around.

And then it's me. With his wrists in my hands. Pinning him to the mattress with my chest—at *what point* did I think this was a good idea? Where, where is the logic? What happened to holier thoughts, Scott?

He's breathless and blinking up at me and grinning, and my face gets warmer with every second that passes. His heart is a jackrabbit against mine.

"I…wanted to take you to Dollywood. Before we fly home," he says as he swallows. Don't you do it—he licks his lips. Wasn't I angry at him 0.5 seconds ago? Can we get back to *those* red-hot emotions, please?

"You're gonna take me to death's door if I fly off your back while you speed down the highway on that thing."

"I'll protect you."

"Impossible."

"You literally have to go; our plane is leaving from Gatlinburg Pigeon Forge."

"Where the heck is Pigeon Forge?"

"Dollywood," he smirks. Why haven't I gotten off him yet? Why hasn't he made me get off him yet?

I shove away from him and turn onto my other side, glaring at Chicken who's glaring at me from the sofa. "Go to sleep, After."

He hums into a yawn and closes the space I've created with an arm around my waist, face pushed to my middle back. "I'm glad you let me talk to you about Jacob," he mumbles, squeezing me. "I needed you here. Thank you."

Don't do that, I want to tell him.

I'm clinging to being upset right now. I have to, I can't forget the fight we had just like that. I don't really care that he's apologized. He can pretend like yesterday didn't happen all he wants. But the shouting, the bringing up old, hateful words, him walking out on the conversation—all that's still fresh in my brain. If this was a real relationship, he wouldn't have—

Well. But it's not, is it? He's not really my boyfriend. We don't really have a mutual trust and respect on that level. And this isn't a partnership where we don't stomp out and slam doors.

And yet…if this wasn't a real relationship, at least a real friendship, would he have made the effort to prove his own commitment to himself by breaking up with a toxic person? Would he have gotten so excited to tell me about it?

If this wasn't a real…whatever this is, he wouldn't have apologized to me in the eye this time so sincerely.

Can't hang onto frustration anymore. Can't get comfortable on my left. Can't turn around with After right up against me— "You need to roll over, don't you?" he says quietly.

I mutter some sleepy nonsense, and he lifts his arm, lets me turn. But he doesn't back away once I'm facing him, and he settles with his forehead to my chest, no doubt feeling every rapid heartbeat straight into his skull.

"What um…" My arm hovers in the air for a moment before I let gravity pull it down, resting it on his shoulder. "What time do we need to leave in the morning for Dollywood?"

He shakes his head and nuzzles in closer. "Sleep as late as you want, Scotty. No rush to go anywhere at all."

Yeah, definitely can't hang onto frustration anymore…

Chapter 46

The motorcycle isn't nearly as terrifying as I thought it'd be. When I start to ball up tight as we pass around a slow-moving semi, or gravel flies a bit too close to comfort near my helmet (thank the Lord After thought to make sure we had helmets and leather jackets, even if I'm sweating bullets in the getup) I just tell myself: Dolly's at the end of this. Do it for Dolly.

I admittedly get a little cocky, and when After says there's only fifteen minutes left until we get there, I take off the helmet and let the wind and smell of open road rush around me.

Slowing to a stoplight, After does the same, handing his back to me with a wild grin and encouraging me to toss them into the sidecar. (The sidecar unfortunately wasn't on the bike when he was doing the bad boy stunts last night. I was told it's usually attached though, as that's Rosamine's special spot.)

He revs the bike at the light, and we take off in a blink, so fast I hardly have time to grip his waist before I'm thrown to the wayside. My cheek presses to the leather between his shoulders, and his laugh shakes through me. Already I know the moment we get back to LA he's gonna buy himself a bike. I'll have to pretend to hate it.

Visiting Dollywood in the late spring means it's the Flower and Food Festival. Which also means there are butterflies everywhere.

Walking around and getting lost one too many times, we're amazed by tulips and daffodils and monarch statues the size of Chicken. (He's getting a ride to the airport by angel Harry and is currently eating his weight in sausage, don't worry.)

I get my picture taken with every poster of the great Ms. Parton I can find, and I buy a pretty white and red China mug for Bevvy. She didn't understand my adoration for Dolly until I made her watch Steel Magnolias three years ago. Now we watch it every Christmas.

Not sure when I did it—but I'm holding onto After's hand. And he's been content to let me drag him around the entire time, taking him from food place to flower sculpture.

It's a good thing we're walking so much or I'd have died after the first trip to get paletas and lobster rolls. To be fair, it is called the flower and *food* festival. The latter of the two being the reason we park ourselves on a bench in the shade, drinking frozen lemonades and munching on a shared waffle sandwich. (Okay, yes Greta, in this *one* instance I will say waffles are better than pancakes.)

After lets out a long, satisfied hum, and drapes his arm along the back of the bench, our leather jackets folded on his other side. "Are you happy, Scotty?" he asks, leaning his head back.

"Currently, I'm eating a waffle filled with coffee ice cream and dipped in chocolate." He chuckles and opens one eye at me. "Ask me again in an hour when I'm dying from overeating."

"Can I ask you another question?"

"If you must interrupt my feast, I can't stop you."

"Did you read the text?"

He's got both eyes on me now. I shake my head, and he nods and rubs a hand across his thigh. "I'm sorry I thought pushing you to do that would help the situation somehow."

"What did you think it would accomplish?"

"I don't know, honestly. It felt like there was a line we'd created and agreed to, and it was starting to get murky. I couldn't figure out if I wanted that or not, or if you did. The text was me trying to build that line. No…" he looks to his lap, "that *wall*. Back up. Remind myself that I can pretend all I want that I'm a good person, but I'm…" His nose twitches and he looks up to the multi-colored umbrellas hanging above us. Kind of wish they let in more rainbow light, like a stained-glass window. Bet he'd look nice, painted in a prism like that.

I offer him a bite of my waffle, and he gives me a shy smile and lets me feed him. "We're friends," he mumbles, nodding to himself. "Whatever I said yesterday was bullshit. We *are* friends, and I trust you."

"Then as your friend, I need to be honest," I reply. He turns and mirrors me, leg crossed under a knee, arm still on the back of the bench. "Your words aren't matching your actions. Your words don't even match your other words. What you said might've been bullshit, but I meant what I said; I can't keep up with how you are around me. I appreciate that you say we're friends and that you've apologized, but it's hard to believe that when you're all over the place."

Maybe there *is* a prism overhead; his face turns a shade of pink, then red, bright over his ears. "You're right. I've been hot and cold and it honestly has nothing to do with you. But…I don't think I'm ready to face the real reasons yet, if that's okay. In the meantime, I'll try to be better."

I give him the rest of my waffle without pushing those reasons. Once he balls up the wrapping paper, he holds it tight in his fist, and his voice catches when he says, "I wanna give you an out."

"What do you mean?"

"So. Obviously the—the fake dating thing is working. It's getting noticed, talked about. We can. Stop now…if you want to." His arm isn't around the back of the bench anymore but pressed to my shoulders. "I'll still help you with your writing, as long as you need me to. Maybe we can uh…I dunno. Get. Coffee sometimes. But we can stop here with all the other stuff. You don't have to go to Spain."

I open my mouth and he drops the trash in his lap and wipes at his temple. Why is his lip shaking? Why does this feel like we're about to be split apart again? I live closer to him than an eight-hour greyhound ride, and this is a worse goodbye than last time. "No."

"No," he repeats to the umbrellas.

"No, I said I'd do the five things with you, and I'm sticking through it."

"But that's just more of me you'll have to put up with—"

"*You'll* have to put up with *me*," I retort. After huffs a short chuckle. "Besides, when else am I gonna get an all-expenses paid trip overseas?"

He laughs then and smiles at me with crinkly eyes. "Who said I was paying for all of it?"

"I got your dads' numbers; they'd buy my ticket in a heartbeat before they ever bought yours."

After snickers, and his shrug leans his arm closer to my back. "True, very true."

"Besides, do you realize how many times I had to go get my passport fixed cause they kept misspelling Everett?"

"What'd you get instead, Everest like in third grade?"

"Got fucking Ervervent." After snorts at me. "There's not even an 'n' anywhere in my name."

Another long breath in. He turns his head away, but not before I watch one tear slip past his lashes. I pat his knee, and I leave my hand there, especially once his fingers clap over mine and press it to his leg. "Can I take you somewhere else before our flight?" he asks.

"Anywhere."

He gets up and leads me by the hand back to the bike.

———

With three hours to go, he takes me to a miles-wide field, covered in big, bouncy green leaves the size of dinner-plates. The stalks of whatever's growing here are thick and nearly as tall as me, and there are thousands of them.

"What am I looking at?" I ask, walking along the edge, expecting to see some little woodland creature beckoning me within to some otherworldly place hidden in the lush foliage.

"C'mere, come back here," After smiles, reaching out for me as I start to wander into the field. He's got his phone out, and before I can look at it, he hides it to his chest.

"Now, we're early. They're not usually out until July. But I thought you'd like to see what's going to be here in a few months." His hand rubs circles on my back. "Maybe…we can plan another trip. Drive all over the country just to get here and see…these," he whispers, showing me his phone.

I look from the screen to the field, then back to his phone, grin widening so much it makes my eyes water.

Every inch of his screen is covered in glorious, yellow sunflowers. A horizon's worth, far as the eye can see. Lower-level painted emerald with stems, sky above crisp and cloudless, just like today. Then a wide line of gold. So much gold.

Don't remember the moment I wrapped my arms around his waist, or when I put my head to his shoulder.

I wish I had my Pashmina. I'd run through the fresh, green fields, holding it out behind me like it could catch a strong wind and take me off into the sky, floating with the umbrellas that hung over our heads at Dollywood.

I wish I had my mom. She'd love this.

Chapter 47

"And you have to go to another event next week, right?"

After hums over the phone line. There's a *tappity-tap* of his fingers on something as he thinks. "No, I had to move that one. I'm trying not to travel that much more before we go to Gibraltar, I don't want to be crunched for time."

"Smart, smart." I get out of the way of a family of six strolling into the movie theater, nodding apologetically to them for standing smack in the middle of the pathway. "How'd the one go last week?"

"In Malibu? Really amazing actually. A lot of LGBTQIA people, so many questions—bro, I went home and read until, like, four AM, just to make sure I could help answer more questions for the next talk."

"That's amazing. So lots of positive receptivity?"

"For sure. I mean, there's the occasional grunt who gets wind that there's a convention and feels the need to butt in and be ugly and homophobic but—" the noise he makes is his shrug noise— "it's kinda funny when they see it's me. Cause I think they're imagining the person doing interviews about being gay as a celebrity, coming to terms with alcoholism—they're expecting a caricature of a victim, or an addict, whatever that looks like to them. But then they get—"

"Tattooed beefcake with a facial scar and two doors for security guards."

After giggles. "Don't forget Chicken."

I pause my circling and cover my smile with my hand, shaking my head. "You're bringing him to your interviews?"

"He's turned into a bit of a guard dog. Some of the kids that come to the conventions are young. Like, ten, eleven years old. They travel in packs with their friends, behind their parents' backs sometimes, looking for someone who understands them. Add Chicken to the mix who loves everyone, he helps a lot of them who get upset calm down. I even bought him a vest. It says: 'Hi, I'm Chicken, and I'll be your friend'."

"That is the cutest thing, oh my gracious."

"I mean, I think back to when I got him—I was low and lonely and scared. Rescuing him helped me, so I thought he'd do a lot of good. I look at these people, young and old, and I'm like, I was you. I'm still you. We're friends. Let's talk, y'know?"

My face warms with pride. "You were born for this, dude. You should do something nice for yourself."

"I am, what do you think I'm doing at the dealership?"

"I cannot believe you're actually buying one."

He laughs, and I check up and around to make sure no one's seeing me standing here giggling like a dumbass. "I'm surprised you're surprised, Scotty," he replies. "You had fun on the bike, admit it."

"I like the Ferrari better."

"About that…"

"Don't you *dare* tell me you sold my car—"

"—*Your* car!"

"—To buy a flipping motorcycle!"

After laughs again, so loud it makes the phone break up. "Oh, man. No, no it's still here, I'm just teasing you."

"You have more money than you know what to do with."

"Nonsense—hey, I gotta go, they're wheeling my shiny new chrome baby out now."

"Are you gonna name it?"

"I'll let you name it. What did you name the Ferrari?"

I grin and turn my back to the bustle of people coming out of the movie theaters into the lobby. "Sugar Shorts."

He snickers like a snake. "I love it. Okay, I'll talk to you later, yeah?"

"Yeah, sure bye—"

Bevett comes racing out of our theater, having stayed behind with Mitch to get to the post credits scene. (I saw After calling me and I tripped on my own feet just to get to the lobby to answer him. Don't need no thirty minutes of credits for a ten second cliffhanger, that's what Wikipedia's for.)

"Guess what, guess what, guess what!" she squawks.

"What, what, what?" I smile, opening my arms for her to collide into. She halts right before she gets to me, does a one-girl wave with her arms, then jumps into mine, squeezing my middle. "What the heck was that?" I laugh, swaying her around.

"My happy dance! Mill and Hattie said they can visit me this summer! And Grandpa said they can stay in the big house with me all! Summer! Long!"

"All summer?" I look over her head to Mitch, one hand in his pocket, grey suit jacket open all casual. He unbuttons the top of his shirt. I haven't seen his so at ease in ages. "All...*all* summer, Grandpa?"

He smiles at...at *me*? "I think she deserves a nice break, don't you?" he replies, putting his hand on the back of Bevett's head. She beams up at him, still pressed to my chest. "After being honest about NJHS, working to bring her grades up to her own standards, she's earned some ridiculous girl fun."

Man, back in my day, we didn't have our 'own standards' when it came to Grandpa. His second hand comes out from his pocket and he sets my back on fire when it lands on my shoulder. "You've earned that, too."

"He's earned some ridiculous girl fun, too?" Bevett giggles. Mitch *laughs*.

"Good grief—he deserves a break! Some time to relax, more fun days like today. You're nearly graduated and your job's been running you ragged, Scotty. Took you all the way to Tennessee two weeks ago, who knows where they'll send you next."

Oooh. About that.

I never told Grandpa I went to Tennessee with After. Never even told him I stayed the night at his house, just that I was working late at the office and couldn't come visit him and Bevett for the weekend.

I didn't think Grandpa Mitch would appreciate that I was still spending time with After, not when the news came out just how drunk he was at the club on the gala night. Even if he was working hard to remain sober now, it did nothing to stop the rumors. And the pictures.

After might've asked me to not seek the photos out, and I know Erica's been working her ass off to get them destroyed somehow. But there wasn't much I could do when yesterday I pulled up Google, and the first article said, "**Things you missed last month: David Después Drunk Debut. Boyfriends and boy-toys galore!**" Photo right there of him lip-locked with Jacob, another random dude with his arms around After from behind, hands quite literally in After's pants.

Caption under the picture made me squirm: "**Gay? Yes. Insatiable? Triple yes!**"

He doesn't know I've seen those photos yet.

I thought today with Bevvy and Mitch, going to get crepes, seeing a movie (not After's new movie, Bevett's seen it six times already) was all because. I mean. I don't know. For her? I had no idea it was meant for me, too.

"T-thanks, Grandpa. Thank you, I appreciate it," I smile at him. His fingers trace through my hair like I'm legit his grandson and he's legit proud of me. I crush Bevett tighter in case this is all a dream. "Um. So. Lunch? Lunch—where do we wanna go?" I sniffle, looking down to her.

She wrinkles her nose at me like she gets the reason why my voice is now ten notches higher. "Where do *you* wanna go?"

"Barbecue?"

"Didn't get enough southern cooking in Tennessee?" Mitch smiles, accepting Bevett's arm behind his waist as she squishes between us.

"No, never," I laugh. My phone starts to go off in my pocket. "Y'all go ahead, I'll be right out."

"We'll get the car—if you're not out in five, we're getting potato salad without you," Mitch says, leading Bevett to the doors.

My face hurts from smiling, and I look at my phone. "Hey, After, two calls in one day? I'm flattered, but—"

"Scotty, where are you?"

I scowl at my phone, goosebumps tickling around my neck at the deep, quiet tone of his voice. "The movies, haven't left the theater yet—"

"Which theater, which one?"

"The one on Paramount, why?"

"Shit, okay that's—that's not too far. You still with Mitch and Bevvy?"

"Yeah, why—what's going on?"

"Stay close to them, Scott, keep together, okay? I'm on my way."

"After—"

"Stay away from the reporters, Bo! Do *not* answer *any* questions!" He hangs up.

My hand trembles and struggles to slide my phone back into my pocket. Is this about the photos? I can't swallow right. I shouldn't feel so anxious; I've handled people being nosy about him before.

Fixing my shirt collar, I go out to join Bevett and Mitch. They're on the sidewalk, the Caddy's hazards flashing as it sits at the curb. Mitch's arm is still around Bevett, and the two are talking to someone in line at a magazine cart.

"Hey, y'all," I smile, jogging down the theater steps toward them. Three heads turn with smiles back for me, and the dude nods. "Bevvy, you make a new friend already?"

She laughs. "Not my friend, he says he knows you!"

"Me?" I tilt my head but accept the guy's handshake. Don't recognize him. Little taller than me, black hair, friendly eyes.

"Yeah man, good to see you again." At my embarrassed chuckle and shake of my head, guy smirks and looks to his shoes. "It's cool, no worries. Greg? Greg Benson? Greggo?"

"Greggo…no, man, I'm sorry I don't think I know you."

"Well, damn," he says, clicking his tongue, "I know *you*. From El Paso."

Greg smiles. Looks like Jacob at the fundraiser; vicious and sneaky and foxlike. My stomach plummets.

He pulls his other hand from his pocket, and in it is a recorder. He holds it up to me. Clicks it on.

"What do you have to say, Scott Boscoe, about the accusations around you becoming a heroin junkie at the ripe age of eighteen, drinking underage, indecent exposure, and assaulting an El Paso police officer?"

All conversation around us freezes in mid-air. I choke on spit and can't manage to swallow, let alone reply. Everyone waiting for a taxi, everyone in line at the magazine kiosk. They all turn and look at me.

To make matters worse, so much worse, he holds up his newly purchased mag.

And there's my face. Eighteen. Bleary-eyed and high as hell, hair a mess. In front of a white backdrop, holding my number for my mugshot. Front and center on *Us Weekly*. "**David's newest catch—throw it back! Scott Boscoe, grandson of Judge Norman, just as much an addict as Lancelot? Match made in heaven!**"

Greg blinks and cocks his head. The wind caresses a piece of his black hair. I can see the steady pulse in his neck from here. Slow and chill.

I don't hear Mitch. He must be holding his breath. I don't hear Bevett breathe, either.

I just hear me breathing, hard, eyes shaking. There's sweat under my arms, at my ears, behind my knees.

Greg's smile stretches wider. "Well? Nothing to say? Silence is just as good as an admission, Scotty."

The recorder jabs at me. Knife, screams my brain, rattlesnake, bomb! I slap his hand away.

That was 1,000% the wrong thing to do. One person in line steps out, comes toward us, and she's got a notepad and pen. I sense movement on our other side, beside Mitch, and here comes another reporter hidden in plain sight. Something flashes, lights of the afterlife blinding me. Across the street, another person has a long-lens camera focused straight on me.

They're multiplying. There's two more, pushing forward through this slowly building crowd, piling between cars stopped in traffic and rubbernecking at the scene. Three more pulling recorders and pens and journals from their pockets like hand grenades.

People all over are lifting their phones up and pointing them at me. I half expect to look at my chest and see myself dotted in red sniper lasers.

Then Judge Norman, esteemed man of court who should know better, shouts the worst possible thing you could ever say to someone with their head on a chopping block.

"*Who did you tell!*"

And they swarm like rats to a corpse, with me as the still bloody and juicy heart in the center. I don't stand a chance.

Chapter 48

"Is it true your alcohol level was over 1% at the time of the arrest—"

"Your boyfriend Gabriel reported that the drugs were your idea—"

"Gabriel Avant claims Devon and Kendra Bates from El Paso got you the cocaine and the heroin—"

"Did you really hit Officer Kingwald with a crowbar—"

"How much did Judge Norman pay the officers of El Paso to keep silent—"

"Dash cam evidence shows you and Gabriel both assaulted officer Kingwald while she was unconscious—"

Mitch's hand clamps around my bicep. Bevett's crushed between us (at least we both thought the same thing at the same time: protect her) but I swear Mitch is straight up steering me to use me as a human shield.

I've never seen so many beady eyes directly in my face at one time.

Am I not human to them? Is this what After deals with on a daily basis? It's no wonder he needs both Thor and Angus to protect him. Who's gonna protect me?

Some asshat on a motorbike revs through traffic and nearly hits Grandpa's Caddy at the curb, scattering leaves and gravel up at the paparazzi in a flash of silver and red.

They screech to a stop in front of us and flip up the visor of their helmet, and furious hazel eyes glint in the sun, shadowed by a scarred brow.

I want to laugh. I want to kiss him. But I'm gonna throw up.

For ten intense seconds, cameras flash and click like beetles.

Then the first person yells out, "Is that David Después?"

Everything explodes a thousand times worse, and people rush at him. Someone goes for the second helmet in his grip, another sends claws for his leather-clad arm. After's hand shoots out, holding the extra helmet and parting the sea of people. "Get on!"

I force my way through reporters and snatch the helmet and shove it around my head. Someone yanks on my sleeve and without looking back, I knock an elbow their way and leap off the curb, scrambling for the seat.

After flips his visor down and revs the engine threateningly. "Hold tight to me." As soon as my arms hook around his middle, he takes off. I squeeze my eyes shut and a scream gets caught in my throat.

There's one single, high-pitched shriek, and I think it might be Bevett calling my name. I send a prayer to Mitch and whoever else is listening to look out for her. Then nothing but the roar of the bike bellows into my ears.

As much as I'm tempted to see where we're going, watch things fly past me at seventy miles an hour, when I open my eyes, my visor is fogging up from tears. I press my helmet into After's back instead.

—

Could be five minutes or fifty. Every second I've been on the bike has been panic inducing, not at all like the pleasure cruise we took through Tennessee on flat, desert land.

I could probably ease up my hold around After's waist, but knowing my luck, the moment I relax, I'd go flying and a helmet ain't gonna do shit for the rest of my broken body. Plus, he hasn't told me to back off yet, so I'm taking it as a sign it's okay.

There's a grunt in front of me, and I open my eyes and look up at him. He keeps darting fast glances back over his shoulder at me. The moment he sees me lifting my head, he stares a second longer and flips up his visor.

"Hey." I startle with a sharp gasp when his voice is suddenly loud and clear in my head. "Don't panic," he says next. I expected him to sound muffled through layers of padding and road noise, traffic moving in the opposite direction back into LA. Hearing him right in my ear is somewhat terrifying.

"Not—not panicking, why would you think I'm panicking?" How the hell is he coming out so perfectly? Like, God? Is that you?

"You literally just squeezed my organs the moment I said 'hey'," After chuckles. He releases a handlebar to tap at his head. "Bluetooth in the helmets. Cost a shit ton, but we have a two-way radio this way."

"Spared no expense," I choke, trying to laugh. Oh, that hurts.

"Yeah—are you good? Got a ways to go."

"I'm still here, aren't I?" I mean, duh, should've said something less obvious. He definitely would've noticed if I was no longer monkeying on his back. Straightening my spine, my lower vertebrae pops. Must've been riding longer than I thought if I was that hunched over. I sit off the seat by an inch and crane my neck.

When he looks back again, I see that green in his iris, bright in the sun. Last thing I should be thinking about right now. But it's either I over-romanticize the flecks of color in my rescuer's hazel eyes, or I think about how I left Bevett alone with Mitch, and how that makes my stomach swirl. "Where are you taking me?" I ask.

"Safe spot," he replies.

"Hey, After…"

He hums and pulls us off the highway, onto a stretch of country road. Sand flies up and hits me in the shins, coating my jean-clad legs with red, but the road noise is softer now as he slows. "How'd you know what was gonna happen?" He's quiet, and I think he might've not heard me even with the headset.

"Was waiting for them to finish up my paperwork at the dealership. Two dudes waiting on an employee kept saying I looked like David Después, but I wasn't actually the actor. Laughed when I pulled out my ID, then Arny—employee helping them with a bike—he stepped in, asked how I felt about my boyfriend's secrets splashed on the cover of *Us Weekly*."

I wish I didn't have a helmet on, just to properly press my face into his back. Or to launch myself into the trees that rush past us. "I said I didn't know what they were talking about. One guy pulled up your…" don't say it, I scream inside at him, please don't say it, "the news article. Anyway…Arny said his brother-in-law works for KRVF in El Paso."

"The radio station?"

"Yeah. Guy was flying here for it—all expenses paid, said Arny, like he was super pumped for his bro to get the details before anyone else. Guess there's a promotion for the guy if he can get more gritty shit aired before any magazines can scoop the rest up. Looked like a lot of people had the same idea, though. Last time I saw that many reporters in one public place was after my first movie, and I got flocked at fucking Target."

"Are you angry at me?" I shout. Didn't need to be so loud, not with the quieter road and fancy telecom shit directly into my skull.

I'm sitting up so close to him that when he shakes his head, his helmet clunks into mine. "Of course not, why would I be?"

"I messed all this up. You said to keep it around you—"

"Stop. Let's talk when we get somewhere."

"Are you okay?"

He laughs. "Are you?"

"No."

His laugh stops. I start to relax my arms, when his hand grips my wrist, keeping me in place. "Don't let go. I don't feel like peeling you off the road today."

My eyes sting. "Right."

Chapter 49

His fingers tug at my hand, nails gently scratching my wrist. "This okay?" After asks.

He's brought us to some teeny daycare set up, the kind with pine around the play mats and under the monkey bars to soften kids when they fall. Scott just this morning would've launched himself at the metal dome. My legs are numb. And I feel like I've had a pillow shoved over my nose and mouth ever since I put on this helmet. So Scott right now isn't launching himself anywhere except maybe into space.

"Yeah, this is fine." I disconnect from his body, snapping bones in my arms just to release his waist. If I'd been there any longer, if he'd let me, I'd have melted into the safety of his strong back and remained there forever.

I get off first and groan, taking off my helmet. I think it ends up on the ground. (So polite. With the Bluetooth, it probably cost five hundred bucks.) I don't look back as I go past the swings and a slide, staggering straight for a seesaw, where I drop to the side that's resting on the ground, my head drooping between my knees.

The seesaw gives a jolt, and I glare up at After on the other end. He smiles at me. When I don't smile back, his face and shoulders droop, and his weight lowers on the seat, raising me up and up and up until my knees are at ninety degrees. "Tell me about the mugshot," he says. Hate that he said it so straight like that.

I'd rather not. Ever. I'd rather bury myself under this playground. "You'll never look at me the same way again."

"I already look at you differently than I did three months ago. Than I did an hour ago, Scott." What does that mean? He sighs and leans his head to the side. "I just want to know if you're okay. If…I want to know what's true. And I want to hear it from you."

"You won't like it."

"Maybe."

"You'll hate me."

"Never."

Lies.

My first inhale does nothing to bring in oxygen. I try again, shoulders reaching my jaw.

"Cassidy and Dad died," I start with a sigh. "Three days after I turned eighteen." After crosses his arms on the handle of the seesaw. So attentive. I'll never get used to his eyes on me. "You know that, of course. Um. We—Devon, Kendra, Bevvy and I—stayed in the house to pack it up, sell it. So Bevett and I could finish out the semesters at our schools.

"It was fine for a while. Devon was great—I'd only known her for a little bit from some holidays. Just met Kendra that spring. They were both nice, young; Devon was barely thirty, fifteen years younger than Mom. They made sure Bevett got to school, made sure I'd have the car if I needed it."

"You seemed okay," After says. Then he winces, scratches his cheek. "Sorry. I mean obviously you weren't. I just…you still went to junior prom. Still came over for my birthday, went on hikes with me and…and uh…"

And Missy. Still saw you holding hands with Missy Davis and making out with Missy Davis and dancing with…

"Yeah. Until summer it *was* okay. But then June hit, and we had to move to El Paso. Devon and Kendra had a much smaller house. Moving day was when a lot of things changed, including them. And. Well, I got my box."

"You mentioned your box. Your journals, hoodies."

"Bevvy got one, too. Paintings, books, some CDs. Anything she could fit."

"Shouldn't estate stuff have gone to you? Y'all could've gotten a storage unit or something."

"Sure, all of that was left to Bevett and me, in Cassidy and Dad's wills, but…to be perfectly honest, I was at a low. I got sick, and I just. Signed it over to Devon. I didn't want to mess with the house. I had no legal guidance; they never got a lawyer to help me. I didn't realize at the time I was signing over everything in it, too."

"So where did all your family's stuff go?" he whispers. I feel like he knows.

"It went to whoever sold it on eBay, Facebook Marketplace. Which happened to be Devon and Kendra."

His brows raise gradually, then wrinkle as his lip curls. "Are you serious? They sold all your stuff and took the money? What about the wills? Money from Cassidy and your dad? Your mom?" After closes his mouth, picking at his nails. "Your mom's ring, man…"

I know, dude. Trust me, I get it. "Will money went to bank accounts. One for me and one for Bevett. Mom had set aside money for me, too, in her will. All accounts were set to go straight to us when we turned twenty." I look to my hands and try to release my fingers on the handlebars of the seesaw.

"I often think maybe Dad knew I'd spiral one day. That he didn't make the age of the will eighteen for a reason. And more often, I think Dad didn't put Devon as co-owner of the bank account for a reason, too. Despite how well they got along when he was alive. As much as she fought, she had no way to get that money. Thank God."

My knees bend and I drop us a few inches, then I let him send me back up, desperate to keep moving, if only to have something to focus on other than my words. "El Paso became a whole ordeal. Devon and Kendra had no idea how to care for us—I mean, I could take care of myself, or I thought I could. But Bevett got ignored, left behind.

"I had to raise her myself while also getting a job at the closest place I could bike to, since I couldn't use the car anymore. Then senior year started and it got so much worse. They'd have parties, by the masses. People bunked around on the sofas, the floor, their office. I went from sleeping in the living room to staying in Bevvy's room, walking her to and from the bathroom, cause strangers were everywhere."

The seesaw sinks, and I'm on the ground again, After standing with his back straight. "Is that. *That's* why you kept wanting to meet in Odessa? Even though it was a four-hour bus ride. You'd bring Bevett—"

"Just to get her out of the house—"

"You never *told* me, man!"

"What was I supposed to say? That the only home—only family I had other than my little sister were horrible? I had a *roof*, they bought me *food*, I still had a *bed* to sleep in. No one was beating me or touching me. Yeah, they wanted my paychecks and they wanted me to change, but it was that or homeless. And I couldn't...I couldn't uproot Bevett again. Not like that. Not after she'd lost her parents. I was keeping her safe from knowing what those people were doing in the house. Taking her away all over again, in the middle of fifth grade—she was barely passing her classes as it was."

He's still glaring at me, but at least he's sitting down. "I begged her repeatedly to go live with Mitch, said I'd help her buy her ticket. She kept saying she didn't want to leave me. Trust me, I regret that I didn't just pack her up anyway."

"I get it. I hate it. But I get it...and I wish you'd told me." He lowers, and we balance each other out. "Can I just say I'm so fucking sorry I called them to meet us for dinner? I had no idea."

"It's okay."

"It's not," he whispers. No, it's not. But it's not his fault, either.

"Anyway um, in late September, some of Devon's friends from Canada came to visit, people she used to work with. One morning there was someone I didn't recognize in the kitchen. He was making Bevett's lunch for school. His name was Gabriel Avant."

"Sounds like a movie character," After says quietly. I chuckle and meet his smile with a weak one of my own.

"Right? He was…he was magnificent. Tall, polite, great taste in music. He was bi, twenty-four, had a wonderful French-Canadian accent. Made Bevvy's sandwiches without the crusts like she liked; he walked so easily into our family that it was like he'd been there the whole time."

My face overheats and I stare at my toes turned out, heels digging into the pine flakes. "He was my first. But, as nice as he was, he knew people, who knew people. Who knew places where kids under twenty-one could get in and um…where they could get a little looser."

After dips, makes me stand on my toes. "Looser with what, Scott?"

I chew at my lip. He's too far away to stop me from breaking the skin and making myself bleed at this point. "Started with tequila. Whiskey. Ended with cigarettes, cocaine. And heroin. A few times."

He looks so shocked. I tell myself he's not disappointed. "Oh, good God. For how long?"

"Until halfway through December. I hid it pretty well from Bevett. She just thought I was sick for a while. I didn't tell her the truth about it all until she turned thirteen."

"What got you to stop?" 'Who' is a better question.

"One night, I was with Gabriel in his—" I falter for the first time during this entire outpour of painful honesty.

After blinks at me. This is going to hurt. "I was with Gabriel in his…Jeep. In a parking lot."

He scowls at his knees, thinking, then his eyes fly up to me. It sinks in. The similarity, the potential. The what-if. The almost. He turns his head like he wants to look away from me. His eyes stay locked in.

"Cop showed up, we were high, drunk. When she forced us out of the car, I was still trying to pull my boxers on. And before I could even turn to Gabriel, thinking this older, smarter guy would help explain us out of this, he punched the cop and took off in his Jeep. Left me standing in my underwear without a phone, with an unconscious police officer. I called 911 on her phone. Three patrol cars showed up. I stayed the night in jail."

I look at my wrists, and my hands run over my chest, feeling my ribs, my collarbone under my button up. Concrete scratched my skin that night when they forced me to the ground to handcuff me, and tiny pebbles under my torso left behind red divots for days. Those handcuffs left marks, too.

"Mitch called in a dozen favors and bailed me out the next morning, and I was sent home to Devon. The cop's dash cam showed everything: Gabriel punching her, me sobbing, trying to stop her bloody nose, sitting on the ground and waiting for someone to show up to help with my face to my knees. Caught me throwing up a few feet away, too."

After's crying. I'm crying. When I wipe my eyes, it does nothing to stop the tears. "Then…I mean that's it. Grandpa came to Devon and Kendra's, didn't even look at his daughter, just had the court order for Bevett to go with him. He paid so much money to the police to keep what happened out of the news; I can't even say the number out loud without revealing just how fucked up this family is with bribery. And Mitch gave me a choice. I go with him and I correct everything by any means, or I never see Bevett again."

"So you left El Paso after Christmas. Came to Lubbock one last time," After whispers behind his fingers. "And I slept right through it." He shakes his head as I nod mine, and he scrubs his hands through his hair. "Then I sent you that horrible fucking text and ignored you for months—oh my God…oh, Scott…"

I want to run to him. I like the distance between us, though. It's safe. Stay on the ground, says Devon, says Grandpa Mitch. I keep my feet on the solid pine and sand.

"I didn't bring all this up to make you feel bad," I tell him. His faces twists from anger to submission, and he scratches at his cheek, trying to dig the tear trails from his skin. "I wanted to explain why I felt like, by the time you and I…ended. When I stole your paper. I was at the end of my rope."

"And why is that?" he sniffles. He picks at his knuckles with a nail. I wonder if he got that habit from spending so much time around me lately.

"It wasn't me trying to get some revenge because of your text, first off. I know that's what you're thinking. I told you when you showed up drunk to my dorm, but I doubt you remember."

He smiles without humor and chews at his lip. He definitely picked that up watching me. "That *was* what I was thinking…"

"It was because I'd blown through Mitch's last straw. Spent the end of Christmas break in California drying out, getting better. Got another job through one of his friends. But it wasn't enough; I was struggling with my final semester in a new school and no direction. Applied to six different Mitch-approved colleges to no avail. Lastly, I picked Jethro. Tried twice, didn't get in. Then you…"

Blew me out of the water. Were incredible, got excited about their theater program, started making your own plans and dreams. 'Let's go together,' he'd said. 'Let's be roommates, be close again'. After peeks at me under his brows.

"When you wrote your own essay, Grandpa found it, thought it was mine. Hugged me, like he was proud. When I pulled out the second rejection letter and showed him that instead, he snapped. He screamed me into a corner, holding the letter in his fist. Last chance, he said. And once he left, I looked at your paper and just…gave up."

"Gave up."

"Gave in."

He mouths 'gave in'. He swallows. Stands tall, sure-footed.

"Was either get into a college by any means, have a roof over my head that wasn't his, or end up on the streets. Or worse, in some sort of conversion center. Bevett was safe and snug in California and no doubt she'd always have a home there, but I wouldn't have anywhere else to live—"

"You could've lived with me."

The seesaw dips heavier on his side, and I reach to my toes. He won't look at me. I choke on a startled laugh. "What?"

"You…you could've lived with Mom and me," he whispers again. After meets my eye. "Sleepovers every night. Get jobs somewhere together, saved money for an apartment, maybe go to community college if you really wanted to."

My throat burns. Anything I could say now just sounds like an excuse, again. Could've got a plane ticket, could've taken busses if I had to with my bike. But he's describing a total dream, and I only thought to focus on the nightmare I was in at the time. Never thought about living with him, not when I was drowning, not when I thought our friendship was broken. I just thought of Bevett and myself.

"I would've come and helped you, Scotty," he sighs. We seesaw back toward me, and I start to sink.

"Seriously? You'd have gone all the way to California?"

There's a glint of amusement in his eye. More sick pity, like, how could I ever doubt otherwise. How could I *not* doubt that? I thought he hated me for months, why would I ever think I could call him and ask him to take me back to Texas, give me a roof and food and security?

"Woulda gone to the ends of the Earth. You were my friend. No matter how horrible I was to you, how angry I was, if you'd have asked, I'd have gone to get you."

"What, like if I'd called in my favor—"

"Forget the favor crap," he scoffs. "Forget it. Favor or not, if you were on the moon and miserable and unsafe, I'd have found a way to come and pick you up and bring you home, no questions asked." Home. There's nothing I can say to that.

"But. You didn't give me a chance to prove that. You just made a decision that hurt us both. And I did that, too, when I broke us up in December, and never healed us right. Couldn't have expected you to trust me afterward." There's nothing I can say to that, either.

I'm on the ground, and he's standing, lifting his leg from the seesaw. I'm 87% sure he's about to get on his bike and leave me here, but he walks over and lowers his hand. "C'mon. Let me take you home."

I accept his hand and he helps me up, and the words are out of my mouth before I have a backup plan. "I don't want to go home."

"Then we'll go back to my place." He leads me to his bike by my hand and I start to shiver.

"No. Just...just take me to Jethro."

He stares back at me for too long. "I don't want to do that."

"I'm fine. I'll be fine once I get back to my dorm. Get a change of clothes, shower...I'll be fine. I only came in for the day anyway, I don't have my laptop or—or anything for homework."

After's still staring. "Please? I have an online final on Monday. Last one on Tuesday—I have to go back. Then we'll do Spain. Soon. In a w-week, yeah? I'll be fine."

He lifts a helmet from his bike and turns to face me with it. "Fine." Before I can put it on myself, he's inching it over my head, and I start to hyperventilate in the padding. He doesn't notice as he puts on his own.

"David." No idea why I said his name; I have nothing else to admit. No more apologies to beg with that I haven't already exhausted a thousand times. But he looks back at me, and just his eyes boring into mine make me hold my breath.

He takes my helmed head in his hands and puts his against it with a plastic thud. I grip hold of his shoulders.

"Breathe," he tells me, taking in a deep breath through his nose. He exhales it with a nod and, "You'll be okay."

"How do you know?"

After's eyes soften. Wish they wouldn't. "Cause you got me, Bo. Breathe. Estás a salvo."

I know those words. I'm seven again. Jaw busted, lip chewed to death, while this other kid with a split brow that's bleeding into his eye holds my face. He's got sweat on his chubby cheeks, and tears, and he still looks at me so strong as he tells me in his baby, cracking voice, "You're safe. Estás a salvo. Estás a salvo." He said it until I stopped crying. Like now. I manage to stop the tears before they scratch up my throat this time.

Chapter 50

I can do this. I *have* to do this.

It's Tuesday, just a Tuesday. I called out sick yesterday at Silversmith, aced an online final like a champ, did some half-assed yoga, ate a salad, and now I feel better than ever. Rejuvenated. Invigorated. Totes thriving.

Saturday's uh…*incident* is already fading from my memory. I don't even flinch when someone walks past me too fast. Not really, anyway. Only if I'm in a crowded hall, and people don't smile back at me when I force a smile, and every stranger who suddenly appears at my side sends heat slicing behind my eyes cause I think it's someone who wants something from me—

Nah, nope, I'm good, Scott Everett is *good*.

If I can get over a brief flirtation with a heroin addiction while struggling through Christmas in a house too big with a grandfather who held my sister as ransom in order for me to get better, I can do this. Just another traumatizing moment in the bag. Add it to the pile.

I made it through my classes without issue, finished my art history final. Ignored the mumbling and whispering and the kids who thought it was amusing to hold my mugshot up with a marker and ask for an autograph. One didn't think it was funny anymore when I took the Sharpie and just walked off with it. Can always use a good Sharpie.

I was in the art building, debating texting Mona that I might need another sick day, when it turned into a *legit* sick day, and I nearly didn't make it to the bathroom in time.

Two hours later, I'm still here, moving in and getting cozy with my legs all splayed out under the neighboring stall. A couple other dudes have walked in, I think I called out to one and asked for help, maybe. Or maybe one just shouted, "You good?" and I replied with, "Ship shape, broski!" Sounds like me.

This is the first moment I can see straight enough to send a text, and there are heeled steps in the bathroom thirty minutes later.

She's clearly startled some random guy, as there's a squawking curse word and a rush of zipper, but I give a wheezy laugh when Charlotte snaps back, "Oh, please, buddy, I haven't been interested in penises since I discovered my fiancée's vagina."

The stall door opens, and I lean on my shoulder and peek up at her, haloed by flickering overhead fluorescents. "An angel," I muster.

She looks wonderful; hair longer in the front but still choppy, no makeup today, rocking a short, white summer dress. I've missed her.

"It smells like a mall in here," Charlotte sighs, kneeling next to me. I try to push her off her knees so I can set my backpack down in front of the toilet first, but she just pats my shoulder. "You're a gentleman even when you reek, my darling."

"I need help…"

"I can see that. What's going on?" I squint and she rolls her eyes. "Other than the obvious."

"So you heard."

"From *you*, dumbass, do you not remember calling me Saturday night?"

Shit, no? Who else did I blackout call? "Um…no, don't remember that…"

"You called me crying, Scotty," she says, pushing my bangs from my face. Her hands are so cold that a groan cracks from my acidic and aching throat. "I'm so sorry. Any idea what happened with the article?"

"Best guess?" I slur, attempting to get my head off my arm. She holds my neck in her hands and her fingers massage at my spine, making my eyes roll. "Oh...that's nice. Thank you. Best guess is...shit, I dunno. Gabriel saw me getting attention, found someone to squeal to, said he had some dirty deets about me. Got paid big money."

"You don't think it was Officer Kingwald?"

"No, highly doubt it. This stinks like Gabriel."

"This *stall* stinks—let's get you off the floor, Scott," she says softly, hooking my arm over her shoulders, letting me lean on her. "Did you eat something bad? Did you...drink? Something bad?"

AKA, did I shoot off the deep end. Not yet, dear Cat-Cat. "No, just stress, I think. I hope. Where's my phone?"

"Oh—uh—" She checks the floor and braces me against the stall wall, stooping for my phone and wiping Lord knows what off of it with her skirt hem. "You've got a few texts."

I attempt to squint at the screen, but my eyes cross. "What looks like the most important?"

"After asks if you're okay. He's got three texts in his thread for you. Bevett has six. There's one from Mona and—"

"Read that one first," I ask as she takes us step by step out of the bathroom.

She shrugs my backpack onto her shoulder, and though I'm a good head and a half taller than her, I'm slouching so much that my arm weighs hard on her neck. "All it says is she needs you to come in today to talk about your promotion?"

Still have a five-minute walk back to my dorm. At the rate we're trudging, it's gonna take us half an hour. "That sounds daunting. Does she say anything else?"

"Not really. 'Dear Scott Everett'—"

"Oh. Oh that's so not good."

"Why? Is that not normal?"

"Let me put it this way: her texts have only ever started with, 'sup, dweeb'."

"You're fucked."

"Royally…okay, so shower is needed. Any other messages? Before I go lose my job or worse?"

Charlotte hums and shifts me on her shoulder, taking us outside. Hot air forces itself into my mouth and nose, and I have to close my eyes to the sun, lead only by her presence.

"One from Jethro. Looks like an email notification. Probably about graduation—I got one this morning."

"Okay, yay, one more thing to stress about."

We get to my dorm a hundred years later and she helps me inside, and I'm successfully standing on my own for the most part. After booting up my laptop, I go through my emails wearing sunglasses with the brightness on my screen turned down low, while Charlotte gathers me up some clean clothes. There's an email from Mona, but it's the same message as the text. Stiff, robotic. **Dear Scott Everett, please come in today as we need to discuss the promotion we spoke about in February.**

Okay, that's not too bad. Maybe someone else sent it from Mona's laptop. Maybe they just want to kick me down from the publicist thing and put me back as her assistant. Or as, like, the janitor.

That's fine, I can live with that. It's Tuesday and I'm still breathing.

I open the email from Jethro. Subject line: **Case of Boscoe, Scott Everett. Senior, JU4322EXP**

Dear Scott Everett Boscoe,

We at Jethro University have received some distressing news regarding an incident that occurred in El Paso, Texas, circa December 2017.

The charges of assault, public intoxication, nudity, and illegal drug abuse have deeply concerned us, and we are not comfortable with letting you continue your education here at JU without discussing said charges.

In order to fulfill your academic career and walk with your peers at graduation on June 5th, 2021, it is required that you write a one (1) page essay stating your case, explaining why you must be allowed to complete your semester, and why these previous problems do not reflect on you as a current student.

We here at Jethro believe in offering equal opportunities to all, no matter their race, gender, sexual orientation, background or other. However, we do not condone the misuse of the legal and educational system for personal gain and nepotism, such as what has happened with you specific situation.

Please email your testimony to staff@jethrouniv.edu by May 24th, 2021, at the latest. We will review your case and make a decision based on your grades, character, and record.

Best regards,
Hannah Montgomery, Dean of Jethro University.

I wake up on the floor, and the first eyes I see are After's.

Chapter 51

By some miracle, I'm standing outside Silversmith in a fresh shirt and clean jeans and sneakers. When I say, 'some miracle', I mean because of After and Charlotte.

Long story short, according to Charlotte, I read the email from JU, made a noise like a donkey being hit by an eighteen-wheeler, and I stumbled backward too fast for her to catch me. Tripping over my own feet, I fell like a tree, hit my head on the opposite desk, and went down, hard. Charlotte called After only once I started mumbling at her that I was okay, begging her to not call EMS, or worse, Mitch.

After ran in (no, really, he sprinted the last mile to campus because traffic was moving too slow, despite Thor doing his best to cut through LA in his monster truck) and he found me and Charlotte on the ground with my head in her lap. He asked her what happened, she tried to explain, but her back had been turned. All she knew was it was something on my laptop, but she didn't know my password to log back in and take a look. They both read the email. She started crying.

After put his hands on my face, and that's the moment my brain kinda kicked into gear, and the hamster hopped back onto the squeaky wheel to get everything up and running again.

Guess that was more long story than short, but I'm delirious, swaying a little as my knee keeps buckling under me.

Charlotte had to go, she got a call from Mei; apparently, Mei received a similar, but much less horrible, letter.

Hers stated that, since she'd been spending time around me, and her fiancée had known me since before El Paso, she's required to talk to the staff about keeping her position. (Surprised Charlotte hasn't gotten her own, 'listen here, you little shit,' letter, but it may only be a matter of time.) The Dean also said Mei needs to come clean and explain that she had no hand in the bribery Mitch did with the cops.

Oh, yeah. Then there's that fun little word that popped up in my own death sentence letter: nepotism. To get *into* Jethro.

That has me asking all *sorts* of questions about how I got accepted. And it makes me wonder if I ever needed to run myself so ragged to get in in the first place.

Boy, that hindsight 20/20 sure sucks, don't it?

I take the stairs up to Silversmith because nope to vertigo and elevators, and even though I'm sweating through my shirt by the time I get to the right floor, at least I've kept down the water and saltines After fed me.

He's not here, by the way, he's not downstairs waiting on me. But I've been amazed and slightly overwhelmed at how empathetic he's been. He got me snacks, helped me change (head injuries make it super difficult to focus on unbuttoning shirts, it would seem) and he offered to help me get a shower. (Like *hell* was I about to accept that. Not gonna add 'seen naked by best friend' to the list of reasons I'm so screwed up today.)

Once After and Thor drove me here, I just sent him home. Or I sent him somewhere. I think I told him I was fine and I'd call him if I needed him. He fidgeted like he wanted to ignore my request, but eventually he left, mentioning that he had to make some calls anyway.

Now I'm facing off against Mona, alone. And I'm wishing I thought to bring him along as a shiny shield. She's in knee length shorts and flip flops and a chunky sweater.

I attempt to raise a hand and say something like, greetings boss, be gentle, but I can't get my voice to work with my destroyed throat.

"Hi, Scott. C'mon, let's go see Jackie," she says, leading me with a light hand on my back. Hope she doesn't care how sweaty I am.

—

So similar to months ago in February, I'm in Jackie's office with clammy palms on my knees and the director of a publishing house across from me. She pinches her mouth to the right, then to the left, looking between my eyes. "So um. Well, this isn't easy, Scott."

I just nod, close my eyes and nod. "You've written some excellent work for us in just the couple months you've been here."

"I had help," I admit. "Friend from school."

Her brow knits and she looks to Mona behind me. "This…Gabriel—"

"No, no. My boyfriend," I reply.

"David Después," Mona adds. I nod again. Should slow down on that nodding or it's gonna be saltines all over Jackie's desk.

"Right," Jackie says, tapping her nails on an armrest. "I have to get this out—I'm furious, Scott. I don't get it. How this happened, why we're just now hearing about it. You had to take a background test; you took a—a goddamn piss test. How'd all that come up clean?"

Can I phone a friend? Use a lifeline? Throw myself out the window? "The pi…the drug test came clean because I've been clean for years—"

"So you admit to using at one point," she says, crossing her arms. "That should've been picked up on the background check."

"Yes, I admit to using, repeatedly. I admit to the charges, all of them. Including the bribery that still makes me sick to this day."

She's glaring, shaking her head, orange curls dancing like fluffy, mesmerizing Cheetos. "Goddammit. Then how did *none* of that come up on the check?"

Mona clears her throat, and she steps into view.

"We uh...we had Oliver do some digging. He spoke with some people in the HR department, they got in contact with the company we're partnered with for the background checks."

She sends me a quick glance that kind of looks like, 'sorry, dude, but it has to be done'. I shrug, and she sets two files down on the desk. Both have my name on them. One very clearly has *many* more red highlights on it than the other.

"There's um...there's quite a lot missing from the one we received. As you can see...here and...here..." Mona mutters into silence. You're doing your best, Mona, don't sweat it. "The one we were given before his employment had been fabricated. Someone paid one of the checkers, got them to change things, send this to HR instead."

Sweet, cool, so I had thought they just accepted the charges as the progressive company they claimed to be. No clue they never saw them to begin with.

Add it to the pile, I think. Add another behind my back bribery to the bucket. Didn't even get this job on my own, cause I didn't do this, and unless Bevett's a secret teenage spy, she didn't either. Only other person who knew about the background check and charges was Mitch.

Jackie's purple. Window option is looking real nice at this point. I'm fighting the urge to smile. I think smiling is definitely a nervous reflex. "Unbelievable," she steams through her nose, squinting at me. "I could have you arrested."

"You could."

She points a long nail at me, and I go cross-eyed looking at it. "You're going to go to Ingrid's Mercy Hospital downtown. I'm going to write them an order for a new piss test *and* a blood test to see that you're *legitimately* clean like you claim. I'm then going to send in a request for a new background check—after getting whatever skeevy shit in that company fired for messing with my employees. And *then* I'll decide if I'm keeping you on to clean the goddamn coffee machines, or if I'm throwing you to the police."

Is a blood test even legal? Even if it weren't, I wouldn't put it past her to grab the letter opener from her desk and use it on my throat to take a sample herself.

Well, at least I know if I was one of her good associates and there was a murderous junkie running loose who'd lied on his checks somehow, she'd have our backs and would keep us safe. So glad the rest of the staff are protected from little ol' me. I think of After's joke, all that time ago in February. Maybe Wendy's will hire me.

"Nah, I'm good."

Her eyes snap wide. Mona coughs. "*Excuse* me?" hisses Jackie.

I stand too fast and everything swims. "I'm gonna go clear out my space. You got a box I can borrow?" Mona makes a noise and holds up a hand. Jackie sends her a look. Mona puts her hand down. "No prob—can I borrow this then?" I stoop and grab the short trash bin by the desk, take the bag out, and leave her office.

There's a barrage of colorful curse words from Jackie that have me snorting into a deranged chuckle. Brain is ticking down the seconds before it forces me to be horizontal again *real* damn quick.

Mona's right behind me with a *flop-flop-flop* of her sandals. "Scotty—wait, wait, you can talk to her, she's just upset she's been lied to! She almost reacted the same way when she found out I was using my bereavement days to go to Lollapalooza and I didn't *actually* have grandmas repeatedly dying around that time annually."

"No offense, Mona, because I really like you and I think this could've been a good friendship between us. But I'm really not interested in being under anyone's thumb anymore."

I get to my cubicle and collect my photo of Bevett, the one of Charlotte and Mei, my notebook, my extra pencils and…wow. Didn't even need the trash can. I don't take the pink lamp.

Once I've gathered my stuff up into my arms, I look at her. There shouldn't be three of her, but there sure are. "I appreciate you. A lot. I wish you luck," I tell her with a pat to her arm, nearly missing entirely.

She closes her fingers over mine, looks past her shoulder, and whispers back to me. "Please, stay. You can work for me. I'll talk to her—you've been great, Scott. Your writing has been amazing." Never been my writing. Not my voice, not my work. I dip my head to look at the tiny amount of things in my arms.

Always so little. I never carry much with me. Most I ever traveled with was to Nashville. Why? Was I secretly hoping I'd get stranded there, have to start a new life?

Geez, maybe. Build me a shabby hut in Arkansas. Or in that sunflower field, waiting for July to bring the golden blanket with it. A place for myself. A perfect, Scotty-sized home.

As it is, if I stay (in El Paso, in Mitch's house, in Silversmith, even in Harry's made-up cabin where his partner is left alone most of the time, happy and floating on a secluded island) then I'm not my own person, all over again.

If I apologize and bend and do what they want from me just to prove I'm enough, prove I'm worthy, then…I'm After's swan. Molded and squashed to fit the picture they crave. How much longer until I explode? Or more, implode, just like he said, taking down an entire block with me.

"Thanks Mona," I tell her. And I leave.

No one's outside for me. Didn't think there would be (lies, always with the lies) so I get a ride to my dorm. Half expected it to be empty, notice of eviction on my door. Nope, everything just where I left it a couple hours ago, when I wandered out in a daze, thinking I'd still have some sort of job when I got back.

I pace around my dorm once. Curl up in each bunk. Sit at each desk, push myself around in each swivel chair, exchange which knee I have pulled to my chest.

On the floor with my back to the wall, head right under the windowsill, I bring my Pashmina around my shoulders and make a call. I make many calls, mentally. But I make one call, literally.

He picks up on the first ring. "Hey, Bo, you okay?"

"Aft…David—"

"Yeah, it's me, you're alright, what's going on?"

"Can you…c-can you come pick me up?"

"Where you at?" Rustling, keys jingling. "Where you at, Bo?"

"My dorm. Please, David. Come get me, please—"

"On my way, pack a bag, honey, pack your shit up, I'm on my way, don't move." Honey? Is he with someone? Does he have someone with a recorder in his face, asking who he's rescuing? Who's in the tower you're going to save, After, why would you use such a sweet name for them if no one was around you?

He talks to me hands-free the entire drive to JU while I pack, when I go get my bike and wheel it into my dorm. Talks to me as he's parking, as he's coming to my room, until I hear his voice in the hall.

Then my unlocked door is open, and I turn in the center of my ransacked room. And there he is, breathing hard, phone in his hand. He hangs up then.

"You're here." Like I doubted it. Didn't doubt it this time.

He hugs me, crushes me, lifts me to my toes. Taking my backpack and suitcase, he leads me to an in-between with his arm around my shoulders as I wheel my bike out, to another home that's not mine. Better than anything else.

Chapter 52

After makes us dinner. Chicken parmesan, spaghetti, broccoli. The healthiest thing I've ever eaten in this house. I don't make it past half the Texas Toast garlic bread.

He says he has some work to do, but I'm free to do whatever I want. "Calls to make," just like earlier. I'm not sure what that means, and I don't ask.

Sitting on the sofa with Chicken half in my lap, there's a plate of brownies on the coffee table and the TV is on. (Think After started Lord of the Rings during dinner. Which one, I couldn't tell you.) He walks behind me on his way out of the living room. I hear his steps pause at the back of the sofa.

I'm about to turn my head, when there's a rush of something soft and cool across my bare neck, and tassels tickle my arms as he drapes my Pashmina around me.

I sit frozen while he works it properly into place, crossing my body with it, tucking it under my arms just so, fixing where it lays over my shoulders.

Looking at him upside down, he smiles, tilts his head. "Got it from your bag, hope that's okay. You cozy?"

"Comforted."

His smile grows, and he nods in satisfaction, heading out of the room while I continue to blink, like the next time I close my eyes and they flash open, that odd, loving moment will make sense to me. It doesn't.

After gets to the threshold and pauses to stare at me. "You'll uh…" He shifts his weight, checks his bare toes.

I check mine, too, feet hidden under me and covered in socks he loaned me. He also gave me shorts and a hoodie. Not my JU one, though. This one's from James Bowie. He let me borrow it before, a thousand years ago, walking to his parents' house for a New Year's sleepover. "You'll still be here when I'm done?" he asks.

"I mean, I may not be in this *exact* spot," I joke. He leans on the threshold. "I'll be. Around."

"Good." He knocks on the doorway and leaves. I fold into Chicken, cloaking us both in my scarf, and bury my face in his fur until it feels like I'm crushing my ribs like a soda can.

—

I end up in the pool outside. Angus came into the living room twenty minutes ago, offering to make me soup or some eggs. As much as I wanted to say yes, my stomach said absolutely not, and I just sighed and muttered that I wanted to go swimming.

Ten minutes later, he reappeared with black swim trunks.

Five minutes later, I stopped crying and shaking enough to change into them. Hence, pool.

Sun started setting when I first got out here. Now everything in After's yard is such a soft pink that I can almost imagine I'll wake up tomorrow and none of this would have happened. Life is too nice and full of this cotton candy hue, like Yvonne's hair. Nightmares don't come to fruition; they don't crawl out of your darkest corners in this lovely world.

With my mouth, almost up to my nose, underwater, I bob. Watch a fat dove splash around in the shallow beach end. No steps, just that pleasant walk-in set up. Like a real coast, if the ocean was made of turquoise pool tiles. The fountain's off, so only my slow kicks under water are causing waves up to that bird taking a bath.

Little bird ain't got no problems.

I think I've gone swimming more the last few months than I have in years. What does that say about me? Feel like I'm drowning mentally, so I swim, tempt fate to drown me in real life?

If I was a...man, I dunno. A water sign. That would make sense. I'd have to text Charlotte and ask what sign I am for my birthday. Or just look it up myself. After's a Gemini, I know that much. Is *he* a water sign? Fluffy bird has a friend now. That's nice.

Won't be texting anyone or looking anything up for a hot minute. I haven't turned my phone on since I called After to come get me.

Since Mitch sent me a novel-long text on the drive over that said I wasn't welcome back in the big house.

Since Jackie emailed me an even shorter notice of end of employment.

When we first got here, I asked After to text Bevett and Charlotte and let them know I was okay. Charlotte tried to call but he screened it. When Bevvy called, he handed me his phone and I locked myself in the big, empty art room. I cut my palms with my nails just to not cry over the phone, hearing her sob like that. Even Harry texted After asking if I was okay. Good to know my fame has made it all the way to lovely Tennessee.

The screen door closes, and I turn my buoyant body to face the back porch. After, holding a 7-11 Big Gulp. "Thor brought you something," he says, coming down the porch steps. He keeps walking, into the beach end, past the birds who don't give a fuck, through the shallow end—

"You're still in your clothes," I remind him, in case he's forgotten the jeans and t-shirt now soaked through.

"Ah, darn, am I?" he replies, handing me the massive drink. It's heavy as hell. "Slurpee. Cherry and Vanilla Coca Cola."

I accept it with pruney fingers. "I didn't ask for this."

"I know. He asked me your favorite comfort drink, since you didn't eat your comfort foods. Not even the chocolate chip and pecan brownies. Angus made you those this afternoon, by the way, while we were driving back from JU."

"How do you know my comfort foods?" Slurpee is so fucking good. Ice cold. I close my eyes and dunk my head to mask the tears on my lashes.

His smile is all blue from the pool lights and pink from the sunset. He'd fit right into my Pashmina scarf.

"How do I know you like beaches for the sole purpose of collecting shells for Bevett? How do I know you love the cream cheese and pumpkin muffins Starbucks sells in the fall?"

Don't like this. Don't like this at all, don't like that he's able to stand flat-footed while I have to kick to keep afloat. "After—"

"Or that you always start off laying on your left side, but you can't ever actually go to sleep until you're on your right? How can I know that sunflowers are your favorite?" Pool's too cold, air's too frigid. I've been in for too long. And he's too close to me.

What would he do if I just hung onto him until all this was over? Is that too much? That's not a friend thing. I don't want it to be a friend thing.

"How do I know your favorite memory of your dad is when he took you to an Astros game and you had to sit on three seat cushions to see over the guy in front of you? And that the moment you first met Cassidy, you said she looked like she walked out of a painting?"

After takes another step, and I don't have to dunk, cause he puts his hands on my face and wipes my tears.

"I know all those things cause I've been with you, Scott. I sat by you in the stadium, when we got mad and just stood in the seats and were loud as hell. I bought you your first Starbucks muffin to celebrate you winning a writing contest in seventh grade. I was with you when we found the sunflower field in Lubbock, when we stayed all day until mosquitos ate us alive. And I might sleep through all sorts of shit, but during sleepovers, I'd never get comfortable until I heard your breathing even out when you laid on your right side."

All surface level.

I can't even draw a breath to say his name. He takes my drink and sets it on the pool tiles. There's not much I can do when he tethers me to him by bringing my face to his neck, one arm around my waist, the other behind my legs, keeping me warm and secure.

No feet on the ground. Weightless. I circle his neck with my arms and cling to After.

—

He insisted I sleep in his bed, but that meant, well, sleeping in his bed. I decided for the both of us where I'd be when I went and curled up on the blanket pallet Thor had set up on the sofa. Staring at the cushions, laying on my left side, of course I can't get comfortable. Never noticed that I sleep on my left then right or whatever After said. Now it's all I think about.

After clears his throat, loud enough to stir me out of that horrid feeling where you're bouncing between awake and sleep but sleep sounds like a really bad idea.

His voice is soft over the white noise machine and low movie he's got turned on for me. "Hey, um…"

I roll over and squint at his back in the dark. "What?"

"You awake?"

"I am now."

"Can I ask a favor?"

"If you wanna do that pinky promise shit, After, you better do it over here cause I ain't moving."

He laughs, and it sounds genuine, but it's also sharp, too high. I rub sleep from my eyes and try to focus on him again. He rolls off his side, onto his back, then onto his other side, facing me. The whites of his eyes glint when he blinks. "Can you um…can you not call me 'After' anymore?"

I mirror him on my side. He moved the sofa from across the room to nearer to the bed while I was in the bathroom earlier. I didn't ask why, and I didn't put it back. Staring at him now, I wish I'd thought to shift the sofa even closer. "Does it bother you?"

He shrugs. "Sometimes. I just um. It's too much like when we were kids. Didn't really like it then, don't like it now."

"Then why'd you let us call you that for years?" Why'd you let me whisper it at you in your Jeep, in my backyard?

"Cause I just…" He closes his eyes, lays on his back. "Just liked being included. No matter what you called me."

"Oh."

"So…"

"Oh…" Shame. That's what this is, burning up my throat. Slurpee, reheated spaghetti and a shit ton of shame. Never thought to ask cause I never thought to care. "What um. What do you want me to call you instead?"

His voice is so small, I swear when I blink, he'll be that kid again, curled up with his Stuffy under his arm. "Can you just call me David?"

I sit up on my elbow, and he tilts his head to me. His eyes are shiny. My chest is tight. "Yeah. David. I like it. It's—that's a good name."

"Thanks," David nods. "Hey, Scotty?"

"Yeah, David."

When he chuckles, it's so much quieter, like he's laughing himself into a light sleep. "I wish you weren't on the sofa."

"I wish I wasn't either."

In unison, like we practiced, we roll over onto our opposite sides, facing away from one another.

—

I can't sleep, so I wander. Chicken joins me for a minute when I reach the kitchen, but I urge him to go back when he falls asleep standing up and leaning on my leg. I find the gym next, there's a gorgeous, cherry red piano in a circular room covered in multi-colored carpet, and what look like three other guest rooms.

Glad he never insisted I stayed in one of those when I slept over. Not After. David. It's been two hours and I keep whispering his name to myself and I'm really not sure why.

There's the library, and I almost pass it, except for the expansive amount of boxes in it that look unopened. I step in with a glance behind me to see if he's bumbling about, too, and I go toward the first box.

It's stuff from Lubbock, looks like James Bowie High. His letterman, some trophies from acting class, a medal from a writing competition senior year. I have to muffle my laughter in the crook of my arm when I find the specific yearbook photo where I made him ugly-laugh from behind the photographer. He was mad at me for days, until he forgot to be.

I set the box aside and go for another, curiosity piqued. This one's heavy with silver-ringed binders full of loose-leaf pages and wrinkled scraps, even some things scribbled on ancient Whataburger napkins. There's one leather-bound journal that's labeled 'finished' and when I lift it, I see a couple others with labels like it, every page full.

Not sure what it says about him that his handwriting is nearly exactly the same now as it was when he was seven. Never messy and illegible like mine. It's careful, slanted, biggest difference is he used to take up two lines per letter until he figured out how to shrink it down. He's clearly practiced how to write for years, perfecting his style.

I check once more over my shoulder and start flipping through. Some are dated as early as when he first moved to Lubbock from New Mexico, July 2005. They're titled with things like *Lunch Box* and *Rainy Day* and one that makes me smile says *Cicadas Galore*. He'd crossed out cicadas three times until he got it right. One makes me stop from August.

It's simply titled *Day of Scott*.

Chapter 53

--August 25th - Day of Scott.

I ate lunch today. New kid, no one wanted to sit by me. Someone said my food ~~smeld~~ smelled bad and didn't care when I said it was made special from my mom. So I was by myself.

But this one guy came and set his lunchbox down. It was Iron Man. Kid had a big pointy nose. Dad says people with pointed noses like that are smart. He had brown eyes. (He said mine aren't brown. Said they're ~~hayzl~~ hazel. After school, I asked Mom what that meant. She said he was right, means there's green in them.)

This kid smiled at me, but he was ~~mizing~~ missing his front teeth. Said I had long lashes, and that his mom would think I was pretty. I said pretty was for girls, he said that's not true, and he said he ~~thoht~~ thought I was pretty.

He said his name was Scott. I said I know. I've heard him laughing in the hall with the others. He said he'd like to laugh with me. I told him to leave me alone. He ~~eggnord~~ ignored me and ate lunch with me anyway. But he shared his oreos.

My finger trails over his words, and I get cozy on the floor, turning another page, as little David used the entire sheet just for those brief lines. The next one is a few days later, and I laugh at the title and have to cover my mouth, checking the door again.

--August 29th - Idiot.

Mom says it's rude to use that word. But this kid Scott hit my face with his face when I was playing football. Hadn't talked to him in days and he came to ~~resees~~ recess and said we were friends.

I said no we were not. Then he wanted to play football. Mark said he could, and so did Jenny, so I said fine.

Then Scott ran for it when I did and his face hit my face and we were both ~~bleding~~ bleeding a lot and I called him an idiot like Dad says at the TV when football players hit each other. Mrs. Hill was worried and sent us to the nurse, but the nurse called our moms, but Scott doesn't have a mom, so they called his dad.

Scott was crying for his mom. Told me she died five months ago. He wouldn't stop crying and it was making me cry. I did what Mom does when I cry.

I held his face and told him he was safe. A lot. I called him Bo, cause all the kids call me After (Dad says Después means after in Spanish, I guess) and some of them call him ~~Bozko~~ Boscoe. He said he liked Bo, and he stopped crying.

Tears race too fast down my cheeks, and I barely catch them at my chin in time before they splotch on his ink. I look over the other entries for that year and others at Navy Glenn, then I move on to a journal with pages about junior high.

The promise we made at twelve. The fights we had sometimes. The sleepovers. The times we got drunk and made up later. How different things would be if we talked through our problems then.

There's one bit when he's fifteen that makes me pause, and my stuttered laugh startles me.

--November 28th - Kissing or Nah?

Mom said it's not normal for guys to kiss guys. But I was at Dad and Vernon's wedding, I laughed and threw the confetti when they kissed, so I don't get that.

They're in love, it's obvious, they love to kiss each other. I understood it at fourteen, I still do at fifteen.

But Mom didn't go to the wedding. She says she loves Dad; says she accepts that he's gay. But would someone who accepts it not support it? I don't get that. I know she's still upset about Tio Nathan. Maybe it has to do with him getting shot. I don't know.

She also said Dad's too old to find out he's gay. That he should have known before. But that doesn't sound nice, or true.

Dad also just recently got into country music. And I just learned I liked acting in theater. So what? I kind of feel like it's okay to find things out about yourself at any point.

Dad got drunk on Jameson after Thanksgiving dinner. He said some things I don't think he meant to say, and I haven't told him he said them. He said she'd get mad when I was little and he would hold my hand, when he still kissed me on the top of my head. I asked him why.

He started crying. Never saw my dad cry except for when we had to put Mango down cause she got too old and her back legs stopped working.

I know that one day, when I was eleven, he picked me up for the last time to help me onto a horse at Meemee's ranch. And he never picked me up again. Never kissed my head, my knuckles, never held my hand again. So I don't know.

I think when I'm old enough to fly to Spain to visit Dad and Vernon, I'll ask for hugs immediately. Cause he hasn't hugged me since I was eleven.

I want to kiss Bo. I really want to hold his hand.

But I don't think I should.

I nearly get up and run to David at just that. It makes me curious…and masochistic. So I find a journal from James Bowie and flip to the year, the month most on my mind.

Maybe I'll get an entry or two about it. Maybe I'll only get Missy on the bench.

I get pages…upon pages. Upon pages.

--March 18th - Rules.

His hand was slender, thin fingers, long palm. It was on my collarbone today. As high as I'd let it go, even if I did want it on my jaw, in my hair. I kept it on my collarbone with my hand over his knuckles.

Bo stared at me for so long I nearly fell asleep with my eyes open, lost in a haze of brown, such a dark comforting oak, bursts of orange coming in through my blinds. A prism crossed over his face and set him ablaze with rainbow.

He leaned toward me, and I pushed him back. I wanted to touch him. ~~I'd been dying to.~~ For months, since Christmas when we bumped into each other going for the kitchen and he didn't notice we were under mistletoe at my mom's house, but I noticed, and he smelled like sugar cookies and his face was so red from laughing all night.

He slept over. He stayed in my bed. I couldn't sleep the entire time he was next to me. Not with his hand so close to mine.

I think I like you, Bo said in my room today.

I know I like you more, I thought. Instead I said no kissing. Cause guys don't kiss or hold hands. Bo agreed. That prism broke and a shadow clouded the sun, and he was cast in gray, but he agreed.

--March 25th - Need.

He wasn't heavy in my lap in my Jeep, in my hands. His jean shorts soft, torn at the knee, his forehead hard on mine, skull to skull, heart to heart, breath held between us in the space I refused to close.

No kissing, no kissing. My rule my stupid rule.

Let me break it, let me feel his lips on mine, I want to put mine on his neck, I've always loved his long, thin neck. ~~God I wanted Bo's mouth on me Mom's going to hate me she'll hate me~~

He breathed on me, warm, too warm. I wanted to swallow every exhale he sighed across my face. I could live off the way he said my name.

I wish he said David.

I'm David, I'm not After.

But if I brought that up then, he might've stopped pressing down on me like that, so I didn't.

I want to feel you, I want to hear you come, he said. God, who says that? Who fucking says that? They don't say that in the porn I watch.

Don't worry about me, I told him. I want you, I want you to first. I felt it, I felt it, sensed it, coiled so hot. The noise Bo made. I could survive forever with only that echoing in my ears. Almost.

~~Mom's gonna never talk to me again just like she ignores Dad if she ever found out.~~

Mom can't fucking find out.

God Mom can't find out I'm so screwed I'm screwed what've I started shit.

--March 27th - What Did I Do

My back itched on the tree trunk. Scratched through my shirt every time he rolled his hips against me, pushing me back into the bark. I told him he's going to drive me crazy if he keeps doing that.

He smiled so wicked and bit his lip. I wanted his lip between my teeth. This is what you get for gripping my thigh during dinner with my fucking parents, Bo said. His voice didn't crack once, not like mine. He sounded like a fucking man.

Then he touched me with his fingers, not just his leg between mine. He pushed his hand into my pants and I couldn't even see him, not with fireworks in my eyes. He said he liked the noise I made.

Are you close, he asked me. God yes, I said, don't stop I begged. ~~Mom I'm sorry I'm so sorry what's wrong with me Dad help me what's wrong with me.~~

My knee shook, my fingers ached from holding his shoulders. I wanted to, I wanted to. I wanted to, I wanted him to drop to his knees and put me in his mouth. I know he wanted to, he said he did. Just his words were enough to have me blazing against the elm, his cheek in flames and sweaty on mine. I bit his shoulder to muffle myself. I've never felt like that in my life. Even drunk I've never felt so amazing. And I ran like a fucking coward.

~~Stupid, stupid, stupid, I hate myself why'd I do that.~~

--March 30th - Him and Me.

~~Bo I miss you, I fucked up, I shouldn't have run, I dream about you, I dream about your hands and your sounds and your smile, I dream about how you feel when you sleep against me at sleepovers and shit it's not enough anymore, I need every inch of you.~~

My pencils keep breaking. Mom wants to know what I'm doing in my room with my door always locked. I think she thinks I'm jacking off.

I'm really just sitting in my room with my face in my pillow and crying. I think if she knew that, she'd prefer me jacking off like a normal teenager, and not one that's so sick in the head and might be in love with his best guy friend.

She's going to hate me like she hates Dad. I have to tell Dad. Tell him what? No, no, no. I'm not gay.

~~I might be gay I don't know how to be gay.~~

I need to breathe.

I'm not myself anymore I'm Bo and me.

--April 3rd - I want to Die.

His hands aren't like mine. Mine are rough, clumsy, scarred, fat fingers and thick palms. His are dexterous and dangerous and long, so long. Bo could wrap a hand around mine and lead me through his favorite fields, pull me across the desert, guide me blindly to the coast of Galveston and I'd happily leap right into the ocean after him.

Destroy me, mold me, hold me with just his hands.

He made me sing.

I don't sound like that when I touch me. It's animal, it's dumb, it's blocky and robotic. I sounded pretty when he touched me. I felt pretty. He's told me I'm pretty before when I first met him as kids. In my Jeep he said I was handsome.

Today after school, with Missy. I felt so ugly.

She had petite fingers, little rings from Claire's. I blame him for why I did what I did. I blame him because I'm scared. I should've called him today for his birthday. I didn't.

--April 4th - Hate Me.

I'm not myself anymore. I'm him and me and Missy. I want to carve her out but I can't. I can only rip up the shirt she touched and cut up the shorts I let her unzip to pull me out and slide myself inside her with that plastic condom. I feel like I can still smell the rubber on my fingers from when I threw it away yesterday. I've thrown up three times just today.

I thought of Bo the whole time, how pink his lips were in my Jeep, inches from my face. When I came, I was thinking of the way he laughed so loud in February when I showed up on his doorstep, covered in snow and sweat and grinning like a dumbass.

You're a dumbass, he said, when I pulled him from his front porch in the snow, cause I found a new trail for us to get lost in. I wanted to kiss him by the pale birches.

I'm your dumbass, I replied, and you're stuck with me forever. He laughed even harder. I didn't kiss him. I made fun of him. I don't remember about what, but it made him laugh so hard he fell into the snow.

Every time I talk to him, it hurts. Every time I think about telling him, I don't. Every time, I want to. But I don't.

--April 8th - I Think I Broke it.

He won't answer my calls. My texts. His parents are dead, and I feel like I'm the one with my heart broken. How selfish is that?

I read them all half a dozen times. I hold his journal to my forehead in hopes of engraving every single word straight into my mind, like aged flowers pressed into my memory. I just want to live in those lines forever.

He goes on about the funeral. How I wouldn't look at anyone, talk to anyone, but Bevett. Apparently I snapped at a few people who were working the funeral, ignored him, ran away that night to try to find my mom's grave, ended up at Bevett's school playground; he found me under a tree and stayed with me until sunrise. Don't remember any of that.

There's more about him and Missy, what it was like to date her and how much he hated it, but Ms. Florence loved her. When Missy would go over to his place, he started pretending he had homework and he'd hide on the roof. Sounds like him and Sasha.

Parts of me moving to El Paso, the times I visited with Bevett. He always says he's happy to have seen me. Sometimes the lines are short. Sometimes he goes on and on about what we did that day, even if it was just getting DQ and sitting on a playground with Bevett.

Then senior year starts, and he stops writing for months at a time. Comes back with, "*Got in another fight today,*" and, "*losing weight, not eating enough anymore, Mom's worried,*" and then, "*I stopped watching porn cause none of it feels the same, and none of it sounds like him, so I started reading it. writing it.*"

Late December, he says he regrets sending me the text. February 2018, his handwriting gets sloppy, and the ink is blotched. "*I reached out,*" he says. "*I think I've got Bo back. But I changed his name in my phone. I don't know why I did that.*"

I go to the last entry in the journal, rest of the pages empty. What I get makes me want to throw up.

--March 30th - He Broke Me

We were supposed to do this together

I'll never write again. ~~I'll never love~~

My head hurts.

"Hey…" I slam the journal closed. David stumbles into the threshold in just his sweatpants, lit up by the moon from the library window and the dim orange lamp I turned on half an hour ago.

"Uh—here, Af-David, I'm sorry." I stand with his journal crushed to my chest.

David staggers in and thumps into the table with the lamp, glaring at it like it jumped out and tripped him on purpose. "Cariño…"

"Car—car-een-yo?" I shake my head, wipe fast at my face, and shove all his journals back into the box, kicking it toward the others. Fumbling to close it like it was before, I walk toward him, turning off the lamp as I go. "I don't—David, what's that mean?"

David pouts and rubs at an eye. "¿Qué estás haciendo?"

My head falls back with a sigh of relief. Oh, thank God, he's sleepwalking. Means he won't remember finding me snooping through his precious secrets.

"Sorry, David, I wasn't doing anything. Not um…not really. Sort of—let's go back to bed."

He nods until his chin hits his chest, and he reaches for me. "Es la hora…de dormir…"

"Yeah, bud, it's bedtime, let's go." I accept his hand and trip as he drags me to him.

Everything about him, his smell, his warmth, his arms envelope me, and I have to unlock his fingers from behind my back just to get him to release me from the hug. I lead him to his room, get him settled on his mattress and lift his legs one by one under the covers.

Before I can turn toward the sofa, he's pulling me down next to him by my hand, wrapping me up in him with his leg across my thigh, face in my neck. He's already asleep by the time I get situated, and locked in his grip, there's no way for me to leave him now.

Chapter 54

I've been at David's for a couple days. Thor's cooked only healthy meals. (Though he still snuck me a lemon loaf from Whole Foods yesterday.) Angus drove me back to JU to get more of my stuff. (Guess in my freaking the fuck out state of mind, I grabbed the most random assortment of shit, like ten pairs of socks, and no laptop.)

Most shockingly (read: wonderfully), David's been attentive and patient with my hours of silence, checking up on me as he goes about working at home.

I'm being cared for in every way. I couldn't imagine a better safe place right now.

Yet I've slept, like, five hours tops.

We're going to Gibraltar tomorrow, early. It's gonna be an insanely long flight, but David's assured me it'll be nice and spacious. I liked the fancy plane on the hop over from Tennessee; was weird having so much wiggle room. Can only hope it's comfortable for a twenty-ish hour-long trip overseas.

David comes into the breakfast room, humming to himself and looking over some papers, readers perched on his nose. Since Nashville, he's started to de-age; his skin is clearer, freckles dark and scattered even more, and his hair—grown out quite a bit these last few months—is a charming, fluffed mess in the mornings. The more sober he is, the happier he is, and he continues to just look…enchanting. Young. Full of life.

He glances up at me and smiles with more sunshine than I think I deserve right now. "Hi, good morning."

"Hi," I reply behind my coffee, turning my back to him in my seat at the kitchen table. Probably don't think I deserve the smile cause I still haven't told him I read his personal journals. "How's your work going?" I ask, flipping the next page of a book out in front of me, one I'm not entirely reading anyway.

"Fine, good. Finished up a call with Erica. Think she's finally, *finally* on board with what I'm doing. Taking a step back from the movies for a couple months. I mean of course she's liking it for the wrong reasons, thinks the non-profit stuff is good for publicity. But…I mean it's a start."

I nod along and close my book. "Shallow of her, not surprised. But it's progress," I agree, hand stroking Chicken's back as he comes under the table to rest on my feet.

"Progress, yeah. Though she keeps bringing up some new actor, Phillip West—guess he's fresh on the scene. Eighteen, tall, handsome. From England. She's worried I'll get, like, thrown aside because of this shiny, unsoiled, straight guy…" He gets quiet and I glance over my shoulder.

David sees me staring and straightens. "Nicholas sent me an article. He meant it in a nice way, I think, like a heads up. But people are saying 'out with the old' when it comes to me and…my previous mistakes. Jacob and Erica are going through uh. Paperwork. To keep him quiet. But some drama has leaked anyway, so the press are saying that I can put on a front, but it doesn't erase the 'bad boy' shit I did before."

That's Hollywood for you, I guess. Months ago that 'bad boy' charm was all the rage. Now it's haunting him.

He sputters out through his lips, cracks his neck, and rolls his shoulders, and I smirk at his sudden pout of determination. "Don't care. I'm standing for what I'm doing, no matter what."

"Damn straight."

"I'm impacting more lives with a single podcast episode these days than I ever did with drama TV shows."

"Heck yeah you are."

"And, when I *do* decide to go back into movies, it'll be the projects I wanna do, not what she thinks will make the most money."

"Here, here," I chuckle, raising my mug to him.

He glows and brings the carafe over to refill my coffee. I swear, if he had let momentum take over, he was about to bend at the waist and kiss the top of my head. Dreams, Scott, just dreams. "Speaking of phone calls, I'm curious; when you dropped me off at Silversmith, you said you had calls to make. Who were you calling?" I ask.

"Ah, right." He returns to the counter and taps his fingers to the marble. "Uh. A realtor called me that morning. Remember Megan, from Charlotte and Mei's party? She's been helping me out, and I had to return her message."

"Message about…?"

"Selling the house," he replies. My eyes widen and I turn my entire body in my chair to better to face him.

"What—this house? Why?"

David shrugs and pours himself some coffee. "I don't fit in it. It was meant for someone else, someone I was never able to become. It's not gonna work right now with me moving forward. I need something smaller, compact. I need to downsize a lot of shit in my life, and this is one of those things."

"Oh, wow…are you gonna sell your stuff?"

"Some of it."

"Maybe Devon can help you find the right buyers," I mutter. His head spins back to me, and neither he nor I can tell if I was joking or not. "Um…okay. What about that night, the other call?"

His shoulders droop so low he rests his elbows on the counter, scratching at the back of his head. "Uh…I actually called up Sasha, had to leave a message."

"Oh yeah…?"

"I need to talk to her. Something's been hanging on me since Nashville." He comes back with coffee and sets it between his hands.

His thumb moves in a circle around the mug before he slumps in his seat, kicking his legs out under the table. His foot taps mine, and before he can dart it back, I trap it between my ankles. "I just...I don't want her to keep thinking it could've worked between us. She was a good person—is. *Is* a good person. She thinks it had something to do with her, and it doesn't, just like Missy."

"What do you mean, like Missy?"

David keeps scratching at the back of his head. I'm surprised he's not balding there somehow. "We um. Well. Missy and I fucked around for five months through summer and fall semester, right? Not very long—cause I couldn't uh. Lead her on. My head was all messed up—I mean, my heart—messed up. I guess both. I was trying to...well, but when your parents died. You got sick—or—I mean, now I know you weren't *just* sick. You. You *left*, and...and no, I'm sorry, I'm not saying it's your fault, it's no one's..."

I don't think he's formed a complete sentence for, like, a whole minute. "Dude, are you okay?"

He winces and sits forward, turning his cup in a circle before lifting it, leaving our legs locked up. "Yeah. I don't know. I'm scared to talk to Sasha. She didn't answer. But I think if I text her, I know she'll get back to me. Then I'd *have* to reply, cause that's how conversation works. But I don't want to talk over text, I wanna do it face to face and *that's* a huge fucking no thanks, not by myself."

"Do you want me to go with you?"

Big ol' eyes blink at me, and he whispers behind his mug, "Would you?"

"Yes, of course. I can be there, if you need me to be."

David sets his drink down and goes for my hands on the table, pulling them toward himself until he's crossed his arms over them, forehead pushed to my knuckles.

His sigh is hot over my fingers, his thanks muffled against my skin. I wiggle one hand free and brush through his hair, smiling when he smiles with his eyes closed.

———

She's early. She's *beautiful*, too.

Sasha's dressed to either go to hot yoga after this or run a pro-choice rally like a boss. Hair pulled up in a ponytail, gym leggings and a loose tie-dye muscle tank. (Homegirl is *ripped*, lemme tell you.) She's looking out at the park, foot tapping in the air while she sits at a metal table next to an assortment of coffee shops and cafés. (Not a Starbucks in sight.)

David's hand is squeezing mine to the point of blood loss. "You'll be okay," I tell him. He hums. "You're safe, dude. I'm here."

That gets a smile. A thank you. And we head over. The moment she sees us, her eyes dart first to our hands, then to my face, and they land on David.

Her smile is so legitimate, I kinda melt a little. "Hi, there," she chuckles, getting up and coming around the table.

He doesn't release my hand when he hugs her; his face appearing over her shoulder is startled as hell. "Uh—hi, hey Sasha, hi."

She looks to me again, and I'm seconds away from raising a hand and waving, when she hugs me, too. She smells like lavender tea. I feel like a dick for thinking she was anything like Missy. And I feel like a dick for thinking anything mean of Missy, in the first place.

"Sit, sit, sit," she says, patting the table. One seat is closer to the other, and I urge David to take the one nearest her. She taps his cheek with a hand, then reaches that hand for me. "Sasha, hi, so nice to meet you in person!"

"Scott, you, too," I smile, accepting her handshake. David still looks confused AF. "Thanks for meeting us."

"Oh, of course. I've been wanting to talk to this one, but he's been busy, busy, busy, finishing up filming, fundraisers, his gala—

I was only there a hot minute, Erica called me, but I had to go early. Then you started showing up all over with interviews and conventions."

Sasha sputters through sparkly pink lips. "I even thought, well, darn, I'll just buy a ticket to his next talk and see him there but—sold out!" she huffs, lifting her hands in the air.

"I had no idea you wanted to talk to me," David mutters, scratching at his shoulder under his short sleeve. "Erica told me you were at the gala and I admittedly ran away. I'm sorry it took me so long to reach out. Guess Instagram comments don't really count as back and forth."

"No, it's okay, I get it." Sasha clasps her hands on the table and stares at him for a long time. I can visibly see his face softening inch by inch the longer he's looking at her.

"David, I won't lie. I was hurting when we first broke up. After what happened with Jacob—"

"Sasha, I'm so sorry—"

"I'm going to finish my sentence," she says. David and I both sit up straighter. "It was painful, that you did that behind my back, and didn't tell me until weeks later. And I will be honest and say I don't understand why you didn't just break up with me before you did so.

"But the way the magazines messed it up for us just wasn't fair. I don't think you're a commitment-phobe—I don't even know what that means! All that phooey they published; I didn't say it. I didn't even give a statement that day, Davy. I think honestly you need to have a long talk with Erica, because I hate to say it, but she's moving a lot of pieces without you knowing, even now."

The silence is long enough that it's a pause he can speak up in, and he says quietly, "I know…I'd hoped she'd changed her mind about me acting, but. Yeah. I figured."

Her hand goes back to his cheek, and her heart-shaped face squishes with a smile. "And I get some of what happened afterward. Jacob is not my favorite person, as I've told you before. Even if I was clearly not what you needed at the time, I'd love to stay your friend. I love you a lot, Davy, that hasn't changed."

His eyes water, and he's got my hand on his face, too, when I reach across the table and wipe a thumb under his lashes.

"I'm sorry I didn't tell you about it sooner. Not just about Jacob, but about me being gay."

"Gosh, I'm not!" She laughs, scoffs, and puts a hand to her chest. "David—I'm *not*. This is...this is you. You need to take time to decide when you're comfortable. I'm not upset with you, babe, people are...some people are cruel. And violent. And some are just so gosh darn *wonderful* and understanding, and you'll be swept in with open arms. Your safety is most important. And your comfort. Tell who you want to tell, shout it to the world, spread your love, and impact if you want to. No matter what, I know you'll change lives. You've already changed mine for the better."

David gives a stuttered cry and reaches for her, and I try to hide my surprise at how quickly he falls apart once her arms are around his back. It's soft in her shoulder, but it's just as body-shaking as it was in my dorm after the party. She holds him in silence, cheek on his head, smiling at me. I smile back.

Chapter 55

With a flight out before six AM tomorrow, we should be packing and making sure last-minute things are ready to go, including going over everything Chicken will need while he's staying home with Thangus.

Should is the keyword. We're on the floor in the piano room, laying on our backs and staring at the high-vaulted ceiling. (I thought David was gonna pee himself, when I told him this particular style of architecture included 'flying buttresses'. I might've been totally wrong, but I was over the moon, seeing him laughing so hard after so much crying earlier.)

The only noise now is coming from an old boom box sitting on a window seat by the piano, playing a local country station. When we first came into the room, David asked me to fiddle around a bit on the piano, play him something.

We both mellowed out in a weird way when I started playing Novo Amor songs. He hummed along with one, and when I asked how he knew it, he shrugged and said since I showed him Gregory Alan Isakov, he went down a rabbit hole of similar artists to help him sleep.

Then his phone lit up like crazy; Megan said someone's already making an offer on the house. With a look of 'please do something with this before I break it,' he passed his phone off to Thor, in exchange for mini red velvet cupcakes. We started with eight. We're down to two.

"How do you think Chicky's gonna do in a smaller house?" I ask, noisily licking cream cheese frosting from my thumb. David throws his arm my way and hands me a napkin, chuckling at the fact that he nearly took my eye out in the process.

"Sure he'll be fine. Angus said his sister could watch over him while we get the house moved. It might stress him out, taking stuff out and all that when we need to show it."

"Is Chicken anxious about being left behind on our trip to Spain? You said you take him everywhere."

"I do, usually." David does a dorky crab walk to get to the cupcake container. (We thought, by setting it on the piano bench, we'd be less inclined to finish them off. We were wrong.) "But when we got home from seeing Sasha—remember, when I couldn't find him anywhere and I was screaming my head off? He was with Angus, sprawled out in his and Thor's room. Didn't budge an inch when I called him to me from the doorway."

"You've been replaced by a hunkier, beefier man," I chuckle, accepting a mini cupcake as he hands it my way.

He devours the last one in a single bite and drops with a snort, tucking an arm under his head. "Seems like it."

Night falls. Thirty minutes later, neither of us have bothered to get up and flip on any lights. Thor finds us and goes wall to wall, turning on a lamp or two, bathing the room in a warm yellow. Angus comes in right behind with hot chocolate. These two, I swear, fairy godfathers of snacks.

"Can I say something?" David asks.

"Say whatever you'd like," I reply, picking marshmallows out of the bottom of my near empty cup.

"I think I was scared of Sasha. Because I didn't want us to become my mom and dad."

I tilt my chin up and look at him upside down. His lashes are so long from this angle. "What do you mean?"

"Mom loved Dad for a long time. Years, they were married for over a decade. But he was always a little...soft. She compared him I think to her brother, my tío Nathan, before she even knew Dad was gay. Her own father was homophobic, always pointing out things about Nathan that he disapproved of, so she saw similarities in how Dad and Nathan talked, laughed, their hobbies."

He scoffs and starts to talk with flailing hands. "She noticed *stereotypes* and got hooked in—y'know, when I first told her I was gay, she didn't believe me? She said I didn't look gay. Who the fuck *looks* gay, what does that mean?"

"It's that scowl you do. Only straight guys glare like that. Big bushy brow lookin' like a Neanderthal."

David laughs. "You might have a point. But Mom was obsessed, it was almost like she thought he was cheating on her. She started pushing Dad at every turn, prodding him about his sexuality. He just kept saying he loved her, why wasn't that enough."

"How do you know all this?" I ask, trying to play ignorant, while his journal entries from junior high swim behind my eyes.

"He told me years ago, then we talked about it again when I first got with Jacob while with Jolene. He was who I called immediately; cause I was confused and afraid. Suddenly, thinking gay thoughts and *acting* on them…I mean…" He wipes a hand under his nose while my face tingles. "I mean acting on them *all the way*. There goes that line I'd built. I asked him, wouldn't it be easier if I just went back to Jolene?

"But Dad said Mom was never satisfied in their marriage the moment she assumed he was something else, so he advised me to be honest to myself. I guess when he and Mom broke up and it came out that he *was* gay, she was furious. Felt played. She never understood the fear, the discomfort with coming out, not like Sasha clearly has."

David sighs and rolls around until he's opposite to me on his side. I mirror him and count his freckles upside down. "I didn't want that with me and Sasha, even if I liked her more than Jolene. I didn't want to just keep saying I loved her—I wanted to need her, to want her. I wanted her happy, to be able to satisfy her in every single way, and I don't think I could ever do that and still be true to myself."

He rubs at an eye, hard, and I reach and tap at his wrist until he lets me take his fingers. "Dad lost fourteen years of his life playing a lie, because he was trying to please Mom. And still she was never happy with him. Shit, even now, she still complains about him. Like all her respect for him went out the window and never came back. A lot of years wasted, Scott…"

His voice fades into silence, until it's just us breathing quietly, content to stare at one another and try to read tangled thoughts without saying anything. If only.

"Do you remember me saying at Dollywood, that there were reasons I wasn't ready to face yet?" he asks. "For why I've felt all over the place about…this."

"I remember. You stole my waffle."

I get a laugh, just as I wanted. "You *gave* me your waffle."

"Never, I don't share waffles. What're your reasons?" I ask, running my thumb over his knuckles like he does to me.

"I love my mom. But she wouldn't let Dad hug me as I got older. Told me when I was eleven that big strong boys don't get kissed by their fathers on the cheek, so I shouldn't look to him for affection."

He closes his eyes and brings our hands toward his chin. "I've always felt. Off. Even with Jacob. If I wasn't the one in control—though, I mean even with him, I was *never* in control. But if I was…accepting. If *I* was being kissed, if someone hugged me. Dad, or Vernon, or any guy at all. If I didn't have that control, then….I'd never get it back. I'd let her down, and she wouldn't love me the same again. I don't know. It makes no sense."

So many puzzle pieces just fell into place that I lost count. "David…"

He inhales deeply and looks at me, watches me shift an inch closer. "You're one of the strongest guys I know. You're allowed to be affectionate. And you're allowed to receive affection if you want it. Your mom is wrong. Big strong boys do need love."

His smile is sunshine. Once, he called me a sunflower, but he's the one with bright gold all over his face as he chuckles with utmost, childish delight. "Can I say something else?" he asks.

"No, you've hit your limit." David bursts a laugh and dips his brow into the carpet to muffle it, and I tug at his hand.

"You're beautiful," he sighs, eyes crossed and right on me. "When I saw you at the gala, on those stairs, I suddenly knew what you meant, when you met Cassidy for the first time. You looked like a hero in a painting."

Did I say his smile is sunshine? I meant that his smile is the ocean, overwhelming, taking you with it. Just like his endless, spectacular writing; you start to drown before you've even realized you left the shore.

Since I'm not sure I'm brave enough yet to get pulled out on the next tide, I swallow and check the clock on the wall by the piano, and say, "It's after midnight. Happy birthday, David." And I leave to pack without waiting on him to reply.

———

It's still dark out when my eyes decide to open. My hand reaches out across the sheets and comes up empty; David's already awake, arms holding his knees to his bare chest. His body is bathed in cool, and his side of the bed has chilled without him laying down. (I didn't think we'd ever have sides of the bed.) (I didn't think I'd ever crave the heat of his body, either.)

He's staring at the dark open windows, thin drapes brushed by a warm breeze. By the time the sun rises, we'll have already lifted off from a private runway. I can hardly hear his shallow breathing.

It must be my creaky voice that asks, "Are you alright?" cause he's the one that turns his head slightly and replies, "I'm scared."

I mean to ask why, or does he want to talk about it. I attempt to push exhaustion aside so I can pay attention to him, now, in the dark, when it feels like this moment may either disappear the second I blink, or it could last for the rest of my life.

I'm sleepy (and beautiful, David said so), and it's making me feel braver than last night. So I sit up, and before he can fully turn around, I circle his waist with my arms and pull him back down to lay with me. I don't say, 'you're safe'. I don't say, 'I love you'. I don't think.

Holding him to me until I hear his breathing match mine, I tell him, "I'll protect you." From what, I don't know. From it all. But I mean it. I hope he knows I mean it.

He doesn't say anything, and he doesn't make me move as I curl around him and feel him drift back to sleep right along with me. Until his alarm goes off, waking us up again, bringing us back into reality.

Chapter 56

There's a moment over the North Atlantic when I'm suddenly awake, Ben Howard still playing quietly in my headphones. I mean, I'm assuming it's the Atlantic; there's only blue out the sliver of my window. Feel like I've been passed out for two days straight. Obviously not possible, as we did our second stop at JFK airport just…uh…well shit, I dunno…

Looking around the spacious cabin, I rub sleep from my eyes, and squint when I notice movement at my side. I turn to David. He's holding his phone up at me, a faint smile on his lips.

"Hi…" Man, my throat definitely *feels* like I've been asleep for two days straight.

"Hiya," he whispers, lowering his phone. That one word shouldn't sound so soft and pleasant.

"Get a good shot of me drooling?" I ask with a long stretch, pointing my toes. Still not used to having so much space in front of me in an airplane. David's chuckle doesn't answer my question, and he continues to stare at his phone. "What're you doing? Picking a good filter?"

"No, don't think I'll post this one," he says, shifting to tuck a leg under him.

"What, that bad?" I yawn. His phone is in front of me, and I blink and roll my eyes around, attempting to focus.

That's not me. There's no way that's me. It's someone else wearing my headphones, using my neck pillow, dressed in my white linen shirt. Someone who isn't as wrecked as I am. Someone peaceful.

Hell, with the sun coming in through the window, lighting this stranger up in pearly fire that illuminates the sharp slant of their nose and turns their hair gold, it almost looks like— "I look like my mom."

David's phone in his hand lowers, his arm lowers, and I stare back at him as his shoulders sink. "Do you?" he asks, starting to pull his hand back. I reach for his wrist so fast I think I startle him, but he doesn't yank away, merely leaning on the armrest so he can look at the photo with me. "Will you ever tell me about her?"

"The moment has to be just right before I tell you about Georgiana Elodie Boscoe," I reply, tearing my eyes from the picture to keep from appearing vain. David chuckles again, a little rumble I feel in my ribs, shaking his shoulder where it's pressed to mine on the shared armrest.

"Maybe the perfect moment will happen before we land. We've got another few hours."

"Do we? I thought we refilled a while ago."

"We did."

"Screw consciousness then, I'ma nap s'more," I grumble, shimmying more into my seat.

"You might be the most boring flight mate I've ever had going to Spain," David smirks, kicking his legs up on the seat across from him.

"Were you expecting a party plane ride? Complete with strippers and confetti cannons?"

"I mean, what do you think the pole is for?"

"What pole—you do *not* have a pole." He grins and I squint up at the lights, looking for a retractable stripper pole and/or the word 'gullible' written on the ceiling. "Have you heard from our dads yet?"

"Which ones? Thangus?" I smile and nod, loving that he's using that name for them now, and he shrugs. "Yeah, they called while you were asleep. Guess Chicken was antsy at first, but the moment they turned on a movie he chilled out."

"Which movie?"

David smiles then. "Up."

"It'll knock *anyone* out, dude, for real."

"For real, for real. You want a snack? Thor made sure to stock us up for our trip over. We got Chex Mix, popcorn, protein bars, microwave meals, you name it. But Angus of course threw in some sweets for us, too. Cupcakes from that place you liked yesterday, donuts. I think he even made a fucking cake."

"You got a pantry large enough for all that?"

"It's huge—I've caught them making out in there once."

"Oooh, didn't know it was seven-minutes-in-heaven sized, that changes things." It doesn't, I'm talking out of my ass. But he's super cute and sitting really close to me and neither of us have stopped smiling this entire conversation.

"I can show you later," he replies. His face turns rosy before I can even take a breath to start laughing. "I didn't—I meant like—we got *snacks*! In the closet!"

"Oh, buddy, I know you got snacks alright! Remind me to never eat anything that comes out of the make out closet," I laugh, pushing him in the shoulder as he groans into his hands. "Okay, okay, I'm awake now, let's play on the Switch or something—"

"No, I wanna go find the escape hatch so I can throw myself from this plane."

"Don't, please, I'll be lost as hell in Gibraltar without you." David gives me the side eye. "Can we stop at London on the way back? Is that a thing we're allowed to do?"

That gets a big smile out of him, and he situates closer, pulling his legs up on the giant seat. Can't find this kind of leg room in Delta, I can tell you that. "Do you want to? Then we can drive to Scotland, it's only nine hours."

"Nine hours—you drive nine hours in Texas, you're still in Texas," I snort. "I'd love Scotland, we can stumble upon a castle."

"Plenty of make out closets in abandoned castles," David mumbles, scratching under his nose. That decides that, then.

—

Pedro had a car sent to pick us up. I teased David that they didn't want to be seen in public with us, and he just laughed. "Knowing them, they're cooking something, and they didn't want to leave it unsupervised, otherwise it'll burn the kitchen down again."

"*Again*?"

"Don't ask."

David might've shown me pictures of Gibraltar, but he refused to share any photos of the actual house, claiming it was a surprise. Already I adore the neighborhood; homes built close enough for neighbors but not so much that you'd drive each other mad with loud music and parties. Porches painted lime green and hot pinks, houses an array of pastels or glowing white brick.

When the car pulls up to one in particular on a steep hill, my jaw just…sags.

Slap me silly and, like—shoot, I dunno, some sort of southern phrase. Throw me down the gosh darn stairs.

I want this house. I *need* this house.

It takes David yanking me out of the car just for me to remember how to function.

Palm trees touch at the tippy top of the pointed, one-story roof. Cream colored stone, bright red brick shingles, hand-painted tiles leading up the walkway to the front door, stained emerald green and hanging wide open. On either side of welcoming columns sit bushels of yellow and red flowers, just like David's tattoo.

Everything glorious and good smelling floats out and lingers in the beach air, from vanilla incense to spiced food and men's cologne, mixing with sea salt from the coast down below the other side of the house.

"Can we move here?" I mutter.

He chuckles, hand on the back of my neck. "You know they'd adopt you before they ever let me move in."

"I know. So. Can *I* move here?"

Vernon's singing is louder than anything else, even the radio blasting The Beatles through the tiled house.

We take our shoes off at the entrance, set our bags down. Wooden wind chimes clink together near the open patio doors leading to the yard and a small but shining pool covered by a cedar pergola. Open water stretches for miles beyond, all the way to the horizon.

The house has no lamps or fans on whatsoever, and yet it doesn't need them; every window is open and glowing with sunlight, breeze coming in enough to send a line of sweat speeding down my back.

I gulp in the largest inhale I can without falling backward.

Haven't felt like this since Lubbock; coming into the old house during a hot summer day to find Mom cooking grilled cheeses, pink lemonade full of strawberries and too much sugar. It seeps into my marrow and hugs around my heart. This is a loving home.

"Oi!" David's shout startles me into his side, and he grins, hand up to his mouth. "¡Papás, ya llegamos!"

There's a yelp from the kitchen with what sounds like a spoon being dropped on the counter. Vernon appears in an old Seahawks t-shirt and jean shorts, russet skin more freckled and aged since I last saw him, particularly up by his green eyes.

He screams and runs for us. "There are *children* in the house again!"

I get a hug first, ha! He lifts me to my toes and I hold on for dear life, breathing in rice, salsa, and grilled vegetables hidden in the threading of his shirt and long black hair tucked behind his ears.

"Hi, Vernon," I groan, tears springing to my eyes.

Vernon drops me, and I hardly have a second to breathe before the spitting image of David leaps at me. He doesn't stop at my toes, and I go flying off the ground. Pedro's round and soft like my mom used to be, though his arms are muscular like David's from working his boat in the summers, and his ashen brown hair has gray at the temples.

He smiles at me with brown, crinkly eyes. "Hola, hi, hi," I laugh, my face smooshed between calloused hands.

Pedro plants a kiss on my forehead, one in my hair, and he dives for David next. I catch a flutter of 'hermoso hijo' and 'God, I've missed you' mumbled between the two of them, David's fist gripping tight to the back of Pedro's muscle tank.

Vernon's arm comes around my shoulders again, and I get another kiss to my cheek. Everyone here is taller than me, Pedro himself standing well over Thor's height. I'm surrounded by the sweetest, most loving giants, and I'm getting kisses left and right.

Never, ever did I get love like this in my home. My parents adored me and Bevett. But this is a different kind of affection.

It's open and it's teary, as both David and Pedro, and now Vernon and—shit, now me, are all kind of crying and blubbering, cause the last time David saw them was a year ago, and the last time I saw them was too fucking long ago.

Pedro lets out one last flustered, weepy sigh and corrects David's leather necklace, before he turns to me with a hand on his hip. I start to laugh all over again when it finally registers that he's in hot pink flamingo shorts. "Hungry? Boys are always hungry."

"Famished," I smile. David winks at me and dips his head as his dad rakes fingers through his hair.

"You need a haircut. I'll fix that for you." A hard thwap hits David's shoulders, leading him to the kitchen with me and Vernon behind.

David snorts and takes two plates from the table set up, passing one to me. "Last time you did that, I had a bowl cut for ninth grade homecoming, so no thank you."

"¡Tan malo! Never cares at all for my feelings, does he," Pedro pouts, serving us what looks like the thickest enchiladas I've ever seen in my life. (Like, *thiccc.*) I'm gonna get so fat and happy and sunburned here, I can't wait.

Chapter 57

We take forever with lunch cause all four of us together means more talking, less eating. They pair the food with peach tea full of fresh lemons and peach chunks, and David doesn't stop me when I steal his drink after downing mine. But when Vernon hints that there's homemade dessert, David and I hit the same wall, and we tap out for naptime.

I figure he'd want to go bunk out in the room we'd be sharing. (Ten steps to the pool, hadn't forgotten that detail.) However, he flops onto the burnt orange sofa next to his dad, who's sitting on the center cushion with his arms outstretched along the back. A gigantic photo from Pedro and Vernon's wedding hangs on the floral-patterned wall behind the couch.

And David, to my absolute delight, squeezes as much of himself as he can fit onto a single cushion, head on his dad's shoulder, pulling his legs to his chest. He lets out a heavy sigh, the kind Chicken does once he gets settled in the perfect position for a nap, and I chuckle at Vernon going to take up the other space under Pedro's opposite arm.

All at once, I notice there's no room for me. I almost don't even care, not with the look of love and peace on David's face.

But he meets my eye with a smile, drops a foot back to the ground and spreads his legs open, waving for me to sit with him in...in his lap. With his dads right there on the sofa.

I point at myself and my brows go up in question. "Get over here," David laughs, almost in unison with Pedro and Vernon ushering me over.

With a shrug of 'if y'all cool with it, I'm jiggy with it', I join them. I sit between David's open legs, drape my own across his thigh, and my cheek fits perfect right on Pedro's chest, David's head dropping onto mine.

We're a puppy piled mess. I can't imagine what we look like. Doesn't even matter. In three minutes, David's breathing deepens, his arms around my waist fall limp, and Pedro's talking soft to Vernon about the show they're watching as I drift off. Never been so warm in my entire life.

—

Once we get naps, a second helping of reheated enchiladas, and break into the flan Vernon made, we go for a walk on the beach.

Straight up forgot that getting paparazzied was one of the reasons we were here to begin with. Had a little flicker of normalcy where I was in food and pleasant smells heaven; the first person we see taking our photo, I legit grin and wave at them like, howdy doodily stranger, how's your day going! David laughs, but he does the same thing seconds later.

By the third person, a dude in trunks and a ratty 'Hang Loose' t-shirt, Pedro and Vernon start to notice we're attracting attention.

Guy ain't slick; he's tripping over his flip-flopped feet, trying to get our photo, rambling off at David in Spanish. I catch bits of him asking what David's doing here if not partying it up, am I still his boyfriend after the pictures of him and Jacob, is he really past the drinking like he claims.

At something that sounds like 'gay' and 'hereditary', Pedro loses it. And I lose it with a gleeful cackle. He chases the dude down and chucks a sandal at him as the nosy jerk attempts to take more photos while running backward. I most *definitely* understand the curse words Pedro shouts out on the public beach, cause many of those were the first Spanish words David taught me when we were thirteen.

"That's right, you better run!" Vernon laugh-screams, shaking David around by the shoulders cause he's in tears and wheezing at this point. "And bring back his chancla, asshole!"

They don't understand that we *want* to get photographed, and we can't really admit to them why. I mean, we *could*; if anyone would be empathetic, it would be them.

But there's a twist in my stomach that says maybe we don't need to fake anything anymore. Or at least, maybe we can just enjoy this as, I dunno. Friends. Who tell each other they're beautiful and fall asleep spooning. (And who *don't* talk about that time two nights ago where one gangly friend accidentally rubbed up against the other's chiseled, warm body in their sleep. Cause *that* fucking happened.)

Pedro and Vernon, after requesting that we to stick to their own private sector of the beach, abandon us to go on a secret mission, refusing to let David and me return to the house with them until they call David's phone.

Their first mistake is leaving two dudes who are hyped up on shaved ice from the street corner and jetlag alone on an empty beach. We run through the water for an hour, chasing each other and tossing layers of clothing at one another's head. I get my sneaker real darn close to his shoulder, and in turn I get a flip flop to the back of my skull.

We cool it after that, cause when I blink again, I'm on the ground, and David's looking like he wants to laugh, while also checking to see if I'm bleeding.

"Any word from the papas?" I ask as he joins me in the sand, flopping backward.

"Nope."

"Did you even bring your phone with you?"

David smirks at me. "Nope."

"You think they'll notice?"

"Doubtful. I'm sure their super-secret whatever the fuck is just them wanting peace and quiet before they're surrounded by millennials every breathing moment for the rest of the weekend."

I smile and lay down on my back, shielding my eyes from the sun as water laps up around us. It reaches all the way to my shoulders, covers me in foam, and tickles back down again. David lets out a sigh and crosses his arms over his eyes.

"Hey, David."

"Yeppers."

"I don't think I'm gonna have a home when I go back to the states."

He looks at me in shock and sits up on an elbow. "What?"

"Mitch texted me. The day you picked me up from Jethro. Said I wasn't welcomed back; it's why Bevvy was so upset when I spoke to her that night on your phone."

"Why can't you go back? Because of the reporters?"

"That's what he said, but I feel like there's gotta be more that he's not sharing. Can I tell you something else, without you getting angry? Just trust that I was angry enough to fuel over six thousand angry elephants when I found out."

He hums and lays back down a few inches closer to me. "No promises, but okay…"

"You read the email JU sent me, right?"

"Right."

"I think Mitch got me into Jethro with connections, behind my back. And I think he faked my background check for Silversmith." I'm not sure if that's rushing water, or David's heavy breathing, but I keep going. "Don't think I ever had to fight my way in like I did. For either of them."

Tears hurt. They mix with salt from my sweat, with sand, with a cut I got on my cheek from when we were screwing around earlier. "Not a damn thing I've worked for has been mine. And I'm gonna leave this fantastical place and be slammed with a reality I thought I was safe from."

He smells like dude and sea and lemonade, and I'm overheated and already sunburnt. But when his hand tucks under my neck and he's curling me closer to him, I let him, fingers looping through his necklace by his collarbone to keep him against me.

"I might have an idea," he says, chin moving on top of my head. "What if...after my house sells. You and I get our own place? Like we planned when we were younger?"

When I look up at him, he doesn't move away, and my breath catches at his mouth right near mine. I want to say yes, I want to scream and wrap him up in my arms. But he keeps talking before I can say anything, and he's smiling, and he thinks he's telling me a dream. But it sinks into my stomach and weighs like a nightmare.

"We can get a place, and you won't have to worry about your job. Or school. I make enough for both of us; we could get a nice flat in Malibu if you wanted. I know it's not cheap, but I can cover it. You'd only have to work if you wanted to."

David nods like he's come up with the most amazing thing ever. In another world, maybe he has. In a world where I'm not centered around myself and my stupid fucking fears, I could move in with him and be cared for, no questions asked.

In this world though, it's horrid and selfish, but all my brain keeps screaming is cage, a cage, this is a cage—

"I just...man. The idea of coming home and you're there, and it's not an empty house with just me, hoping Thor and Angus are nearby. We can make dinner together, you can help me with my talks, and we can write."

If he'd suggested this weeks ago on the flight back from Tennessee, I would've had a job to go to, I would've had just a little bit left before I got a degree. I could cover half the rent of a flat in Malibu. We could go on road trips; I could drive the damn Ferrari and not feel like I'm maneuvering glass that doesn't belong to me.

As it stands, I have five grand in my bank account from the wills, and maybe nine grand from my job at Silversmith before they cut me out. I've got a phone I need to figure out how to pay for. I have no health insurance.

In a blink, I could get all that with David. And it would all just be another handout I could lose on the next unpredictable tide.

"I'll...think about it." He smiles at me all happy and tan, and I do my best to return it for the sake of saving face. "Think we can uh...can go see what the lovebirds are cooking up?" I sniffle, rolling away from him. David stares at me long after I've stood and started to gather up our shirts and shoes, shaky hands not as sneaky as I'd hoped they'd be.

—

We must be back earlier than intended. As soon as we come into the back door, Pedro's hollering at Vernon, and Vernon's screaming something back like, "I'm trying, amor, shut up, shut up!"

David gets a wily grin and darts away from my side, straight for the kitchen, where Vernon's shriek kicks up even louder, and there's a ripple of uncontrollable laughter.

"I've been caught, Pedro," Vernon yells. I get into the kitchen and throw my head with a laugh.

David's pinned Vernon to the kitchen counter with one hip, hand over the long-reach lighter, sheet of chocolate birthday cake laid out on the island with twenty-three candles in it.

"It says happy birthdays, plural," David tells me, nodding his head to the icing written out on the top, half-covered in sprinkles. I come to his side and tilt my head and he steps back so Vernon can light the candles.

"What for, why?"

"We didn't celebrate you, mijo," Pedro says, joining us, squeezing me in a one-armed hug. "This is for you both."

"Oh. Oh, no, no wait—" I look fast to David and can't shake my head enough. "No, y'all, that's not—this is for David—"

"I don't mind." He reaches behind him for something, and there's a snap of a rubber band under my chin as he adjusts a pointy party hat on my head. "We've shared parties before. When you got home late from Galveston we shared mine. Or when I was gonna be in Nebraska, you shared yours."

He puts on his own polka dot party hat. He's never looked more ridiculous and attractive at the same time as long as I've known him. "Besides. I've got a gift for you."

"I didn't get shit for you," I blurt out. His grin makes his eyes close.

"*Didn't* you?"

Vernon thumps into me, and he and Pedro take up a horrific chorus of Feliz Cumpleaños, complete with Vernon making the last note linger much longer than anyone would like, until Pedro force feeds him a slice of cake.

We eat half the cake in one fell swoop, continuing to nibble off it and lick icing from the serving spoon, until Pedro and Vernon call it quits. "We didn't get a nap like you sweet puppies," Pedro says, tucking hair behind my ear.

David sees his dad putting things away and getting ready for bed, and he hops off the counter where we were sitting, chasing after Pedro with a rushed, "Can I talk to you." Vernon kisses my cheek goodnight, puts the rest of the cake away, and I'm left alone in the kitchen, eating icing from my fingers and listening to the sound of the pool cleaner through the open doors, sea rushing in the distance.

Chapter 58

David comes back an hour later, just as my ass was starting to get numb from the hard counter. He holds something small at his side, looks like a box, or a book. "You okay?" I yawn, getting down and stretching my back.

"You're not tired, are you?"

"A little…but I can stay up a bit, I think."

David nods and looks to the package in his hand, wrapped in white paper. "Wanna sit by the pool?" I hum to his suggestion, but he makes no move to start walking.

"You okay, dude?" I repeat, standing in front of him.

He sets the package on the counter and scratches at his shoulder under his navy unbuttoned shirt. "Would you…I think I could use a hug."

My brow goes up, and I bend my knees to try to meet his eye. "Would you like me to hug you?" He nods. "Do I have permission to land hug?"

David chuckles and drops his hand with a limp shrug. "Permission granted."

I pretend to make a big fuss of where to put his arms, posing him this way and that, until he's laughing, and I go for around his waist. His arms circle my shoulders, face digging into my neck by my baggy shirt collar.

When I pull back, he's crying. "Hey, David…"

He sniffs and shakes his head. "I um. Can I give you your gift?"

"Yeah, let's go sit." He keeps an arm around my back as I lead him outside, and we sit on the blue and white tile circling the edge of the pool, hanging our feet into the water. "Talk to me, what's going on?"

David holds the package out to me. "Happy birthday."

"It's *your* birthday."

"*Yesterday* was my birthday," he corrects me. "Technically, you slept through most of it on the plane over."

"Whatever," I grumble, taking the gift anyway and opening the wrapping. Soft, worn leather runs under my fingers, crisp pages made of cream paper. It's a journal, and a pit in my stomach plummets at just how similar it looks to the ones I found in his library. "It's beautiful, David, thank you," I say, flipping through the empty sheets.

"I asked Dad to get this for you weeks ago. When we got back from Nashville. There's a maker here, he does them—vegan leather, recycled paper. I've got a couple at home from him."

"Do you?" I clear my throat, hold it to my chest. "Um. I think um…I gotta…" I look back to him, and my heart thumps at the utter look of devastation on his face. "Oh, Jesus, David, what is it, what's wrong?"

"I—I talked…" He hangs his head, pushes his forehead into his hands with a choked cry. "I talked to Dad about the college party—how—how bad it almost was, how Erica refused to help me. About Jacob and the b-breakup, and Mom—God, *Mom*. She called me, saw the gala pictures. And…she saw your picture; your news. Said she was d-disappointed in me, wouldn't listen when I told her you're not like Jacob. She said this wouldn't have happened if I was with Sasha. Fuck, I feel like how you must've felt with Devon and Kendra."

He gulps in an inhale and shivers out an exhale. "It just hit me, hearing Dad today on the beach, going on and on about what they wanted to fit into our trip before we leave Tuesday m-morning—hit me that I'm not gonna stay here. I visit and I'm just *covered* in love. I'd die for my mom but—but even when I'm with her, I'm not heard.

"Dad and Vernon, they're like Thor and Angus, back home. They're like, like guardians, they fit around me and protect me and...shit, Scotty, the biggest reason I haven't moved yet is I'm so fucking scared. I know moving and giving up acting might mean no more Thor and Angus. No more someone else in the silence with me, caring for me, helping me. I'm gonna be alone—I wanna cut my heart out and leave it here for safe keeping but I—I can't—"

David curls forward with one more sharp gasp and weeps into his palms, so loud it echoes against the brick and tiled patio and disturbed water around our legs.

I can't do anything for him but wrap him in a hug, push my fingers through his hair by his neck and let him sob into my shirt. This is an implosion. This is a splintered soul, one held together all this time finally shattering. He sounds like I felt in El Paso.

I wish I could hold him in my hands. I wish he was small enough I could fit him in the collar of my hoodies, hide him in the pocket of my shirts. Tuck him into a home built out of worn leather journals and colorful scarves.

The world is massive. And cruel like Erica said.

And wonderful like Sasha said. Full of beautiful people who truly want him with wide, open arms and so much kindness. Yet here come Devon's words again, reminding me that the love we want isn't always something that exists. In this moment, looking at someone who's cherished by his mother, but may never be understood by her, I think I get it.

"You're safe, David," I tell him, with nothing else to say but I love you, I love you, I'd give you the stars and hold your heart for you if you let me.

He pulls a hand up to wipe his eyes but I'm faster, catching his tears before he can. "When we get back...I'm dropping the house fast as I can and I'm finding you and me a place. I'm desperate for a home. I'm home here and never...not..." He pushes his cheek into my hand and sighs, shaking all over. "Scotty. I got um. A big request."

Can't be bigger than asking me to move in with him, but sure. "What is it?"

"You can say no…and maybe it's weird, but. Can you tell me about *your* mom?"

If now's not the perfect time, when is? Maybe it'll distract him from the idea of us moving in together, one I hadn't agreed to yet. "What do you want to know?"

"Read one of your poems. What was her favorite song? Anything."

"Anything," I repeat. David nods, closes his eyes and sits back on one hand, leaning into my shoulder. His foot kicks slow in the water, and with the pool light casting a blue glow on his tear-covered chin, he could be something from another world.

"So." He blinks and looks over to me, and I make a big show of pulling imaginary sleeves to my elbows, hands out like 'picture this'. He starts to smile.

"Imagine. You take a sunflower. Find the tallest, most beautiful one, with perfect yellow petals and a fresh green stem. The one that stands with pride and the occasional cocky hip. Wrap it in a dazzling Pashmina scarf, painted like a sunrise at sea, with blue eyes like a clear pool on a summer day. Give that sunflower a laugh like a river, the kind that bubbles, loud and infectious. It'll have gentle petals, hands that are larger than yours and perfect for holding, but strong, too, for lifting you up and spinning you around.

"Make it obsessed—*obsessed*, I tell you—with scary story podcasts and Chai vanilla tea and salt and vinegar chips. Give it soft edges, curves you fit into with your knees to your chest, safe and sound. Top it off with a love for Elton John and orange tabby cats. That was my mom. Georgiana Elodie Boscoe."

He's crying again. "She sounds magnificent," he whispers, taking one of my still raised hands before it can fall to my lap.

"She would have loved you," I reply, so quiet the words hardly leave my mouth.

David runs my fingertips over his lips. "Do you?" he murmurs. Swallowing is impossible. So is looking away from those eyes.

As brave as I thought I was that last night in his room, wrapping around him and being his shield for once, I feel three times as brave now. "Yes. I love you."

"I love you, too—"

"Don't. Don't say that." His brow wrinkles. He starts to let go of my hand, and I grab his fingers. "I…I have to tell you something."

I get to pick and choose my admission.

I could tell him that I can't move in with him without having a grasp on something that's my own, or something I earned. That I can't just hop from one shelter to the next, because when I lived with Devon and Kendra and thought I had safety, it was all a ruse to get my money and my youth.

And when I lived with Mitch, it was a trick to get me to change into the thing he wanted me to be, and there was nothing I could do about it, because it was either accept it, or be mentally twisted and thrown to the streets.

Ah, there it is, hello darkest fear: What's David going to want from me if he lets me in without carrying my own weight? How soon down the line is he going to say, so, now that you're comfortable, you have to do something for me, and you don't get a choice, because I feed you and give you a roof.

Second option here? I tell him about me reading his journals. Better sword to fall on at this time, I think. Fuck bravery, but here goes nothing…

With a deep breath, I expel it out. "I read your journals. In your house in LA. Found your pages about when we met, when we got hurt playing football. When your dad told you he wasn't allowed to hug you. Found your pages of…us. And of Missy. And after."

The reaction isn't immediate, and I don't think that's a good thing. It's like it simmers. The first bubble on the surface pops when his nose twitches once, then twice. His lip curls, and his brow sinks over his eyes.

"You fucking serious?"

He hasn't ripped his hand from mine yet, but maybe that's cause it's closer to my neck, less of a reach to strangle me.

"I'm really sorry. I couldn't sleep that first night. You found me, actually, you were sleepwalking and talking in Spanish. Said a word I didn't recognize, um…car…car-een-yo?"

Then he rips his hand from mine, shoving the heels of his palms into his eyes. Even with the colors from the pool lights, I can see just how flushed his neck is. What is this mystery word? Now I'm incredibly curious, even if it means he's pissed off at me. "Fucking *shit*, Scott! Fuck!"

"I'm sorry—"

"Stop it, stop, just shut up, saying you're sorry isn't gonna change—you read—that was all personal, man! You, *you* should know what it's like to have your privacy breached!"

"I'm—" he sneers at me and I sputter the rest of my apology out. At least he's not crying anymore. "Um…for what it's worth, you wrote beautifully."

"Fuck you," he spits. Is that a smile? No, stop Scott, you're hallucinating.

"You did. Never knew you could write like that. I liked your shorter sentences. Sometimes you wrote like me."

"Not on purpose, I don't write like *your* stuttery trash."

I can't even accept that as an insult, not since he's crossed his arms and his ankles like a toddler. I should be taking this more seriously, I hurt him by reading that stuff. But yay, biggest secret safe for now. I'm gonna ride this struggle bus straight into the sea.

"David, I mean it. I won't say 'sorry' again—"

"You *just* did—"

"But I'd love if you wrote some more. You should. Write poems, love stories. You're so talented." He huffs. I'm smiling, I can't help it. "I liked how you wrote about hands. Your memories. If anyone writes with their heart, it's you."

He keeps glaring at the pool, refusing to look my way now. What've I got to lose if I do this and he hates me? I'm left in Spain with no way home? Ha, what home? I'd figure something out. Maybe Pedro and Vernon would take pity on me and let me hunker down in the pool shed, feeding me cold enchiladas.

But I can't *not* do this.

I lift a hand and trail a finger from his cheek to his ear, around in his hair and down his neck. His eyes roll closed and he breathes in like it's the first time in his life. "You wrote that you like my hands," I whisper, letting my thumb circle near his shirt collar, "how much do you like them?"

David tilts his head without opening his eyes, and sighs when I gently grasp the back of his neck, turning him more toward me. "I *love* your hands."

I bring my mouth inches to his. "May I kiss you, David?"

"I think I'd die if you didn't, Bo."

And on his exhale, my lips are on him.

His fingers are in my hair immediately, keeping me in place. Like I'd go anywhere else, not when he gives that lovely gasp and dives in deeper. He's salty from tears and tastes like birthday cake, and at the touch of his palm on my knee, I melt into him. Before my other hand can go to his shoulder, David starts to smirk.

"What?" I chuckle, feeling him smile.

"You smooth motherfucker."

My laugh is too giddy to keep kissing him. "What did I do?"

"'You like my hands,' he says—like you don't know…"

"What?" I grin, getting a kiss on my cheek. He leans back and gets to his feet, and my smile flees. "Wait, where—"

"I'm jetlagged to shit, and I'm still peeved at you," he snorts, reaching down for me. "Bedtime? Please? We can go to the beach tomorrow, after breakfast. Dad and Vernon will be out until eleven at the market, when they get back we can go shopping."

"More of your perfect shed-yule?" I ask, accepting his help up.

He wraps me in his arms and squeezes me, lips to the scar on my jaw. I kiss his brow in response, making him grin. "If we don't plan something, we'll be lazy fucks the entire time."

"I wouldn't mind a lazy fuck," I smirk.

He squints at me. I'm seconds away from super big regrets, when he kisses me again, fingers in my hair giving a light tug, until it's me who's gasping and bending back at the waist from his sheer force and filthy smooching.

And we're about to go to bed? *Together*? Fuck me. (No literally, I'm begging you.)

"I love you," he says into my mouth.

I think I like you more. "I love you more."

Chapter 59

I get up earlier than him, but not earlier than Pedro and Vernon (like hell, they were up before eight to get groceries at the market; I'm on vacation, I ain't doing that shit) so I get coffee started. There are all sorts of chrome contraptions and espresso makers, and I stand in the kitchen in my boxers and one of David's shirts with a glare on my face, until I discover a Mr. Coffee hidden under the counters.

"You're making *American* coffee? In *Gibraltar*?" David grunts over the rumbling machine, walking in shirtless with delightful bedhead. And boxers cut *much* higher up the thigh than mine. Dude knows how to swagger, dear Lord. "You're such a tourist."

"Yep." Sound like a mouse that got stepped on. I clear out my throat and get to work, death-gripping a pan and going for eggs.

Or, I mean, I'm halfway to the fridge for the eggs, when a wide hand plants on my abdomen from behind me under my shirt, and I look up to the face of David as he brings me back toward him. "What—uh, hey—hi."

He smiles and dips his head down. "Good morning."

"You smell like morning breath."

"So do you," he replies. He *sure* is close, holy *shit*. Couple kisses last night and this is what we're doing? Hell, this holiday just got so much better. He takes my jaw in one hand and angles my face up more, makes me rest my head on his collarbone. His fingers splay over my stomach, pinky dancing along the line of my boxers. "May I kiss you?" he says, hovering over my lips.

I manage a super convincing, "Uh-huh," and I end up reaching to my toes. To think, this was what I was missing out on years ago. I give seventeen-year-old Scott a swift kick in the head.

Not even a make out session, it's just one slow kiss, and I have to be held up by his arm around my waist. He smiles, kisses my ear, and smacks me on the ass, sending me back to the fridge. "Grab the creamer while you're at it," he says.

"Hmbokay." David laughs, and I glare at the fridge and debate shoving my face into the bag of vegetables in the freezer instead. Better yet, I might just launch myself into the pool to cool off. That would be a mistake; I know he'd follow me. Then I'd be seeing those high cut boxers soaking wet and clinging to him and—hooboy, nope. (Yes, *please*.)

—

Breakfast was pretty light, just eggs and coffee. I blame David. (Homeboy knew exactly what he was doing; practicing fucking yoga in the living room in his underwear while I cooked. Asshole.) After swimming in the pool, I get settled on one of the pool chairs with my fancy new journal, drying off in the heavy sun.

David took one look at my sunburned back and offered me his navy button up. Meanwhile he remains, distressingly, unfortunately, shirtless; I think it's cause he caught me staring five or fifteen times.

He comes out from the kitchen and sets an iced tea down on the table next to my elbow. I get a kiss on the head. He reaches above us and pulls the pergola shade across the pool and deck. "That okay?" he asks, cracking his neck, swim trunks dripping water and marking his path around the tile.

"Sure, thank you," I smile, going back to my scribbling. I'm on page five. First four pages I scratched out cause I wrote them in a dreamy, whacked out state of mind last night. They were all about waking up with David's firm, tight body against me, and…yeah, yikes, sleep deprived Scotty is a horny idiot, clearly. With another failed attempt at writing, I go to the next page.

There's a light groan ahead of me, and I look up to David. "You okay?"

He sends me a tense smile. "Too much driving with the conventions, haven't had much time to exercise lately."

"You had time for yoga," I snort. He chuckles evilly and my burning ears tell me I was right; he *did* do downward dog for an unnecessary amount of time. "You can go running or something," I suggest.

"Run wouldn't help my back," he grunts, fingers digging into his neck as he rolls his arm. "I'm okay."

"Do you want a massage?" I ask, turning the page of my journal to fill up another sheet. I've given up on writing at this point, I'm now doodling, to the best of my ability, what looks like the deck and pool and one hunky David.

His barefoot steps pause, and I peek at him. He's either horrifically sunburned, or he's lost control of his thoughts, much like I have. My nostrils twitch as I try to keep a straight face.

"Um. S-sure—do you even know how to give massages? I don't want you messing something up in my spine."

"Just like you didn't want me jamming my tongue down your throat when you claimed I didn't know how to kiss?" I think he's holding his breath.

Everything I could say sounds so sensual, but I want to say all of it. I know how to help you relax, I know how to loosen you up, I can help you if you lay down. There's no PG way to say this.

"Do you want one or not?"

He grumbles and I look up to see him flattening a pool chair and getting on it, laying chest down. He sends me a fast, red-cheeked glare, and crosses his arms, turning his head away from me. When I don't get up right away, he snarks, "This is a 'yes', Scott."

"Right," I smirk, setting my journal down and wandering over.

Where do I start? I rub my hands together like I'm looking at a meal. Maybe I am. "Can I straddle you?" That sounded a lot more innocent in my head...

"Fine."

I get situated on his upper thighs, ask if he's good, and begin at his neck. My thumbs dig into the divots of his shoulder blades. His muscles ripple as his back arches to my touch. I press deeper.

"Your back feels nice." Nice. What an understatement. But it covers everything. Nice and solid, nice and muscular, nice and goddamn sexy.

"Thank you," he mumbles, mouth hidden by his arm. He shifts his shoulder, and I catch a pleased smile.

With one more glance at the sliding doors, knowing full well we're the only two here, and I've got a large, incredible man, soft as putty in my hands, laying between my legs, I swallow and turn back to David.

Why am I doing this?

This isn't for any magazine. There's no sneaky cameras, his dad and stepdad live in a safe and secure home. The beach is another story; whatever we did down there yesterday in the public sector, walking hand in hand and taking photos, was for spectators. I think. But now I don't think any of that matters.

Cause I love him. He loves me. This is beyond any kind of fake dating. And up here…there's no reason for me to do this at all. There are a million reasons.

David sighs, asks me to keep going.

A million and *one* reasons I'm doing this, then.

The kisses from last night, the one so sweet this morning, could feed me for an eternity. But still I want more.

I adjust my legs and press my whole torso down along every inch of that tan and freckled landscape. My mouth drops close to his ear. All I have to do is whisper, "*You* feel nice, David," and he trembles.

He makes a soft noise, muffled with his face still pressed in his crossed arms. I'm not sure if that was a 'you're the worst masseuse ever' grumble or a…

"Say it again," he murmurs.

"That you feel nice?"

"Say 'David'."

When I drag my knuckles up his back toward his shoulders, I roll my body with it and grind against his ass. He wiggles below me and his low groan matches my own. "David," I breathe over his ear. When I brush my lips against his shoulder, his lashes flutter, and the one eye visible closes. "*My* David."

I grip his waist by my thighs, kneading the muscle. He's got a faded tan line at his hips, where his shorts hang an inch too low. He lifts up, enough for my fingers to touch his abdomen, the waistband of his trunks, and I send my hands snaking between him and the pool chair.

Before I can travel them south toward his obliques, David flips around underneath me to lay on his back, sending me flying up to my feet. He shoots forward to a sit, makes me trip backward on my heels, and there's panic in my gasp as I nearly fall into the pool.

When he leaps up, he grips my open shirt collar, slamming me to his bare chest. I feel every rapid thump of his heart.

I'm thinking maybe I prodded him too much and now this is about to be more than I bargained for. "Sorry, I'm sorry—was that not okay? Are you—"

"Unless you tell me not to in the next five seconds, I'm going to eat you alive *right* fucking now."

I stutter and clack my mouth shut. He glares at me like he might punch me or destroy my face with his own. Five seconds pass full of choppy breathing. Then his wild grin matches mine.

I don't even get to take another breath before our lips clash.

He guides me backward to the house. Those ten steps into our room take a thousand years. The three from the porch to the door, the five to the bed. We don't bother with those five. We collapse on the floor.

He steals a pillow from the mattress, shoves it under my head. Grabs another. It goes behind the small of my back.

And we're seventeen again. But with hands on faces, fingers raking through hair. Kisses with teeth, with gasps and fumbling tongues.

With David, not After. This is *David*. More than I bargained for but I want it all, even if I drown it in. Every shift of his hips, his moan breaks, and mine cracks. If my back was cold on the tile, I don't feel it anymore.

David pins my wrists above my head with one hand, palms at me on top of my swim trunks, making me beg for what feels like an eternity before he rips at the laces. He spits into his hand; his fingers slide under the waistband and wrap around me as he puts his mouth right on the pulse point under my jaw. My spine arches off the pillow and my head flings back with a groanmoanwhateverthefuck. Who cares. I'm not breathing.

"Jesus, Scott, *fuck*—" He's shuddering more than I am, hand pumping ruthlessly. I catch up to his rhythm, desperate to follow every stroke. "You sound so good, so good," he gasps.

I'm good. I'm good, he says. "Say it again," I choke. He releases my wrists, and I claw at his shoulders, whimpering out a thousand yesses.

"Say what," he whispers between kisses, dropping his forehead to mine.

"That I'm good." I won't cry while he touches me. I won't cry as this feels like something old and yet entirely new and terrifying and overwhelming. I won't.

David chuckles into a sigh, sucks the life right out of me with another slow, aching kiss. "You're incredible. You're magnificent. Honey, I wanna see you come apart."

He moans when I do, rolls when I do, in unison, wave after wave. He's all coiled muscle and hooded hazel eyes and gaping mouth, holding himself up on one elbow, fingers in my hair as he talks so sweet and so dirty at the same time.

Long lashes flutter down as he watches what he's doing to me. He wants to see me. He's gonna see me.

His teeth sink into my throat and the broken cry that scratches out of me bounces off the tiles. If I'm this loud, I can only imagine him when he's not muffled into my t-shirt clad shoulder.

He's a man. He'll tear down mountains.

That's it, he says, let me take care of you, he says.

Then it's nothing but, "Bo, *yes* Bo, come for me, I got you. God, you're so good, you're *so* damn good."

Then I'm nothing. I'm fucking nothing.

Chapter 60

He won't stop kissing me and I'm never going to complain about it. Except for right now, maybe, when I'm starving and he keeps insisting he'll go make dinner, but he's yet to actually get off of me. At least we're on the bed now and not on the floor anymore.

It takes me threatening to jump his frigging bones, like I did in the shower after we got back from the beach, for him to finally groan and sit up on his hands and knees, squinting down at me. "Fine, but I'm making dessert first."

"I will not stop you," I reply, pulling him back down by his necklace to give him one last kiss. His feet pad on the tile toward the kitchen, and my stretch takes up the whole bed, his t-shirt lifting past my stomach.

Pedro and Vernon came home hours ago from the market, and I'm not sure if we just looked like we'd been thoroughly sexed into idiocy or what. But they very nonchalantly said they'd be watching a movie in their room, on the other end of the house, with the volume up and the door closed, if we happened to need anything.

So subtle. I would've been embarrassed had I cared, but my feet are yet to touch the ground.

When David offered to make us all lunch after they first came in (attempting to include them, as we did come to see *them* and this is *their* house), Pedro just kinda hummed and said something in Spanish along the lines of, "No, thank you, you've got your hands busy with other things."

Then Vernon came out of their room and *very* loudly and *very* un-casually asked if anyone had seen him and Pedro's full bottle of lube.

I knew for a fact that a nearly empty bottle was under our shared bed, one David magically 'discovered' earlier. (The frantic conversation took place in the living room with us half-naked, and was followed by, "Don't worry 'bout where I got it from", then, "Stop laughing, do you wanna do this or not", and it ended with him lifting me up and running with me when I gave an enthusiastic, "Yes, obviously, you dumbass".)

Pedro snorted his tequila while Vernon tapped his chin with a squint, and David turned crimson, abandoning the quesadillas he was making to shuffle back to our room. I cackled so hard I nearly threw up.

There's an insistent vibrating coming from near the bedside. I roll onto my stomach, crawl across the bed and give a quiet 'aha!' when I find my phone hanging off the nightstand by the charger. David's is on the floor, and I pick them both up.

Mine is blank except for one email notification, from Jethro. Subject line: **Regarding Case JU4322EXP, Senior, Boscoe, Scott Everett.**

First line of the email: **Dear Scott Everett, as a reminder, you have until May 24th, 2021, to send us your letter of…**

Smells like David's making churros. Yeah, Jethro can wait.

It's his phone that goes off again while in my hand, locked screen lighting up with another block of text. "Hey, dude, your phone—"

[Killory, Megan] 18:22: Hi, David, I don't mean to interrupt super awesome family fun times! But as soon as I got word an hour ago, I wanted to let you know I've got some great news on your…

[Killory, Megan] 18:27: Then the last offer is almost twice the asking price, outbidding the other three we've received, and they're wanting to pay in cash. At this rate, you could be looking at having your house sold by the end of…

[Killory, Megan] 18:29: Oh! Another thing. That request you sent me last night—I think I've got a few condos in mind for you and your bf Scott. They're high in price range, but nothing more than you and I have discussed in the...

[Killory, Megan] 18:32: You mentioned him not working, and that's not a prob, since it will be in your name. Depending on how much he's made in the last year, he could potentially be written down as your dependent for taxes, if his income is under...

David's talking at me from the kitchen. I can hear the sea from our room, but it's like when you think you hear it in a seashell; muffled, loud, too close.

Feel the wind brushing over the hairs on my bare legs, making the frayed cuffs on my shorts tickle above my knees. Don't remember getting off the bed, standing in the middle of the room.

He's saying something, his voice grows louder through the house. I look up. The breeze turns the ceiling fan blades slow, even though it's off. Makes the chain hanging down swirl.

It shouldn't feel like the world is crashing, but it does. I've experienced hurricanes before. This isn't a horrific assault of rain and debris and lighting with an eye of calm in the center.

This is a tsunami, a slow pull back, water rushing away from my feet, before it's bound to come barreling down on top of me.

David appears in the threshold, still talking. He sees me holding his phone and tilts his head. "Whatchya doing?" he asks, walking over with a paper plate full of churros.

"Um. Your phone kept going off," I mutter, handing it to him. David nods and looks over the messages. His brows go up, his grin widens. He sends it my way. Muscles in my face refuse to work and help me fake a smile. "What is..." My lips come back together to form another word, but nothing comes to mind that won't hurt him.

He shakes his head. I mirror him, and there's a horrible laugh scorching up my throat. "You already...David, I didn't agree to moving in with you."

He opens his mouth just to close it, looks back to his phone, and drags in a breath. "Ah."

"Yeah."

"That um....ah."

I turn and rush fingers through my hair. I want to vomit, I'm gonna vomit all over this lovely blue and orange Spanish tile. Do I apologize? Do I cry? Do I drop to my knees and sob and hope he won't get angry at me? Why are my first instincts to beg for mercy and forgiveness? What's this world done to me?

He brings in a sharp gulp of air, coughs, and the bed creaks. I look back, thinking he's sitting on the edge of it, but he's on the ground, feet kicked out. One heel is on the pillow that was under my back this morning. "David—"

"It's...no, it's fine. It's *not*. But. Eat a churro."

I stutter and take a step to him. "David, no—"

"Please, I burnt the fuck out of my forearm making these, eat a goddamn churro."

I eat a churro. He shoves one in his mouth and chokes on it, rubs cinnamon all over his face with trembling hands.

"I don't think you're going to understand why I can't move in with you right now," I whisper, pressing my fingers together to feel the grain of brown sugar on my thumb.

"Try me," he sighs. His eyes say try me, please. They're not asking for an apology.

"I just need...to not. Be a dependent," I scratch out. He frowns and looks back to the text on his phone before setting it on the bed behind him.

I reach for him, and he reaches for me, giving my wrist a light tug down. "I'm not sitting on the floor again, c'mon, bed," I scoff, yanking him up to his feet.

"Churros in bed—we're gonna get crumbs everywhere."

"I don't care, I refuse to be on the tile, it's cold as hell."

He crawls on top of me and collapses while I hold the plate in the air. "You weren't complaining earlier."

I glare at him and the twitch in his smile, even as his eyes water. "That's cause earlier you were screwing me stupid."

"If I did it again, would you move in with me?" He asks it like a joke, or I tell myself he does. But the sincerity all over his face is pleading and desperate, and I just pull his temple to my chest and let him feed me another churro.

"You can do what you want to, Scotty, if we live together. You could…you could write. You could do whatever you want and never worry about the money."

I push my face into his hair until it hurts and I see stars. "I don't know if you'll ever get this, David, and it's okay if you don't. But it's ingrained in me to be afraid of words like that. I can't be something in your house that you come back to with nothing to my name but the words I type on a laptop I don't own." I taste copper and I realize I bit right through my lip. My head throbs.

"I mean maybe, with a lot of time, I'll outgrow it. Maybe I'll be okay on my own, or maybe I'll end up dead or homeless—"

David groans. "Don't, don't say that Bo."

"I'm sorry, but I can't, I *can't* just float from one safe haven to the next. I did with Devon and I thought I was okay, but she used me. I did with Mitch, and I thought I was okay, but then—"

"Please don't say you think I'm gonna use you, Scott," he gapes, cupping my cheeks. "I won't. I couldn't. I mean the favor thing—like, that was…that was mutual. I thought. But now you're helping me, and for once I feel like just me is enough."

We're both crying, and I don't know if it'll stop, or when, or how. This is us, more open and aching and bloody than ever. "But am I enough for you? Is just me, with everything I've done and survived through, everything I offer to the table, even if it's just myself. Am I enough?"

David stares at me for a hundred years before he sighs, deflated. Closing his eyes, he says words that solidify me and wash me into the sea at the same time. "Is it going to matter what I say, if you don't believe it?"

Inside, I'm thinking…maybe. Possibly, if he told me right now that I'm enough, I could try to believe it.

But even after everything, after being brave enough to tell him I love him, to look him in the eyes. I'm not brave enough for that. To ask that.

And since we're exposed and this might be the end of it all, I take his hands from my face, kiss his fingers, and reply, "No."

His heart just broke, I saw it right then and there. "No…"

"Because…I'm too. There's too much going on with me. Too many sharp pieces, like you once said. I'm shattered and—and I can't expect you to take care of those pieces, not when you have your own struggles. It's the same reason I didn't tell you about Gabriel and El Paso; not just because of what was going on between us, but because it would be selfish of me to ask you to do that. To care for me like that."

Not selfish, I tell myself. If he asked me to care for him, I'd give him all that he needed. But he's worthy of that and…I'm not sure I am yet.

He shifts up on the bed and presses his brow to my cheek. "Can we have this weekend? Can we have until Tuesday?" he whispers.

One kiss to my neck has me simmering. Another, longer, up to my ear as his leg twines with mine and presses in, has me fading.

His words go through my skin and pulse along with my heartbeat. "I don't want to think about any futures past this room. Past the salt water below us, past the colors coming in through open windows."

Such a poet. I have half a mind to tell him to write that down.

But when he kisses me, it's already different than the other times. So much hungrier, even more than before. I bend willingly, and I give him that last request.

We pretend to not care that we're both still crying, he pretends to not still be bothered by this insane need I have to be my own person, and to not sit on someone else's laurels. Especially when that haven could turn on me at any moment. Unhealthy. Untrustworthy. But I'm yet to be proven otherwise.

David's hands shake. And I was wrong about how loud he'd be when I touch him. I thought he'd be ferocious and gruff with a thick voice and deep moans.

He trembles, whimpers at me between his legs, loses his mind and gasps in rhythm with my movement. He doesn't try to tell me I'm good anymore, or I'm enough, or I'm spectacular.

He says he loves me a thousand times, until he can't string words together anymore, and the message has to be conveyed through his lips on mine, kisses wet from both our tears.

He just sounds like David. He's my David. And I'm the idiot that's gonna let him go.

Because I already decided that I can't do this until Tuesday, until a teary goodbye with Pedro and Vernon and a twenty-hour luxurious flight back. I can't live this dream one minute longer, and I'll be buying a ticket back to California the moment he leaves the room for anything.

What's more in tune with Scott Everett Boscoe's self-destructive tendencies, than leaving in the dead of night, while his loved ones rest and think they'll see him in the morning?

—

Pedro and Vernon both call me, Pedro six times, Vernon seven. No calls from David. Pedro's voicemail, the last one, begs for me to let him know when I've made it to the airport safely.

Once I'm through security with a last-minute ticket back to LA that cost me way too much money, I text him that I got a ride with a taxi. He replies immediately that he thinks I'm making a mistake. Add it to the pile, Pedro.

I'm in LA, doing one last sweep through my dorm. (Anything I leave behind now they can sell for all I care.) Next is the big house, to pack up my one box and shove everything I can into a couple suitcases. Have one more stop on the way first.

I call Thor. He opens the garage of David's house for me so I can grab my bike. I didn't ask, but he brings out my other items from the house, including my scarf.

He doesn't offer to get Chicken or Angus so I can say goodbye. I don't bother to explain to him what's happened, and he doesn't push. Though he hugs me like he might have an idea anyway.

In the big house, I write a letter to Bevett for her to read when she comes home from Willa's, letting her know I'll call her when I can. I almost leave her my Pashmina, but I think she'd hate me if I did. So it ends up in my backpack.

Mitch is in the kitchen. He looks like he's stumbled upon a ghost, the moment he sees me with my bags and my box.

Before he can kick me out or beat me to death or ignore me, I walk straight up to him and hug him, hard as I can. I don't think I imagine his hand coming to rest on my back.

When I pull away with my hands on his shoulders, he looks like the old man I pictured, when I first got a call from someone named 'Grandpa Mitch'; soft eyes, gentle white brow, relaxed mouth behind a beard. Maybe he did what he did out of some sort of love. An attempt to get me the life he thought I deserved. More likely, he did it all to save his own face. I don't know. And I don't think I'll ever find out.

"You watch over Bevett or I'm going to kill you," I tell him.

A flash of fury crosses behind his stare. He stands up taller, nearly out of the reach of my hands, and I straighten my back, too. As much as I used to think I got my anger from my dad, I wonder how much I get it from Mitch.

"With my life, Scott," is all he says back. That's all I need.

I'm in Charlotte and Mei's house on the floor in the bathroom, emailing JU staff and telling them they won't be getting two hundred bucks outta me for a cap and gown I'll never wear again.

And I tell them, no, I will not be ripping myself open for them so they can judge whether or not my 'depressive episodes' and horrific experiences are traumatic enough that I should get to keep hold of my grades and the wonderful honor of representing Jethro as an alumni.

I will not be accepting my diploma or dabbing on stage and collecting a $100 bill from Charlotte. She gives me a wad of too much cash anyway.

One day later, I'm on a greyhound with my bike locked on the front, riding for El Paso.

And David doesn't come for me. Though I know the letter I left behind told him he wouldn't need to, that I'd see him soon.

One day maybe. After all this is over.

Epilogue

--

Of course they started celebrating the Fourth of July an hour ago. It's four in the afternoon. It's still sunny outside—y'all can't even see those expensive fireworks you're blasting.

Yet, I'd expect nothing less from gun blazing Texans.

And I'm learning this tiny side of San Marcos I've been living in hosts some of the most unhinged people I've ever met.

Someone could walk up to me, and all I gotta do is smile, and then it's either they threaten to kick my teeth out, or they burst into tears and say I'm the first person who's smiled at them all week. Both those things happened just yesterday, actually. God bless Texas.

Being a holiday and a Sunday, there aren't that many people coming in for coffee right now, not since the morning rush we had. I'm finally on my break, and I'm halfway through a Lean Cuisine, scrolling the news on my phone, when I remember why I don't look at the damn news, or eat Lean Cuisine. Both have me feeling nauseous as soon as one article pops up, and lo and behold, there's that darling mugshot again.

Only had to see it daily the first week I got started here at Rodrigo's Coffee. (No one here is named Rodrigo. No one has a damn clue who this mystery Rodrigo is.) My manager Mike thought it was funny to post it on the board in the breakroom and draw mustaches on it.

I relaxed a little when he said it wasn't a big deal to anyone that worked there. (Obviously, or I wouldn't have gotten the freaking assistant manager job.)

He was arrested when he was fourteen for dealing pot and stealing cassettes (he's old enough for that to have been a big deal) and darling Kitty, who could jab your eye out with her baby nails, has been caught three times shoplifting from Forever 21.

When I politely reminded them of the charges that were on another page in that edition of *Us Weekly*, written in bulleted format and labeled A through Lord knows what, Mike just shrugged and said, "It don't mean no thang." I like him. He's forty, wears primarily anime t-shirts, and on occasion, he brings me and Kitty some homemade cannoli or a beaded bracelet he made while watching House Hunters with his guinea pigs.

So that's why news like today still startles me on occasion. I may or may not have gotten used to the teasing, and the hugs when sometimes the teasing poked right at a hot button, but this isn't a 'lol, let's give Scotty's mugshot a Fu Manchu'. This is a 'hey, remember this kid? And the rumors around his arrest that spiraled out of control until he fled the state? No? Well, here's a reminder'.

Looks like Melanie Kingwald had to issue her own statement. There's a nice photo of her with her blonde hair pulled into that official policewoman bun, blue eyes sharp and still kind. Just like they were that night in the parking lot, when she first approached me and Gabriel. Concerned, cautious, but patient with kids half her age, until…yeah, anyway.

She says the issue has been handled. She's asking again for the news to leave me alone. Good on you, Mels, good luck with that. Got a call from her the moment I stepped back into Texas (how she knew is beyond me, honestly) and she asked to meet up.

As soon as I saw her in the school parking lot, she said she forgave me a long time ago, and it's all settled. Whatever people are picking at is old and dumb, they're just bored.

I hated the moment where I nearly blurted out how much she looked like my mom. Hated the moment where I actually *did* blurt that out, and she gave me a hug.

Then she let me know something that had me almost skirting back to California, or anywhere else on the planet.

They know Gabriel's somewhere in Texas again, they just don't know where.

Only confirms what Devon told me when I stayed with her that first week back. "Keep your eyes open, Scott," Melanie said, just like Devon had, when she finally believed my side of things once the dash cam footage got leaked. "Stay safe. And call me." Devon and Melanie both said that. I thanked them both with a hug, too, even if one hurt more than the other. Not sure which, though.

At a new Buzzfeed article that says, "**Five stars who've disappeared without a trace. Where are they now? Number three will surprise you,**" I click my phone closed. With a mix of a groan and a yawn, I lean back in my seat and scowl at microwaved macaroni and processed cheese.

Kitty darts her head into the break room, multiple earrings jingling. "Scott. Ohemgee."

"Kitty, ohemgee, what is it?" I ask, poking at the pathetic remnants of my Lean Cuisine.

She prances in, pats her thighs with a drum roll. "There's a dog outside."

"There are, usually."

"But you need to *see* this dog."

I grin and look over at her. Day I met her, I took a selfie with her and sent it to Charlotte, telling her I found her long lost twin. Kitty's got black hair that goes to her shoulders, bangs cut over her brow, sweet, chubby cheeks that push to her glasses when she grins. Found it so perfect that I now have a 'Kitty' in my phone, right under 'Cat-Cat' in my text threads.

"You interrupted my lunch to tell me about a dog outside?" She beams with pride. "Thank you, you're too kind," I chuckle, standing. She wiggles her hands at me, and I pass off the rest of my frozen macaroni. "Which way?"

"Go left, super pretty one," she mumbles around cheesy elbows. "The one all by his lonesome."

"No owner?"

"For now, until I steal 'im."

I snort and leave the break room, nodding at Mike behind the register. "Big dog?" he asks, espresso machine steaming loud and fluffing up his black ringlets, long arms grabbing what he needs without him having to step away from his spot on the comfort mat.

"Apparently. Love that I've been here a month and this is what I'm known for, as the dude who loses his mind over dogs."

Mike laughs, points to the side door, and crooks a finger left. "Look for the ears."

"Excellent." I adjust the loop of my apron behind my neck and push the door open, looking left and down—

I'm knocked back by a blur of black fur, sharp, clipped barking, pointed ears and white sock paws that are oh, so familiar.

"Oh—hi! Hi, Chicky!" Chicken's ruthless with the kisses, weight making me trip with his paws on my shoulders, nipping at my chin.

My glee at seeing Chicken slams to a halt.

As *he* comes around the corner.

I'm so pent up and anxious, that even with Chicken dropping down and circling around me, my brain still says: Gabriel. Right in front of me. Pale skin and freckles and lanky limbs and auburn curls and tight smile.

The one Devon and Kendra and Melanie warned me to look out for.

But it's not, and Chicken nudges a wet nose into my palm, reminding me. This is David. Only David.

And he doesn't look surprised to see me, which is confusing.

"You're a hard man to find," David says.

He's not wearing a ball cap, no way to hide the brow scar or his all over movie star-ness. His hair looks freshly cut, faded by his ears, and his white linen button up is so thin you can see his tattoo through it at his shoulder.

Cargo shorts. Maybe that's his new baseball cap. What celebrity would wear ratty, tan cargo shorts? He's in white Vans. Haven't seen him in Vans since high school.

"What're you doing here?" I ask, reaching instinctively for the door handle. Someone comes barreling outside, hits me with the door, and I glare at them and stumble toward the curb.

"Did you see the dog, did you see—oh—" Kitty blinks and looks to David. Seeing as she's the only nineteen-year-old I know who doesn't own a DVD player, let alone a TV, and she uses her phone solely for Words with Friends, I'm not shocked that she doesn't know who the hell he is. "Do y'all know each other?"

"Um. Yeah."

David puts on a smile and raises a hand. "Hi, David. From L-Lubbock."

"Hi, Kitty, San Marcos," she scoffs, squinting at him. "You good, Scott? You okay out here?" Her chest puffs out an inch. (I've seen her go at customers who think they can sneak a hand into the tip jar. She'd tear him apart.)

"I'm okay, Kitty, thank you," I tell her. She sniffs, sends David her best 'watch it, buddy' stare, and goes back inside.

I look back at David and he shifts his weight. "How've you been?" he asks.

"Hungry," I blurt out. My lunch was interrupted, after all.

"Do you have a break?"

"Just had it."

"Are you off soon? We can get an early dinner."

"Not in my budget."

His brow drops. "Well, I would b—"

"I'm good, I've got food at home." I don't, I hope he doesn't expect to come over and be fed. Of course the week he appears, I haven't gone grocery shopping yet, just have the essentials like coffee and creamer and questionable leftovers.

"I've got…I've got ice cream, instant ramen—don't ask how many cups of those I eat a day, I won't give you an honest answer." He smiles. I'm rambling. "I've got another two hours to go."

"We can wait," he says. Chicken's sitting on my feet. I stare at him just to not look at David. "Brought my truck for a reason. I saw your bike, and I've got room in the truck bed."

"I…yeah, I bike." I open the door and dislodge my foot from under Chicken's butt to step one sneaker inside. "You're really gonna wait out here for two hours?"

"We might walk around. Or find somewhere to sit inside, if there's a shaded park nearby. It's getting hotter out here, and Chicken's not used to July in Texas—"

"You can stay inside here, it's fine. C'mon, Chicky!" I pat at my thigh and wave him in, and Chicken swats me with his tail as he passes. Kitty squeals behind the counter, and I hear Mike give a loud laugh and ask if Chicken wants a puppy drink.

David hesitates. "David, y'all are fine to hang out inside."

He looks to his shoes, gives a little nod, and holds the door open for me. I pretend I feel the slide of his fingers on the back of my neck as I step in ahead of him, a ghost of something he used to do.

When I glance back, his hand is falling to his side.

—

On the drive to my place, he asks about me, no surprise. What have I been up to for the last month or so, what happened with my degree.

"Didn't get it," I tell him. He stares at me at a stoplight and I shrug. "Didn't stick around for final grades, didn't graduate. Never wrote them that stupid essay that explained just how messed up I was, and I didn't beg them to give me another chance."

He has to keep us moving, but he continues to send me looks. I remind him to focus on the road, and I direct him down the next street. "What about financial aid? How're you paying all that back?"

"Gonna do the income-based repayment thingy—it'll suck, hefty chunk taken out of my income every month, but I've crafted up a budget so I'll make do. Mitch tried to pay them off; I got a call from the school a month ago—guess he's so hellbent on pretending I don't exist that he was willing to drop all that cash on me."

"That sounds shifty," David mutters. At least he agrees with me on that.

"Yeah, obviously I declined. Don't want him showing up one day demanding something from me in return."

"What about Bevett?"

"What about her?" Another stoplight, another chance for him to stare me down. "I still talk to her, David, she's my sister. We talk almost daily. Mitch doesn't prohibit her from that; I'm the only blood she's actually got left."

"Do you think you'll visit her soon?"

Visit California soon? I shiver and turn the a/c away from me. "She wants to move here when she turns eighteen. We're looking at getting her an internship at the Art Institute or something—I don't know how it all works, she jabbered it off at me in June, but I was half-awake after being on my feet for seventeen hours for the first time in my life. Comfy boots are great and all for working but holy shit, there's only so much coffee a guy can take until he's, like, hearing colors and…and stuff."

David didn't chuckle at my hand flailing like I thought he would, and he turns us left when I tell him to. That's twice now I've shot my mouth off. Would rather shoot my own foot than be in this truck. (Hello, pants on fire.) "So, uh. Not sure. About visiting."

"What were you doing on your feet for seventeen hours?"

"Working my two jobs."

"You don't just work at the coffee shop?"

"No, I work at the library, too. Neither pays me enough on its own, but I'm getting the hang of it, figuring out a good sleep schedule and all that. At least I'm not on Devon's couch anymore."

He glares at me then. "When the hell were you on her couch?"

"When I first got to Texas. Got really sick for five days straight. Once I finally stopped seeing double, I hopped onto another bus and went to San Marcos. Been here since June, when I got the library job. Got the coffee one right after."

"And how was…that? How was she?"

"Honestly? We hardly spoke to each other the entire time. She didn't have anyone over, which surprised me. Kendra actually cooked food. Devon did work at home. Wasn't until I was leaving that they told me to be safe."

From my ex, who according to them, might come find me. That's a super fun thought I didn't think to keep in mind when I ran to Texas.

I shrug and pull on the threading of my apron in my lap. "But I guess I'm close enough that if I did need her for whatever reason, I can call her. Or. If I ended up dead. She and Kendra could come get my body without too much hassle. Win-win."

David inhales long, exhales longer. Guess I shouldn't joke like that. Not to him.

"Anyway uh…it's been good. Mike—my manager—he lets me pin my poems on the bulletin board. Sometimes a customer buys one or pays me to write them something. The library has me scribe for meetings. Little extra buck in my pocket. More than I've ever made with my writing otherwise."

"You were gonna make sixty k at Silversmith," he sighs.

"*My* writing, David," I reiterate. He doesn't argue then.

Epilogue

Unlocking my door has never seemed so daunting before. I swing it open, and Chicken runs in first, going for the space I've got set up in the corner of the studio, where my bed hides behind a drawn aside curtain.

David goes in second, and I suck in a breath, frozen outside with the door open. I love my place, and I've had friends from the shop over a couple times who like it, too.

I try to remember that, despite the house he owns and the money he has, David's never been one to decorate fancy or judge. And at least here, unlike my dorm, I don't feel lonely.

He turns and grins at me. "It's amazing," he says.

"Yeah?" I wheel my bike in and close the door behind me, kick off my sneakers. He does the same with his Vans and socks and steps off the square of tile at the threshold to wander further in.

"Where'd you get the sofa? I like the blue," he adds, scratching his nails on the corduroy texture.

"Uh—Mike. Just last week actually, got it for a hundred bucks in exchange for watching his guinea pigs for a weekend while he went on a date with his partner."

"What about the coffee table? It's so small, I've never seen such a perfect Scotty-sized coffee table," he chuckles, bending at the waist to run his hands over the fake oak.

"Got that at Goodwill. Buy one, get one furniture sale. When I got my desk, too." I point to the corner of the flat, where my Pashmina hangs over my desk chair. "Chair is an extra from the shop. Kitty was gonna toss it cause it wobbled, I said I'd give it a new home. And I fixed the wobble."

Everything he points at, he asks where I got it, is there a story behind it. The Mr. Coffee I bought at a garage sale, the bookshelf with a slight tilt but lots of character. The mattress from a neighbor who was moving out the week I got in and didn't have room for it. Wanted to give it to me for free, but I exchanged it for my nicest pair of jeans I didn't need.

Then there's the random painting by my desk of a couple frogs, sitting on a log, dressed in bizarre yet fashionable outfits. I rescued that from the side of the road. David laughs and says it's us.

"It's all yours," he whispers, standing in the center with his hands on his hips.

He looks to the kitchenette, neon green boom box on the counter next to my laptop, where I left it this morning mid writing session while making coffee. He gives a couple nods, checks his feet, then turns back to me with a lopsided smile. "I can make dinner, if you want."

Realizing I'm still in the threshold with my backpack on, I shrug it off and toss it by our shoes, tripping as I pull off my socks.

"I don't have anything for you to cook." Chicken dances around my legs, hops onto the armrest of the sofa, and pokes me in the cheek with a cold snoot. "Sorry, bubba, I have no food for you, either."

"Nothing? No spaghetti, hamburger meat or buns or anything?" asks David. I hear my freezer door open as I stretch down to touch my toes, getting Chicken's tongue in my ear since he's still balanced on the armrest. David scoffs and I peek up at him.

"I thought you said you had ice cream."

"I did at one point. There's a toaster strudel in there, but don't get your hopes up; I had a rough day and ate all the icing first."

"Been there." Fridge door opens. "I found whipped cream—wait no, this has couscous in it—what *do* you have?"

"Maybe leftover ravioli from Kitty's aunt and half box of Cinnamon Toast Crunch. It might be Cheerios though, I don't remember."

David puts the couscous back in the fridge. "I love both those, we can share."

I rub at my arm and shift my weight. His smile fades. My three hundred square foot apartment has never felt smaller. Chicken runs and noses David right in the crotch like, hello, I'm here, too, and I'm hungry. "I'll um. I can order a pizza," David mutters, pulling out his phone.

"Fine. I'm gonna change out of my work clothes. The bathroom is literally the only other door in this flat." I walk past him toward my tallboy dresser, squashed between my bed and the wall.

He's staring at me when I close the drape to my 'room'. Never thought to care before, but now I really hope these curtains are opaque enough that he can't see me.

—

"I mean, that's what they told me, but I highly doubt Thor *actually* road the zipline," David scoffs, going for another slice of pizza. "I guess they're enjoying their time at the set in New Zealand. They're still getting to work together, didn't have to split up like Angus thought."

"I'm glad they're with Sasha. Though I feel like she'd be the one to drop kick someone before either of them could even jump into action," I add.

David laughs with a nod, choking on pepperoni, which makes me laugh and reach and thump at his back without thinking. My hand darts into my lap, hopefully before he noticed that it lingered on his shoulder a second too long.

He still hasn't told me what he's doing here, or why Thangus aren't with him anymore. And I've asked him two more times since he found me, since we ordered pizza, and since it arrived.

"So...San Marcos," he says, nibbling on pizza crust. I hum in response, and he pulls a leg up to rest his arm on his knee, passing Chicken a pepperoni over the coffee table. "How long you planning to stay here?"

"Awhile. I like it here."

"Me, too. Been here a week—"

"What?" Now *I'm* choking on pepperoni. David doesn't pat my back. "Why hadn't you—I mean...you didn't..." 'You didn't say anything' sounds so weak. Guess who also didn't say anything before they escaped in the night?

"Yeah, sorry it took me so long. I had a few things I had to get squared away before I could come find you on the moon," he explains. Explains, bullshit, that explains nothing.

"What um. What did you have to get squared away?"

"Well first, I was moving everything out of the house in Cali. Next was figuring out what the hell to do with all that money from selling it, cause I sure as shit didn't need it, not on top of my income. Went through a list of non-profits—surprisingly, that took way too long, but only cause I think half of them thought I was prank calling. I had to go there to be like, yo, take my money, please."

"Which non-profits?" I ask, accepting the last slice with hesitant hands. Chicken gives me a look that says, bro, if you don't eat it, I will.

"A couple in California for homeless youths. One in New Mexico, another shelter, then one in Nebraska for LGBTQ. Visited some super distant relatives in St. Paul."

"Who do you know in St. Paul?"

"It was all Tío Nathan's family, his partner's. Didn't even know he had a partner he left behind until I got up there." He lets out a sigh and angles his elbows back to rest on the sofa cushions behind him. "Really good people; I hope to go back sometime soon. I was the whitest one there," he says with a laugh.

David waves a hand along like he's losing track of what he was saying. "Anyway, I said some goodbyes in LA, grabbed my truck, and now I'm here."

"But you've been here a week doing what? Why Texas of all places?"

"I came to find you, obviously," he snorts at me. I just raise a brow and blink at him like, pardon? "Yeah, man. I admit I got this dumb idea in my head that I'd find you, and you'd be all woebegone and suffering, and I'd be like, aha, tis I, Lancelot, here to save you with my millions of dollars and fancy new plan—"

"Don't worry about me and *my* peasant sensibilities," I chuckle.

His ears pink and he grins, wiping greasy fingers on his cheek, before leaning his head back to the cushions.

"I just mean. Look at you. I had a whole script planned, but when I saw you outside your shop, I was at a loss for words. Cause you seem amazing. And you're doing fantastic."

The swell of pride in my chest makes me float.

I'm stressed as hell about a lot of things. But I'm not waking up every day feeling guilty about the electricity I use, or the water. We're not gonna talk about the guilt of walking out on David, though.

I'm not waiting for the other shoe to drop, for someone to demand something. I celebrated paying my first phone bill with Whataburger. I earn above minimum wage from two separate jobs. Got health insurance, a dental plan. I'm also capable of making monthly payments on my loans or financial aid or whatever. (Know there's a difference. Truly don't care. I'll pay what I need to and I take a power nap afterward.)

Every little thing about my life right now is mine. From the Marketing Books for Dummies that sits in my bookshelf, annotated out the wazzoo, to the dirty dishes in the sink and the Swiffer that's become my new best friend. I'm owning it.

"Hell yeah," I reply, shoving my face with pizza and giving such an affirmative nod that my grown-out bangs fluff over my brow. "I'm doing phenomenal. I'm thriving. I might even get a plant. Maybe I'll self-publish a book of poems."

David shifts to face me, eyes and face glowing. "You totally should, you can do both those things. You're doing this on your own, just like you said you wanted to. I'm so proud of you, Bo." And whoop, I'm up, on my feet, grabbing the empty box and throwing it in the garbage.

"Thank you, thanks, yeah," I grunt over my shoulder. I'm proud of me, *I'm* proud of me, don't need his pride—even if it felt *so nice* hearing that—

There's a rushed rustling behind me, a little whispered kissy noise to Chicken, and I turn to David coming right up toward me, holding a second, smaller box. "Want me to make coffee? Don't forget I got us brownies—"

"Why are you *here*, David?" Better question, why can't I just appreciate that he *is* here? "Why aren't you—why aren't you angry at me?" David's shock makes me more frustrated.

"I just *left* you, like you always said I did. I ran and didn't look back, and it's fucking July, and you've been in town a week and didn't say anything—was it an accident that you were outside the coffee shop? If you didn't find me there, were you gonna look at the library?"

"I mean, I didn't know you worked at the library, Charlotte only said you worked at the coffee shop—"

"David, oh my God—"

"If I had known you worked at the library, too, then yeah," he shrugs. "Had I not found you at Rodrigo's, I'd have gone there. I saw your bike before I saw the coffee shop sign and literally did the most illegal of u-turns to get back toward the parking lot—"

"There are *thousands* of silver bikes in San Marcos."

He snorts a small chuckle through his nose like I should know better. "But only one is yours, Bo."

I start making coffee, cause it's either that or I start screaming, or crying.

He takes the carafe and stands right beside me. Now I'm boxed into my tiny kitchen, and I'm panicking. I want to blurt out that he could've just called, but I *also* could've called, and *neither* of us called and— "I knew you were going to leave," he says.

My hands press into the counter and my breathing hurts. "How?" His palm is warm on my back, running between my shoulder blades.

"Cause you were on your left side for an hour. You don't sleep on your left. I knew the moment you got up, too. When you kissed me and took your suitcase. I didn't get angry, so take that idea outta your head."

"I find that hard to believe," I blurt with a sharp scoff.

"I never told you. When I first saw you again in February, I went home and sobbed on the floor for hours before I came up with that fake dating plan."

My stare flies up and I gawk at him. He shakes his head. "This time, I didn't cry. I understood. And I formed another plan. Sell the house, get my shit together, and come find you. You woke me up, Scott. Back then, and in Spain. To a lot of things, a lot of dreams, all at once."

For the life of me, I can't stop shaking. I shove around him and get back to my living room, planting one hand on my crooked bookshelf, cradling my face in the other.

The sink turns on then off, water fills the Mr. Coffee. The grounds scoop taps in the filter, and the machine rumbles to life.

Apartment is so tight and quiet; I think David could be breathing right on me. When I open my eyes, he's mirroring me, balanced with a hand on the counter, watching the machine.

It's only then that I realize we probably shouldn't drink coffee, cause it's nearly seven, and we'll both be up for hours now. At least I will, whether I have caffeine or not. Like hell am I sleeping now that he's reappeared.

Clearing his throat, David breaks up the quiet with, "I've been looking for a job."

"A job? Why?"

"I do a talk here and there online, started a blog. But I wanted something with a schedule I could keep more often, since I stopped acting in LA."

"You stopped entirely? How'd you get out of your contract with Erica?"

David smiles as he pulls down mugs, but it doesn't look happy. "By ripping myself apart inch by inch, going through the last few years and gathering proof of mental abuse I've experienced since I signed with her at eighteen. She actually picked up that guy I told you about—Phillip West—so her hands have been full with attempts at keeping her shiny newbie ignorant."

He jams a thumb into the Mr. Coffee button as it croaks to the finish line. "In a way, it's helping me. She's trying her hardest to cut ties with me and my failing stardom, so she's been pretty easy to deal with. Though I'm still managing some legalities, might have to do a Zoom call every now and then, but—" The smile he sends me looks a lot happier, and he passes me a cup of coffee. "It's that room to breathe I've been desperate for."

"It's freedom," I reply.

"It is." He clinks his mug to mine. "Feels good, doesn't it?"

My laugh is through a sore throat, but I nod. "Yeah, it does…"

He doesn't say anything else, and the space around us grows cold despite how hot it is in here. Chicken stops pacing and lays down on my sofa. There's a shaky inhale from one of us in the room, and I stare at David and the tears on his cheeks.

"So did you? Find a job?" I ask, chancing a wary few steps into the kitchen, going for creamer from the fridge.

"Almost, I think. There's a TA position at Blevins Community College ten miles from here; it's for the English department. I sent in a resume; guess you don't need a teaching degree to be a TA in Texas. Or something. I'm still figuring it out."

I nod along to his rambling, working the seal off the new bottle of creamer, keeping my back to him so he can't see my growing smile. "If not that, I got an application for the bookstore on campus. It's all so close together, like a little civilization. I got some help from Mei, too—she said she'd be a reference for me. So…it's—I mean—"

Epilogue

His chuckle goes up in pitch. "Shit, man, I'm nervous, haven't had a job interview since high school, and that was for the YMCA. And I—I even—I gotta tell you cause I'm so damn excited—I applied to attend BCC. To get a degree. I got in on late admission."

Creamer splashes too enthusiastically into my coffee and lands on the counter. I spin and my jaw drops. "What?"

He grins, teary-eyed, and wipes his chin with the back of his hand. "I'm going to college."

"I—David, are you serious?" Ecstatic nod from him, hesitant but delighted smile from me. "That's...congratulations. That's incredible." He takes the creamer from me, and I half expect him to chug a swig of it, by the look of joy on his face.

"Thank you. And I got a storage unit, too. You didn't see all the stuff I had in my truck before I came to pick you up."

"Where's the Ferrari?" I'm still stuck on the idea of David in college. David graduating. David *teaching*—God, he'd be brilliant at it.

"Mom's got it. I knew you'd wanna know, she said she can ship it here, if I want her to."

"Fuck no, did you see the parking lot here? Turn your back on Sugar Shorts for five seconds and she *gone*."

"Fine, maybe once I get a place. With a gate and a..." He glances over to my curtain with a tiny smirk. "A bedroom."

"Right, cause community college means no dorms. Have you started looking for apartments yet?" I ask. David hums and tries to hide a flush by raising his mug. "David—frigging hell in a handbasket, were you just gonna pray I let you in so you can bunk *here*?"

"It's not the *best* plan—"

"It's a *terrible* plan, what if I said no!"

"You wouldn't though, would you?"

"Never."

He sets his drink down to lean on the counter by me. "Figured you wouldn't mind having to protect me for once, huh? I'd be the one eating all the groceries, stinking the place up with my socks."

His fingers reach to fiddle with my short sleeve. "Jokes aside," he sighs, "can I say something?" I try to reply verbally and can only nod. He swallows, and his mouth opens as he stumbles for words. Finally, he comes up with, "You never hog the bedsheets."

I croak on a reply. Does he *want* a reply? "Um. What?"

"You…you took the coat off your back for me. When we were little. Did it again as adults. I still have your hoodie. You tore through my liquor cabinet when no one else had offered to help like that. You let me play my music all the way to Nashville. You fed my dog before you made breakfast for yourself. You're too giving to everyone; you never keep anything for yourself."

My eyes sting. "Sounds unhealthy when you say it like that."

"I mean that you're kind, and generous. You're selfless. I should've said all that back in Spain. Whether you believed me or not, I know you needed to hear it, and I gave up too easy. You're worth a trip to the moon, a thousand trips, to find you."

He pinches his mouth to the side, then sucks in deep breath that puffs out his chest. His look of determination tells me he's got more to say, but my head won't stop spinning with just this.

"You once claimed you were sharp. Made of shattered pieces, and that it was selfish of you to ask to be cared for." He takes my elbow and pulls me to him. "I don't think it's selfish to ask for help. To need love. You taught me that. But it doesn't matter what I think. Do *you* still think that it's selfish?"

"I don't think so." He smiles with that sunshine-ocean smile, and my kitchenette starts to shrink when he relieves me of my mug. "I'm getting stronger. I feel…less like the bad guy in my own story. Maybe like Lancelot's jaunty sidekick with all the snappy one-liners."

"You're not a sidekick," he chuckles, searching all over my face. "You're the hero. You're *my* hero."

I squint at him. "You're stupid."

He grins and it's a little blurry now. "But even as a hero, I want you to know: if you have bad days, I'll pick up your pieces. Even if some really are sharp and cut my skin. From the largest ones that are heavy, and reflective, to the tiniest pieces that are like grains of sand. I'd hold you together."

"I'd hold *you* together," I manage to reply. "And…I'll have Spider-man band aids for your fingers."

"We're all set," he says softly. "Bo. If I can. If you let me. I want to cash in my favor." I laugh without meaning to, and he seems to melt at the sound of it. "I'm…I'm asking you to make this all real, with me. I'm scared, I'll admit. But I'm in a better place than I could ever have imagined. Just a few months ago, I didn't know where I was going, who would be in my life."

His fingers hook into my belt loop and he tugs me a few inches closer. I make up the rest of the distance on my own until I can feel his heartbeat straight through mine. "Now, here you are—again. For good this time. And you have no idea how long I've loved you. I've never let myself feel it. I'm dying to feel it now."

"What does this look like to you, David?" I ask, unable to hide the shake in my voice when his hand on my hip slides up my ribs, behind my back. "Me fulfilling this favor."

He chews on his lip, and there goes my thumb, tapping at his mouth to get him to stop. His startled expression at my touch softens, and he leans his cheek into my palm.

"Can I stay with you? Maybe um. Put off finding my own place for now…?"

"You wanna squeeze into this box with me? For how long?"

"For as long as you let me." He looks down, staring at our bare toes. His right hand raises between our chests. When I hold it in mine, he brings my knuckles up, kissing my fingers with an inhale.

"Think we can just start with dessert?" I whisper. "You *did* order brownies."

David nods and puts the back of my hand to his cheek. "I like dessert."

"And you *just* made us coffee," I remind him, both our mugs forgotten already. "I'm sure we'll be wired for hours."

"Coffee and brownies…"

"As a start."

"That sounds like a great start." He lifts his left hand, and though it's a cramped fit with us standing so close, he extends his pinky finger. "What about after?"

I accept it with my own. No fingers, no toes crossed, just our hands tangled together, his forehead bowed against mine. "What about it?"

Acknowledgements

I want to extend a massive thank you to those who read this book long before it was finished, including my wonderful friends Jo M. Arianie, Shabi and Nyanda. Also thank you to Sophie, who went above and beyond as not just a reader, but a friend who believed in this story, and in me. And of course the first reader, my mom, who asked all the right questions and continues to ask for a Lancelot book. (I'm trying, I promise.) Thank God for all of you and your heart, patience, and generosity. Every inch of feedback y'all provided helped fuel the fire to get this published so I can share it with the world.

I hope it's cool I thank Aron Wright, too, who unknowingly wrote the song that I'd hear on a long commute home, which would then inspire this entire story. David and Scott arrived when I needed them, *before* I needed them. In a way, they embody the lines from Look After You that Aron wrote. When I thought I was alone, they brought me home.

Lastly, I'd like to throw it back to the dedication: you all know who you are. Those of you who've struggled to find your own purpose, to figure out what exactly your story is supposed to be. Take it from me—actually, even better. Take it from Pedro Después, who discovered who he was and who he loved long after society said he could start new. He's cheering you on just as much as he cheers on David and Scott. They're all rooting for you.

Take your time, shake it off T Swift style, and do your best. We'll all be okay in the end.

-Love and cheers, Quinn

About the Author

Quinn Coleman is a cat parent and French fry fan. They're nonbinary and located currently in Austin, Texas.

Coleman enjoys long walks by the sea (as long as water and a bathroom are nearby) and staying up impossibly late to write books. (Only to forget what they've written in a day or two, then they're pleasantly surprised by what they apparently wrote in a state of 'is eight PM too late to have coffee, probably, but what is time but a made-up construct'.)

They fought tooth and nail to get the bloody page numbers how they like for this book. Let it be known that tears were nearly shed, but they succeeded. By God, they succeeded.

www.linktr.ee/quinncoleman

Printed in Great Britain
by Amazon